# Songs of the Church

Anatiposi

**George C. Davies**

# Songs of the Church

Reprint of the original, first published in 1859.

1st Edition 2023 | ISBN: 978-3-38230-718-9

Anatiposi Verlag is an imprint of Outlook Verlagsgesellschaft mbH.

Verlag (Publisher): Outlook Verlag GmbH, Zeilweg 44, 60439 Frankfurt, Deutschland
Vertretungsberechtigt (Authorized to represent): E. Roepke, Zeilweg 44, 60439 Frankfurt, Deutschland
Druck (Print): Books on Demand GmbH, In de Tarpen 42, 22848 Norderstedt, Deutschland

# SONGS OF THE CHURCH:

OR

# PSALMS AND HYMNS

OF

# The Protestant Episcopal Church,

ARRANGED TO APPROPRIATE MELODIES.

WITH

A FULL SET OF CHANTS

FOR

Each Season of the Christian Year.

BY

GEORGE C. DAVIES.

---

THE WHOLE CAREFULLY HARMONIZED IN FOUR PARTS AND FORMING

A COMPLETE CHORAL SERVICE

FOR

The Church;

WITH SPECIAL REFERENCE TO THE USE OF CONGREGATIONS,
WITH OR WITHOUT CHOIRS.

---

*Venite, Exultemus Domino.*

---

NEW YORK:
Delisser & Procter, 508 Broadway.
1859.

TO

THE BISHOPS, CLERGY AND LAITY

OF

The Protestant Episcopal Church

OF THE UNITED STATES,

THIS,

THE FIRST COMPLETE CHORAL SERVICE OF THE CHURCH

EVER PUBLISHED

IS RESPECTFULLY DEDICATED, BY

GEO. C. DAVIES.

# CONTENTS

# PREFACE.

John Playford, in the preface to his Psalter, published in 1671, quotes: "It is the saying of a learned divine, in his sermon on the subject, that prayer shall cease, and preaching shall cease, but praising of God shall never cease, neither in this world, nor in the world to come. To sing praises to God is an angelic office; it is a taste of the first-fruits of heaven while we are on earth. Music (the learned say) is the handmaid to divinity; and there is no science except that admitted into the service of the Church." I trust, therefore, that no apology will be deemed necessary for the publication of this the first complete Choral Service of the Protestant Episcopal Church ever published.

There can be no doubt that the association of music with the worship of the Supreme Being, is of the highest antiquity, although the earliest mention made of it in the Scriptures occurs after the destruction of the Egyptians in the Red Sea; but Metrical Psalmody, which originated with the United Brethren, or Moravians—who derived their first psalm tunes from the chants of the Church of Rome, as may be seen by inspecting their first hymn-book, published with musical notes, in 1538—only became general in public worship about the time of the Reformation, when, it is said, it was no unusual occurrence to hear five or six thousand voices fill the air with the simple yet noble melodies of our old church tunes.*

What a contrast does this afford to the present mode of praising God in His holy temple, when four feeble voices, yclept a "Quartette Choir," "do up" the praises of the sanctuary in the most approved style, in scraps from the opera, or secular songs, that are caviare to the congregation, and in which they can take no part, save that of silent listeners—and to the exclusion of those majestic melodies that, in the olden time, borne on the breath of thousands of worshipers, shook the massive walls of the grand old cathedrals of Europe, or awakened the echos of the forests of the new world.

It is much easier, however, to point out this sad defect, than to remedy it; yet the total neglect of the study of music by the clergy, with few exceptions, and the want of a carefully prepared psalter or music-book for the use of, and within the comprehension of ordinary church-goers, lie unquestionably at the root of the evil. To provide a remedy for the latter, this book has been prepared—the former can only be remedied by the clergy themselves.

It has been well said by a cotemporary, that, "happily, the day is gone by, when any person who shall affirm, with some degree of boast, that they can not discern

---

* See *Psalmist* and *Cantica Ecclesiastica*. London.

the difference between the Old Hundred psalm tune and some popular lively air, will excite any other feeling than pity for their infirmity; certainly no true Christian would make such an assertion, except in sorrow. Music is a science that requires long and intense study to excel in it; yet neither much skill nor instruction is requisite to join in the services of the Church; and as we are to *sing* to God, as well as to *pray* to him, it would appear an imperative duty, that all who hope, through his mercy, to bear a part in the heavenly choir, should, to the best of their ability bear a part in the songs of his Church in this present world." It is, therefore, incumbent upon parents, pastors, and teachers, to see that all young persons under their charge have proper facilities for acquiring a good elementary knowledge of vocal music. An intimate acquaintance with the fine congregational songs of the Church, from the hands of the grand old masters—from Tallis, Farrent, and Ravenscroft, down to the commencement of the present century, can not fail to have a beneficial influence upon the character of youth; besides, in the language of another, providing for them a recreation of the most delightful kind—vocal music being regarded by all competent persons, as "the most perfect mode of giving expression to the deepest emotions of the soul, as well as calling them into action."

In the present work, which has been a labor of love, there has been no attempt at origiuality; but an earnest effort to improve congregational singing, by supplying such a music book, that every one who wishes may join in the praises of the sanctuary with that degree of confidence that every Christian should possess. For this purpose the music has been arranged for four voices, and printed side by side with the words to which it is to be sung, and put into the most convenient form for use in churches or in the family circle. The words embrace the whole choral service of the Church, save the *Kyrie* and the Psalter, which are not sung in this country, except in a few churches. The music has been selected with great care, from the old, well-known, and much-loved melodies in general use—the great majority of which were designed, originally, for psalmody only, and for the words to which they are now set; while many of them are glittering with the rime of a hundred years or more, and were in daily use in the Mother Church long before the revolution. Most of the harmonies are by the best harmonists of the present day.

In making these selections free use has been made of "*The Royal Psalmodist Compleat*, by W. Tans'ur, 1742," containing a tune for each of the psalms; The 150 Psalms, by D. Weyman, Dublin—with sequel by Dr. John Smith and Richard Beatty; Cantica Ecclesiastica, by Thomas Ions, Oxford; Harmonia Sacra, by Baxter & Davies, London; The Psalmist, by Vincent Novello, London; Simple Chants and Gregorean Tones, by Novello; One Hundred Chants, by George Bird, London; Marsh's 250 Cathedral Chants, etc., etc. Earnest effort has been made to exclude every thing not worthy to be heard in the sanctuary; while all tunes, hallowed by time and association, have been retained, as far as was possible, and placed with the words, to which churchmen in America have been accustomed to sing them.

Many of these tunes have been, for a long time, excluded from public use, much to the annoyance of the lovers of genuine church music; "in consequence," says a late writer, "of the productions of a class of men, who would have been much better employed in learning to sing and appreciate what men of genius had already composed, than in obtruding their own crude, dissonant and tasteless performances upon the public; which they have done in a way that has tended to degrade the popular taste, and to deprive this delightful part of public worship of its due solemnity, as well as every other attraction it originally possessed. The apparent simplicity of the genuine psalm tune seems to have seduced these persons into the serious mistake of supposing themselves capable of composing in that style; and so prolific have they proved, and such has been the extent of their influence, that they have not only succeeded in banishing, from many places of worship, the noble compositions of the fathers of English psalmody, but by closely occupying the ground by incessant novelties of the same spurious order, have deprived the legitimate musical talent of the present day of almost every chance of successfully developing itself in this description of music. That some of these pseudo-musicians were capable of forming a pleasing melody, it would be unjust to deny; but an examination of many of these performances, discloses the lamentable fact, that very many of them which have gained popularity, prove their authors to be not only destitute of musical knowledge, but equally incapable of appreciating that spirit of devotion and humble reverence which should ever characterize our devotional engagements."

In the present volume, consequently, but few tunes from modern composers will be found,* owing to the fact that few of the later composers have seen fit to follow in the steps of the originators of the "English Psalm Tune," as developed and perfected by such writers as Purcell, Ravenscroft, Tallis, Boyce, Croft, Milgrove, Burney, Wainwright, and a host of others whose names are so familiar to the lovers of the solemn, but soul-stirring "Songs of the Church" of the past century or two. It is from this school that the great mass of material, of which the following volume is composed, has been drawn — the editor deeming it the only true style of church music; for English psalm tunes in their purity and finish, when properly studied, will prove to be the best adapted for common use, in public worship, of any other; and when properly understood, will be sure to gain the hearts and voices of all who use them.

And now, in the words of honest John Playford, "I have nothing more to add; but as the glory of God, and the service of His Church, was my sole end and aim, so shall I account my labor and pains herein sufficiently recompensed, if it prove useful to such as endeavor to sing the praises of their Creator here on earth, that hereafter they may eternally sing hallelujahs among the blessed choirs of saints and angels."

GEORGE C. DAVIES.

CINCINNATI, *July*, 1858.

* The editor is greatly obliged to Doctor Lowell Mason for his kindness in granting the use of his beautiful "Missionary Hymn," and other copyright publications.

## SUGGESTIONS.

It will be seen, on examination, that the following work is not, strictly speaking, a congregational tune book, but one that requires, for its perfect rendering, an organ and choir. Yet no tunes will be found in it, that can not be sung by the great majority of singers — whether learned in music or not — especially when led by a judicious organist; while there are a vast number of them that are well known, and can be sung by the congregation, independent of organists and choirs.

Upon this subject of congregational singing, the great mass of church-goers have very erroneous opinions—a large proportion of them think it a work of easy accomplishment: that all we have to do is to gather together a lot of such tunes as Old Hundred, Mear, St. Ann's, Dundee, etc., and drive out everything of a different class, and the thing is done. But such persons will find, when they come to arrange the details of such a work, that they have undertaken a task that will exclude from public worship the great majority of our finest psalms and hymns, and that the musical taste of this country is too far advanced to tolerate, for any length of time, only simple chorals of the type of those named.

The experience of the editor is, that those tunes which have a decided and flowing melody, when sung with appropriate words, and in correct style, are those which give the best satisfaction; and when used sufficiently often, are those in which congregations most heartily join. It is upon this fact, that the arrangement of the following work has been based: and it is hoped congregations will give it a fair trial, without being deterred by any seeming difficulties in the music or arrangement—for they may rest assured that there are no difficulties in the way of securing good congregational music—that a little study and attention on the part of church-goers, who can sing, will not readily overcome.

In order to achieve the greatest results in the shortest possible time, it is recommended that the book be placed in the hands of every child, and every other person who can sing in the congregation, and then used precisely as arranged, without alteration or amendment — for any alteration in the division of the words of the chants, because they happen to differ from those formerly used, or a change in the harmonies to suit certain tastes or fancies in one church, will only tend to confuse worshipers from other churches, where no changes, or different ones have been made. No two persons can exactly agree upon such points, for there is no absolutely "right way" in such matters. Beside, by so doing, they defeat the leading object of the book, which is designed to render the choral service of the Church as uniform and *common* as are its prayers and liturgies; so that the churchman, into whatsoever church he may enter, may join in the same praises, with the same strains of melody with which he is accustomed, and with which, perhaps, his kindred and friends at home are, at the same moment, "lifting up their voices in songs of praise in the sanctuary of the Lord of lords and King of kings." How beautiful the thought, that the same outburst of song which, borne on thousands of voices on the rock-bound coasts of Maine, welcomes the morn, with

"Awake my soul and with the sun,
Thy daily course of duty run,"

shall flow on in one continual wave of harmony to the golden sands of the Pacific and the far-off "Isles of the Sea," to be followed by that grand old anthem

"Glory to thee, my God, this night,
For all the blessings of the light."

Who would not sacrifice something of caprice, or fancy, or taste, it may be, to secure so gratifying a result?

It will be seen, from examination, that this work contains seven full sets of chants for each of the canticles, and the Gloria tibi Domini—besides chants for occasional offices; Trisagion; and Burial of the Dead—all arranged, in the order of the prayer-book, under appropriate heads for the great divisions of the Christian year—thus securing enough of change to maintain freshness, while the great object is obtained, of sufficient repetition of each chant, to fix it in the mind of the worshiper; at the same time the divisions of the ecclesiastical year, as set forth by the Church, are distinctly marked.

The psalms and hymns are printed in full, with their appropriate doxologies, and face the music to which they are to be sung—thus obviating the trouble and confusion consequent upon the selection of suitable tunes during service—a labor to choristers always troublesome, and, at times, very perplexing, and involving the use of a multitude of books and manuscripts.

It will be observed that the division of words in the chants is somewhat different from that in most American publications. In this, the best English models have been followed; and it is to be hoped that choristers, and others in authority, will not make any alterations in these divisions, for, independent of the reasons given above, they may rest assured that these divisions have the sanction of the best authorities of the day, and are in accordance with the true style of chanting—which is "musical reading," not the singing, so common in American churches. And should there be any difficulty in making the words chime in properly, they may be certain that the fault is in their mode of chanting, and not in the division of the words. The practice of putting only one word to each note of the cadence, or one accented word to two notes, so prevalent in this country, has destroyed the beauty of the chant, by giving it a heavy, drawling character, totally at variance with its truer and more spirited rendering.

It will be also observed, that the music, in this volume, is printed without the usual marks of expression. This has been done so that every organist can exercise his own taste in rendering the music, and giving to it the expression required by the words, untrammeled by arbitrary signs or accents. The editor would, however, remark, that church psalmody, in this country, is, as a general rule, sung too slow, and with too dolorous and monotonous an accent. Singers and players would do well, in all cases, to enter into the spirit of the words; and, when cheerful and exultant, sing them so; but when penitential, prayerful, or solemn, let them be given accordingly.

In chanting, that portion of the words which is recited should never be given in the loud and noisy manner which children are apt to employ, but in a quiet and subdued tone—in the time of a good reader—care being taken to prolong the last word, or the next to the last, as the case may be, as a preparation to the cadence, which should be distinctly given in marked time and accent; but *with the same rate of movement* as the words of the recitative. It is a want of attention to these two points that has destroyed the beauty of the chant, and given it a heavy, dragging character, totally at variance with its true rendering. Care, however, should be taken not to hurry over the words, especially the recited ones, as is the case in many churches, which also arises from neglect of the points above mentioned. All "regular singers," with scarce an exception, make *too great an effort in chanting;* while organists, as a general thing, accompany the voices with too much organ—covering up and destroying the enunciation of the words. These latter gentlemen will pardon the suggestion, that those little interludes and cadences with which many of the more indifferent performers introduce at the beginning and end of each line of the chant had better be left out altogether, or left to the hands of the master, for they almost always destroy the smoothness and beauty of the chant, by interrupting the easy flow of the words, unless very skillfully and appropriately introduced. They should also bear in mind, that interludes between the verses of the psalms and hymns, to be effective, should be *very brief,* seldom exceeding four or eight measures, and in the key of the piece. Long interludes, without point, rythm, idea, beginning, or end, in all keys, and no key at all, such as are heard in far too many of our churches, are unworthy the place, and seriously interrupt the praises of the people. Those who can not extemporize fluently—and but few can—would do well to prepare or study their voluntaries and interludes beforehand, so as not to bore their listeners with unmeaning sounds and rambling phrases.

All, however, should bear in mind the great truth, that "any thing that is worth doing at all, is worth doing well," and that to sing or play in a manner worthy of the Church or Him whose praises they celebrate, is no easy matter, and requires time and study, both of which should be freely given; for there is no nobler task in which they could engage, for the "Songs of the Church" furnish a stronger bond of union among Christians, than creeds and liturgies, and have done as much, perhaps, for the salvation of souls as even "the foolishness of preaching." They are, therefore, worthy the closest study and attention of every Christian in the land. But no singing or playing can be effective in the church, unless the heart prompts the lips or fingers; for it is from the heart that all prayer and praise, to be acceptable, must come.

## DIRECTIONS TO SINGERS.

Throughout the chants, in the following collection, the *Melody* or *Air* is at the top of the staff; as is also the case in some of the psalms and hymns, which are printed in short, or condensed score. It can readily be distinguished from the second treble or alto, which is always associated with it, by the stems all turning upward. In the psalms and hymns, with the exceptions above-named, the air is always at the top of the second line of the score, and may be similarly recognized. This part, for the due effect of the harmony, should be sung by a female or boy's voice only.

The *Second Treble* or *Alto* is on the same staff with the melody, and may be recognized by the stems turning downward. Where there is but one note on the staff, both voices sing that note.

The *Tenor*, in the chants and condensed score of the psalms and hymns, is on the same staff with the base, and may easily be recognized by the upward stems. In the psalms and hymns, with the exceptions named, the tenor is always on the upper line of the score, to which the treble or G clef has been prefixed, for the convenience of those persons who find it difficult to read that part on the proper clef. But no errors can arise from this, if the part is confined to *male voices*, to which it belongs—for, though nominally an octave higher than it ought to be, when sung by *male* voices it takes its proper place in the harmony. It is a common mistake, especially in the country, for *female* singers to sing the *Tenor* part, leaving the *Air* to *male* voices, for which it is not intended. This causes an inversion of the harmony highly displeasing to cultivated ears, and a false progression of the parts that is intolerable.

The *Bass* is always on its own clef, and when associated with the tenor, may be easily recognized by its downward stems.

With regard to *all the parts*, it is absolutely necessary, says a late authority, for the perfection of the harmony, *that the duration of all the notes*, in singing, should be *strictly* that assigned them by the composers. A slight departure from this rule will sometimes convert the most beautiful *harmony* into *dissonance*, and utterly ruin the effect of the composition. It may be further added, that the too general custom of altering the tunes by the introduction of *appoggiatura* or *passing notes*, is frequently injurious to the effect of both harmony and melody. Such deviations can never be safely practiced by persons unacquainted with musical science.

No directions are given with regard to the *time* or *style* of performance of the tunes, for reasons previously assigned. But as the words in all instances accompany the music, there will be no difficulty in giving the proper expression to either, if singers and players will enter into the spirit of the poetry, and sing and play like Christian men and women — as the "sweet Singer of Israel" did in the olden time, and not like a parcel of anchorites "wailing in tombs and catacombs"

# VENITE EXULTEMUS DOMINO.

ADVENT AND CHRISTMAS.

MORNINGTON.

TREBLE.
SECOND.
TENOR.
BASS.

| | | | |
|---|---|---|---|
| 1 O come let us sing | un- | to the | Lord: |
| 3 For the Lord | | is a great | God: |
| 5 The sea is His | | and He | made it: |
| 7 For He is | the | Lord our | God: |
| 10 Glory be to the Father, | and | to the | Son, |

| | | | |
|---|---|---|---|
| Let us heartily rejoice in | the | strength of our | sal- vation. 2 |
| And a great | | King a bove | all Gods. 4 |
| And his hands | pre- | par - ed the | dry land. 6 |
| And we are the people of his pas- | ture | and the sheep | of his hand. 8 |
| And | | to the Ho - | ly Ghost. 11 |

| | | |
|---|---|---|
| 2 Let us come before his presence | with thanks- | giving: |
| 4 In His hand are all the corners | of the | earth: |
| 6 O come, let us worship | and fall | down: |
| 8 O worship the Lord in the beauty of | ho - li- | ness: |
| 9 For he cometh, for he cometh to | judge the | earth, |
| 11 As it was in the beginning, is now, and | ev - er | shall be, |

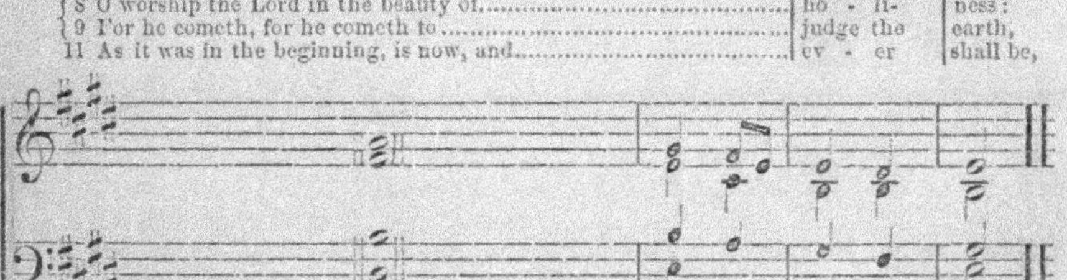

| | | | |
|---|---|---|---|
| And show ourselves | glad in | Him with | psalms. 3 |
| And the strength of the | hills — | is His | also. 5 |
| And kneel be- | fore the | Lord our | Maker. 7 |
| Let the whole earth | stand in | awe of | Him. 9 |
| And with righteousness to judge the world, and the | peo - ple | with His | truth. 10 |
| World | with - out | end. *A-* | *men.* |

# VENITE EXULTEMUS DOMINO.

EPIPHANY TO QUINQUAGESIMA. KENT.

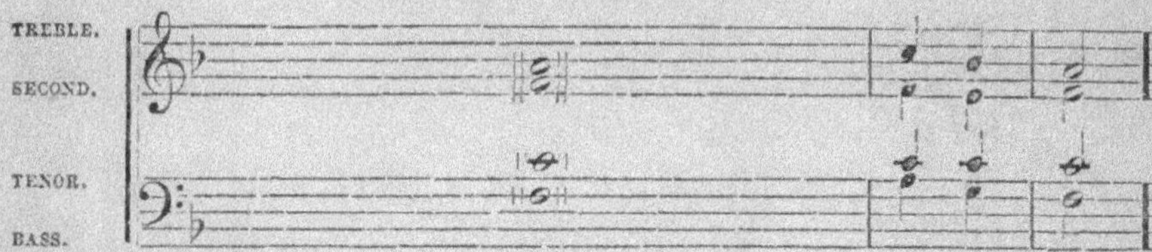


| | | |
|---|---|---|
| 1 O come let us sing un- | to the | Lord: |
| 3 For the Lord | is a great | God: |
| 5 The sea is His | and He | made it: |
| 7 For He is the | Lord our | God: |
| 10 Glory be to the Father, and | to the | Son, |

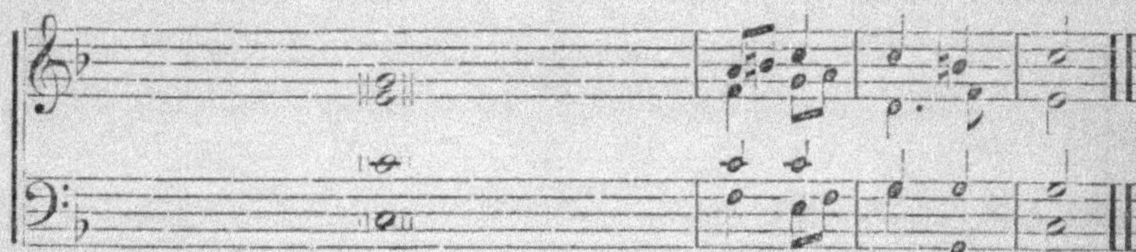

| | | | |
|---|---|---|---|
| Let us heartily rejoice in the | strength of | our sal- | vation. 2 |
| And a great | King a | bove all | Gods 4 |
| And his hands pre- | par - ed | the dry | land. 6 |
| And we are the people of his pasture | and the | sheep of his | hand. 8 |
| And | to the | Ho - ly | Ghost. 11 |

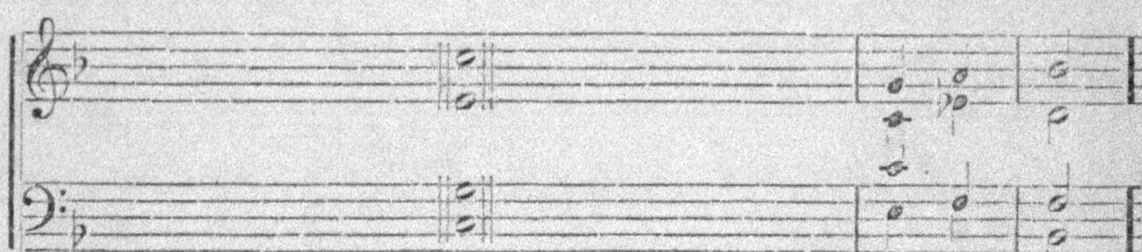

| | | |
|---|---|---|
| 2 Let us come before his presence | with thanks- | giving: |
| 4 In His hand are all the corners | of the | earth: |
| 6 O come, let us worship | and fall | down: |
| {8 O worship the Lord in the beauty of | ho - li- | ness: |
| {9 For he cometh, for he cometh to | judge the | earth, |
| 11 As it was in the beginning, is now, and | ev - er | shall be, |

| | | | |
|---|---|---|---|
| And show ourselves | glad in | Him with | psalms. 3 |
| And the strength of the | hills — | is His | also. 5 |
| And kneel be- | fore the | Lord our | Maker. 7 |
| Let the whole earth | stand in | awe of | Him. 9} |
| And with righteousness to judge the world, and the | peo - ple | with His | truth. 10} |
| World | with - out | end. *A-* | *men.* |

## VENITE EXULTEMUS DOMINO.

LENT. R. LANGDON.

TREBLE.
SECOND.
TENOR.
BASS.

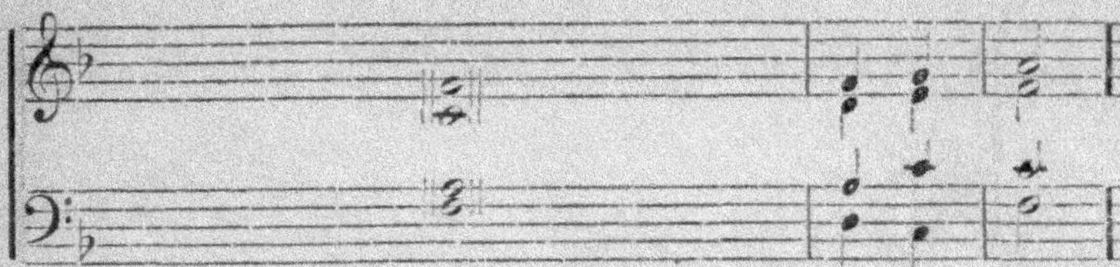

| | | |
|---|---|---|
| 1 O come let us sing un-........................................ | to the | Lord: |
| 3 For the Lord ........................................ | is a great | God: |
| 5 The sea is His........................................ | and He | made it: |
| 7 For He is the........................................ | Lord our | God: |
| 10 Glory be to the Father, and........................................ | to the | Son, |

| | | | |
|---|---|---|---|
| Let us heartily rejoice in the........................................ | strength of | our sal- | vation. 2 |
| And a great........................................ | King a | bove all | Gods. 4 |
| And his hands pre-........................................ | par - ed | the dry | land. 6 |
| And we are the people of his pasture........................................ | and the | sheep of his | hand. 8 |
| And........................................ | to the | Ho - ly | Ghost. 11 |

| | | |
|---|---|---|
| 2 Let us come before his presence........................................ | with thanks- | giving: |
| 4 In His hand are all the corners........................................ | of the | earth: |
| 6 O come, let us worship........................................ | and fall | down: |
| {8 O worship the Lord in the beauty of........................................ | ho - li- | ness: |
| {9 For he cometh, for he cometh to........................................ | judge the | earth, |
| 11 As it was in the beginning, is now, and........................................ | ev - er | shall be, |

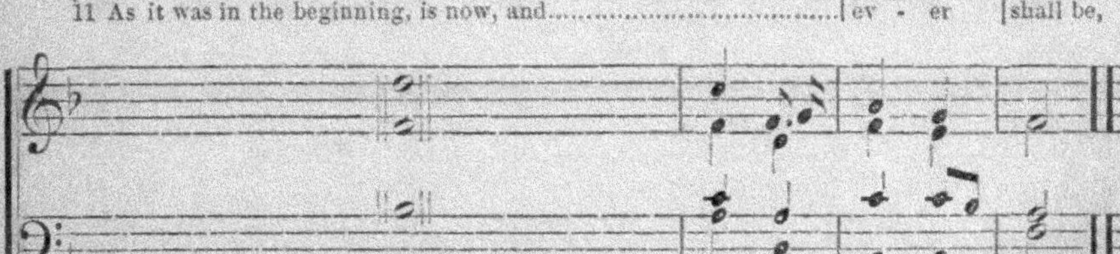

| | | | |
|---|---|---|---|
| And show ourselves........................................ | glad in | Him with | psalms. 3 |
| And the strength of the........................................ | hills — | is His | also. 5 |
| And kneel be-........................................ | fore the | Lord our | Maker. 7 |
| Let the whole earth........................................ | stand in | awe of | Him. 9 } |
| And with righteousness to judge the world, and the.... | peo - ple | with His | truth. 10 |
| World........................................ | with - out | end. *A-* | *men.* |

# VENITE EXULTEMUS DOMINO.

EASTER DAY. DR. BECKWITH.

TREBLE.
SECOND.
TENOR.
BASS.

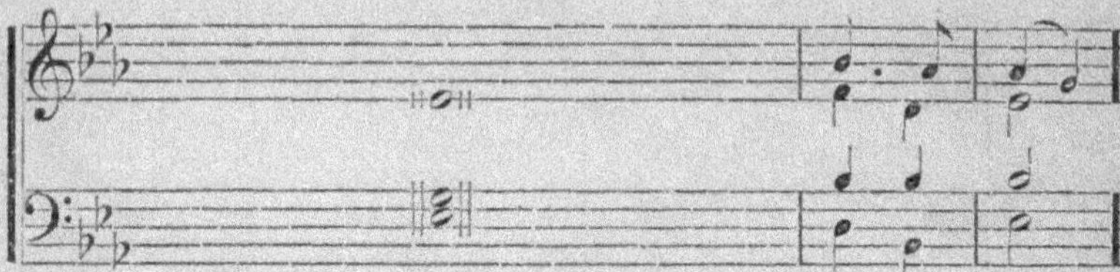

| | | |
|---|---|---|
| 1 Christ our passover is | sacri-ficed | for us: |
| 3 Christ being raised from the dead, | dieth no | more: |
| 5 Likewise reckon ye also yourselves to be dead indeed | un - to | sin: |
| 7 For since by | man came | death: |
| 9 Glory be to the Father, and | to the | Son, |

| | | | |
|---|---|---|---|
| Therefore | let us | keep the | feast. 2 |
| Death hath no | more do- | min - ion | over him. 4 |
| But alive unto God through | Je - sus | Christ our | Lord. 6 |
| By man came also the resur- | rec - tion | of the | dead. 8 |
| And | to the | Ho - ly | Ghost. 10 |

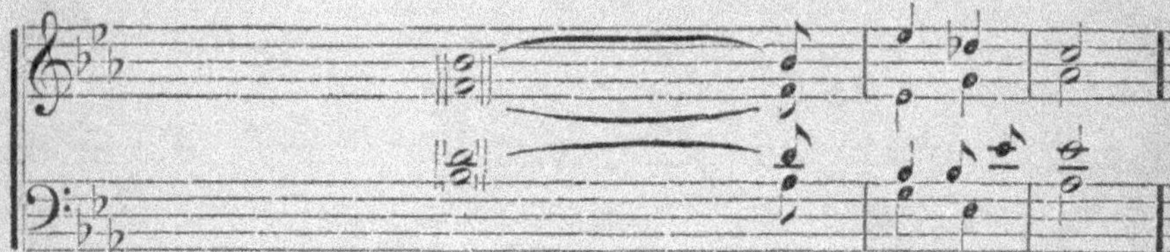

| | | |
|---|---|---|
| 2 Not with the old leaven, neither with the leaven of | malice and | wickedness: |
| 4 For in that he died, he died | unto sin | once: |
| 6 Christ is ris- en | from the | dead: |
| 8 For as in | Adam all | die: |
| 10 As it was in the beginning, is now, and | ev - er | shall be: |

| | | | |
|---|---|---|---|
| But with the unleaven- ed | bread of sin- | cerity and | truth. 3 |
| But in that he liveth, he | liv - eth | un - to | God. 5 |
| And become the first | fruits of | them that | slept. 7 |
| Even so in Christ shall | all be | made a- | live. 9 |
| World | with - out | end. *A-* | *men.* |

## VENITE EXULTEMUS DOMINO.

EASTER WEEK TO WHITSUNDAY. Dr. Boyce, 1750.

TREBLE.
SECOND.
TENOR.
BASS.

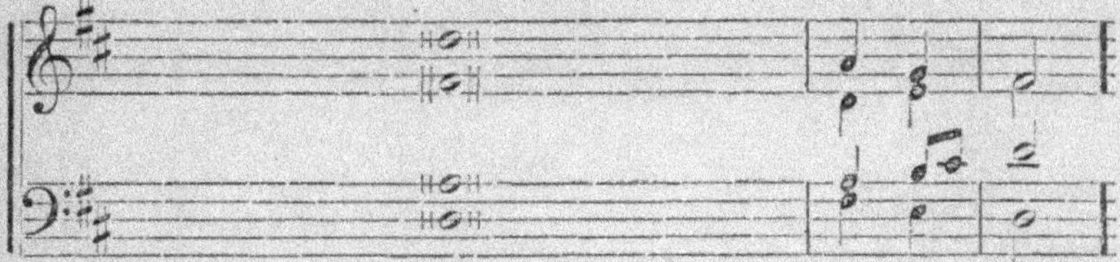

| | | |
|---|---|---|
| 1 O come let us sing un-........ | to the | Lord: |
| 3 For the Lord........ | is a great | God: |
| 5 The sea is His........ | and He | made it: |
| 7 For He is the........ | Lord our | God: |
| 10 Glory be to the Father, and........ | to the | Son, |

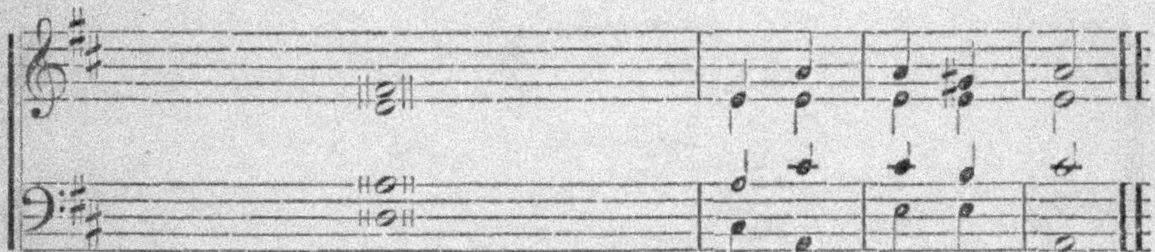

| | | | |
|---|---|---|---|
| Let us heartily rejoice in the........ | strength of | our sal- | vation. 2 |
| And a great........ | King a- | bove all | Gods. 4 |
| And his hands pre-........ | par - ed | the dry | land. 6 |
| And we are the people of his pasture........ | and the | sheep of his | hand. 8 |
| And........ | to the | Ho - ly | Ghost. 11 |

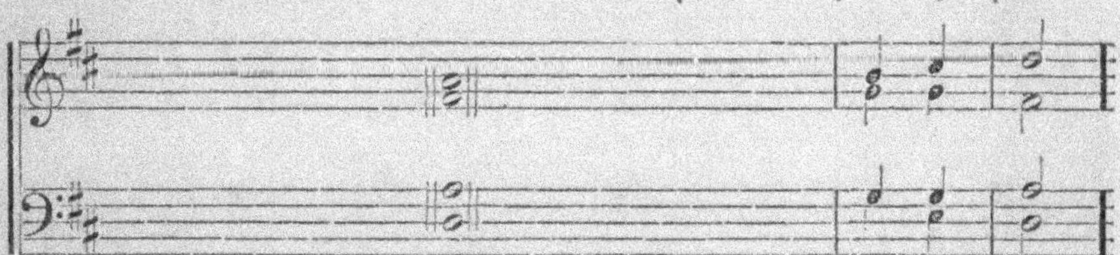

| | | |
|---|---|---|
| 2 Let us come before his presence........ | with thanks- | giving: |
| 4 In His hand are all the corners........ | of the | earth: |
| 6 O come, let us worship........ | and fall | down: |
| {8 O worship the Lord in the beauty of........ | ho - li- | ness: |
| {9 For he cometh, for he cometh to........ | judge the | earth, |
| 11 As it was in the beginning, is now, and........ | ev- - er | shall be, |

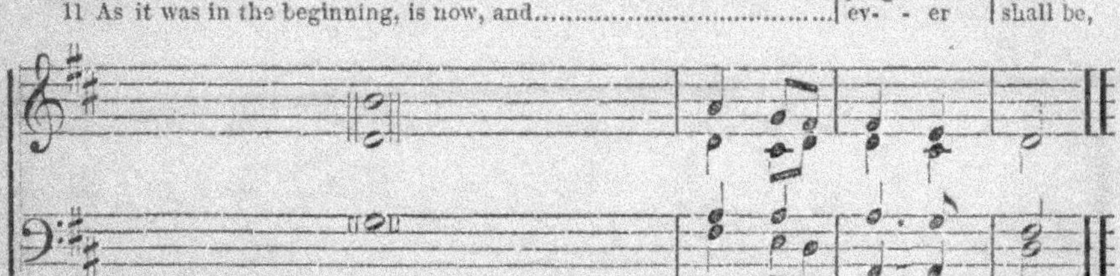

| | | | |
|---|---|---|---|
| And show ourselves........ | glad in | Him with | psalms. 3 |
| And the strength of the........ | hills — | is His | also. 5 |
| And kneel be-........ | fore the | Lord our | Maker. 7 |
| Let the whole earth........ | stand in | awe of | Him. 9} |
| And with righteousness to judge the world, and the........ | peo - ple | with His | truth. 10} |
| World........ | with - out | end. A- | men. |

## VENITE EXULTEMUS DOMINO.

17TH TO 27TH SUNDAY AFTER TRINITY. DR. CROTCH.

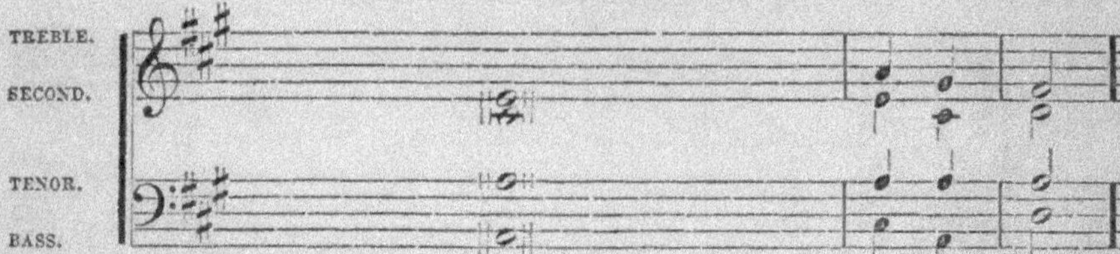


| | | |
|---|---|---|
| 1 O come let us sing un-............ | to the | Lord: |
| 3 For the Lord............ | is a great | God: |
| 5 The sea is His............ | and He | made it: |
| 7 For He is the............ | Lord our | God: |
| 10 Glory be to the Father, and............ | to the | Son, |

| | | | |
|---|---|---|---|
| Let us heartily rejoice in the............ | strength of | our sal- | vation. 2 |
| And a great............ | King a | bove all | Gods. 4 |
| And his hands pre-............ | par - ed | the dry | land. 6 |
| And we are the people of his pasture............ | and the | sheep of his | hand. 8 |
| And............ | to the | Ho - ly | Ghost. 11 |

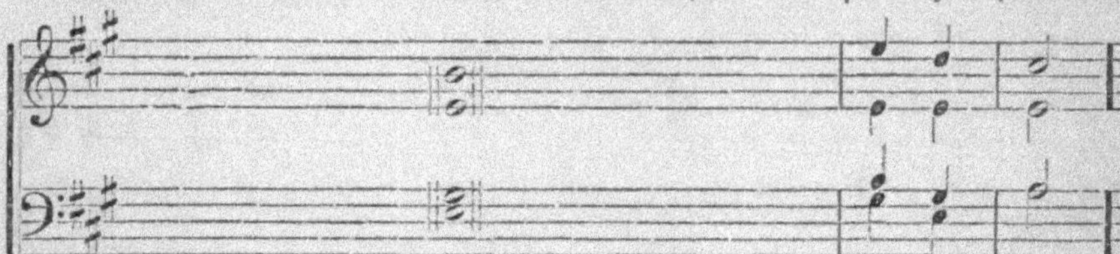

| | | |
|---|---|---|
| 2 Let us come before his presence............ | with thanks- | giving: |
| 4 In His hand are all the corners............ | of the | earth: |
| 6 O come, let us worship............ | and fall | down: |
| {8 O worship the Lord in the beauty of............ | ho - li- | ness: |
| {9 For he cometh, for he cometh to............ | judge the | earth, |
| 11 As it was in the beginning, is now, and............ | ev - er | shall be, |

| | | | |
|---|---|---|---|
| And show ourselves............ | glad in | Him with | psalms. 3 |
| And the strength of............ the............ | hills — | is His | also. 5 |
| And kneel............ be-............ | fore the | Lord our | Maker. 7 |
| Let the whole earth............ | stand in | awe of | Him. 9 } |
| And with righteousness to judge the world, and the... | peo - ple | with His | truth. 10 } |
| World............ | with - out | end. *A-* | *men.* |

# VENITE EXULTEMUS DOMINO.

THANKSGIVING. JOHN DAVY.

TREBLE. SECOND. TENOR. BASS.

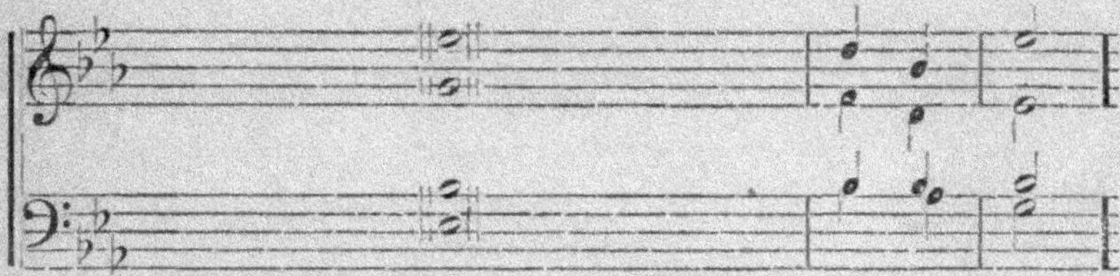

| | | |
|---|---|---|
| 1 Praise ye the Lord, for it is good to sing praises un-.................... | to our | God: |
| 3 He healeth those that are .................................................... | broken in | heart: |
| 5 He giveth to the ................................................................ | beast his | food: |
| 7 For he hath strengthened the................................................ | bars of thy | gates: |
| 9 Glory be to the Father and.................................................... | to the | Son: |

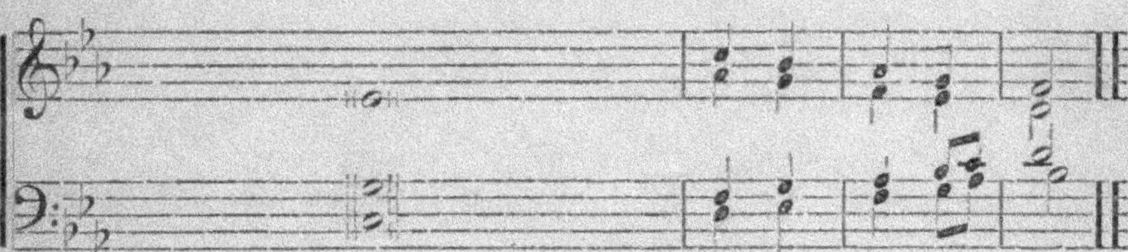

| | | | |
|---|---|---|---|
| For it is..................................................................... | pleasant and | praise is | comely. |
| And........................................................................... | bind - eth | up their | wounds. |
| And to the.................................................................... | young — | ravens which | cry. |
| He hath blessed thy........................................................ | child - ren | with- — | in thee. |
| And .......................................................................... | to the | Ho - ly | Ghost. |

| | | |
|---|---|---|
| 2 The Lord doth build up Je-................................................ | ru - sa - | lem: |
| 4 He covereth the heavens with clouds and prepareth.................. | rain for the | earth: |
| 6 Praise the Lord, O Je-........................................................ | ru - sa - | lem: |
| 8 He maketh........................................................................ | peace in thy | borders: |
| 10 As it was in the begining is now and .................................. | ev - er | shall be |

| | | | |
|---|---|---|---|
| He gathereth together ...............................the........ | out- — | casts of | Israel. |
| He maketh the grass ....................................to........ | grow up | on the | mountains. |
| Praise................................................................... | thy — | God, O | Zion. |
| And fillest thee with ..................................the......... | fin - est | of the | wheat. |
| World.................................................................... | with - out | end. *A* - | *men.* |

## GLORIA IN EXCELSIS.

ADVENT AND CHRISTMAS. Thos. Ions.

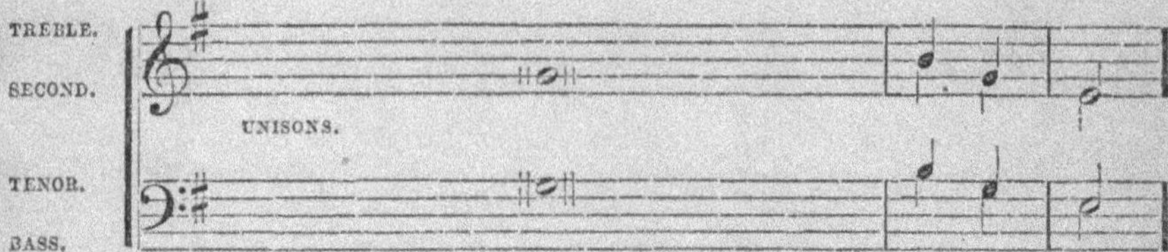


| | | | |
|---|---|---|---|
| 1 Glory be to | God on | high, | |
| 3 O Lord God | heaven-ly | King: | |
| 5 That takest away the | sins of the | world: | |
| 7 Thou that takest away the | sins of the | world: | |
| 9 For Thou | only art | holy: | |

| | | | | |
|---|---|---|---|---|
| And on earth | peace, good | will towards | men. | 2 |
| God, the | Fa - ther | Al- — | mighty. | 4 |
| Have | mer - cy | up - on | us. | 6 |
| Re- | ceive — | our — | prayer. | 8 |
| Thou | on - ly | art the | Lord. | 10 |

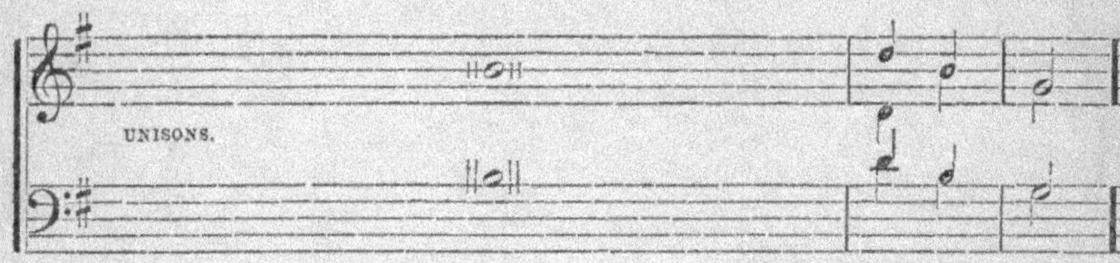


| | | |
|---|---|---|
| 2 We praise Thee, we bless Thee, we | wor - ship | Thee: |
| 4 O Lord, the only begotten Son | Je - sus | Christ: |
| 6 Thou that takest away the | sins of the | world: |
| 8 Thou that sittest at the right hand of | God the | Father: |
| 10 Thou only, O Christ, with the | Ho - ly | Ghost: |

| | | | | |
|---|---|---|---|---|
| We glorify Thee, we give thanks to | Thee for | Thy great | glory. | 3 |
| O Lord God, Lamb of | God, — | Son of the | Father. | 5 |
| Have | mer - cy | up - on | us. | 7 |
| Have | mer - cy | up - on | us. | 9 |
| Art most high in the glory of | God the | Father. *A-* | *men.* | |

## GLORIA IN EXCELSIS.

EPIPHANY TO QUINQUAGESIMA. JOSH. GARNETT.

| | | |
|---|---|---|
| 1 Glory be to............ | God on | high, |
| 3 O Lord God............ | heaven-ly | King: |
| 5 That takest away the............ | sins of the | world: |
| 7 Thou that takest away the............ | sins of the | world: |
| 9 For Thou............ | only art | holy: |

| | | | |
|---|---|---|---|
| And on earth............ | peace, good | will towards | men. 2 |
| God,............ the...... | Fa - ther | Al- — | mighty. 4 |
| Have............ | mer - cy | up - on | us. 6 |
| Re............ | ceive — | our — | prayer. 8 |
| Thou............ | on - ly | art the | Lord. 10 |

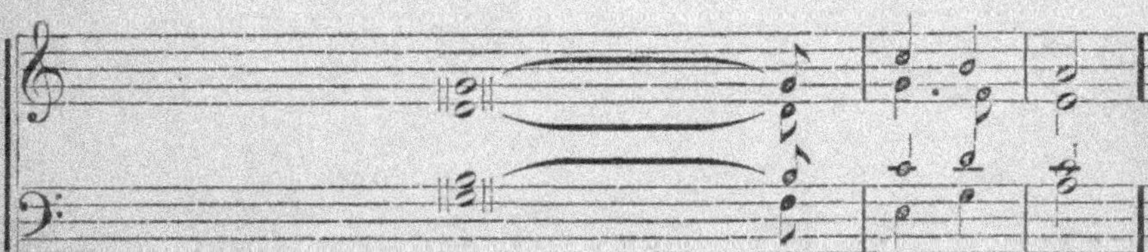

| | | |
|---|---|---|
| 2 We praise Thee, we bless Thee,............ we...... | wor - ship | Thee: |
| 4 O Lord, the only begotten Son............ | Je - sus | Christ: |
| 6 Thou that takest away............ the...... | sins of the | world: |
| 8 Thou that sittest at the right hand............ of...... | God the | Father: |
| 10 Thou only, O Christ, with............ the...... | Ho - ly | Ghost: |

| | | | |
|---|---|---|---|
| We glorify Thee, we give thanks to............ | Thee for | Thy great | glory. 3 |
| O Lord God, Lamb of............ | God, — | Son of the | Father. 5 |
| Have............ | mer - cy | up - on | us. 7 |
| Have............ | mer - cy | up - on | us. 9 |
| Art most high in the glory of............ | God the | Father. *A-* | *men.* |

## GLORIA IN EXCELSIS.

LENT. JACKSON.

TREBLE.
SECOND.
TENOR.
BASS.

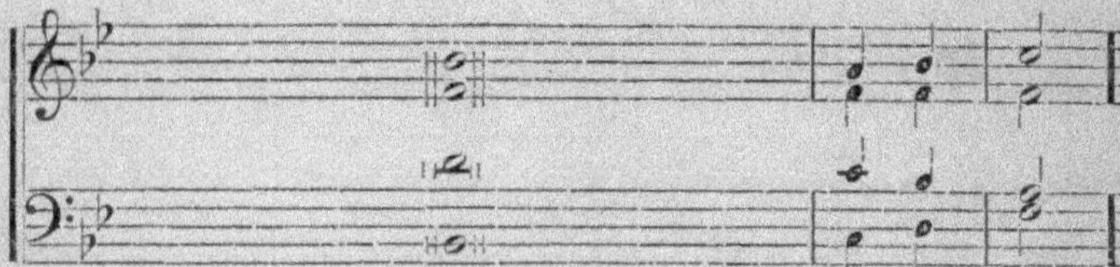

1 Glory be to.......... God on high,
3 O Lord God.......... heaven-ly King:
5 That takest away the.......... sins of the world:
7 Thou that takest away the.......... sins of the world:
9 For Thou.......... only art holy:

And on earth.......... peace, good will towards men. 2
God, the.......... Fa - ther Al- — mighty. 4
Have.......... mer - cy up - on us. 6
Re-.......... ceive — our — prayer. 8
Thou.......... on - ly art the Lord. 10

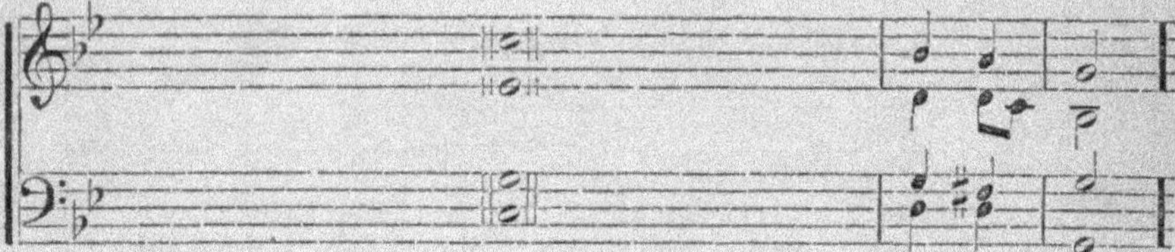

2 We praise Thee, we bless Thee, we.......... wor - ship Thee:
4 O Lord, the only begotten Son.......... Je - sus Christ:
6 Thou that takest away the.......... sins of the world:
8 Thou that sittest at the right hand of.......... God the Father:
10 Thou only, O Christ, with the.......... Ho - ly Ghost:

We glorify Thee, we give thanks to.......... Thee for Thy great glory. 3
O Lord God, Lamb of.......... God, — Son of the Father. 5
Have.......... mer - cy up - on us. 7
Have.......... mer - cy up - on us. 9
Art most high in the glory of.......... God the Father. *A- men.*

## GLORIA IN EXCELSIS.

EASTER TO WHITSUNDAY. JOSH. GARNETT.

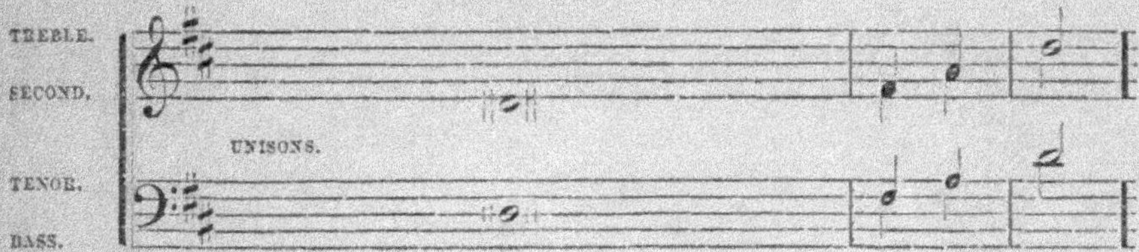


| | | |
|---|---|---|
| 1 Glory be to.......................... | God on | high, |
| 3 O Lord God.......................... | heaven-ly | King: |
| 5 That takest away the.......................... | sins of the | world: |
| 7 Thou that takest away the.......................... | sins of the | world: |
| 9 For Thou.......................... | only art | holy: |

| | | | |
|---|---|---|---|
| And on earth.......................... | peace, good | will towards | men. 2 |
| God, the .......................... | Fa - ther | Al- — | mighty. 4 |
| Have.......................... | mer - cy | up - on | us. 6 |
| Re. .......................... | ceive — | our — | prayer. 8 |
| Thou.......................... | on - ly | art the | Lord. 10 |

| | | |
|---|---|---|
| 2 We praise Thee, we bless Thee, we.......................... | wor - ship | Thee: |
| 4 O Lord, the only begotten Son.......................... | Je - sus | Christ: |
| 6 Thou that takest away the.......................... | sins of the | world: |
| 8 Thou that sittest at the right hand of.......................... | God the | Father: |
| 10 Thou only, O Christ, with the.......................... | Ho - ly | Ghost: |

| | | | |
|---|---|---|---|
| We glorify Thee, we give thanks.................. to ...... | Thee for | Thy great | glory. 3 |
| O Lord God, Lamb.................. of ...... | God, — | Son of the | Father. 5 |
| Have.......................... | mer - cy | up - on | us. 7 |
| Have.......................... | mer - cy- | up - on | us. 9 |
| Art most high in the glory.................. of ...... | God the | Father. *A-* | *men.* |

## GLORIA IN EXCELSIS.

TRINITY TO 8TH SUNDAY AFTER. JOSH. GARNETT.

TREBLE.
SECOND.
TENOR.
BASS.

| | | |
|---|---|---|
| 1 Glory be to | God on | high, |
| 3 O Lord God | heaven-ly | King: |
| 5 That takest away the | sins of the | world: |
| 7 Thou that takest away the | sins of the | world: |
| 9 For Thou | only art | holy: |

| | | | | |
|---|---|---|---|---|
| And on earth | peace, good | will towards | men. | 2 |
| God, the | Fa - ther | Al- — | mighty. | 4 |
| Have | mer - cy | up - on | us. | 6 |
| Re- | ceive — | our — | prayer. | 8 |
| Thou | on - ly | art the | Lord. | 10 |

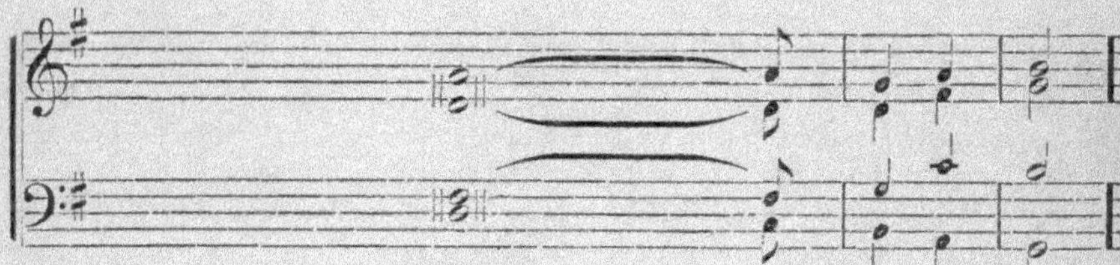

| | | |
|---|---|---|
| 2 We praise Thee, we bless Thee, we | wor - ship | Thee: |
| 4 O Lord, the only begotten Son | Je - sus | Christ: |
| 6 Thou that takest away the | sins of the | world: |
| 8 Thou that sittest at the right hand of | God the | Father: |
| 10 Thou only, O Christ, with the | Ho - ly | Ghost: |

| | | | | |
|---|---|---|---|---|
| We glorify Thee, we give thanks to | Thee for | Thy great | glory. | 3 |
| O Lord God, Lamb of | God, — | Son of the | Father. | 5 |
| Have | mer - cy | up - on | us. | 7 |
| Have | mer - cy | up - on | us. | 9 |
| Art most high in the glory of | God the | Father. *A-* | *men.* | |

## GLORIA IN EXCELSIS.

9TH TO 16TH SUNDAY AFTER TRINITY. DR. CHARD.

| | | |
|---|---|---|
| 1 Glory be to | God on | high, |
| 3 O Lord God | heaven-ly | King: |
| 5 That takest away the | sins of the | world: |
| 7 Thou that takest away the | sins of the | world: |
| 9 For Thou | only art | holy: |

| | | | |
|---|---|---|---|
| And on earth | peace, good | will towards | men. 2 |
| God, the | Fa - ther | Al- — | mighty. 4 |
| Have | mer - cy | up - on | us. 6 |
| Re- | ceive — | our — | prayer. 8 |
| Thou | on - ly | art the | Lord. 10 |

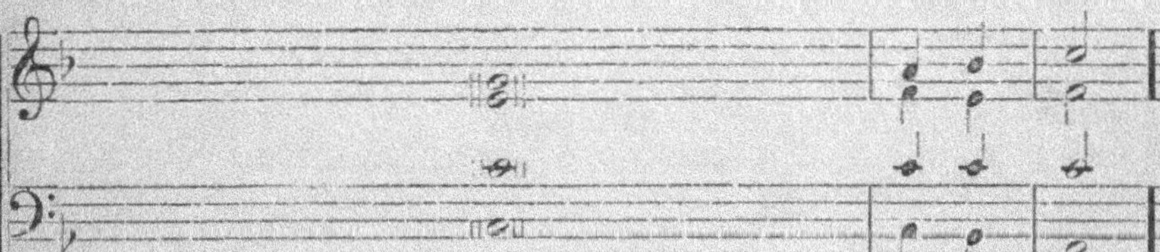

| | | |
|---|---|---|
| 2 We praise Thee, we bless Thee, we | wor - ship | Thee: |
| 4 O Lord, the only begotten Son | Je - sus | Christ: |
| 6 Thou that takest away the | sins of the | world: |
| 8 Thou that sittest at the right hand of | God the | Father: |
| 10 Thou only, O Christ, with the | Ho - ly | Ghost: |

| | | | |
|---|---|---|---|
| We glorify Thee, we give thanks to | Thee for | Thy great | glory. 3 |
| O Lord God, Lamb of | God, — | Son of the | Father. 5 |
| Have | mer - cy | up - on | us. 7 |
| Have | mer - cy | up - on | us. 9 |
| Art most high in the glory of | God the | Father. *A-* | *men.* |

3

## GLORIA IN EXCELSIS.

17TH TO 27TH SUNDAY AFTER TRINITY. GREGORIAN.

1 Glory be to............ | God on | high,
2 We praise Thee, we bless Thee, we ............ | wor - ship | Thee:

9 For Thou............ | only art | holy:
10 Thou only, O Christ, with the............ | Ho - ly | Ghost:

And on earth............ | peace, good | will towards | men. 2
We glorify Thee, we give thanks to ............ | Thee for | Thy great | glory. 3

Thou............ | on - ly | art the | Lord. 10
Art most high in the glory of ............ | God the | Father. *A-* | *men.*

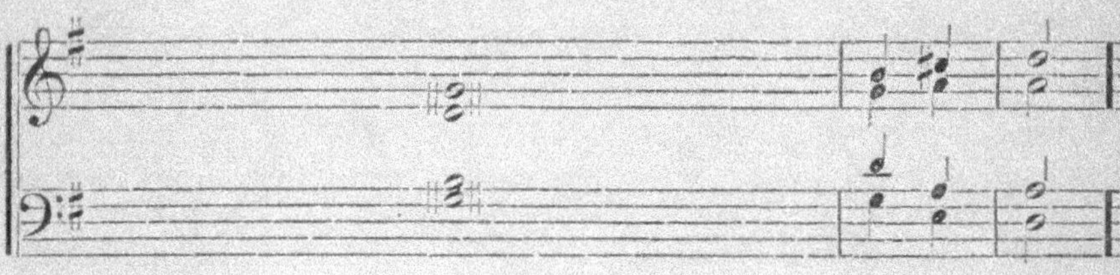

3 O Lord God,............ | heaven-ly | King:
4 O Lord, the only begotten Son............ | Je - sus | Christ:

God, the............ | Fa - ther | Al- — | mighty. 4
O Lord God, Lamb of............ | God, — | Son of the | Father. 5

(*Next page.*)

## GLORIA IN EXCELSIS.

CONTINUED.

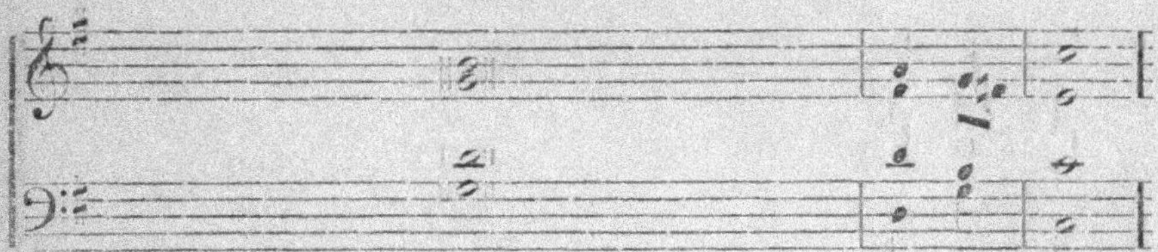

| | | |
|---|---|---|
| 5 That takest away the | sins of the | world: |
| 6 Thou that takest away the | sins of the | world: |
| 7 Thou that takest away the | sins of the | world: |
| 8 Thou that sittest at the right hand | God the | Father: |

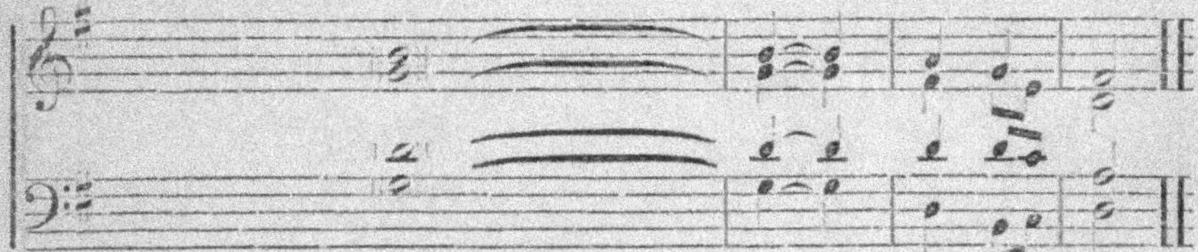

| | | | | |
|---|---|---|---|---|
| Have | mer - cy | up - on | us. | 6 |
| Have | mer - cy | up - on | us. | 7 |
| Re- | ceive — | our — | prayer. | 8 |
| Have | mer - cy | up - on | us. | 9 |

(*Page* 26.)

---

## GLORIA PATRI.

ADVENT AND CHRISTMAS. W. HAYES.

TREBLE.
SECOND.
TENOR.
BASS.

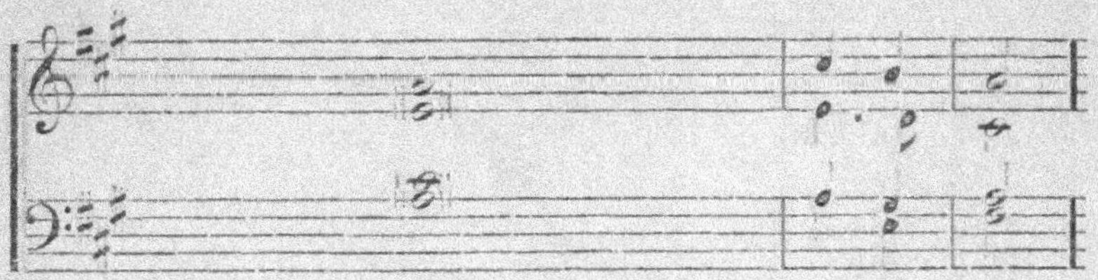

| | | |
|---|---|---|
| 1 Glory be to the Father and | to the | Son: |
| 2 As it was in the beginning, is now, and | ev - er | shall be, |

| | | | |
|---|---|---|---|
| And | to the | Ho - ly | Ghost. |
| World | with - out | end. A- | *men.* |

## GLORIA PATRI.

EPIPHANY TO QUINQUAGESIMA. P. HUMPHREYS, 1670.

Glory be to the Father, and ........ | to the | Son,
As it was in the beginning, is now, and ........ | ev- - er | shall be,

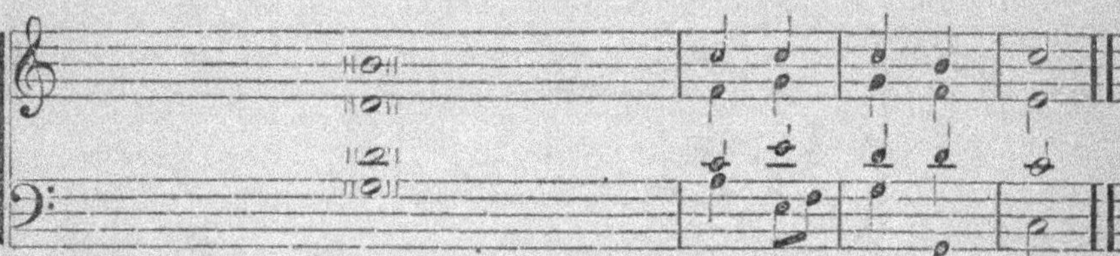

And ........ | to the | Ho - ly | Ghost.
World ........ | with - out | end. *A-* | *men.*

---

## GLORIA PATRI.

LENT. TALLIS, 1560.

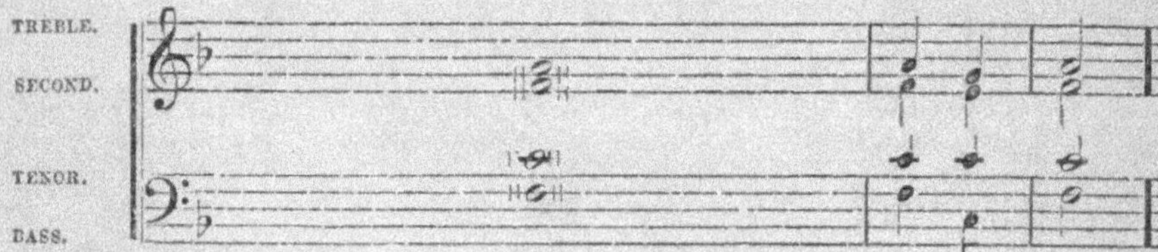


Glory be to the Father, and ........ | to the | Son:
As it was in the beginning, is now, and ........ | ev - er | shall be:

And ........ | to the | Ho - ly | Ghost.
World ........ | with - out | end. *A-* | *men.*

## GLORIA PATRI.

EASTER TO WHITSUNDAY. JOSH. GARNETT.

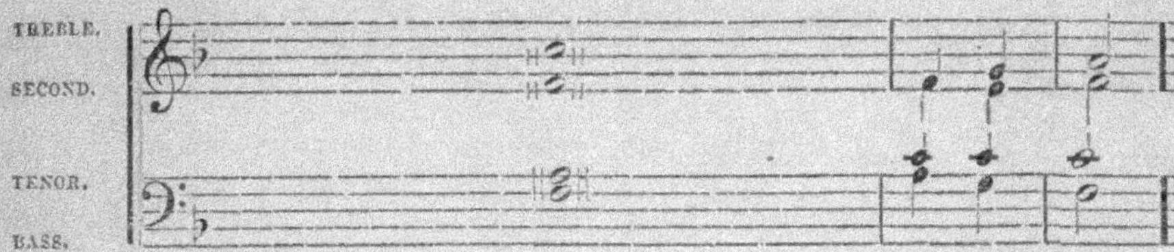


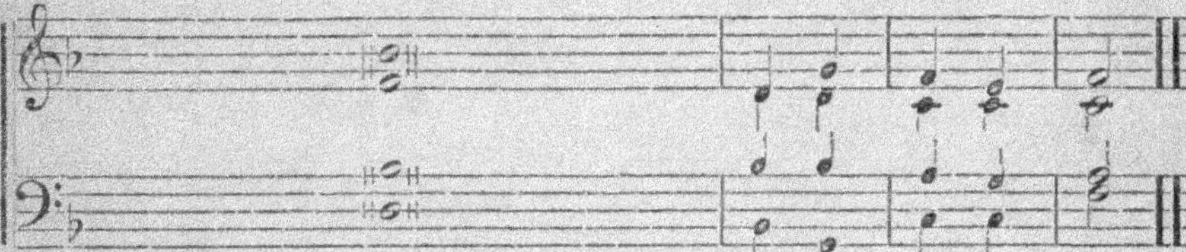


---

## GLORIA PATRI.

TRINITY TO 8TH SUNDAY AFTER. GREGORIAN.

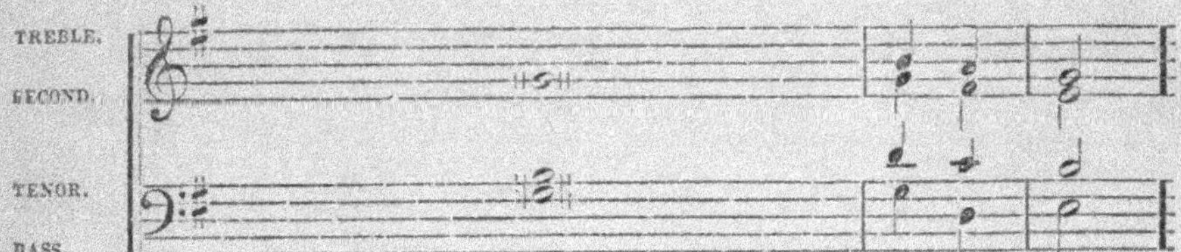


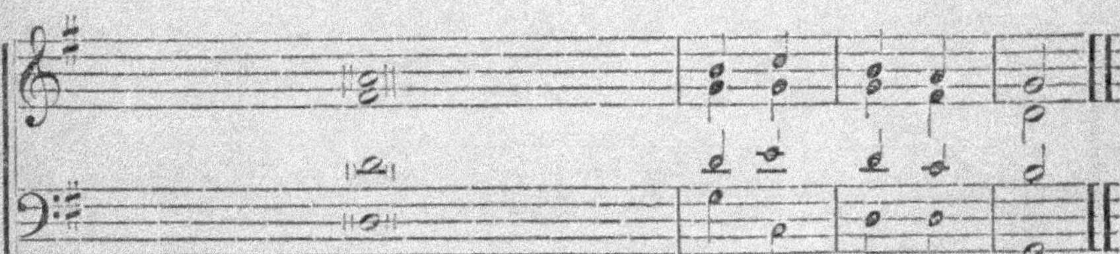

## GLORIA PATRI.

9TH TO 16TH SUNDAY AFTER TRINITY. FARRANT, 1570.

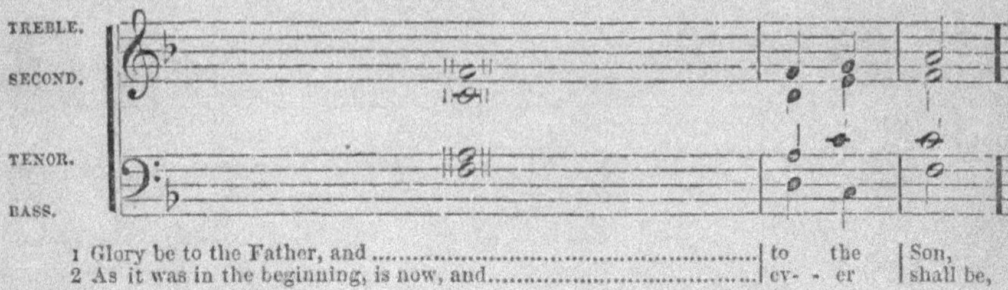


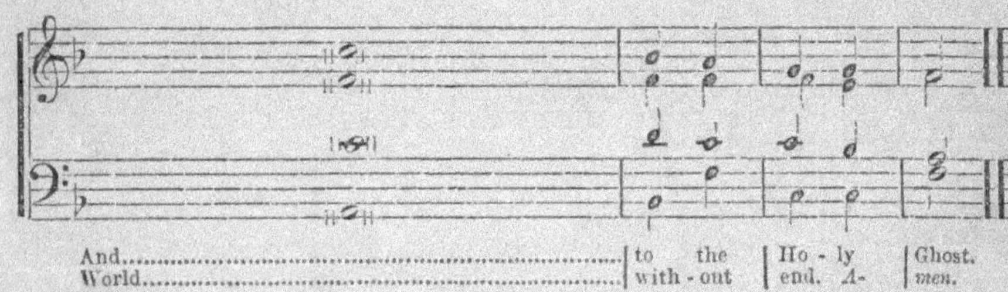


---

## GLORIA PATRI.

17TH TO 27TH SUNDAY AFTER TRINITY. DR. ALCOCK.

# TE DEUM LAUDAMUS.

ADVENT AND CHRISTMAS. JONES, 1760.

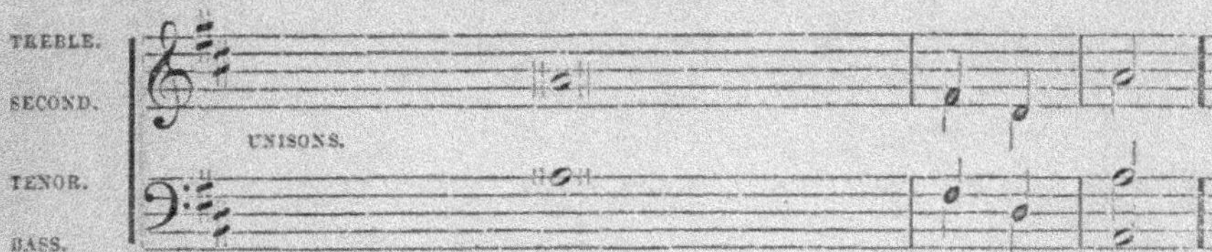


| | | |
|---|---|---|
| 1 We praise Thee, O God, we acknowledge Thee to | be the | Lord: |
| 4 Heaven and earth are full of the majesty | of thy | Glory: |
| 6 The Holy Church throughout all the world, doth ac- | know-ledge | Thee: |
| 8 Thou art the King of | glory, O | Christ: |
| 10 When thou hadst overcome the | sharpness of | death, |
| 12 We therefore pray Thee | help thy | servants: |
| 14 O Lord save thy people, and | bless thine | heritage: |
| 16 Vouchsafe, O Lord, to keep us this | day without | sin. |

| | | | | | |
|---|---|---|---|---|---|
| All the earth doth worship thee, | the | Fa - ther | ev - er- | lasting. | 2 |
| The glorious company of the | A- | pos - tles | praise — | Thee. | 5 |
| The Father of | an | infi - nite | ma - jes- | ty. | 7 |
| Thou art the ev- | er- | last - ing | Son of the | Father. | 9 |
| Thou didst open the Kingdom | of | heaven to | all be- | lievers. | 11 |
| Whom thou hast redeem- | ed | with Thy | pre - cious | blood. | 13 |
| Govern them, | and | lift them | up for- | ever. | 15 |
| O Lord, have mercy upon us, | have | mer - cy | up - on | us. | 17 |

| | | |
|---|---|---|
| {2 To Thee all angels cry aloud; the heavens and all the | powers there- | in: |
| {3 Holy | Ho - ly, | Holy, |
| 5 The goodly fellowship of the prophets | praise — | Thee: |
| 7 Thine adorable, true and | on - ly | Son: |
| 9 When thou tookest upon Thee to de- | liv - er | man, |
| 11 Thou sittest at the right hand of God, in the glory | of the | Father: |
| 13 Make them to be numbered | with Thy | saints, |
| 15 Day by day, we | mag - nify | Thee, |
| 17 O Lord, let Thy mercy be upon us as our | trust is | in Thee: |

| | | | | |
|---|---|---|---|---|
| To Thee Cherubim and Seraphim con- | tin - ual- | ly do | cry. } | 3 |
| Lord | God of | Sab - a- | oth. } | 4 |
| The noble army of | mar - tyrs | praise — | Thee. | 6 |
| Also the Holy | Ghost the | Com - fort- | er. | 8 |
| Thou didst humble Thy- | self to be | born of a | Virgin. | 10 |
| We believe that Thou shalt | come to | be our | Judge. | 12 |
| In | glo - ry | ev - er- | lasting. | 14 |
| And we worship Thy | name ever | world without | end. | 16 |
| O Lord, in Thee have I trusted; let me | nev - er | be con- | founded. | |

## TE DEUM LAUDAMUS.

EPIPHANY TO QUINQUAGESIMA. JOHN DAVY.

TREBLE. SECOND. TENOR. BASS.

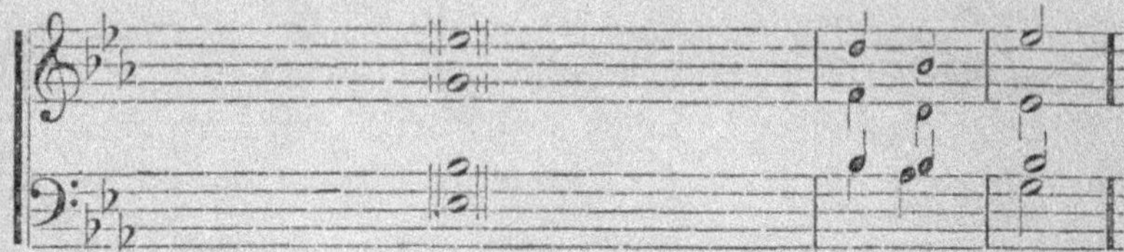

| | | |
|---|---|---|
| 1 We praise Thee, O God, we acknowledge Thee to | be the | Lord : |
| 4 Heaven and earth are full of the majesty | of thy | Glory : |
| 6 The Holy Church throughout all the world, doth ac- | know-ledge | Thee : |
| 8 Thou art the king of | glory, O | Christ : |
| 10 When thou hadst overcome the | sharpness of | death : |
| 12 We therefore pray Thee | help thy | servants : |
| 14 O Lord save thy people, and | bless thine | heritage : |
| 16 Vouchsafe, O Lord, to keep us this | day without | sin. |

| | | | | |
|---|---|---|---|---|
| All the earth doth worship thee, the | Fa - ther | ev - er | lasting. | 2 |
| The glorious company of the A- | pos - tles | praise — | Thee. | 5 |
| The Father of an | infi - nite | ma - jes- | ty. | 7 |
| Thou art the ever- | last - ing | Son of the | Father. | 9 |
| Thou didst open the Kingdom of | heaven to | all be- | lievers. | 11 |
| Whom thou has redeemed | with Thy | pre - cious | blood. | 13 |
| Govern them, and | lift them | up for | ever, | 15 |
| O Lord, have mercy upon us, have | mer - cy | up - on | us. | 17 |

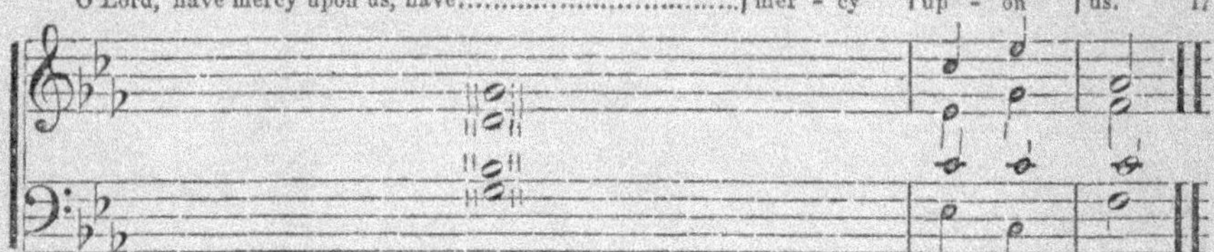

| | | |
|---|---|---|
| {2 To Thee all angels cry aloud ; the heavens and all the | powers there- | in : |
| {3 Holy | Ho - ly, | Holy : |
| 5 The goodly fellowship of the prophets | praise — | Thee : |
| 7 Thine adorable, true, and | on - ly | Son : |
| 9 When thou tookest upon Thee to de- | liv - er | man : |
| 11 Thou sittest at the right hand of God, in the glory | of the | Father : |
| 13 Make them to be numbered | with Thy | saints : |
| 15 Day by day we | mag - nify | Thee : |
| 17 O Lord, let Thy mercy be upon us, as our | trust is | in Thee : |

| | | | | |
|---|---|---|---|---|
| To Thee Cherubim and Seraphim con- | tin - ual- | ly do | cry. } | 3 |
| Lord | God of | Sab - a- | oth. } | 4 |
| The noble army of | mar - tyrs | praise — | Thee. | 6 |
| Also the Holy | Ghost the | Com - fort- | er. | 8 |
| Thou didst humble Thy- | self to be | born of a | Virgin. | 10 |
| We believe that Thou shalt | come to | be our | Judge. | 12 |
| In | glo - ry | ev - er | lasting. | 14 |
| And we worship Thy | name ever | world without | end. | 16 |
| O Lord, in Thee have I trusted ; let me | nev - er | be con- | founded. | |

## TE DEUM LAUDAMUS.

EASTER TO WHITSUNDAY. EBDON.

TREBLE.
SECOND.
TENOR.
BASS.

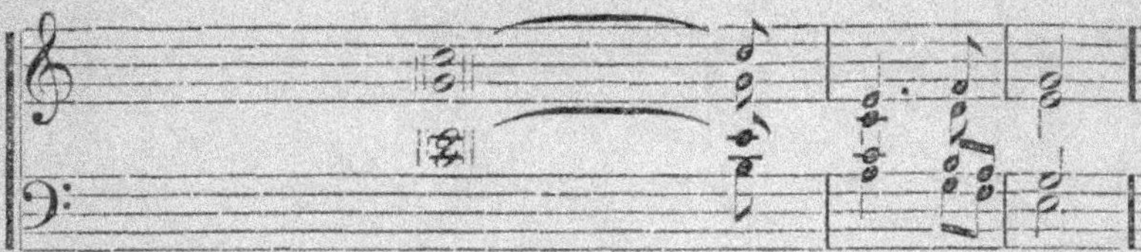

1 We praise Thee, O God, we acknowledge Thee........................ to ...... | be the | Lord :
4 Heaven and earth are full of the majesty........................................ | of thy | Glory
6 The Holy Church throughout all the world, doth.......................... ac-...... | know ledge | Thee :
8 Thou art the king.................................................................... of ...... | glory, O | Christ :
10 When thou hadst overcome ...................................................... the..... | sharpness of | death :
12 We therefore pray Thee .............................................................. | help thy | servants :
14 O Lord save thy people,.......................................................... and .... | bless thine | heritage ;
16 Vouchsafe, O Lord, to keep us.................................................. this .... | day without | sin.

All the earth doth worship thee,........................... the ...... | Fa - ther | ev - er- | lasting. 2
The glorious company of ..................................... the A-... | pos - tles | praise — | Thee. 5
The Father of.......................................................... an ...... | infi - nite | ma - jes- | ty. 7
Thou art the ev-...................................................... er- ...... | last - ing | Son of the | Father. 9
Thou didst open the Kingdom.................................. of ...... | heaven to | all be- | lievers. 11
Whom thou hast redeem-......................................... ed ...... | with Thy | pre - cious | blood. 13
Govern them,............................................................ and ...... | lift them | up for- | ever. 15
O Lord, have mercy upon us,................................... have .... | mer - cy | up - on | us. 17

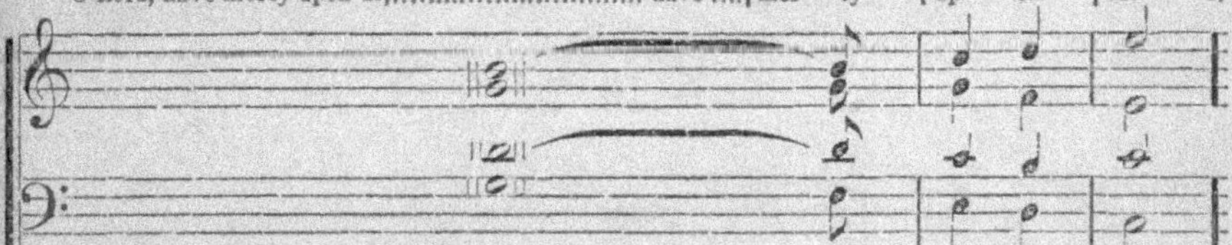

{2 To Thee all angels cry aloud; the heavens and all.......................... the ...... | powers there- | in:
{3 Ho-................................................................................................ ly ....... | Ho - ly, | Holy,
5 The goodly fellowship of the pro-..................................................... phets ... | praise — | Thee:
7 Thine adorable, true.......................................................................... and,...... | on - ly | Son:
9 When thou tookest upon Thee to....................................................... de-...... | liv - er | man,
11 Thou sittest at the right hand of God, in the glo- .............................. ry ...... | of the | Father:
13 Make them to be num-...................................................................... bered... | with Thy | saints,
15 Day by day,...................................................................................... we ...... | mag - nify | Thee,
17 O Lord, let Thy mercy be upon us as................................................ our..... | trust is | in Thee:

To Thee Cherubim and Seraphim,......................... con-..... | tin - ual- | ly do | cry. } 3
Lord.......................................................................... | God of | Sab - a- | oth. } 4
The noble army................................................... of ...... | mar - tyrs | praise — | Thee. 6
Also the Ho-....................................................... ly ...... | Ghost the | Com - fort- | er. 8
Thou didst humble Thy-.............................................. | self to be | born of a | Virgin. 10
We believe that Thou.................................. shalt,... | come to | be our | Judge. 12
In............................................................................. | glo - ry | ev - er- | lasting. 14
And we worship.............................................. Thy ...... | name ever | world without | end. 16
O Lord, in Thee have I trusted; let.................... me..... | nev - er | be con- | founded.

# TE DEUM LAUDAMUS.

TRINITY TO 8TH SUNDAY AFTER. J. GARNETT.

TREBLE.
SECOND.
TENOR.
BASS.

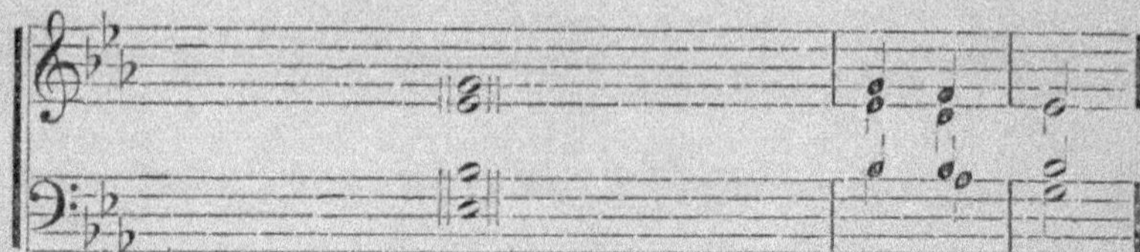

| | | |
|---|---|---|
| 1 We praise Thee, O God, we acknowledge Thee to | be the | Lord: |
| 4 Heaven and earth are full of the majesty | of thy | Glory: |
| 6 The Holy Church throughout all the world, doth ac- | know-ledge | Thee: |
| 8 Thou art the King of | glory, O | Christ: |
| 10 When thou hadst overcome the | sharpness of | death, |
| 12 We therefore pray Thee | help thy | servants, |
| 14 O Lord save thy people, and | bless thine | heritage: |
| 16 Vouchsafe, O Lord, to keep us this | day without | sin. |

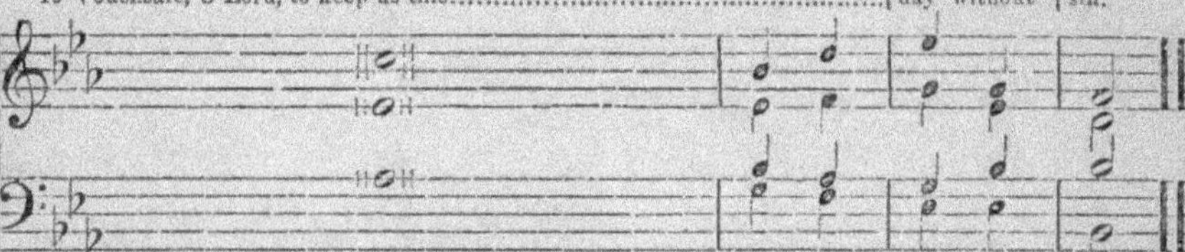

| | | | |
|---|---|---|---|
| All the earth doth worship thee, the | Fa - ther | ev - er | lasting. 2 |
| The glorious company of the A- | pos - tles | praise — | Thee. 5 |
| The Father of an | infi - nite | ma - jes- | ty. 7 |
| Thou art the ever- | last - ing | Son of the | Father. 9 |
| Thou didst open the Kingdom of | heaven to | all be- | lievers. 11 |
| Whom thou has redeemed | with Thy | pre - cious | blood. 13 |
| Govern them, and | lift them | up for | ever, 15 |
| O Lord, have mercy upon us, have | mer - cy | up - on | us. 17 |

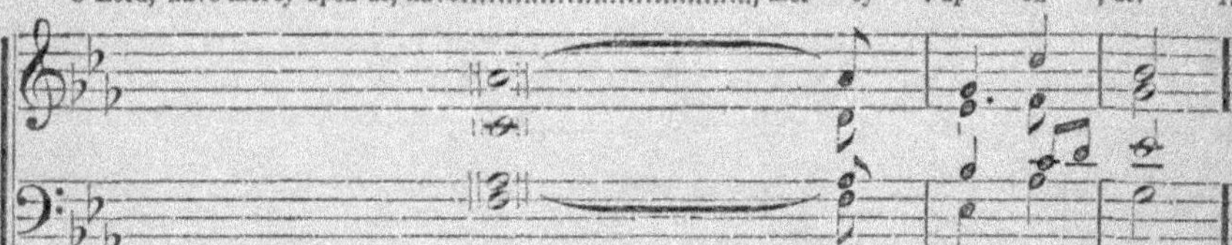

| | | | |
|---|---|---|---|
| {2 To Thee all angels cry aloud; the heavens and all | the | powers there- | in: |
| {3 Ho- | ly | Ho - ly, | Holy, |
| 5 The goodly fellowship of the pro- | phets | praise — | Thee: |
| 7 Thine adorable, true | and | on - ly | Son: |
| 9 When thou tookest upon Thee to | de- | liv - er | man, |
| 11 Thou sittest at the right hand of God, in the glo- | ry | of the | Father: |
| 13 Make them to be num- | bered | with Thy | saints, |
| 15 Day by day | we | mag - nify | Thee, |
| 17 O Lord, let Thy mercy be upon us as | our | trust is | in Thee: |

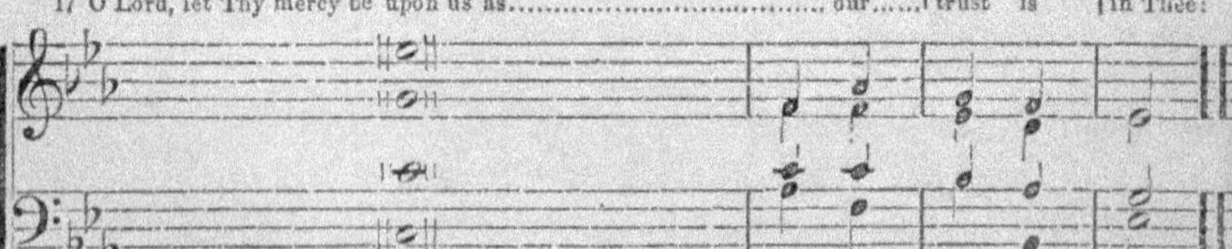

| | | | |
|---|---|---|---|
| To Thee Cherubim and Seraphim con- | tin - ual- | ly do | cry. } 3 |
| Lord | God of | Sab - a- | oth. } 4 |
| The noble army of | mar - tyrs | praise — | Thee. 6 |
| Also the Holy | Ghost the | Com - fort- | er. 8 |
| Thou didst humble Thy- | self to be | born of a | Virgin. 10 |
| We believe that Thou shalt | come to | be our | Judge. 12 |
| In | glo - ry | ev - er | lasting. 14 |
| And we worship Thy | name ever | world without | end. 16 |
| O Lord, in Thee have I trusted; let me | nev - er | be con- | founded. |

## TE DEUM LAUDAMUS.

9TH TO 16TH SUNDAY AFTER TRINITY. DR. CHARD.

TREBLE. SECOND. TENOR. BASS.

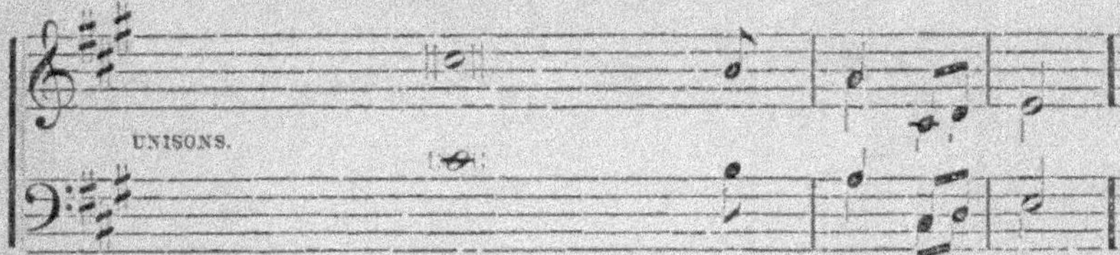


| | | | |
|---|---|---|---|
| 1 We praise Thee, O God, we acknowledge Thee.......... | to | be the | Lord: |
| 4 Heaven and earth are full of the majesty.......... | | of thy | Glory: |
| 6 The Holy Church throughout all the world, doth.......... | ac- | know-ledge | Thee: |
| 8 Thou art the King.......... | of | glory, O | Christ: |
| 10 When thou hadst overcome.......... | the | sharpness of | death, |
| 12 We therefore pray Thee.......... | | help thy | servants, |
| 14 O Lord save thy people,.......... | and | bless thine | heritage: |
| 16 Vouchsafe, O Lord, to keep us.......... | this | day without | sin. |

| | | | |
|---|---|---|---|
| All the earth doth worship thee, the.......... | Fa - ther | ev - er | lasting. 2 |
| The glorious company of the A-.......... | pos - tles | praise — | Thee. 5 |
| The Father of an.......... | infi - nite | ma - jes- | ty. 7 |
| Thou art the ever-.......... | last - ing | Son of the | Father. 9 |
| Thou didst open the Kingdom of.......... | heaven to | all be- | lievers. 11 |
| Whom thou has redeemed.......... | with Thy | pre - cious | blood. 13 |
| Govern them, and.......... | lift them | up for | ever. 15 |
| O Lord, have mercy upon us, have.......... | mer - cy | up - on | us. 17 |

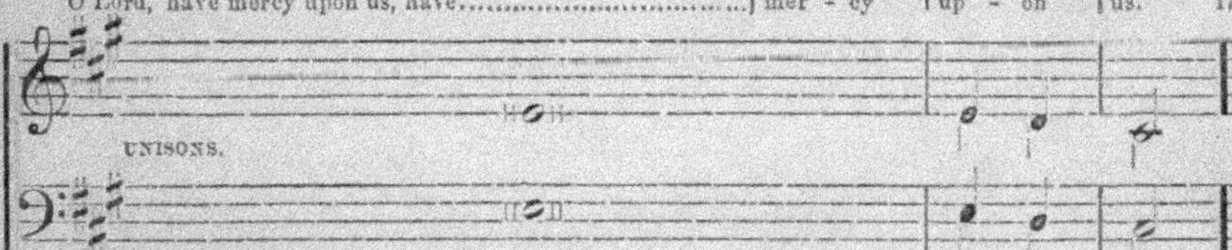


| | | |
|---|---|---|
| {2 To Thee all angels cry aloud; the heavens and all the.......... | powers there- | in: |
| {3 Holy.......... | Ho - ly, | Holy: |
| 5 The goodly fellowship of the prophets.......... | praise — | Thee: |
| 7 Thine adorable, true, and.......... | on - ly | Son: |
| 9 When thou tookest upon Thee to de-.......... | liv - er | man: |
| 11 Thou sittest at the right hand of God, in the glory.......... | of the | Father: |
| 13 Make them to be numbered.......... | with Thy | saints: |
| 15 Day by day we.......... | mag - nify | Thee: |
| 17 O Lord, let Thy mercy be upon us, as our.......... | trust is | in Thee: |

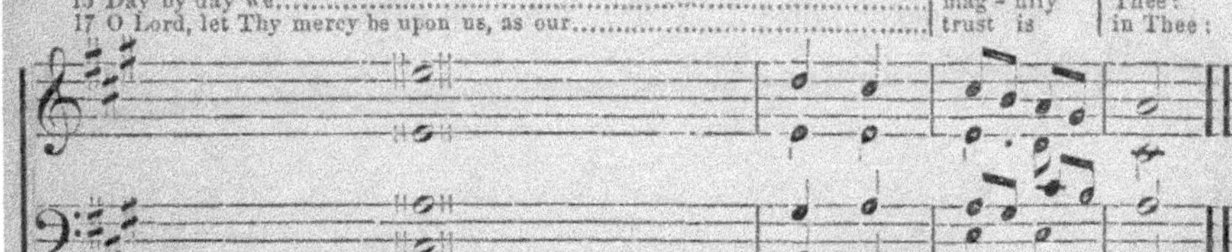

| | | | |
|---|---|---|---|
| To Thee Cherubim and Seraphim con-.......... | tin - ual- | ly do | cry. } 3 |
| Lord.......... | God of | Sab - a- | oth. } 4 |
| The noble army of.......... | mar - tyrs | praise — | Thee. 6 |
| Also the Holy.......... | Ghost the | Com - fort- | er. 8 |
| Thou didst humble Thy-.......... | self to be | born of a | Virgin. 10 |
| We believe that Thou shalt.......... | come to | be our | Judge. 12 |
| In.......... | glo - ry | ev - er | lasting. 14 |
| And we worship Thy.......... | name ever | world without | end. 16 |
| O Lord, in Thee have I trusted; let me.......... | nev - er | be con- | founded. |

## TE DEUM LAUDAMUS.

17TH TO 27TH SUNDAY AFTER TRINITY. J. GARNETT.

TREBLE.
SECOND.
TENOR.
BASS.

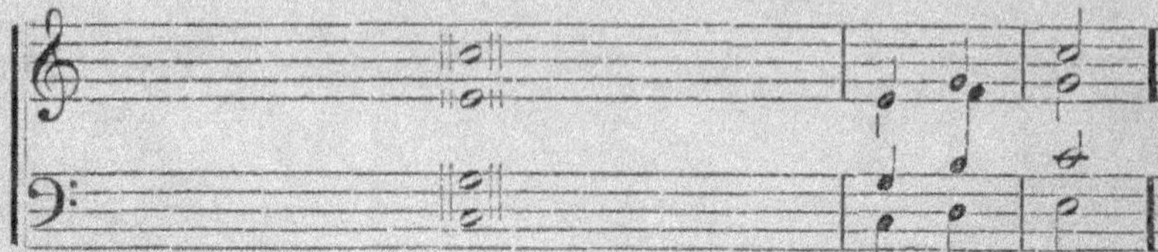

| | | |
|---|---|---|
| 1 We praise Thee, O God, we acknowledge Thee to.......... | be the | Lord: |
| 4 Heaven and earth are full of the majesty.......... | of thy | Glory: |
| 6 The Holy Church throughout all the world, doth ac-.......... | know-ledge | Thee: |
| 8 Thou art the king of.......... | glory, O | Christ: |
| 10 When thou hadst overcome the .......... | sharpness of | death: |
| 12 We therefore pray Thee .......... | help thy | servants |
| 14 O Lord save thy people, and.......... | bless thine | heritage: |
| 16 Vouchsafe, O Lord, to keep us this.......... | day without | sin. |

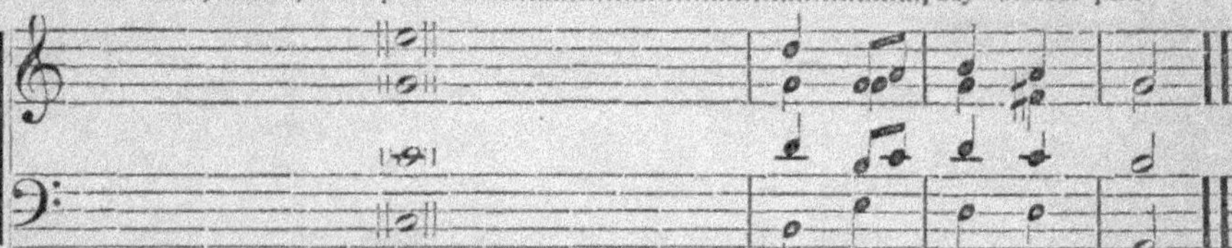

| | | | |
|---|---|---|---|
| All the earth doth worship thee, the.......... | Fa - ther | ev - er- | lasting. 2 |
| The glorious company of the A-.......... | pos - tles | praise — | Thee. 5 |
| The Father of an.......... | infi - nite | ma - jes- | ty. 7 |
| Thou art the ever-.......... | last - ing | Son of the | Father. 9 |
| Thou didst open the Kingdom of.......... | heaven to | all be- | lievers. 11 |
| Whom thou hast redeemed.......... | with Thy | pre - cious | blood. 13 |
| Govern them, and.......... | lift them | up for- | ever. 15 |
| O Lord, have mercy upon us, have.......... | mer - cy | up - on | us. 17 |

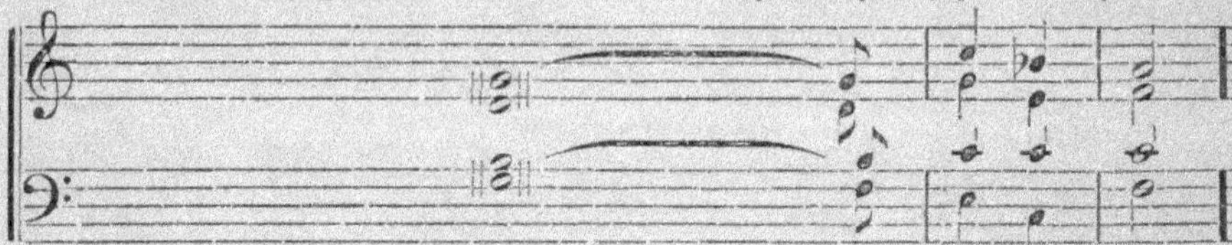

| | | | |
|---|---|---|---|
| {2 To Thee all angels cry aloud; the heavens and all.......... | the..... | powers there- | in: |
| {3 Ho-.......... | ly..... | Ho - ly, | Holy: |
| 5 The goodly fellowship of the pro-.......... | phets... | praise — | Thee: |
| 7 Thine adorable, true,.......... | and .... | on - ly | Son: |
| 9 When thou tookest upon Thee to .......... | de-..... | liv - er | man: |
| 11 Thou sittest at the right hand of God, in the glo-.......... | ry ..... | of the | Father: |
| 13 Make them to be num-.......... | bered... | with Thy | saints: |
| 15 Day by day.......... | we..... | mag - nify | Thee: |
| 17 O Lord, let thy mercy be upon us, as.......... | our..... | trust is | in Thee: |

| | | | |
|---|---|---|---|
| To Thee Cherubim and Seraphim con-.......... | tin - ual- | ly do | cry. } 3 |
| Lord.......... | God of | Sab - a- | oth. } 4 |
| The noble army of.......... | mar - tyrs | praise — | Thee. 6 |
| Also the Holy.......... | Ghost the | Com - fort- | er. 8 |
| Thou didst humble Thy-.......... | self to be | born of a | Virgin. 10 |
| We believe that Thou shalt.......... | come to | be our | Judge. 12 |
| In.......... | glo - ry | ev - er- | lasting. 14 |
| And we worship Thy .......... | name ever | world without | end. 16 |
| O Lord, in Thee have I trusted; let me.......... | nev - er | be con- | founded. |

# BENEDICITE, OMNIA OPERA DOMINI.

HAVERGALL.

| | | | | | | | |
|---|---|---|---|---|---|---|---|
| 1 O all ye Works of the Lord, | bless ye the | Lord, | praise Him, and | magnify | Him for | ever. | 2 |
| 3 O ye Heavens,.................... | bless ye the | Lord, | praise Him, and | magnify | Him for | ever. | 4 |
| 5 O all ye powers of the Lord, | bless ye the | Lord, | praise Him, and | magnify | Him for | ever. | 6 |
| 7 O ye Stars of Heaven,......... | bless ye the | Lord, | praise Him, and | magnify | Him for | ever. | 8 |
| 9 O ye Winds of God,............ | bless ye the | Lord, | praise Him, and | magnify | Him for | ever. | 10 |
| 11 O ye Winter and Summer,.. | bless ye the | Lord, | praise Him, and | magnify | Him for | ever. | 12 |
| 13 O ye Frost and Cold,......... | bless ye the | Lord, | praise Him, and | magnify | Him for | ever. | 14 |
| 15 O ye Nights and Days......... | bless ye the | Lord, | praise Him, and | magnify | Him for | ever. | 16 |
| 17 O ye Lightnings and Clouds | bless ye the | Lord, | praise Him, and | magnify | Him for | ever. | 18 |
| 19 O ye Mountains and Hills... | bless ye the | Lord, | praise Him, and | magnify | Him for | ever. | 20 |
| 21 O ye Wells,......................... | bless ye the | Lord, | praise Him, and | magnify | Him for | ever. | 22 |
| 23 O ye Whales, and all that move in the Waters...... | bless ye the | Lord, | praise Him, and | magnify | Him for | ever. | 24 |
| 25 O all ye Beasts and Cattle,. | bless ye the | Lord, | praise Him, and | magnify | Him for | ever. | 26 |
| 27 O let Israel,....................... | bless ye the | Lord, | praise Him, and | magnify | Him for | ever. | 28 |
| 29 O ye Servants of the Lord,.. | bless ye the | Lord, | praise Him, and | magnify | Him for | ever. | 30 |
| 32 Glory be to the Father, and | to the | Son | and — | to the | Ho - ly | Ghost: | 33 |

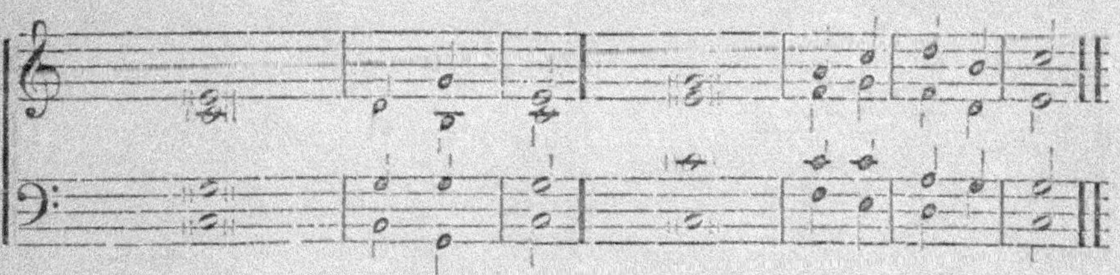

| | | | | | | | |
|---|---|---|---|---|---|---|---|
| 2 O ye Angels of the Lord, | bless ye the | Lord, | praise Him, and | magnify | Him for | ever. | 3 |
| 4 O ye Waters that be above the Firmament,........... | bless ye the | Lord, | praise Him, and | magnify | Him for | ever. | 5 |
| 6 O ye Sun and Moon,........... | bless ye the | Lord, | praise Him, and | magnify | Him for | ever. | 7 |
| 8 O ye Showers and Dew,...... | bless ye the | Lord, | praise Him, and | magnify | Him for | ever. | 9 |
| 10 O ye Fire and Heat,........... | bless ye the | Lord, | praise Him, and | magnify | Him for | ever. | 11 |
| 12 O ye Dews and Frosts,........ | bless ye the | Lord, | praise Him, and | magnify | Him for | ever. | 13 |
| 14 O ye Ice and Snow,............ | bless ye the | Lord, | praise Him, and | magnify | Him for | ever. | 15 |
| 16 O ye Light and Darkness,... | bless ye the | Lord, | praise Him, and | magnify | Him for | ever. | 17 |
| 18 O let the Earth,................ | bless ye the | Lord, | praise Him, and | magnify | Him for | ever. | 19 |
| 20 O all ye Green Things upon the Earth,............... | bless ye the | Lord, | praise Him, and | magnify | Him for | ever. | 21 |
| 22 O ye Seas and Floods,......... | bless ye the | Lord, | praise Him, and | magnify | Him for | ever. | 23 |
| 24 O all ye Fowls of the Air,.... | bless ye the | Lord, | praise Him, and | magnify | Him for | ever. | 25 |
| 26 O ye Children of Men,......... | bless ye the | Lord, | praise Him, and | magnify | Him for | ever. | 27 |
| 28 O ye Priests of the Lord,...... | bless ye the | Lord, | praise Him, and | magnify | Him for | ever. | 29 |
| 30 O ye Spirits and Souls of the Righteous,............. | bless ye the | Lord, | praise Him, and | magnify | Him for | ever. | 31 |
| 31 O ye holy and humble Men of heart,..................... | bless ye the | Lord, | praise Him, and | magnify | Him for | ever. | 32 |
| 33 As it was in the beginning, is now, and.................. | ev - er | shall be | world — | without | end. A- | *men.* | |

## JUBILATE DEO.

ADVENT AND CHRISTMAS. BATTISHILL & JACKSON.

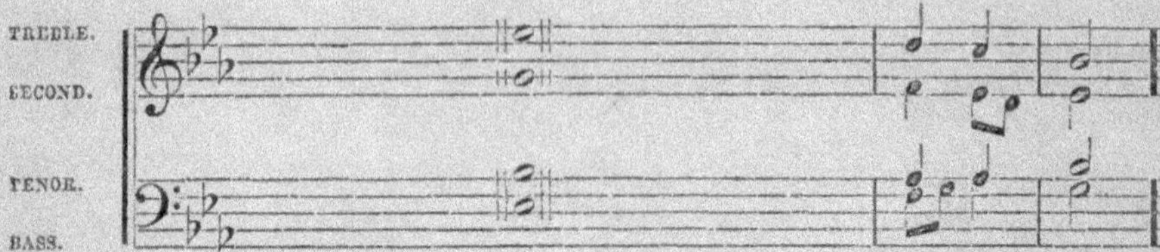


1 O be joyful in the Lord............ | all ye | lands:
3 O go your way into his gates with thanksgiving, and into his............ | courts with | praise:
5 Glory be to the Father, and............ | to the | Son:

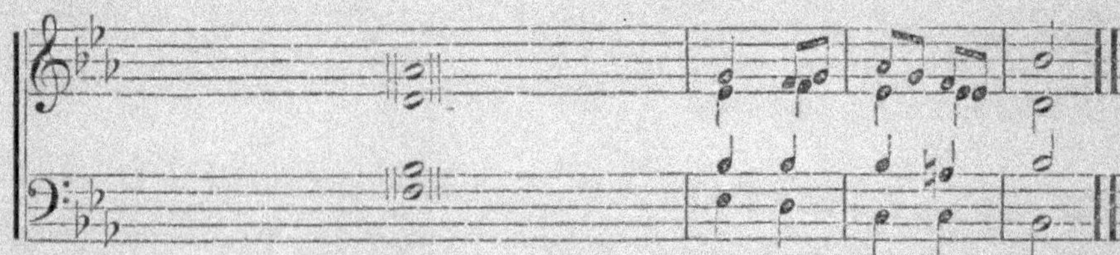

Serve the Lord with gladness, and come before his............ | pres - ence | with a | song. 2
Be thankful unto Him, and............ | speak good | of his | name. 4
And............ | to the | Ho - ly | Ghost. 6

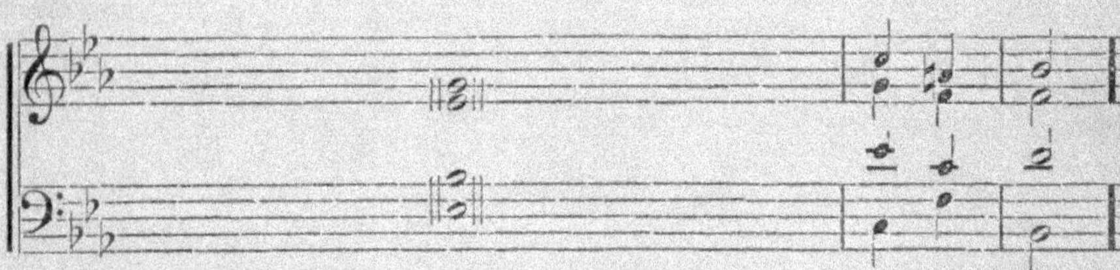

2 Be ye sure that the Lord,............ | He is | God:
4 For the Lord is gracious, his mercy is............ | ev - er | lasting:
6 As it was in the beginning, is now, and............ | ev - er | shall be,

It is he that hath made us, and not we ourselves, we are his | people and the | sheep of his | pasture. 3
And his truth endureth from gene-............ | ration to | gen - e- | ration. 5
World............ | with - out | end. *A-* | *men.*

# JUBILATE DEO.

EPIPHANY TO QUINQUAGESIMA. ALDRIDGE.

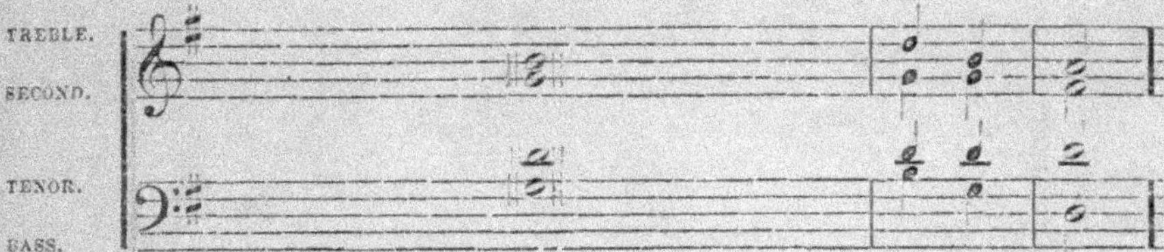


1 O be joyful in the Lord.................................................. | all ye | lands:
3 O go your way into his gates with thanksgiving, and into his.............. | courts with | praise:
5 Glory be to the Father, and.................................................. | to the | Son:

Serve the Lord with gladness, and come before...... his ...... | pres - ence | with a | song. 2
Be thankful unto Him,......................................... and...... | speak good | of his | name. 4
And .................................................................. | to the | Ho - ly | Ghost. 6

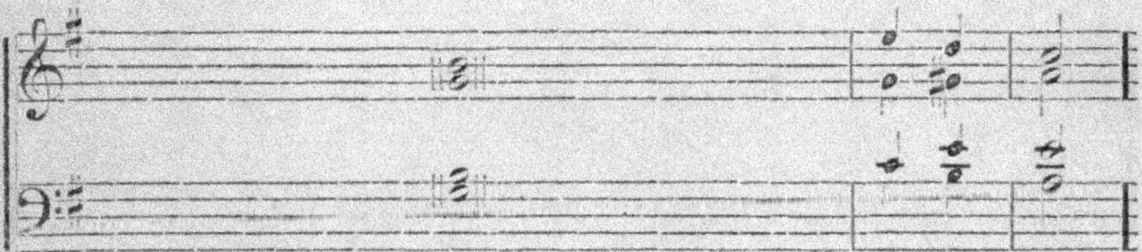

2 Be ye sure that the Lord,................................................. | He is | God:
4 For the Lord is gracious, his mercy is..................................... | ev - er | lasting:
6 As it was in the beginning, is now, and.................................... | ev - er | shall be,

It is he that hath made us, and not we ourselves, we are his | people and the | sheep of his | pasture. 3
And his truth endureth from gen-.......................... e- ...... | ration to | gen - e- | ration. 5
World .................................................................. | with - out | end. *A-* | *men.*

## JUBILATE DEO.

LENT. T. PARNELL.

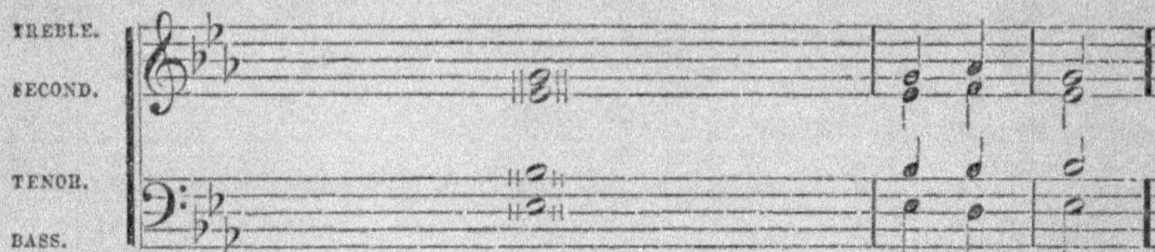


| | | |
|---|---|---|
| 1 O be joyful in the Lord.................................................... | all ye | lands: |
| 3 O go your way into his gates with thanksgiving, and into his.............. | courts with | praise: |
| 5 Glory be to the Father, and .................................................... | to the | Son: |

| | | | | |
|---|---|---|---|---|
| Serve the Lord with gladness, and come before his............ | pres - ence | with a | song: | 2 |
| Be thankful unto Him and.................................... | speak good | of his | name. | 4 |
| And .................................................................. | to the | Ho - ly | Ghost. | 6 |

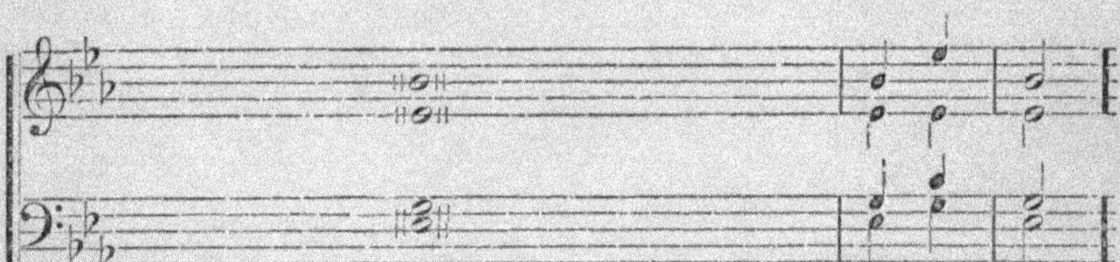

| | | |
|---|---|---|
| 2 Be ye sure that the Lord,.................................................... | He is | God: |
| 4 For the Lord is gracious, his mercy is.................................... | ev - er | lasting: |
| 6 As it was in the beginning, is now, and.................................. | ev- - er | shall be, |

| | | | | |
|---|---|---|---|---|
| It is he that hath made us, and not we ourselves, we are his | people and the | sheep of his | pasture. | 3 |
| And his truth endureth from gene-........................................ | ration to | gen- e- | ration. | 5 |
| World........................................................................ | with - out | end. A- | *men.* | |

# JUBILATE DEO.

EASTER TO WHITSUNDAY. ISAAC BARROW.

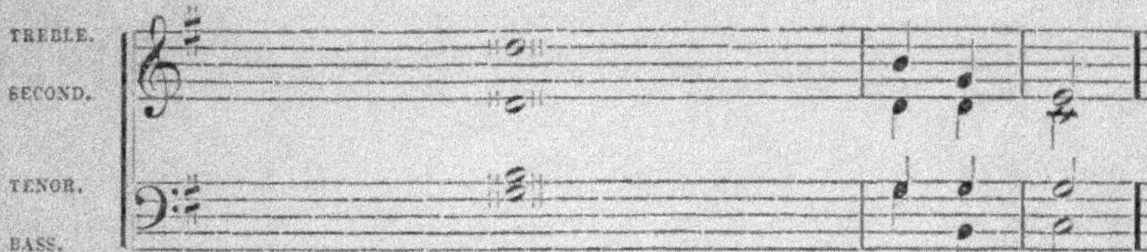


1 O be joyful in the Lord.......... | all ye | lands:
3 O go your way into his gates with thanksgiving, and into his.......... | courts with | praise:
5 Glory be to the Father, and.......... | to the | Son:

Serve the Lord with gladness, and come before...... his ...... | pres - ence | with a | song. 2
Be thankful unto Him,.......... and...... | speak good | of his | name. 4
And.......... | to the | Ho - ly | Ghost. 6

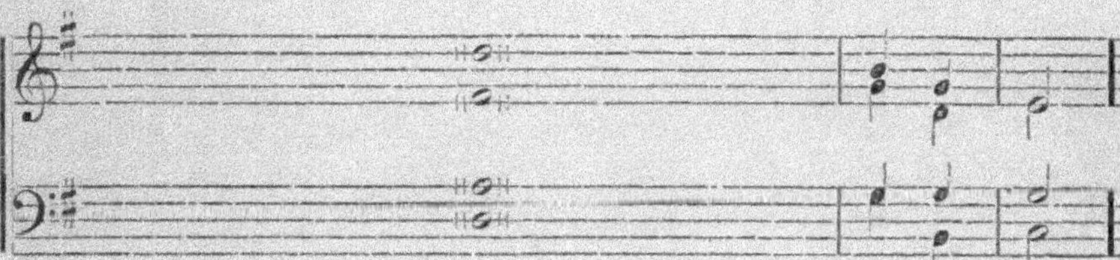

2 Be ye sure that the Lord,.......... | He is | God:
4 For the Lord is gracious, his mercy is.......... | ev - er | lasting:
6 As it was in the beginning, is now, and.......... | ev - er | shall be,

It is he that hath made us, and not we ourselves, we are his | people and the | sheep of his | pasture. 3
And his truth endureth from gene-.......... | ration to | gen - e- | ration. 5
World.......... | with - out | end. *A-* | *men.*

## JUBILATE DEO.

TRINITY TO 8TH SUNDAY AFTER. REV. T. PEARS.

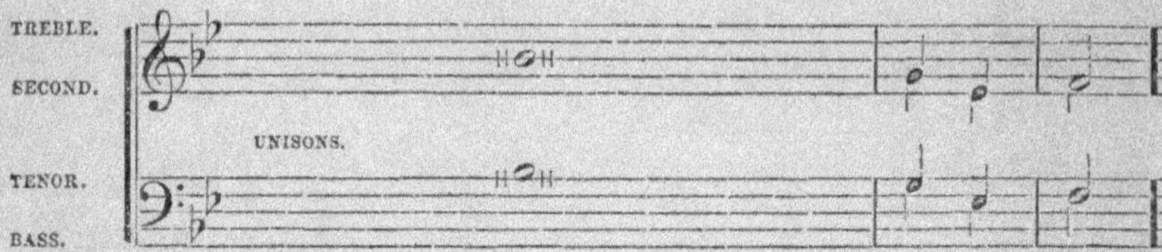


1 O be joyful in the Lord............ | all ye | lands:
3 O go your way into his gates with thanksgiving, and into his............ | courts with | praise.
5 Glory be to the Father, and............ | to the | Son:

Serve the Lord with gladness, and come before his............ | pres - ence | with a | song. 2
Be thankful unto Him and............ | speak good | of his | name. 4
And............ | to the | Ho - ly | Ghost, 6

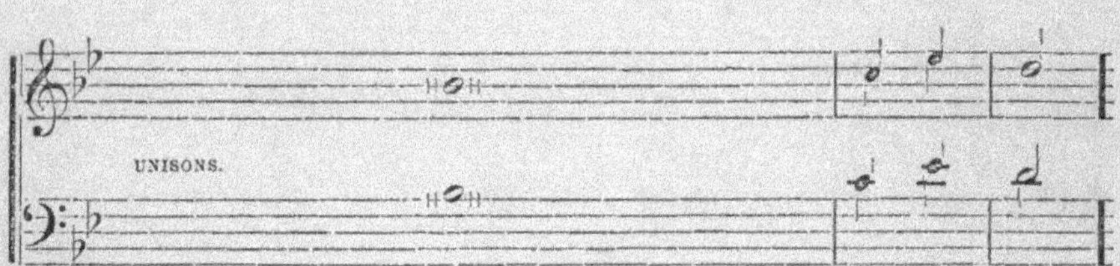


2 Be ye sure that the Lord............ | He is | God:
4 For the Lord is gracious, his mercy is............ | ev - er | lasting;
6 As it was in the beginning, is now, and............ | ev - er | shall be,

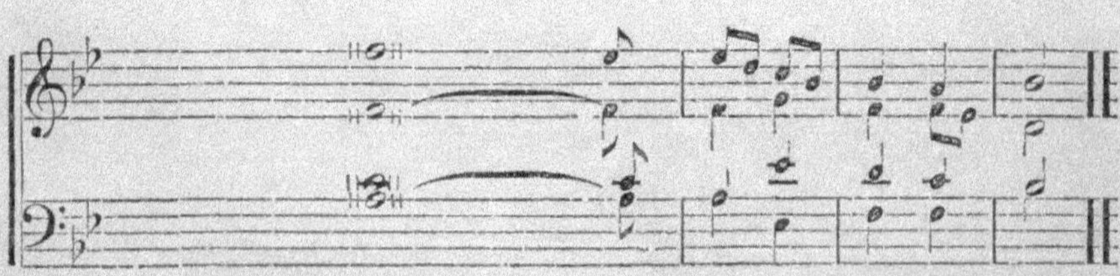

It is that hath made us, and not we ourselves, we are his... | people and the | sheep of his | pasture. 3
And his truth endureth from gene............ | ration to | gen - e- | ration. 5
World............ | with - out | end. *A-* | *men.*

## JUBILATE DEO.

9TH TO 16TH SUNDAY AFTER TRINITY. SOAPER.

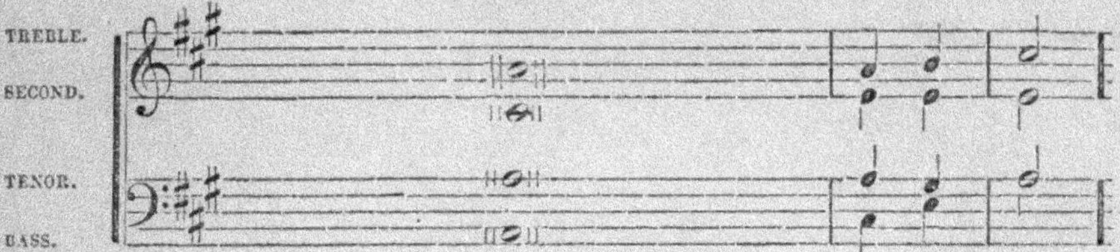


1 O be joyful in the Lord.......................................................... | all ye | lands:
3 O go your way into his gates with thanksgiving, and into his.............. | courts with | praise:
5 Glory be to the Father, and.......................................................... | to the | Son:

Serve the Lord with gladness and come before...... his ...... | pres - ence | with a | song. 2
Be thankful unto Him,........................................ and ...... | speak good | of his | name 4
And ........................................................................ | to the | Ho - ly | Ghost. 6

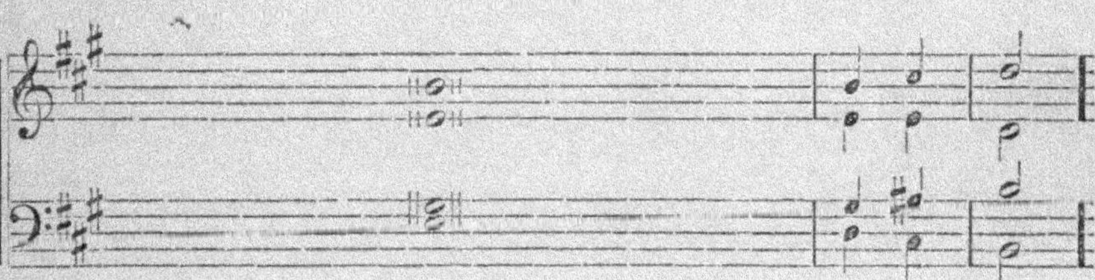

2 Be ye sure that the Lord,.......................................................... | He is | God:
4 For the Lord is gracious, his mercy is.......................................... | ev - er- | lasting:
6 As it was in the beginning, is now, and.......................................... | ev - er | shall be,

It is he that hath made us, and not we ourselves, we are his | people and the | sheep of his | pasture. 3
And his truth endureth from gen-........................ e- ...... | ration to | gen - e- | ration. 5
World.................................................................... | with - out | end. *A-* | *men.*

## JUBILATE DEO.

17TH TO 27TH SUNDAY AFTER TRINITY. DAVIS.

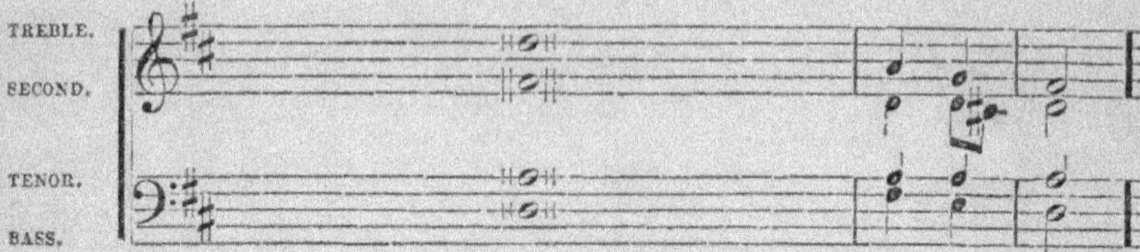


| | | |
|---|---|---|
| 1 O be joyful in the Lord........................ | all ye | lands: |
| 3 O go your way into his gates with thanksgiving, and into his.............. | courts with | praise: |
| 5 Glory be to the Father, and........................ | to the | Son: |

| | | | |
|---|---|---|---|
| Serve the Lord with gladness, and come before...... his ...... | pres - ence | with a | song. 2 |
| Be thankful unto Him,........................ and...... | speak good | of his | name. 4 |
| And........................ | to the | Ho - ly | Ghost. 6 |

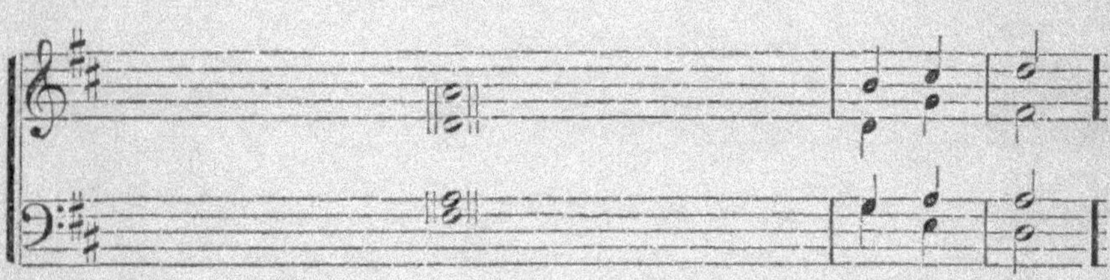

| | | |
|---|---|---|
| 2 Be ye sure that the Lord,........................ | He is | God: |
| 4 For the Lord is gracious, his mercy is........................ | ev - er | lasting: |
| 6 As it was in the beginning, is now, and........................ | ev - er | shall be, |

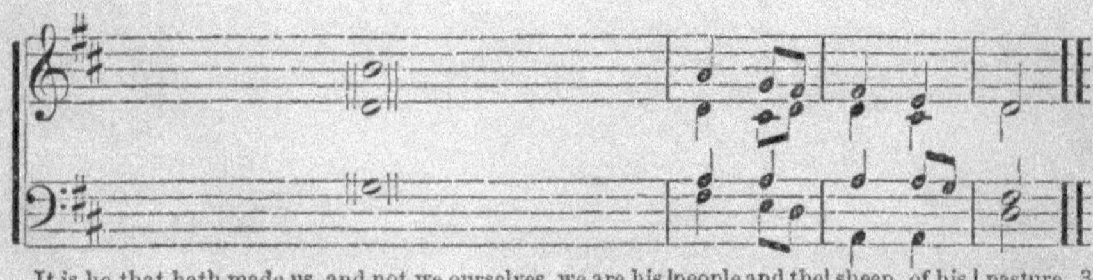

| | | | |
|---|---|---|---|
| It is he that hath made us, and not we ourselves, we are his | people and the | sheep of his | pasture. 3 |
| And his truth endureth from gene-........................ | ration to | gen - e- | ration. 5 |
| World ........................ | with - out | end. *A-* | *men.* |

## BENEDICTUS.

ADVENT AND CHRISTMAS. DR. CROTCH.

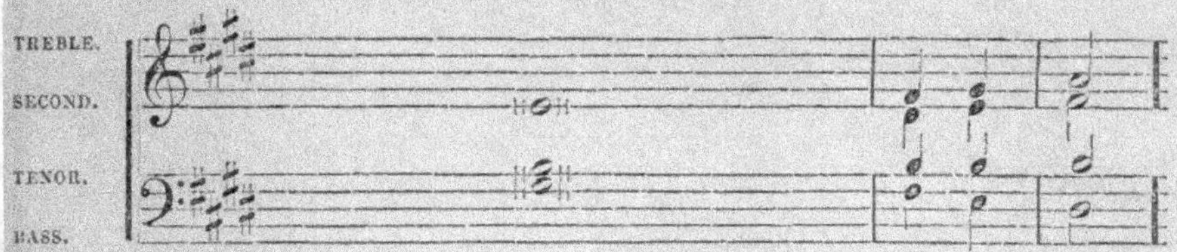


| | | |
|---|---|---|
| 1 Blessed be the Lord........ | God of | Israel: |
| 3 As he spake by the mouth of his........ | ho - ly | prophets: |
| 5 Glory be to the Father, and........ | to the | Son: |

| | | | |
|---|---|---|---|
| For he hath visited........ | and re- | deemed His | people: 2 |
| Which have been........ | since the | world be- | gan: 4 |
| And........ | to the | Ho - ly | Ghost: 6 |

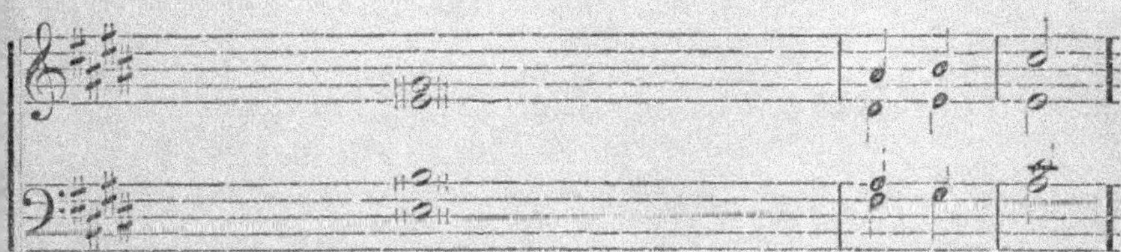

| | | |
|---|---|---|
| 2 And hath raised up a mighty sal-........ | va - tion | for us: |
| 4 That we should be saved........ | from our | enemies: |
| 6 As it was in the beginning, is now, and........ | ev - er | shall be: |

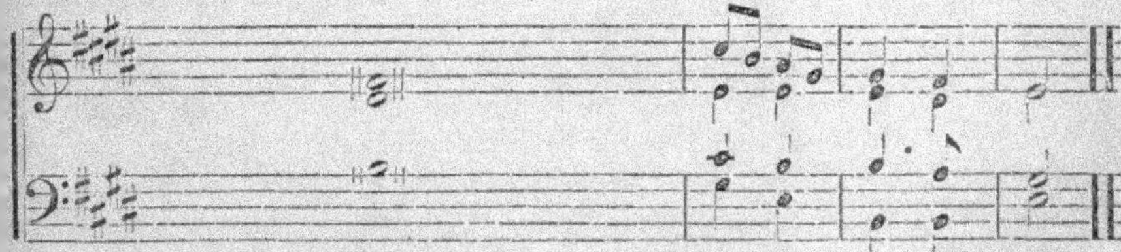

| | | | |
|---|---|---|---|
| In the house........ | of His | ser - vant | David. 3 |
| And from the........ | hand of | all that | hate us. 5 |
| World........ | with - out | end. *A-* | *men.* |

## BENEDICTUS.

EPIPHANY TO QUINQUAGESIMA. JOHN ROBINSON, 1730.

TREBLE.
SECOND.
TENOR.
BASS.

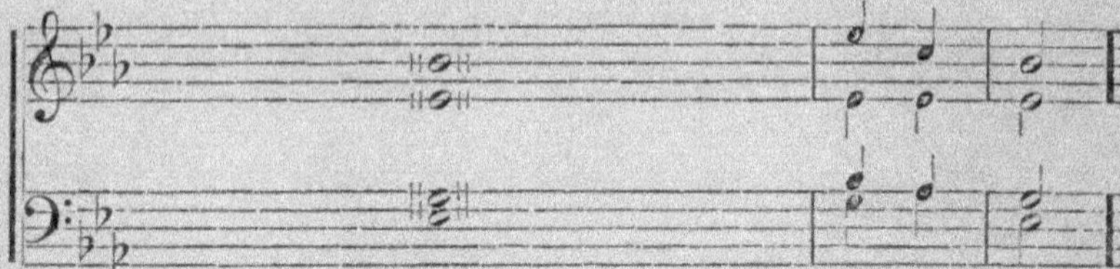

1 Blessed be the Lord............ | God of | Israel:
3 As He spake by the mouth of His............ | ho - ly | prophets:
5 Glory be to the Father, and............ | to the | Son:

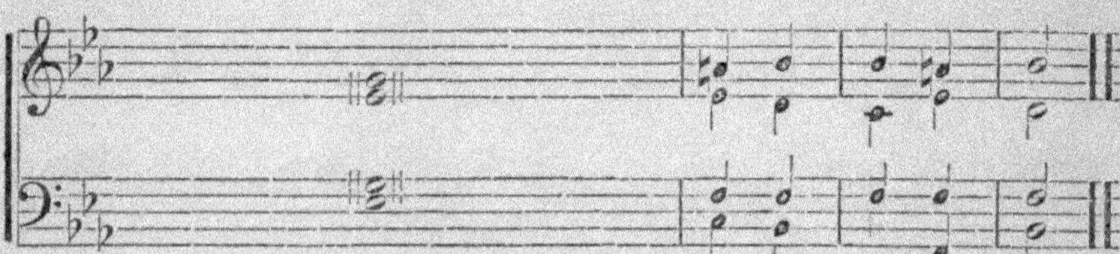

For He hath visited............ | and re- | deemed His | people. 2
Which have been............ | since the | world be- | gan. 4
And............ | to the | Ho - ly | Ghost. 6

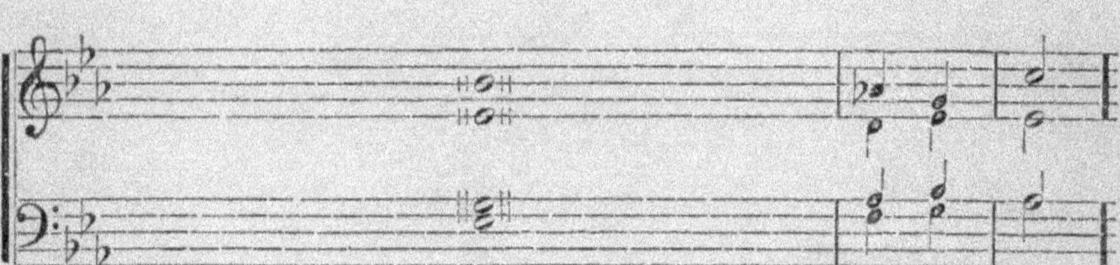

2 And hath raised up a mighty sal-............ | va - tion | for us:
4 That we should be saved............ | from our | enemies:
6 As it was in the beginning, is now, and............ | ev - er | shall be,

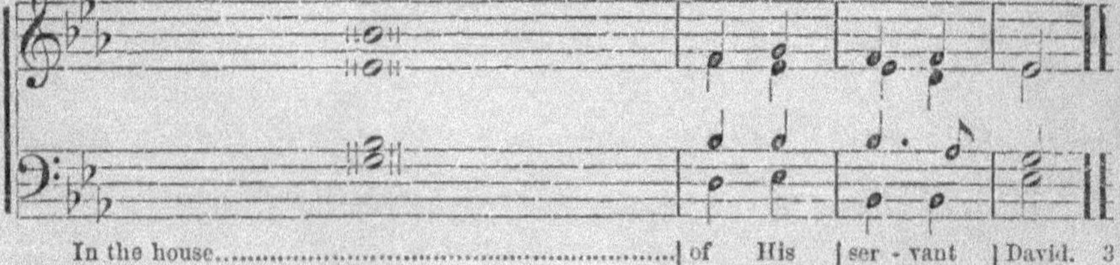

In the house............ | of His | ser - vant | David. 3
And from the............ | hand of | all that | hate us. 5
World............ | with - out | end. *A-* | *men.*

## BENEDICTUS.

LENT. GREEN.

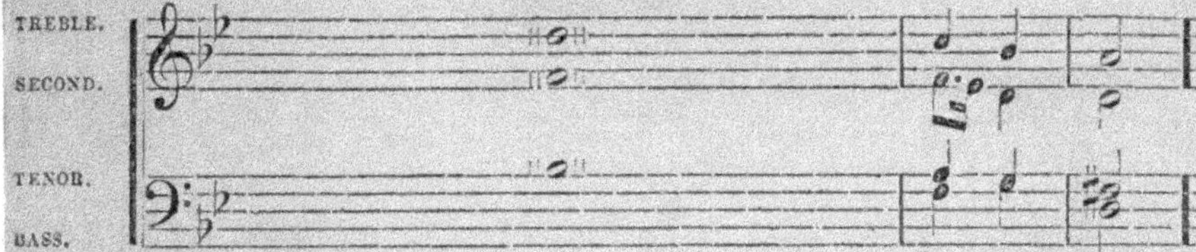


| | | |
|---|---|---|
| 1 Blessed be the Lord........ | God of | Israel: |
| 2 And hath raised up a mighty sal-........ | va - tion | for us: |
| 3 As he spake by the mouth of His........ | ho - ly | prophets: |
| 4 That we should be saved........ | from our | enemies: |
| 5 Glory be to the Father, and........ | to the | Son, |
| 6 As it was in the beginning, is now, and........ | ev- - er | shall be, |

| | | | | |
|---|---|---|---|---|
| For He hath visited........ | and re- | deemed His | people. | 2 |
| In the house........ | of His | ser - vant | David. | 3 |
| Which have been........ | since the | world be- | gan: | 4 |
| And from the........ | hand of | all that | hate us. | 5 |
| And........ | to the | Ho - ly | Ghost. | 6 |
| World........ | with - out | end. *A-* | *men.* | |

## BENEDICTUS.

EASTER TO WHITSUNDAY. WOODWARD.

| | | |
|---|---|---|
| 1 Blessed be the Lord........ | God of | Israel: |
| 2 And hath raised up a mighty sal-........ | va - tion | for us: |
| 3 As He spake by the mouth of His........ | ho - ly | prophets: |
| 4 That we should be saved........ | from our | enemies: |
| 5 Glory be to the Father, and........ | to the | Son, |
| 6 As it was in the beginning, is now, and........ | ev - er | shall be, |

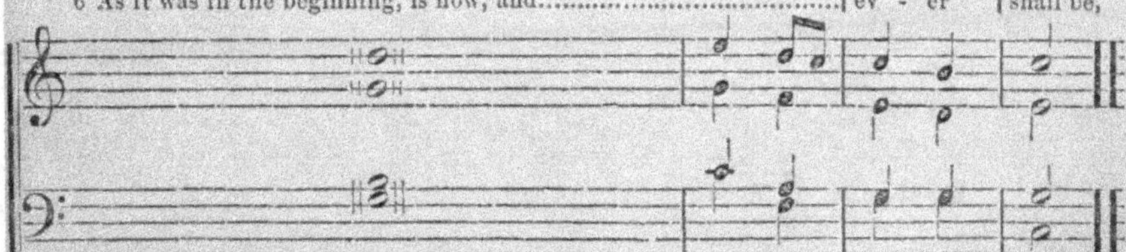

| | | | | |
|---|---|---|---|---|
| For He hath visited........ | and re- | deemed His | people. | 2 |
| In the house........ | of His | ser - vant | David. | 3 |
| Which have been........ | since the | world be- | gan: | 4 |
| And from the........ | hand of | all that | hate us. | 5 |
| And........ | to the | Ho - ly | Ghost. | 6 |
| World........ | with - out | end. *A-* | *men.* | |

## BENEDICTUS.

TRINITY TO 8TH SUNDAY AFTER. DR. CROTCH.

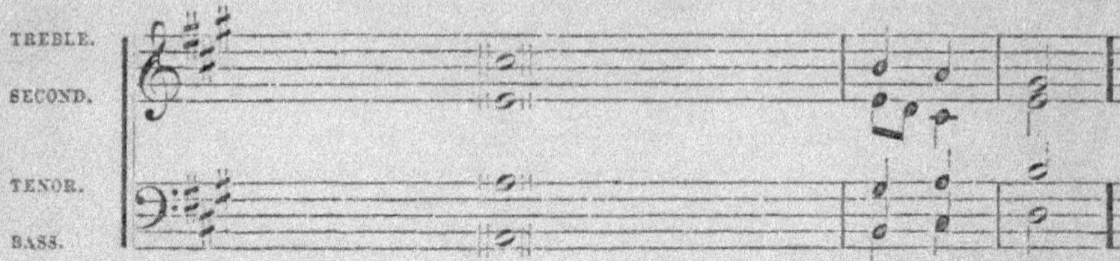


1 Blessed be the Lord.......... | God of | Israel:
3 As He spake by the mouth of His.......... | ho - ly | prophets:
5 Glory be to the Father, and.......... | to the | Son:

For He hath visited.......... | and re- | deemed His | people. 2
Which have been.......... | since the | world be- | gan: 4
And.......... | to the | Ho - ly | Ghost. 6

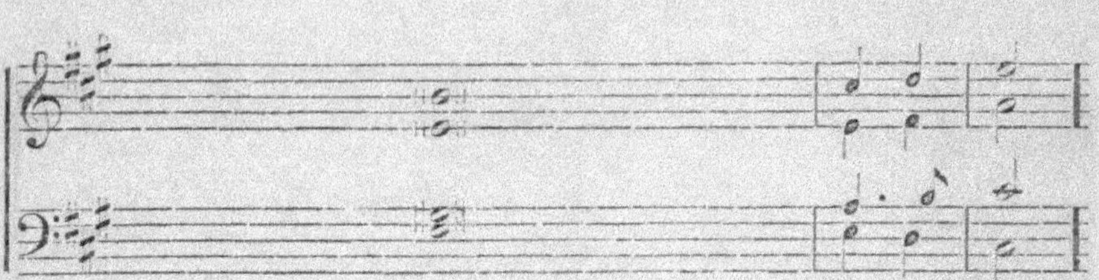

2 And hath raised up a mighty sal-.......... | va - tion | for us:
4 That we should be saved.......... | from our | enemies:
6 As it was in the beginning, is now, and.......... | ev - er | shall be,

In the house.......... | of His | ser - vant | David. 3
And from the.......... | hand of | all that | hate us. 5
World.......... | with - out | end. A- | *men.*

## BENEDICTUS.

9TH TO 16TH SUNDAY AFTER TRINITY. DR. ARNOLD.

TREBLE. SECOND. TENOR. BASS.

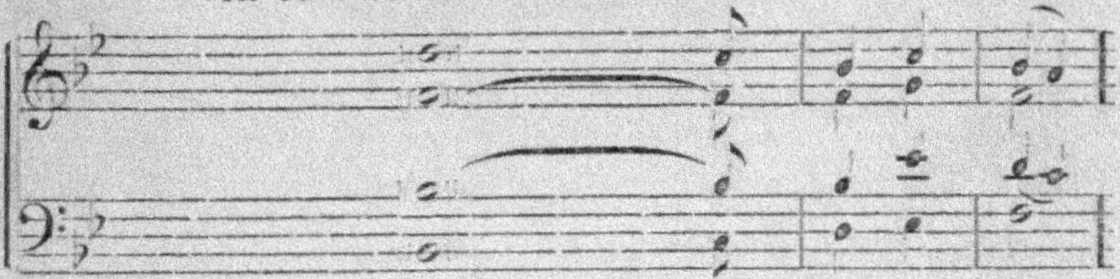

| | | |
|---|---|---|
| 1 Blessed be the Lord | God of | Israel: |
| 2 And hath raised up a mighty sal- | va - tion | for us: |
| 3 As he spake by the mouth of His | ho - ly | prophets: |
| 4 That we should be saved | from our | enemies: |
| 5 Glory be to the Father, and | to the | Son, |
| 6 As it was in the beginning, is now, and | ev- - er | shall be, |

| | | | |
|---|---|---|---|
| For He hath visit- ed | and re- | deemed His | people. 2 |
| In the house | of His | ser - vant | David. 3 |
| Which have been | since the | world be- | gan: 4 |
| And from the | hand of | all that | hate us. 5 |
| And | to the | Ho - ly | Ghost. 6 |
| World | with - out | end. A- | *men.* |

## BENEDICTUS.

17TH TO 27TH SUNDAY AFTER TRINITY. H. F. HEMY.

TREBLE. SECOND. TENOR. BASS.

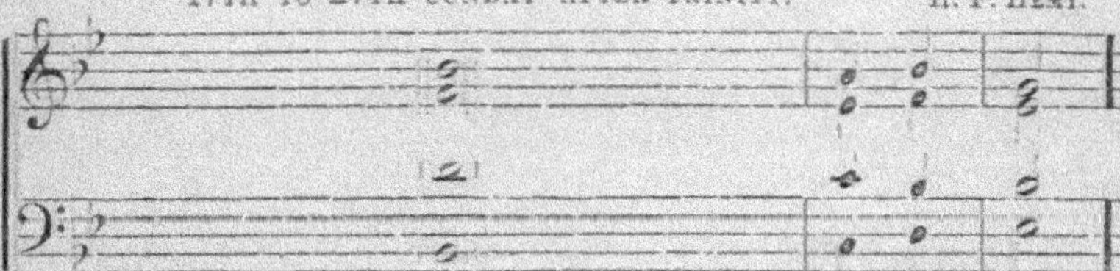

| | | |
|---|---|---|
| 1 Blessed be the Lord | God of | Israel: |
| 2 And hath raised up a mighty sal- | va - tion | for us: |
| 3 As He spake by the mouth of His | ho - ly | prophets: |
| 4 That we should be saved | from our | enemies: |
| 5 Glory be to the Father, and | to the | Son, |
| 6 As it was in the beginning, is now, and | ev - er | shall be, |

| | | | |
|---|---|---|---|
| For He hath visit- ed | and re- | deemed His | people. 2 |
| In the house | of His | ser - vant | David. 3 |
| Which have been | since the | world be- | gan: 4 |
| And from the | hand of | all that | hate us. 5 |
| And | to the | Ho - ly | Ghost. 6 |
| World | with - out | end. A- | *men.* |

## GLORIA TIBI DOMINE.

ADVENT AND CHRISTMAS. SWAFFIELD.

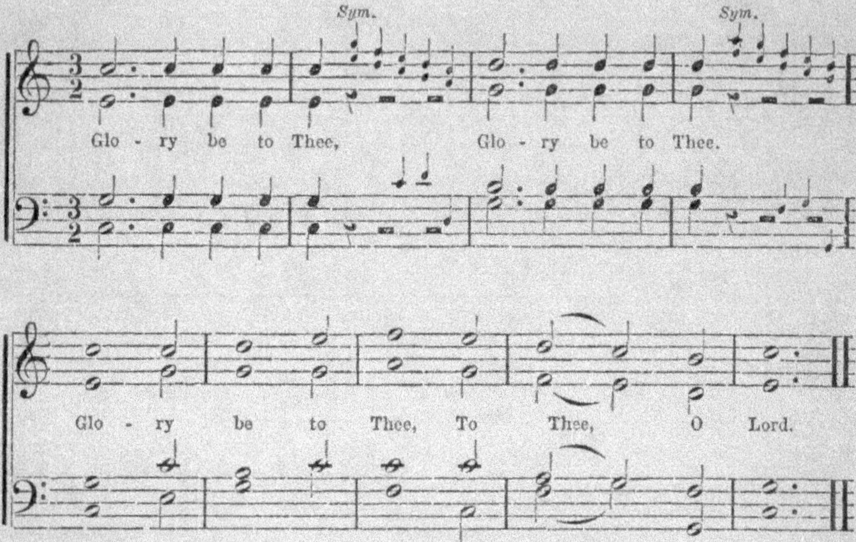


EPIPHANY TO QUINQUAGESIMA. ROGERS.

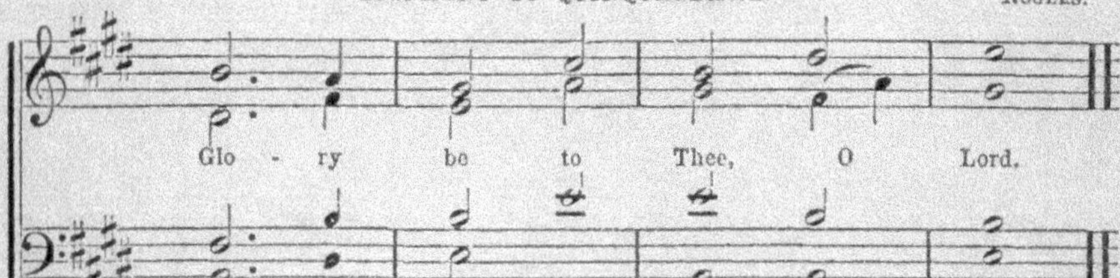


LENT. J. B. SALE.

## GLORIA TIBI DOMINE.

EASTER TO WHITSUNDAY. A. THOMPSON.

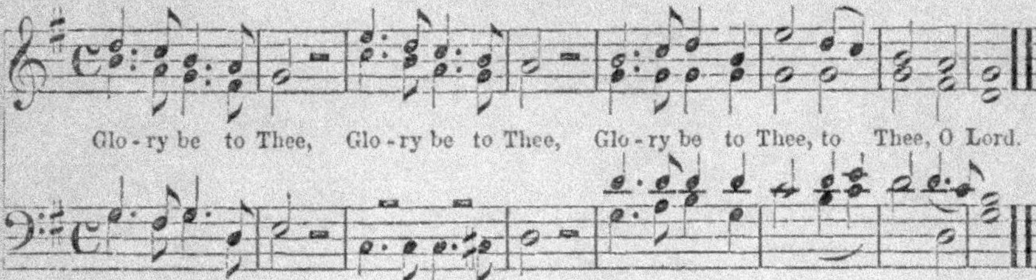


TRINITY TO 8TH SUNDAY AFTER. KING.

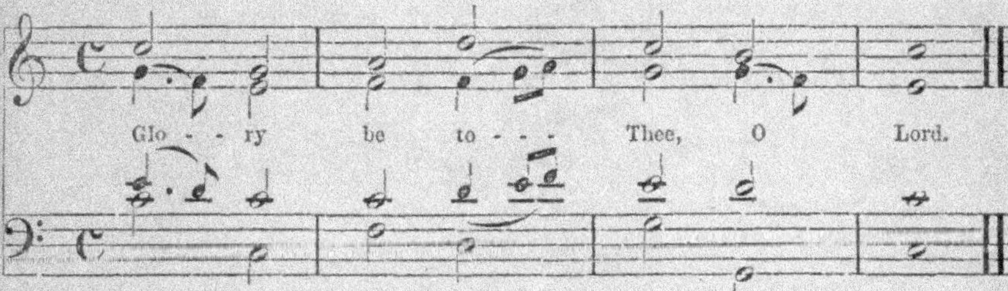


9TH TO 16TH SUNDAY AFTER TRINITY. T. IONS.

17TH TO 27TH SUNDAY AFTER TRINITY. SHORT.

# TRISAGION.

ADVENT TO WHITSUNDAY. R. Taylor.

## TRISAGION.

TRINITY TO 27TH SUNDAY AFTER. DR. G. K. JACKSON.

## GLORIA PATRI.

ADVENT AND CHRISTMAS. HAYES.

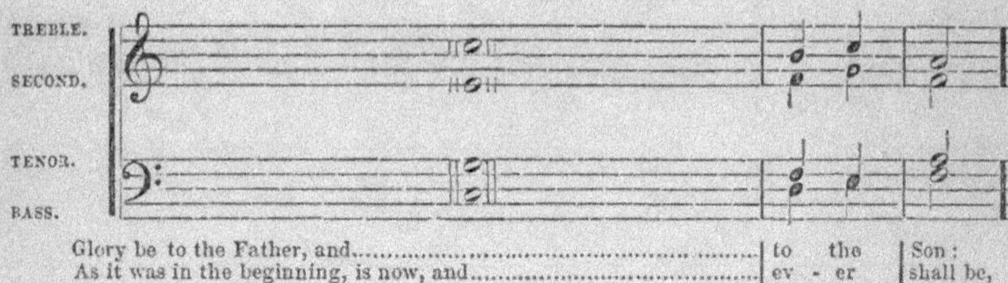


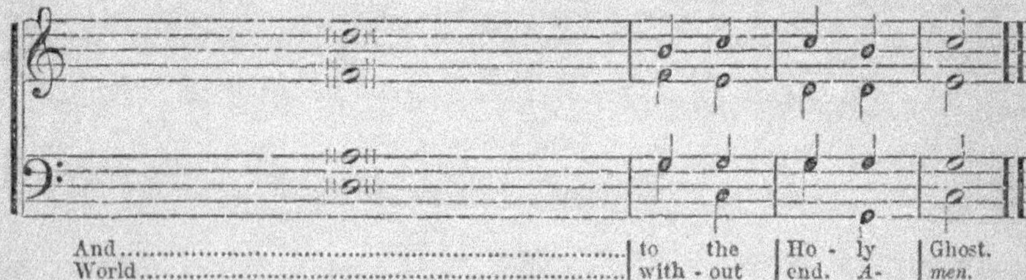


---

## GLORIA PATRI.

EPIPHANY TO QUINQUAGESIMA. FUSSELL.

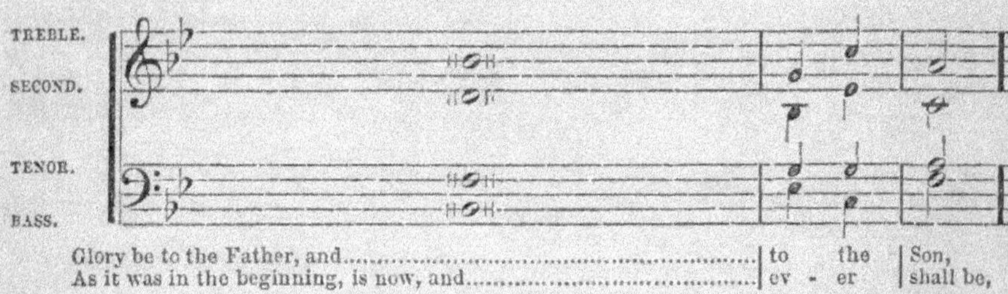

## GLORIA PATRI.

LENT. LANGDON.

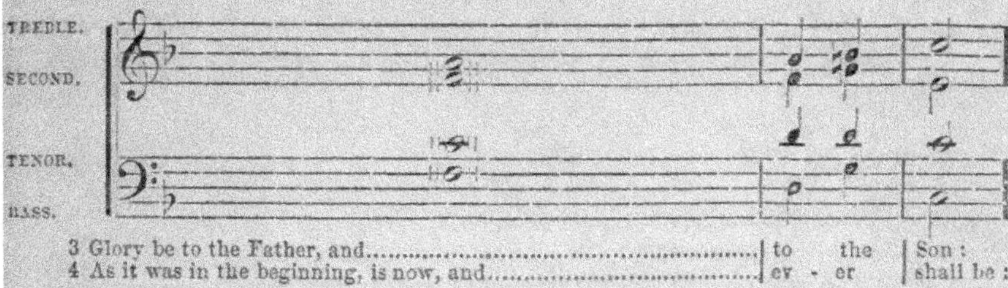


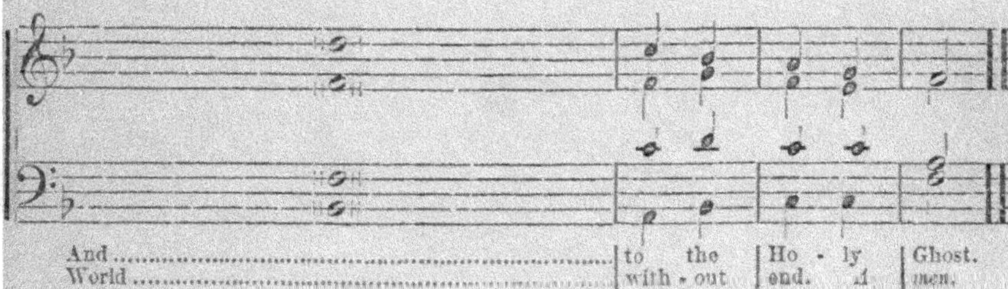


## GLORIA PATRI.

EASTER TO WHITSUNDAY.

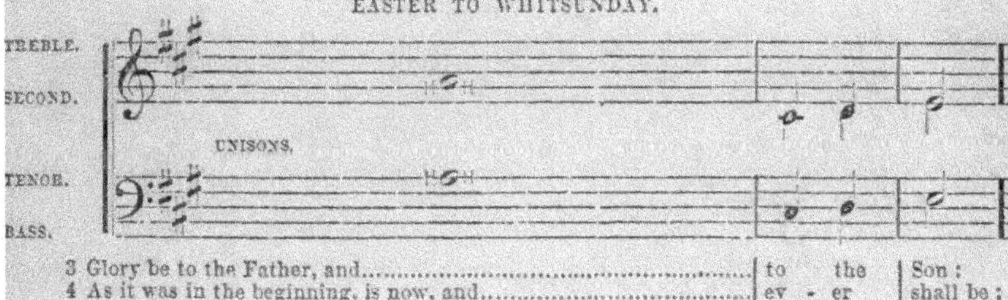

## GLORIA PATRI.

TRINITY TO 8TH SUNDAY AFTER. JOHN GOSS.

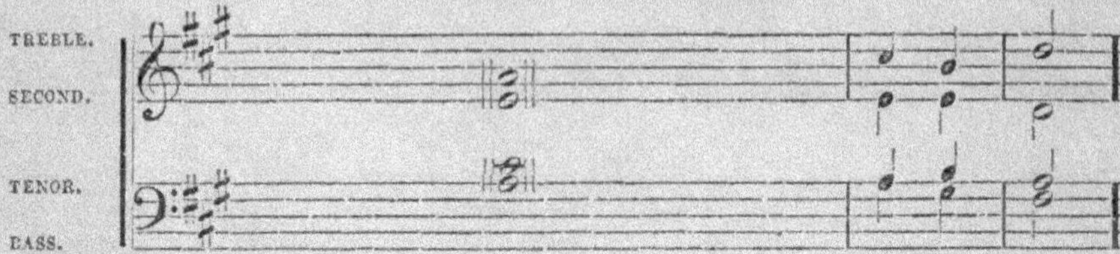


Glory be to the Father, and............ | to the | Son :
As it was in the beginning, is now, and............ | ev - er | shall be,

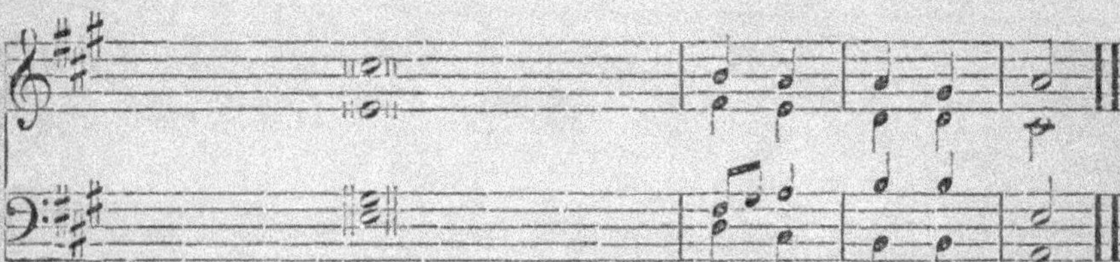

And............ | to the | Ho - ly | Ghost.
World............ | with - out | end. A- | men.

---

## GLORIA PATRI.

9TH TO 16TH SUNDAY AFTER TRINITY. BARROW.

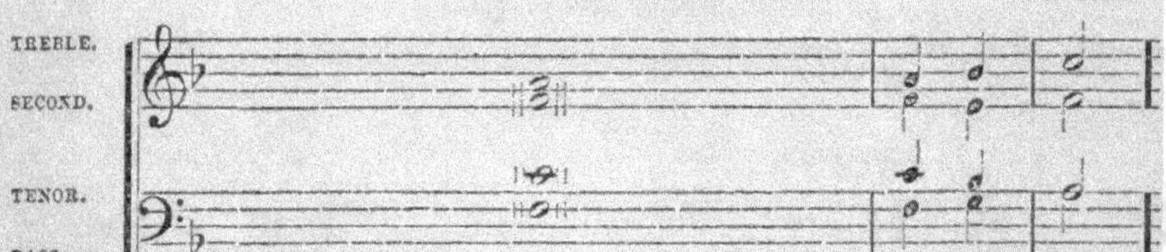


Glory be to the Father, and............ | to the | Son,
As it was in the beginning, is now, and............ | ev - er | shall be,

And............ | to the | Ho - ly | Ghost,
World............ | with - out | end. A- | men.

## GLORIA PATRI.

17TH TO 21ST SUNDAY AFTER TRINITY. JOSH. GARNETT.

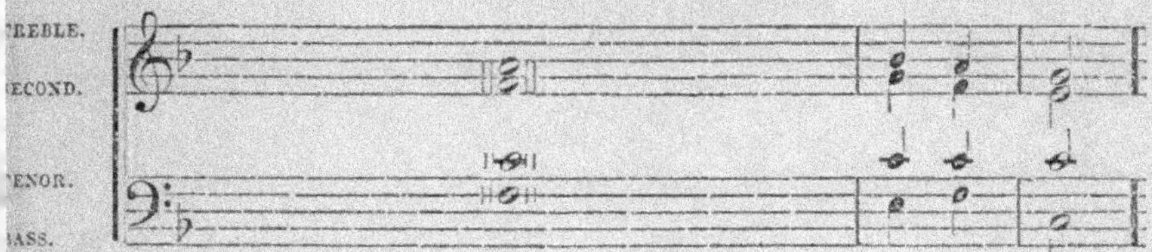

Glory be to the Father, and.......................... | to the | Son,
As it was in the beginning, is now, and.......................... | ev - er | shall be,

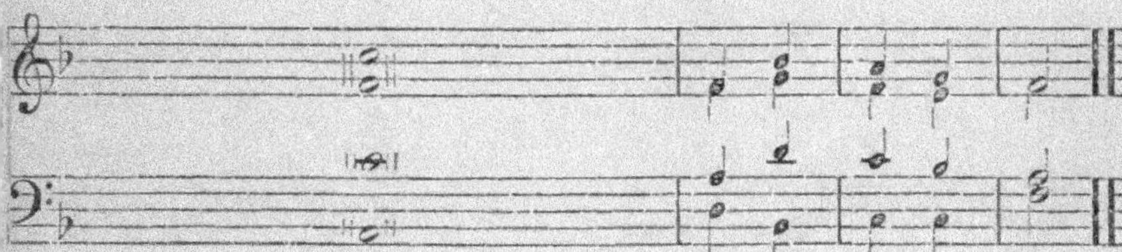

And.......................... | to the | Ho - ly | Ghost.
World.......................... | with - out | end. *A-* | *men.*

## GLORIA PATRI.

22D TO 27TH SUNDAY AFTER TRINITY. T. PURCELL, 1687.

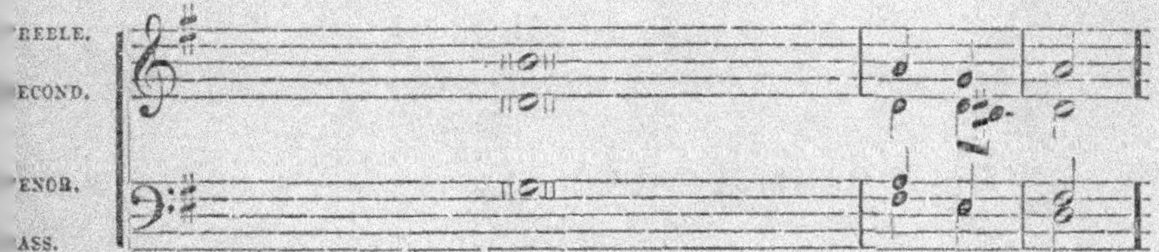

Glory be to the Father, and.......................... | to the | Son,
As it was in the beginning, is now, and.......................... | ev - er | shall be,

And.......................... | to the | Ho - ly | Ghost.
World.......................... | with - out | end. *A-* | *men.*

## CANTATE DOMINO.

ADVENT AND CHRISTMAS. DR. RANDALL.

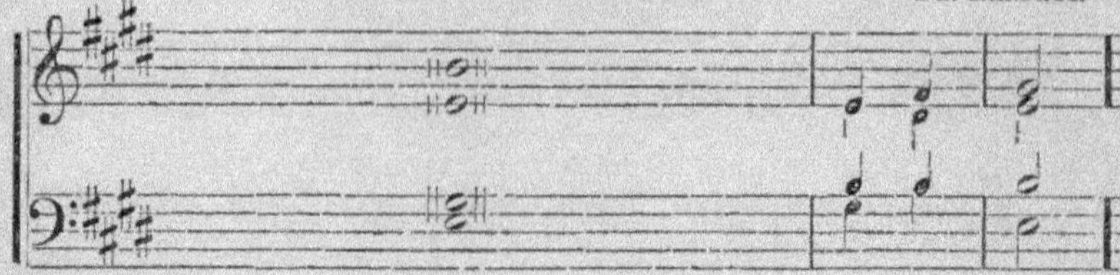


| | | |
|---|---|---|
| 1 O sing unto the | Lord a new | song: |
| 3 The Lord declared | His sal- | vation: |
| 5 Show yourselves joyful unto the Lord | all ye | lands: |
| 7 With trumpets | also and | shawms: |
| 9 Let the floods clap their hands, and let the hills be joyful together be- | fore the | Lord: |
| 11 Glory be to the Father, and | to the | Son: |

| | | | |
|---|---|---|---|
| For He | hath done | marvellous | things. 2 |
| His righteousness hath he openly showed | in the | sight of the | heathen. 4 |
| Sing, re- | joice — | and give | thanks. 6 |
| O show yourselves joyful be- | fore the | Lord the | King. 8 |
| For He | cometh to | judge the | earth. 10 |
| And | to the | Ho - ly | Ghost. 12 |

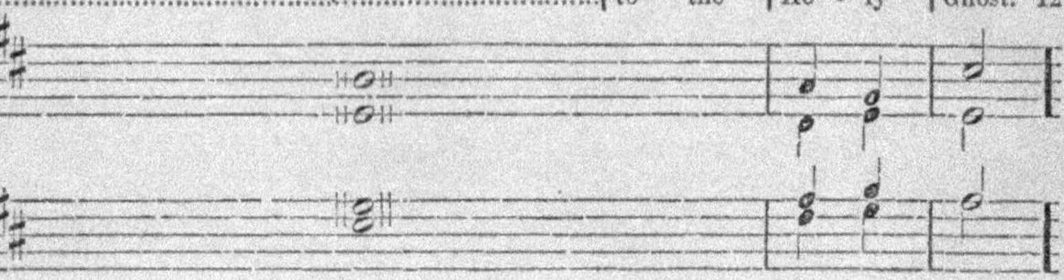

| | | |
|---|---|---|
| 2 With his own right hand, and with His | ho - ly | arm: |
| 4 He hath remembered his mercy and truth towards the | house of | Israel: |
| 6 Praise the Lord up- | on the | harp: |
| 8 Let the sea make a noise, and all that | there - in | is: |
| 10 With righteousness shall he | judge the | world: |
| 12 As it was in the beginning, is now, and | ev - er | shall be, |

| | | | |
|---|---|---|---|
| Hath he | gotten him- | self the | victory. 3 |
| And all the ends of the world have seen the sal- | va - tion | of our | God. 5 |
| Sing to the harp | with a | psalm of thanks- | giving. 7 |
| The round world, and | they that | dwell there- | in. 9 |
| And | — the | people with | equity. 11 |
| World | with - out | end. A- | *men.* |

## CANTATE DOMINO.

EPIPHANY TO QUINQUAGESIMA. HINDLE.

| | | | |
|---|---|---|---|
| 1 O sing unto | the | Lord a new | song: |
| 3 The Lord declar- | ed | His sal- | vation: |
| 5 Show yourselves joyful unto the Lord | | all ye | lands: |
| 7 With trum- | pets | also and | shawms: |
| 9 Let the floods clap their hands, and let the hills be joyful together be- | | fore the | Lord: |
| 11 Glory be to the Father, | and | to the | Son: |

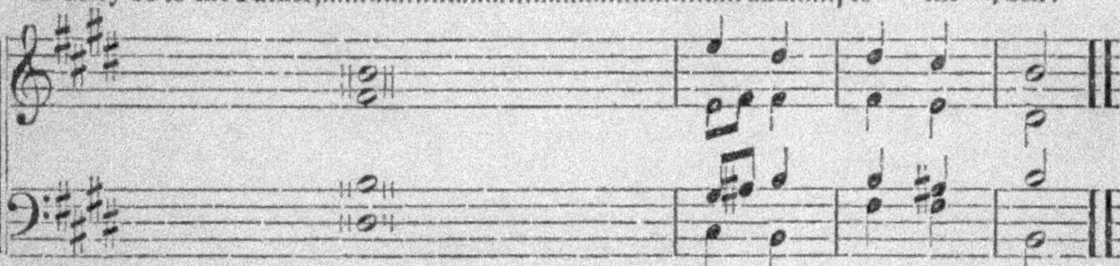

| | | | |
|---|---|---|---|
| For He | hath done | marvellous | things. 2 |
| His righteousness hath he openly showed | in the | sight of the | heathen. 4 |
| Sing, re- | joice — | and give | thanks. 6 |
| O show yourselves joyful be- | fore the | Lord the | King. 8 |
| For He | cometh to | judge the | earth. 10 |
| And | to the | Ho - ly | Ghost. 12 |

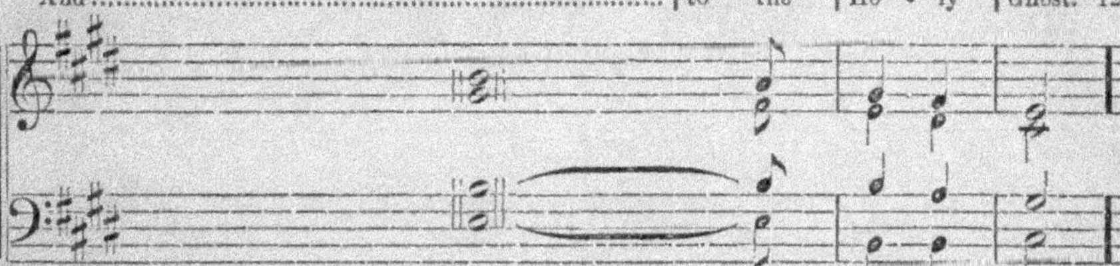

| | | | |
|---|---|---|---|
| 2 With his own right hand, and with | His | ho - ly | arm: |
| 4 He hath remembered his mercy and truth towards | the | house of | Israel: |
| 6 Praise the Lord | up- | on the | harp: |
| 8 Let the sea make a noise, and all | that | there - in | is: |
| 10 With righteousness shall | he | judge the | world: |
| 12 As it was in the beginning, is now, | and | ev- - er | shall be, |

| | | | |
|---|---|---|---|
| Hath he | gotten him- | self the | victory. 3 |
| And all the ends of the world have seen the sal- | va - tion | of our | God. 5 |
| Sing to the harp | with a | psalm of thanks- | giving. 7 |
| The round world, and | they that | dwell there- | in. 9 |
| And | — the | people with | equity. 11 |
| World | with - out | end. *A-* | *men.* |

# CANTATE DOMINO.

## LENT.

(*Commemoration Chant.*) DR. WOODWARD.

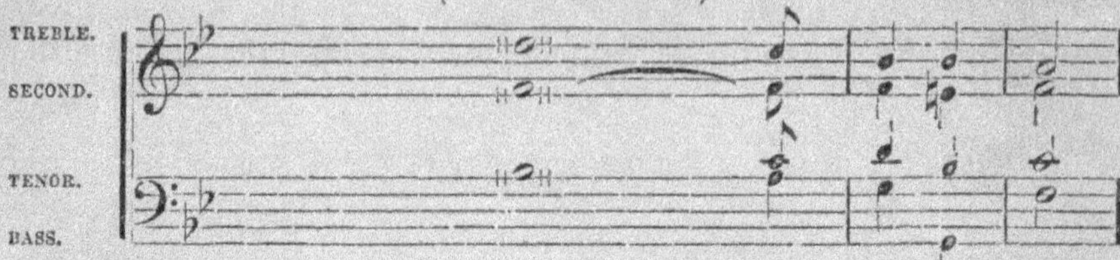


| | | | |
|---|---|---|---|
| 1 O sing unto.......the....... | Lord | a new | song : |
| 3 The Lord declar-.......ed....... | His | sal- | vation : |
| 5 Show yourselves joyful unto the Lord,....... | all | ye | lands : |
| 7 With trum-.......pets,....... | also | and | shawms : |
| 9 Let the floods clap their hands, and let the hills be joyful together be- | fore | the | Lord : |
| 11 Glory be to the Father,.......and....... | to | the | Son : |

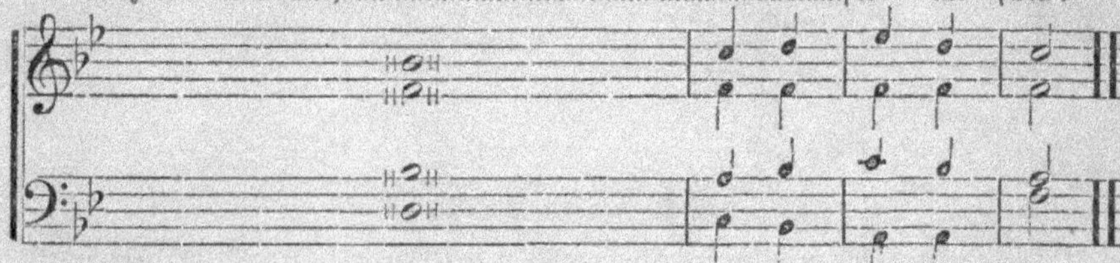

| | | | | | |
|---|---|---|---|---|---|
| For He....... | hath done | | marvellous | | things. 2 |
| His righteousness hath he openly showed....... | in | the | sight of the | | heathen. 4 |
| Sing, re-....... | joice | — | and | give | thanks. 6 |
| O show yourselves joyful be-....... | fore | the | Lord | the | King : 8 |
| For He....... | cometh to | | judge | the | earth. 10 |
| And....... | to | the | Ho - | ly | Ghost. 12 |

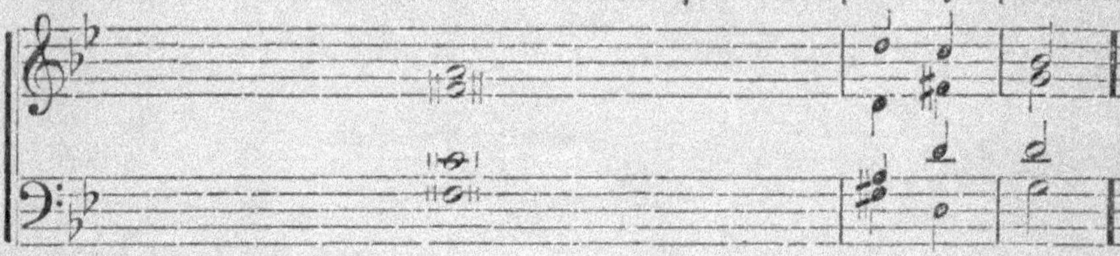

| | | | |
|---|---|---|---|
| 2 With his own right hand, and with His....... | ho - | ly | arm : |
| 4 He hath remembered his mercy and truth towards the....... | house | of | Israel : |
| 6 Praise the Lord up-....... | on | the | harp : |
| 8 Let the sea make a noise, and all that....... | there - | in | is : |
| 10 With righteousness shall he....... | judge | the | world : |
| 12 As it was in the beginning, is now, and....... | ev - | er | shall be, |

| | | | | | |
|---|---|---|---|---|---|
| Hath he....... | gotten him- | | self | the | victory. 3 |
| And all the ends of the world have seen the sal-....... | va - | tion | of | our | God. 5 |
| Sing to the harp....... | with | a | psalm of thanks- | | giving, 7 |
| The round world, and....... | they | that | dwell there- | | in. 9 |
| And....... | — | the | people | with | equity. 11 |
| World....... | with - | out | end. | *A-* | *men.* |

## CANTATE DOMINO.

EASTER TO WHITSUNDAY. DR. BECKWITH.

TREBLE.
SECOND.
TENOR.
BASS.

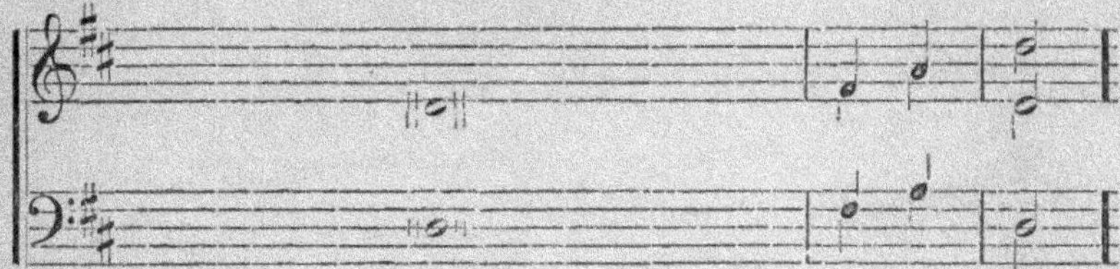

| | | |
|---|---|---|
| 1 O Sing unto the | Lord a new | song: |
| 3 The Lord declared | His sal- | vation: |
| 5 Show yourselves joyful unto the Lord | all ye | lands: |
| 7 With trumpets | also and | shawms: |
| 9 Let the floods clap their hands, and let the hills be joyful together be- | fore the | Lord: |
| 11 Glory be to the Father, and | to the | Son; |

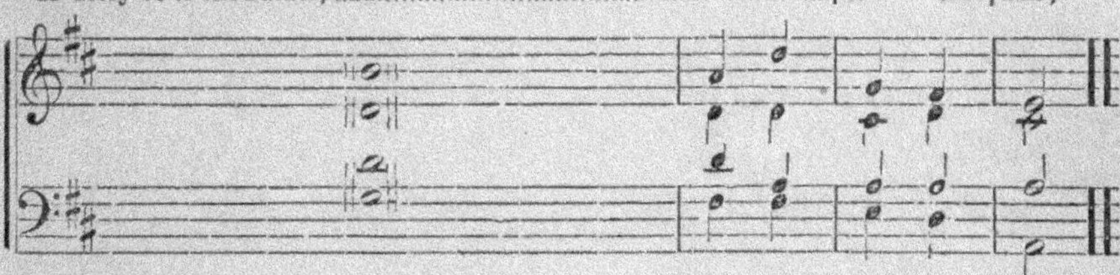

| | | | |
|---|---|---|---|
| For He | hath done | marvellous | things. 2 |
| His righteousness hath he openly showed | in the | sight of the | heathen. 4 |
| Sing, re- | joice — | and give | thanks. 6 |
| O show yourselves joyful be- | fore the | Lord the | King. 8 |
| For He | cometh to | judge the | earth. 10 |
| And | to the | Ho - ly | Ghost. 12 |

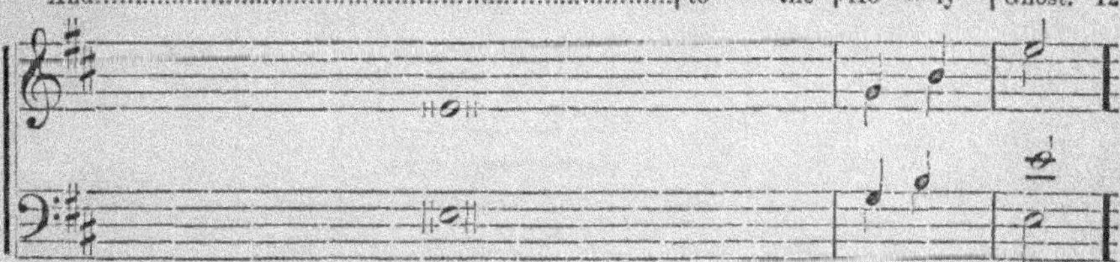

| | | |
|---|---|---|
| 2 With his own right hand, and with His | ho - ly | arm: |
| 4 He hath remembered his mercy and truth towards the | house of | Israel: |
| 6 Praise the Lord up- | on the | harp: |
| 8 Let the sea make a noise, and all that | there - in | is: |
| 10 With righteousness shall he | judge the | world: |
| 12 As it was in the beginning, is now, and | ev - er | shall be: |

| | | | |
|---|---|---|---|
| Hath he | gotten him- | self the | victory. 3 |
| And all the ends of the world have seen the sal- | va - tion | of our | God. 5 |
| Sing to the harp | with a | psalm of thanks- | giving. 7 |
| The round world, and | they that | dwell there- | in. 9 |
| And | — the | people with | equity. 11 |
| World | with - out | end. *A-* | *men.* |

## CANTATE DOMINO.

TRINITY TO 8TH SUNDAY AFTER. DR. ALCOCK, 1755.

TREBLE.
SECOND.
TENOR.
BASS.

| | | |
|---|---|---|
| 1 O sing unto.................................the ...... | Lord a new | song: |
| 3 The Lord declar-...............................ed ...... | His sal- | vation: |
| 5 Show yourselves joyful unto the Lord.................. | all ye | lands: |
| 7 With trum-.....................................pets..... | also and | shawms: |
| 9 Let the floods clap their hands, and let the hills be joyful together be- | fore the | Lord: |
| 11 Glory be to the Father,........................and...... | to the | Son: |

| | | | |
|---|---|---|---|
| For He................................................ | hath done | marvellous | things. 2 |
| His righteousness hath he openly showed .............. | in the | sight of the | heathen. 4 |
| Sing, re-............................................. | joice — | and give | thanks. 6 |
| O show yourselves joyful be-.......................... | fore the | Lord the | King. 8 |
| For He................................................ | cometh to | judge the | earth. 10 |
| And .................................................. | to the | Ho - ly | Ghost. 12 |

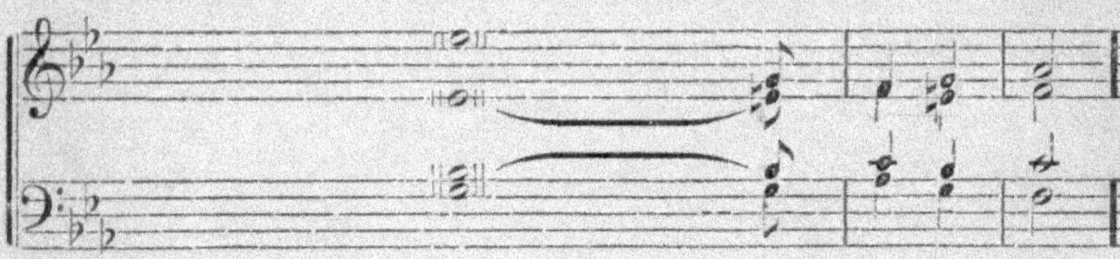

| | | |
|---|---|---|
| 2 With his own right hand, and with.................His...... | ho - ly | arm: |
| 4 He hath remembered his mercy and truth towards..........the ...... | house of | Israel: |
| 6 Praise the Lord .......................................up- ...... | on the | harp: |
| 8 Let the sea make a noise, and all......................that..... | there - in | is: |
| 10 With righteousness shall...............................he ...... | judge the | world: |
| 12 As it was in the beginning, is now,....................and...... | ev- - er | shall be, |

| | | | |
|---|---|---|---|
| Hath..........................................he...... | gotten him- | self the | victory. 3 |
| And all the ends of the world have seen the sal-......... | va - tion | of our | God. 5 |
| Sing to the harp.......................................... | with a | psalm of thanks- | giving. 7 |
| The round world,...............................and.... | they that | dwell there- | in. 9 |
| And ...................................................... | — the | people with | equity. 11 |
| World .................................................... | with - out | end. *A-* | *men.* |

## CANTATE DOMINO.

9TH TO 16TH SUNDAY AFTER TRINITY. DR. CROTCH.

| | | |
|---|---|---|
| 1 O sing unto the | Lord a new | song: |
| 3 The Lord declared | His sal- | vation: |
| 5 Show yourselves joyful unto the Lord | all ye | lands: |
| 7 With trumpets | also and | shawms: |
| 9 Let the floods clap their hands, and let the hills be joyful together be- | fore the | Lord: |
| 11 Glory be to the Father, and | to the | Son: |

| | | | |
|---|---|---|---|
| For He | hath done | marvellous | things. 2 |
| His righteousness hath he openly showed | in the | sight of the | heathen. 4 |
| Sing, re- | joice — | and give | thanks. 6 |
| O show yourselves joyful be- | fore the | Lord the | King. 8 |
| For He | cometh to | judge the | earth. 10 |
| And | to the | Ho - ly | Ghost. 12 |

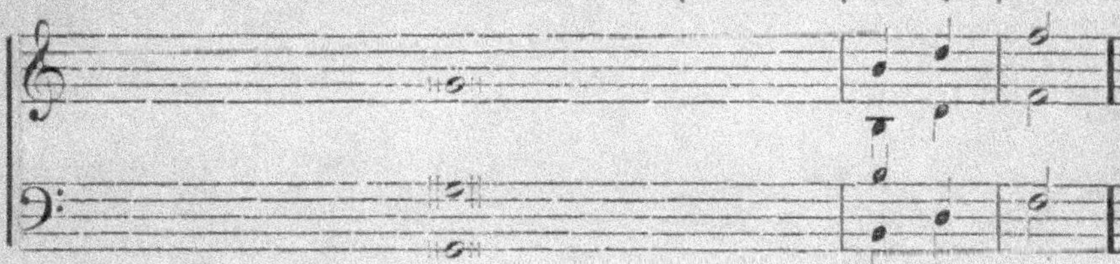

| | | |
|---|---|---|
| 2 With his own right hand, and with His | ho - ly | arm: |
| 4 He hath remembered his mercy and truth towards the | house of | Israel: |
| 6 Praise the Lord up- | on the | harp: |
| 8 Let the sea make a noise, and all that | there - in | is: |
| 10 With righteousness shall he | judge the | world: |
| 12 As it was in the beginning, is now, and | ev - er | shall be, |

| | | | |
|---|---|---|---|
| Hath he | gotten him- | self the | victory. 3 |
| And all the ends of the world have seen the sal- | va - tion | of our | God. 5 |
| Sing to the harp | with a | psalm of thanks- | giving. 7 |
| The round world, and | they that | dwell there- | in. 9 |
| And | — the | people with | equity. 11 |
| World | with - out | end. A- | *men.* |

## CANTATE DOMINO.

17TH TO 27TH SUNDAY AFTER TRINITY.

PRATT.

TREBLE.
SECOND.
TENOR.
BASS.

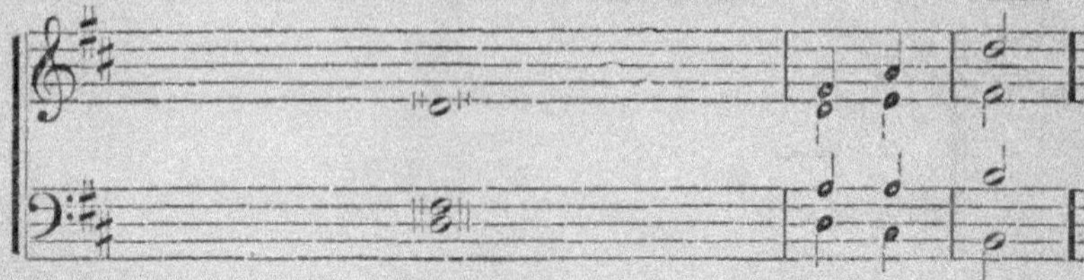

| | | |
|---|---|---|
| 1 O sing unto the........................................................ | Lord a new | song : |
| 3 The Lord declared........................................................ | His sal- | vation : |
| 5 Show yourselves joyful unto the Lord........................................ | all ye | lands : |
| 7 With trumpets........................................................ | also and | shawms : |
| 9 Let the floods clap their hands, and let the hills be joyful together be- | fore the | Lord : |
| 11 Glory be to the Father, and........................................ | to the | Son : |

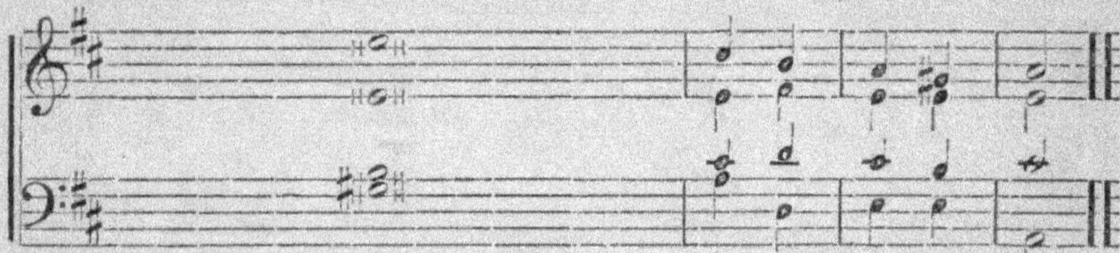

| | | | |
|---|---|---|---|
| For He........................................................ | hath done | marvellous | things. 2 |
| His righteousness hath he openly showed.................... | in the | sight of the | heathen. 4 |
| Sing, re-........................................................ | joice — | and give | thanks. 6 |
| O show yourselves joyful be-........................................ | fore the | Lord the | King. 8 |
| For He........................................................ | cometh to | judge the | earth. 10 |
| And........................................................ | to the | Ho - ly | Ghost. 12 |

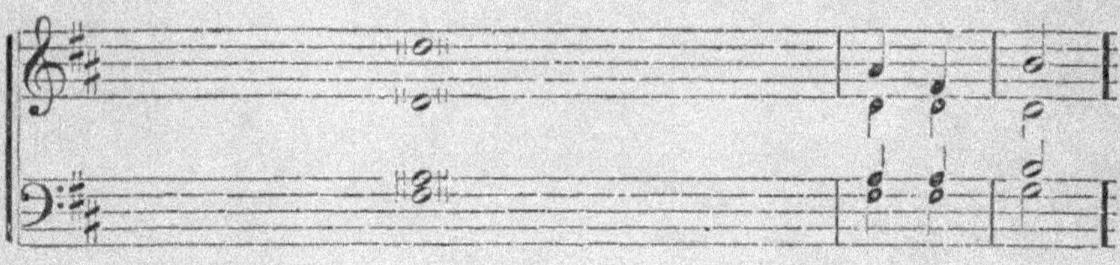

| | | |
|---|---|---|
| 2 With his own right hand, and with His........................................ | ho - ly | arm : |
| 4 He hath remembered his mercy and truth towards the.................... | house of | Israel : |
| 6 Praise the Lord up-........................................................ | on the | harp : |
| 8 Let the sea make a noise, and all that........................................ | there - in | is : |
| 10 With righteousness shall he........................................ | judge the | world : |
| 12 As it was in the beginning, is now, and........................................ | ev - er | shall be, |

| | | | |
|---|---|---|---|
| Hath he........................................................ | gotten him- | self the | victory. 3 |
| And all the ends of the world have seen the sal-.................... | va - tion | of our | God. 5 |
| Sing to the harp........................................................ | with a | psalm of thanks- | giving. 7 |
| The round world, and........................................................ | they that | dwell there- | in. 9 |
| And........................................................ | — the | people with | equity. 11 |
| World........................................................ | with - out | end. A- | *men.* |

## BONUM EST CONFITERI.

ADVENT AND CHRISTMAS. GREGORIAN

TREBLE. SECOND. TENOR. BASS.

| | | |
|---|---|---|
| 1 It is a good thing to give thanks un-........ | to the | Lord: |
| 2 To tell of thy loving kindness early........ | in the | morning: |
| 3 Upon an instrument of ten strings, and up-........ | on the | lute: |
| 4 For thou Lord hath made me glad........ | through thy | works: |
| 5 Glory be to the Father, and........ | to the | Son, |
| 6 As it was in the beginning, is now, and........ | ev - er | shall be, |

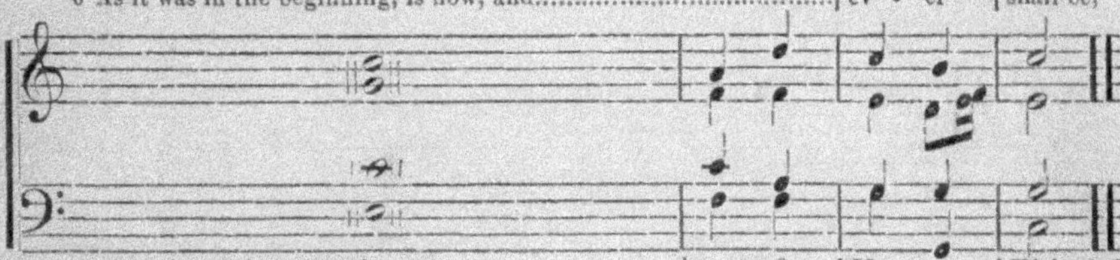

| | | | |
|---|---|---|---|
| And to sing praises unto thy........ | name O | Most — | Highest. 2 |
| And of thy........ | truth in the | night — | season. 3 |
| Upon a loud instrument........ | and up- | on the | harp. 4 |
| And I will rejoice in giving praise for the oper-........ | a - tions | of thy | hands. 5 |
| And........ | to the | Ho - ly | Ghost. 6 |
| World........ | with - out | end. A- | *men.* |

---

## BONUM EST CONFITERI.

EPIPHANY TO QUINQUAGESIMA. HAYES.

TREBLE. SECOND. TENOR. BASS.

| | | | |
|---|---|---|---|
| 1 It is a good thing to give thanks........ | un- ...... | to the | Lord: |
| 2 To tell of thy loving kindness ear-........ | ly ...... | in the | morning: |
| 3 Upon an instrument of ten strings, and........ | up- ...... | on the | lute: |
| 4 For thou Lord hath made me glad........ | ...... | through thy | works: |
| 5 Glory be to the Father,........ | and ...... | to the | Son, |
| 6 As it was in the beginning, is now,........ | and ...... | ev - er | shall be, |

| | | | | |
|---|---|---|---|---|
| And to sing praises unto........ | thy........ | name O | Most — | Highest. 2 |
| And of........ | thy........ | truth in the | night — | season. 3 |
| Upon a loud instrument........ | ........ | and up- | on the | harp. 4 |
| And I will rejoice in giving praise for the o-... | per-........ | a - tions | of thy | hands. 5 |
| And........ | ........ | to the | Ho - ly | Ghost. 6 |
| World........ | ........ | with - out | end. A- | *men.* |

## BONUM EST CONFITERI.

LENT. R. COOKE.

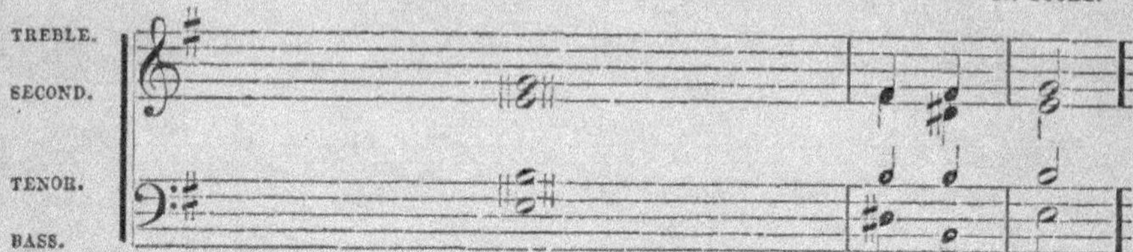


1 It is a good thing to give thanks un-........................ | to the | Lord:
3 Upon an instrument of ten strings, and up-........................ | on the | lute:
5 Glory be to the Father, and........................ | to the | Son,

And to sing praises unto thy........................ | name O | Most — | Highest. 2
Upon a loud instrument,........................ | and up- | on the | harp. 4
And........................ | to the | Ho - ly | Ghost, 6

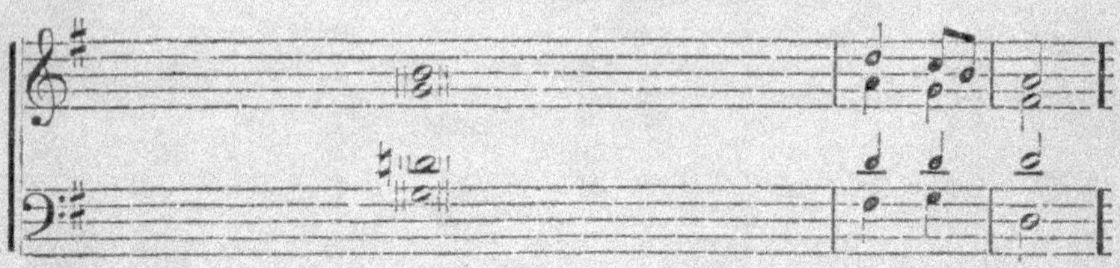

2 To tell of thy loving kindness early........................ | in the | morning:
4 For thou Lord hath made me glad........................ | through thy | works:
6 As it was in the beginning, is now, and........................ | ev - er | shall be,

And of........................thy...... | truth in the | night — | season. 3
And I will rejoice in giving praise for the o-...per-...... | a - tions | of thy | hands. 5
World........................ | with - out | end. *A-* | *men.*

## BONUM EST CONFITERI.

EASTER TO WHITSUNDAY. F. LINGARD.

1 It is a good thing to give thanks un-… | to the | Lord:
3 Upon an instrument of ten strings, and up-… | on the | lute:
5 Glory be to the Father, and… | to the | Son:

And to sing praises unto… thy… | name O | Most — | Highest. 2
Upon a loud instrument… | and up- | on the | harp. 4
And … | to the | Ho - ly | Ghost. 6

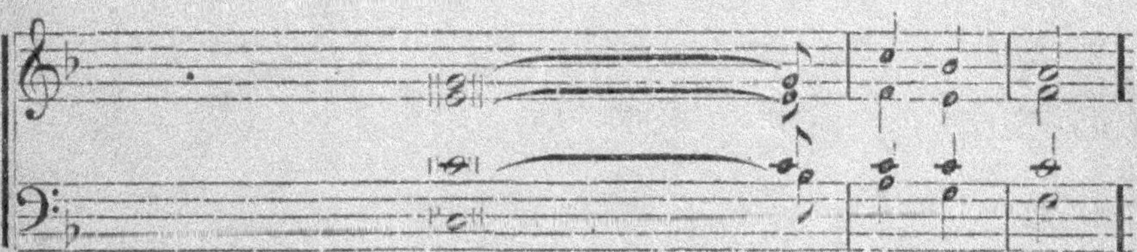

2 To tell of thy loving kindness ear-… ly… | in the | morning:
4 For thou Lord hath made me glad… | through thy | works:
6 As it was in the beginning, is now,… and… | ev - er | shall be,

And of… thy… | truth in the | night — | season. 3
And I will rejoice in giving praise for the o-…per-… | a - tions | of thy | hands. 5
World… | with - out | end. *A-* | *men.*

## BONUM EST CONFITERI.

TRINITY TO 8TH SUNDAY AFTER. MORNINGTON.

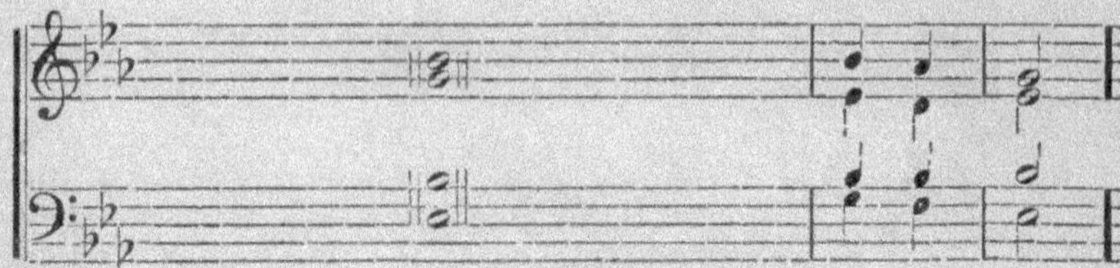


1 It is a good thing to give thanks un- | to the | Lord:
3 Upon an instrument of ten strings, and up- | on the | lute:
5 Glory be to the Father, and | to the | Son,

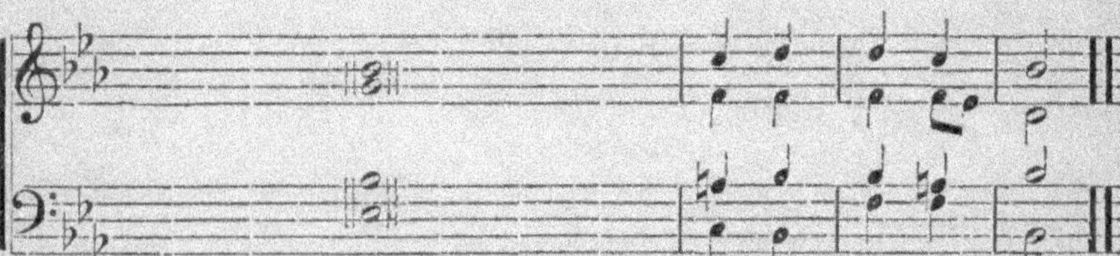

And to sing praises unto thy | name O | Most — | Highest. 2
Upon a loud instrument, | and up- | on the | harp. 4
And | to the | Ho - ly | Ghost. 6

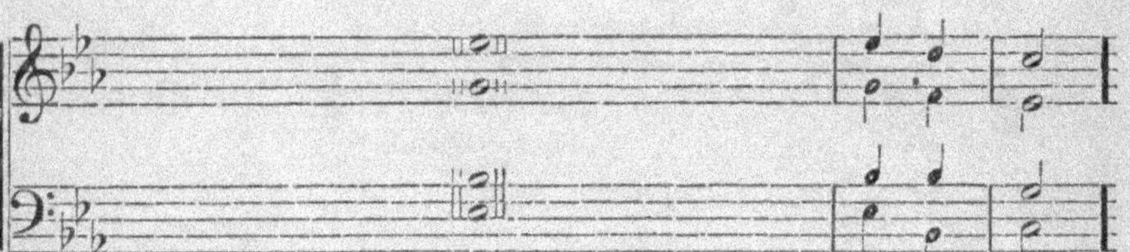

2 To tell of thy loving kindness early | in the | morning:
4 For thou Lord hath made me glad | through thy | works:
6 As it was in the beginning, is now, and | ev - er | shall be,

And of thy | truth in the | night — | season. 3
And I will rejoice in giving praise for the oper- | a - tions | of thy | hands. 5
World | with - out | end. *A-* | *men.*

## BONUM EST CONFITERI.

9TH TO 16TH SUNDAY AFTER TRINITY. J. JONES.

TREBLE.
SECOND.
TENOR.
BASS.

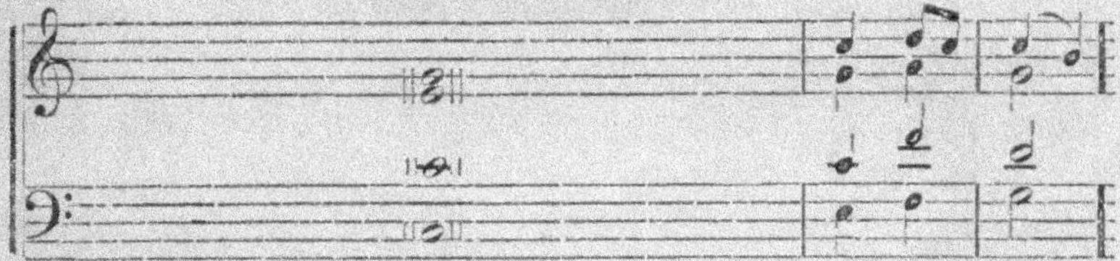

| | | |
|---|---|---|
| 1 It is a good thing to give thanks un-........ | to the | Lord: |
| 2 To tell of thy loving kindness early........ | in the | morning: |
| 3 Upon an instrument of ten strings, and up-........ | on the | lute: |
| 4 For thou Lord hath made me glad........ | through thy | works: |
| 5 Glory be to the Father, and........ | to the | Son, |
| 6 As it was in the beginning, is now, and........ | ev - er | shall be, |

| | | | |
|---|---|---|---|
| And to sing praises unto........thy..... | name O | Most — | Highest. 2 |
| And of........thy..... | truth in the | night — | season. 3 |
| Upon a loud instrument........ | and up- | on the | harp. 4 |
| And I will rejoice in giving praise for the o-.... per-... | a - tions | of thy | hands. 5 |
| And........ | to the | Ho - ly | Ghost. 6 |
| World........ | with - out | end. *A-* | *men.* |

## BONUM EST CONFITERI.

17TH TO 27TH SUNDAY AFTER TRINITY. REV. W. FELTON.

TREBLE.
SECOND.
TENOR.
BASS.

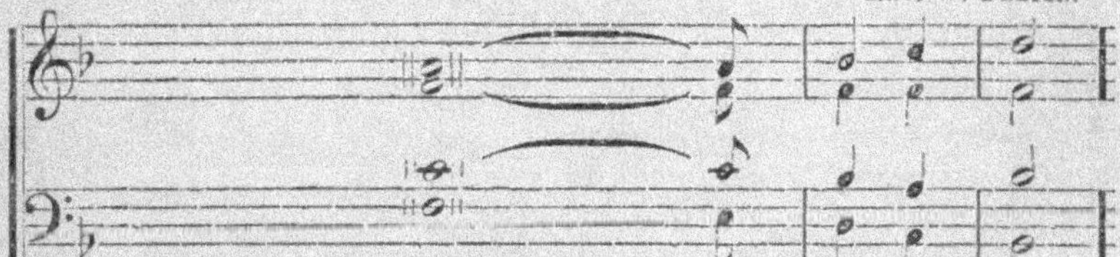

| | | |
|---|---|---|
| 1 It is a good thing to give thanks........ un-...... | to the | Lord: |
| 2 To tell of thy loving kindness ear-........ ly ...... | in the | morning: |
| 3 Upon an instrument of ten strings, and........ up- ...... | on the | lute: |
| 4 For thou Lord hath made me glad........ | through thy | works: |
| 5 Glory be to the Father,........ and ...... | to the | Son, |
| 6 As it was in the beginning, is now,........ and ...... | ev - er | shall be, |

| | | | |
|---|---|---|---|
| And to sing praises unto thy........ | name O | Most — | Highest. 2 |
| And of thy........ | truth in the | night — | season. 3 |
| Upon a loud instrument........ | and up- | on the | harp. 4 |
| And I will rejoice in giving praise for the oper-........ | a - tions | of thy | hands. 5 |
| And........ | to the | Ho - ly | Ghost. 6 |
| World........ | with - out | end. *A-* | *men.* |

# DEUS MISEREATUR.

ADVENT AND CHRISTMAS. BISHOP WAINWRIGHT.

TREBLE.
SECOND.
TENOR.
BASS.

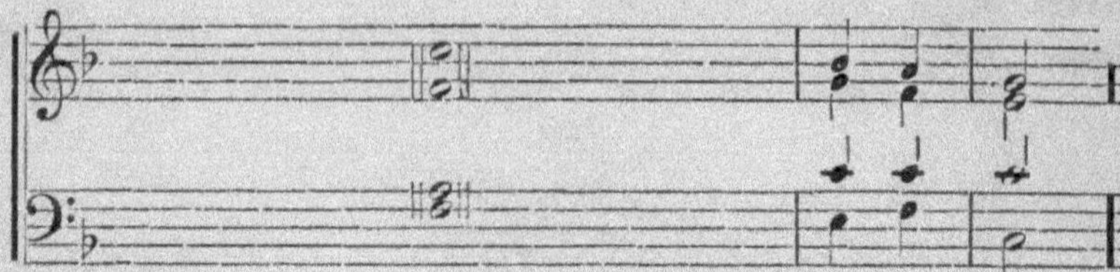

| | | |
|---|---|---|
| 1 God be merciful unto | us and | bless us: |
| 3 Let the people | praise thee, O | God: |
| 5 Let the people | praise thee, O | God: |
| 8 Glory be to the Father, and | to the | Son, |

| | | | |
|---|---|---|---|
| And show us the light of his countenance, and be | mer - ci- | ful un- | to us. 2 |
| Yea, let | all the | peo - ple | praise thee. 4 |
| Yea, let | all the | peo - ple | praise thee. 6 |
| And | to the | Ho - ly | Ghost. 9 |

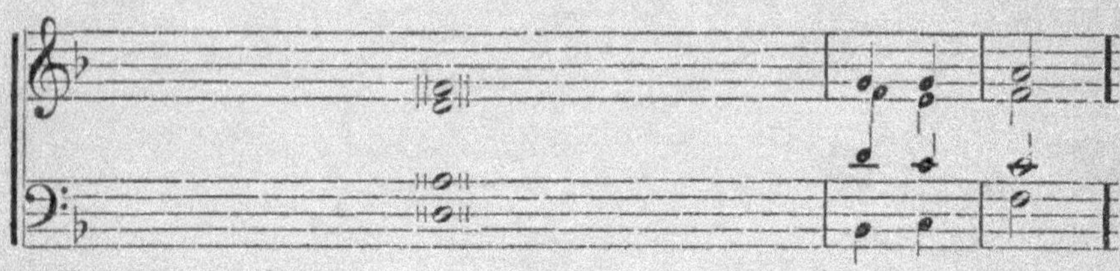

| | | |
|---|---|---|
| 2 That thy way may be | known upon | earth: |
| 4 O let the nations rejoice | and be | glad: |
| 6 Then shall the earth bring | forth her | increase: |
| 7 :‖: God | — shall | bless us, |
| 9 As it was in the beginning, is now, and | ev - er | shall be, |

| | | | |
|---|---|---|---|
| Thy saving | health a- | mong all | nations. 3 |
| For thou shalt judge the folks righteously, and govern the | na - tions | up - on | earth. 5 |
| And God, even our own | God shall | give us his | blessing. :‖: 7 |
| And all the | ends of the | world shall | fear him. 8 |
| World | with - out | end. *A-* | *men.* |

## DEUS MISEREATUR.

EPIPHANY TO QUINQUAGESIMA. Rev. P. Henley.

TREBLE.
SECOND.
TENOR.
BASS.

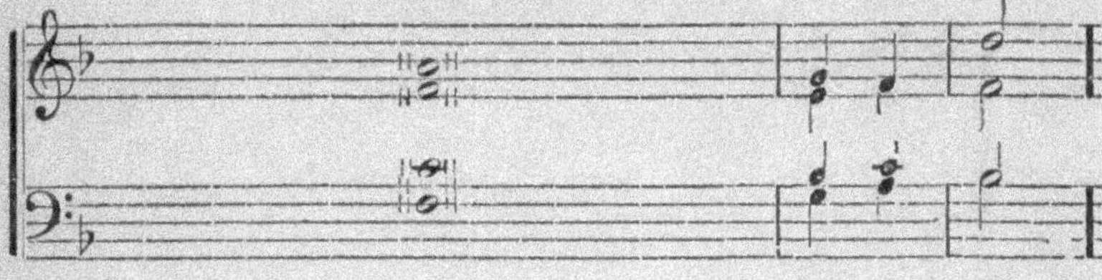

| | | |
|---|---|---|
| 1 God be merciful unto..... | us and | bless us: |
| 3 Let the people.... | praise thee, O | God: |
| 5 Let the people.... | praise thee, O | God: |
| 8 Glory be to the Father, and.... | to the | Son, |

| | | | |
|---|---|---|---|
| And show us the light of his countenance, and be.... | mer - ci- | ful un- | to us. 2 |
| Yea, let .... | all the | peo - ple | praise thee. 4 |
| Yea, let .... | all the | peo - ple | praise thee. 6 |
| And .... | to the | Ho - ly | Ghost. 9 |

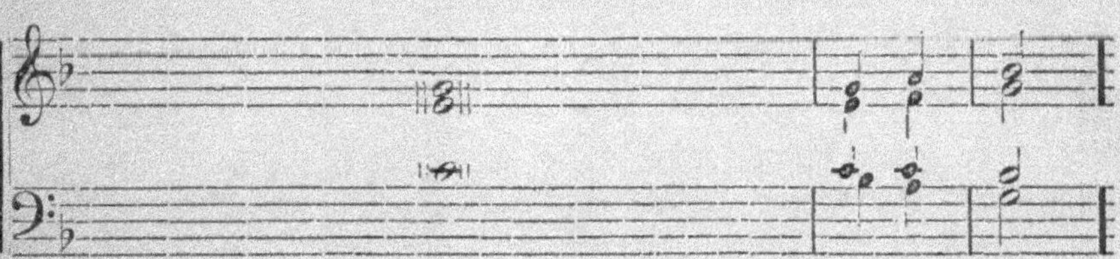

| | | |
|---|---|---|
| 2 That thy way may be.... | known upon | earth: |
| 4 O let the nations rejoice.... | and be | glad: |
| 6 Then shall the earth bring.... | forth her | increase: |
| 7 :‖: God.... | — shall | bless us, |
| 9 As it was in the beginning, is now, and.... | ev - er | shall be, |

| | | | |
|---|---|---|---|
| Thy sav-.... ing... | health a- | mong all | nations. 3 |
| For thou shalt judge the folk righteously, and govern the.. | na - tions | up - on | earth. 5 |
| And God, even our own.... | God shall | give us his | blessing.:‖:7 |
| And all.... the... | ends of the | world shall | fear him: 8 |
| World .... | with - out | end. *A-* | *men.* |

## DEUS MISEREATUR.

LENT. Dr. Camidge.

1 God be merciful unto ........ | us and | bless us :
3 Let the people ........ | praise thee, O | God :
5 Let the people ........ | praise thee, O | God :
8 Glory be to the Father, and ........ | to the | Son :

And show us the light of his countenance, and be ........ | mer - ci- | ful un- | to us. 2
Yea, let ........ | all the | peo - ple | praise thee. 4
Yea, let ........ | all the | peo - ple | praise thee. 6
And ........ | to the | Ho - ly | Ghost. 9

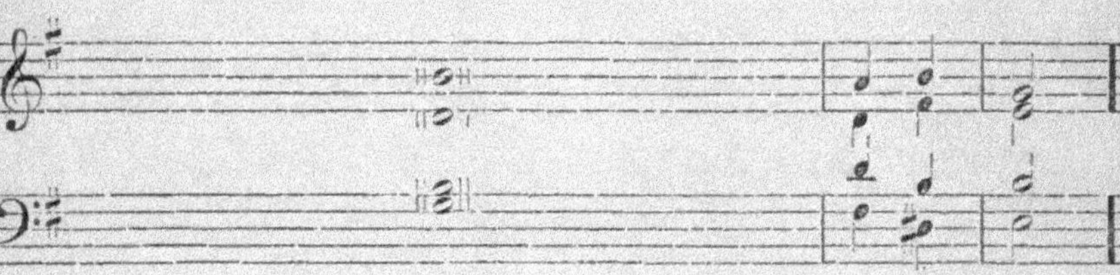

2 That thy way may be ........ | known upon | earth :
4 O let the nations rejoice ........ | and be | glad :
6 Then shall the earth bring ........ | forth her | increase :
7 :‖: God ........ | — shall | bless us,
9 As it was in the beginning, is now, and ........ | ev - er | shall be,

Thy saving ........ | health a- | mong all | nations. 3
For thou shalt judge the folks righteously, and govern the | na - tions | up - on | earth. 5
And God, even our own ........ | God shall | give us his | blessing. :‖: 7
And all the ........ | ends of the | world shall | fear him. 8
World ........ | with - out | end. A- | *men.*

## DEUS MISEREATUR.

EASTER TO WHITSUNDAY. G. BIRD.

TREBLE. SECOND. TENOR. BASS.

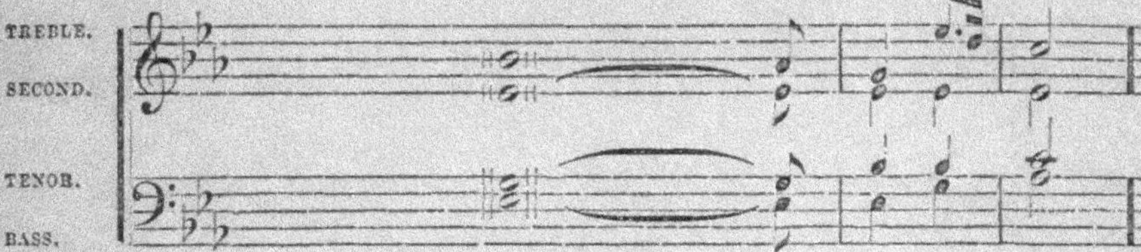

1 God be merciful un-............ to .... | us and | bless us:
3 Let the peo-............ ple ... | praise thee, O | God:
5 Let the peo-............ ple ... | praise thee, O | God:
8 Glory be to the Father,............ and... | to the | Son,

And show us the light of his countenance, and...... be...... | mer - ci- | ful un- | to us. 2
Yea,............ let ..... | all the | peo- ple | praise thee. 4
Yea............ let ..... | all the | peo- ple | praise thee. 6
And ............ | to the | Ho - ly | Ghost. 9

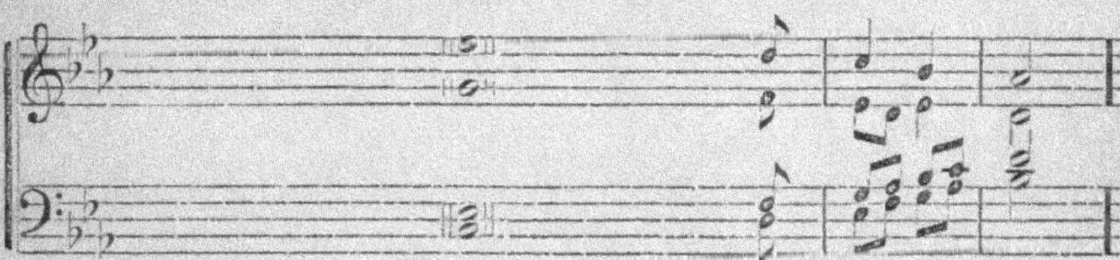

2 That thy way may............ be...... | known upon | earth:
4 O let the nations rejoice............ | and be | glad:
6 Then shall the earth............ bring.. | forth her | increase:
7 :‖: God............ | — shall | bless us,
9 As it was in the beginning, is now,............ and ... | ev - er | shall be,

Thy saving............ | health a- | mong all | nations. 3
For thou shalt judge the folk righteously, and govern the | na - tions | up - on | earth. 5
And God, even our own............ | God shall | give us his | blessing. :‖: 7
And all the............ | ends of the | world shall | fear him. 8
World ............ | with - out | end. A- | *men.*

## DEUS MISEREATUR.

1st to 8th Sunday after Trinity. Dr. O. Gibbons.

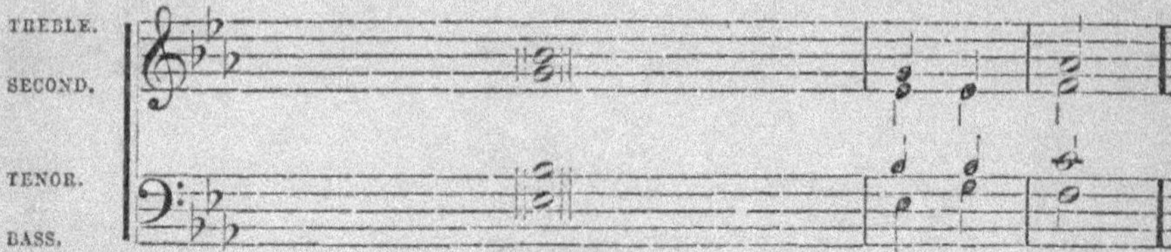


1 God be merciful unto.......... | us and | bless us.
3 Let the people.......... | praise thee, O | God:
5 Let the people.......... | praise thee, O | God:
8 Glory be to the Father, and.......... | to the | Son,

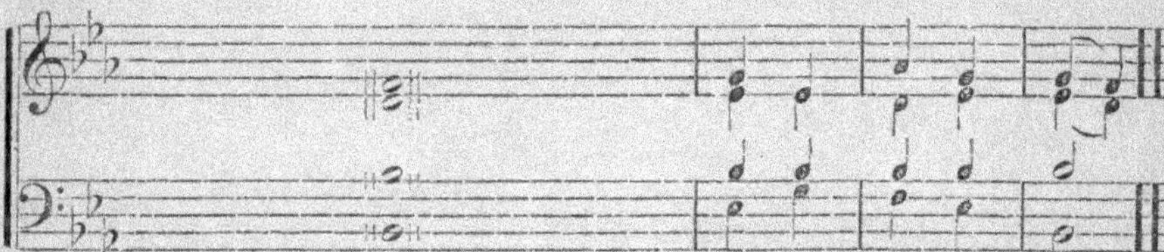

And show us the light of his countenance, and be.......... | mer - ci- | ful un- | to us: 2
Yea, let.......... | all the | peo - ple | praise thee. 4
Yea, let.......... | all the | peo - ple | praise thee. 6
And.......... | to the | Ho - ly | Ghost. 9

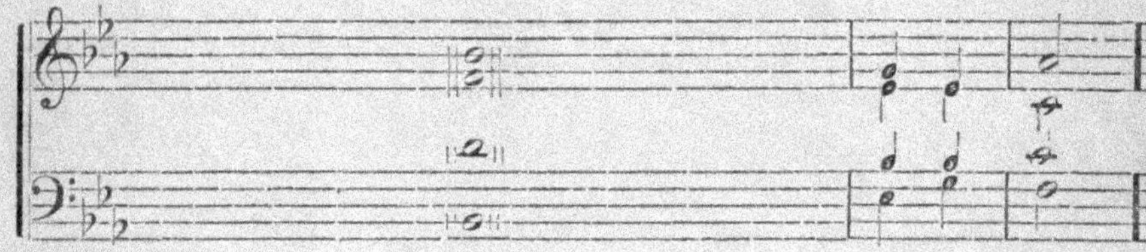

2 That thy way may be.......... | known upon | earth:
4 O let the nations rejoice.......... | and be | glad;
6 Then shall the earth bring.......... | forth her | increase:
7 :‖: God.......... | — shall | bless us,
9 As it was in the beginning, is now, and.......... | ev - er | shall be.

Thy saving.......... | health a- | mong all | nations. 3
For thou shalt judge the folk righteously, and govern the | na - tions | up - on | earth. 5
And God, even our own.......... | God shall | give us his | blessing.:‖:7
And all the.......... | ends of the | world shall | fear him. 8
World.......... | with - out | end. A- | *men.*

## DEUS MISEREATUR.

9TH TO 16TH SUNDAY AFTER TRINITY. REV. DR. BECKWITH.

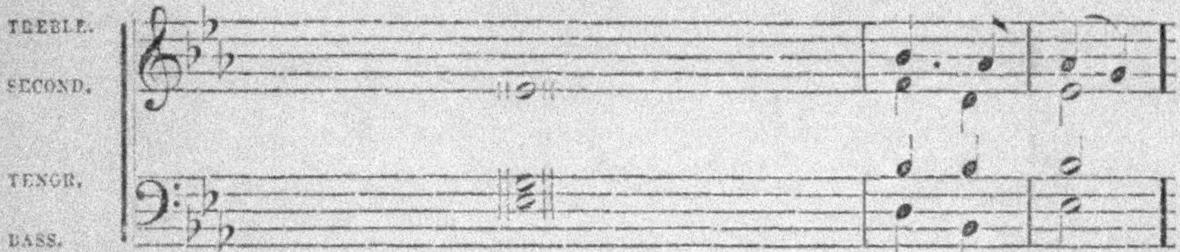


| | | |
|---|---|---|
| 1 God be merciful unto...... | us and | bless us : |
| 3 Let the people...... | praise thee, O | God : |
| 5 Let the people...... | praise thee, O | God : |
| 8 Glory be to the Father, and...... | to the | Son : |

| | | | |
|---|---|---|---|
| And show us the light of his countenance, and be...... | mer - ci- | ful un- | to us. 2 |
| Yea, let...... | all the | peo - ple | praise thee. 4 |
| Yea, let...... | all the | peo - ple | praise thee. 6 |
| And...... | to the | Ho - ly | Ghost. 9 |

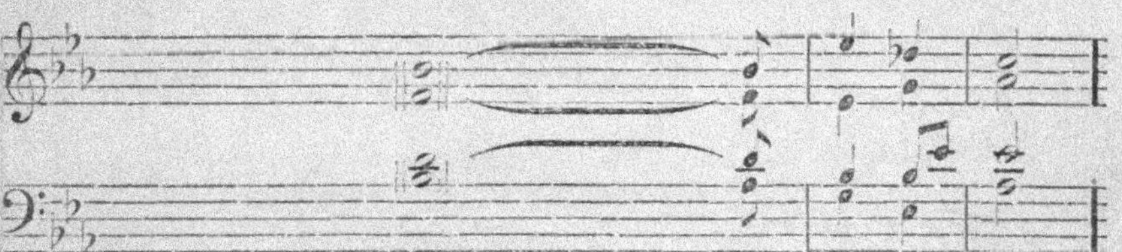

| | | |
|---|---|---|
| 2 That thy way may...... be...... | known upon | earth : |
| 4 O let the nations rejoice...... | and be | glad : |
| 6 Then shall the earth...... bring.. | forth her | increase : |
| 7 :‖: God...... | — shall | bless us, |
| 9 As it was in the beginning, is now,...... and... | ev - er | shall be, |

| | | | |
|---|---|---|---|
| Thy sav-...... ing ... | health a- | mong all | nations. 3 |
| For thou shalt judge the folk righteously, and govern the. | na - tions | up - on | earth. 5 |
| And God, even our own...... | God shall | give us his | blessing.:‖: 7 |
| And all...... the... | ends of the | world shall | fear him. 8 |
| World...... | with - out | end. A- | men. |

# DEUS MISEREATUR.

17TH TO 27TH SUNDAY AFTER TRINITY. DR. CROTCH.

TREBLE.
SECOND.
TENOR.
BASS.

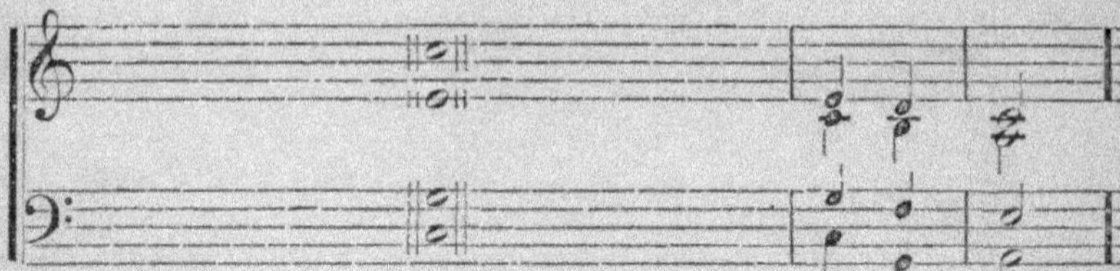

| | | |
|---|---|---|
| 1 God be merciful unto | us and | bless us : |
| 3 Let the people | praise thee, O | God : |
| 5 Let the people | praise thee, O | God : |
| 8 Glory be to the Father, and | to the | Son : |

| | | | |
|---|---|---|---|
| And show us the light of his countenance, and be | mer - ci- | ful un- | to us. 2 |
| Yea, let | all the | peo - ple | praise thee. 4 |
| Yea, let | all the | peo - ple | praise thee. 6 |
| And | to the | Ho - ly | Ghost. 9 |

| | | |
|---|---|---|
| 2 That thy way may be | known upon | earth : |
| 4 O let the nations rejoice | and be | glad : |
| 6 Then shall the earth bring | forth her | increase : |
| 7 :‖: God | — shall | bless us, |
| 9 As it was in the beginning, is now, and | ev - er | shall be, |

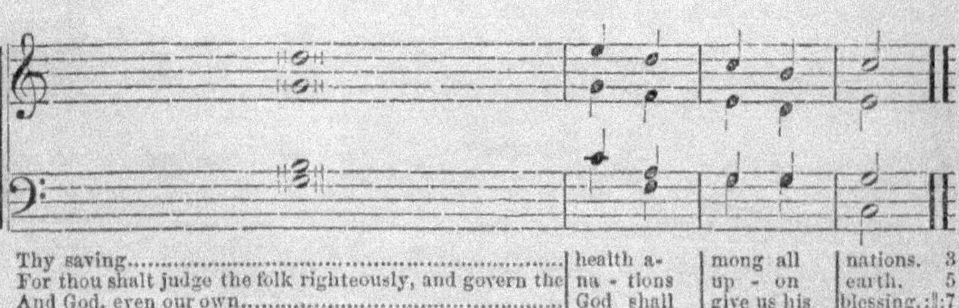

| | | | |
|---|---|---|---|
| Thy saving | health a- | mong all | nations. 3 |
| For thou shalt judge the folk righteously, and govern the | na - tions | up - on | earth. 5 |
| And God, even our own | God shall | give us his | blessing. :‖: 7 |
| And all the | ends of the | world shall | fear him. 8 |
| World | with - out | end. *A-* | *men.* |

## BENEDIC ANIMA MEA.

ADVENT AND CHRISTMAS. BECKWITH.

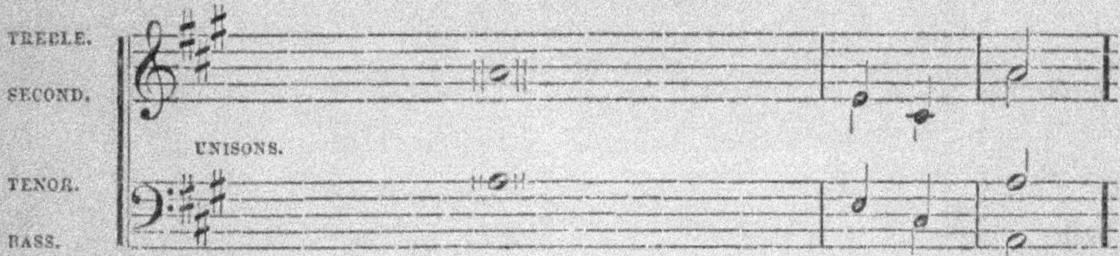


| | | | |
|---|---|---|---|
| 1 Praise the Lord........ | O | my | soul: |
| 3 Who forgiveth........ | all | thy | sins: |
| 5 O praise the Lord ye angels of his, ye that ex-........ | cel | in | strength: |
| 8 Glory be to the Father and........ | to | the | Son: |

| | | | | |
|---|---|---|---|---|
| And all that is within,........ me.. | praise his | ho - ly | name. | 2 |
| And........ | healeth all | thine in- | firmities. | 4 |
| Ye that fulfill his commandment, and hearken........ un.. | to the | voice of his | word. | 6 |
| And........ | to the | Ho - ly | Ghost, | 9 |

| | | |
|---|---|---|
| 2 Praise the Lord........ | O my | soul: |
| 4 Who saveth thy........ | life from de- | struction: |
| {6 O praise the Lord, all........ | ye His | hosts; |
| {7 O speak good of the Lord, all ye works of His, in all places of........ | His do- | minion: |
| 9 As it was in the beginning, is now, and........ | ev - er | shall be, |

| | | | |
|---|---|---|---|
| And for-........ | get not | all his | benefits: 3 |
| And crowneth thee with........ | mercy and | lov - ing | kindness :5 |
| Ye servants of........ | His, that | do his | pleasure:‖:7 |
| Praise thou the........ | Lord — | O my | soul; 8 |
| World........ | with - out | end. A- | *men.* |

## BENEDIC ANIMA MEA.

EPIPHANY TO QUINQUAGESIMA. NUTLOW.

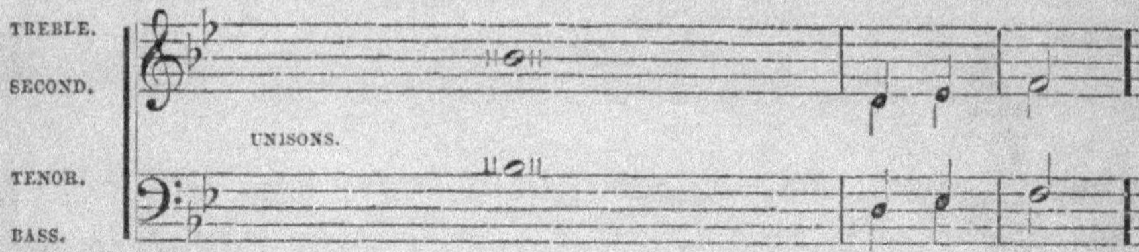


| | | |
|---|---|---|
| 1 Praise the Lord........ | O my | soul: |
| 3 Who forgiveth........ | all thy | sins, |
| 5 O praise the Lord ye angels of his, ye that ex-........ | cel in | strength: |
| 8 Glory be to the Father, and........ | to the | Son, |

| | | | |
|---|---|---|---|
| And all this is within........ me ... | praise his | ho - ly | name. 2 |
| And........ | healeth all | thine in- | firmities. 4 |
| Ye that fulfill his commandment, and hearken...... un-... | to the | voice of his | word. 6 |
| And........ | to the | Ho - ly | Ghost. 9 |

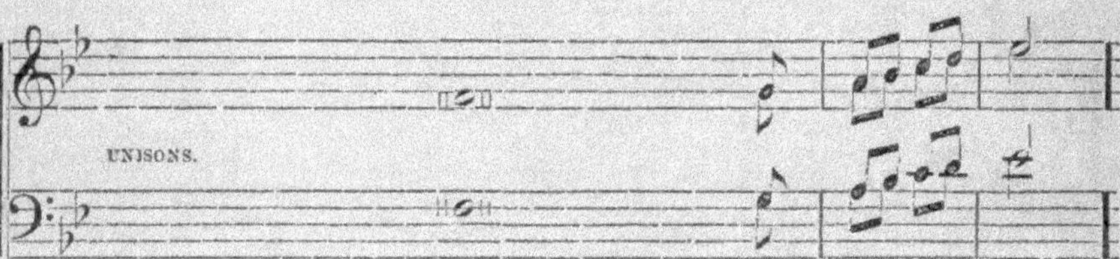


| | | |
|---|---|---|
| 2 Praise the Lord,........ | O my | soul: |
| 4 Who saveth........ thy... | life from de- | struction: |
| { 6 O praise the Lord,........ all.... | ye His | hosts: |
| { 7 O speak good of the Lord, all ye works of His, in all places...... of..... | His do- | minion: |
| 9 As it was in the beginning, is now,........ and... | ev - er | shall be, |

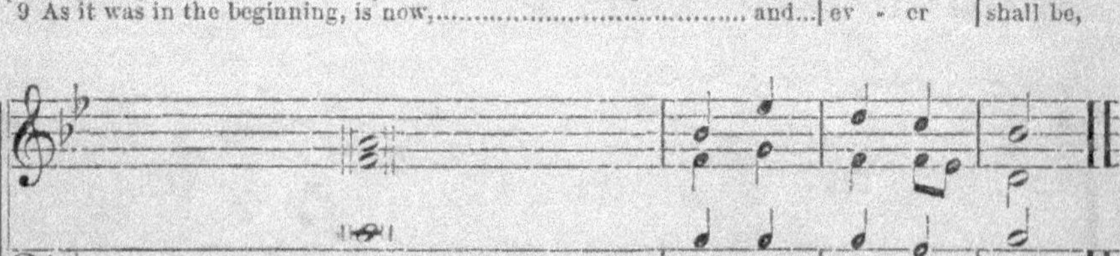

| | | | |
|---|---|---|---|
| And for-........ | get not | all his | benefits. 3 |
| And crowneth thee with........ | mercy and | lov - ing | kindness. 5 |
| Ye servants of........ | His that | do His | pleasure.:‖:7 |
| Praise thou the........ | Lord — | O my | soul. 8 |
| World........ | with - out | end. *A-* | *men.* |

## BENEDIC ANIMA MEA.

LENT. DR. CROTCH.

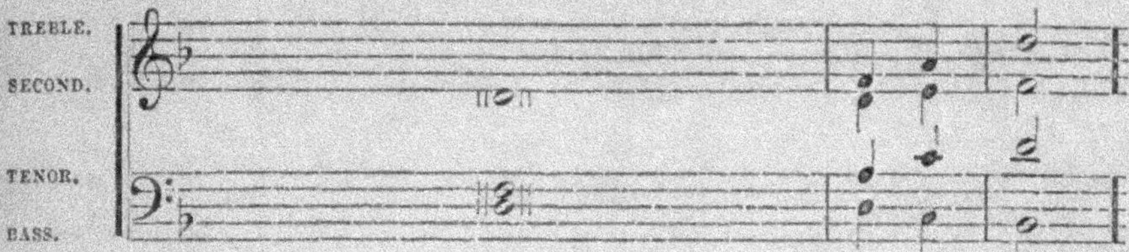


| | | |
|---|---|---|
| 1 Praise the Lord,......................................... | O my | soul : |
| 3 Who forgiveth......................................... | all thy | sins, |
| 5 O praise the Lord ye angels of his, ye that ex-................ | cel in | strength : |
| 8 Glory be to the Father, and ................................ | to the | Son, |

| | | | |
|---|---|---|---|
| And all this is within me.................................... | praise his | ho - ly | name. 2 |
| And ........................................................ | healeth all | thine in- | firmities. 4 |
| Ye that fulfill his commandment, and hearken un-......... | to the | voice of his | word. 6 |
| And ........................................................ | to the | Ho - ly | Ghost. 9 |

| | | |
|---|---|---|
| 2 Praise the Lord......................................... | O my | soul : |
| 4 Who saveth.......................................... thy.... | life from de- | struction : |
| {6 O praise the Lord,.................................. all .... | ye His | hosts : |
| {7 O speak good of the Lord, all ye works of His, in all places...... of...... | His do- | minion : |
| 9 As it was in the beginning, is now,........................ and.... | ev - er | shall be, |

| | | | |
|---|---|---|---|
| And for-.................................................... | get not | all his | benefits. 3 |
| And crowneth thee with...................................... | mercy and | lov - ing | kindness. 5 |
| Ye servants of.............................................. | His, that | do His | pleasure.:‖:7 |
| Praise thou the............................................. | Lord, — | O my | soul. 8 |
| World....................................................... | with - out | end. *A-* | *men.* |

## BENEDIC ANIMA MEA.

EASTER TO WHITSUNDAY. NORRIS.

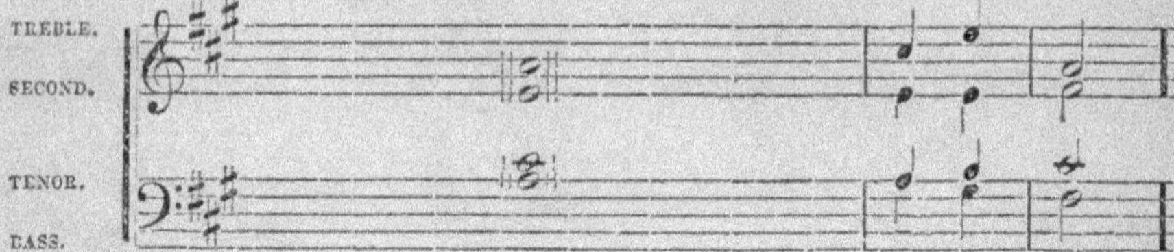


| | | | |
|---|---|---|---|
| 1 Praise the Lord, | O | my | soul: |
| 3 Who forgiveth | all | thy | sins; |
| 5 O praise the Lord ye angels of his, ye that ex- | cel | in | strength: |
| 8 Glory be to the Father, and | to | the | Son: |

| | | | |
|---|---|---|---|
| And all that is within me | praise his | ho - ly | name. 2 |
| And | healeth all | thine in- | firmities. 4 |
| Ye that fulfill his commandment, and harken un- | to the | voice of His | word. 6 |
| And | to the | Ho - ly | Ghost. 9 |

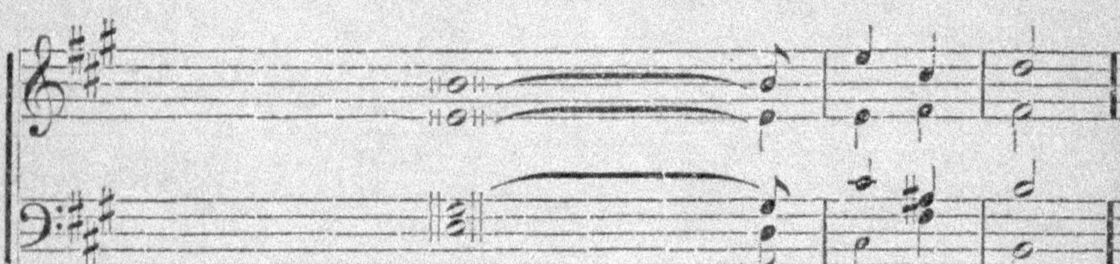

| | | | |
|---|---|---|---|
| 2 Praise the Lord | O | my | soul: |
| 4 Who saveth ... thy | life from | de- | struction, |
| {6 O praise the Lord, ... all | ye | His | hosts: |
| {7 O speak good of the Lord, all ye works of His, in all places ... of | His | do- | minion: |
| 9 As it was in the beginning, is now, ... and | ev - | er | shall be, |

| | | | |
|---|---|---|---|
| And for- | get not | all his | benefits. 3 |
| And crowneth thee with | mercy and | lov - ing | kindness. 5 |
| Ye servants of | His, that | do His | pleasure.:‖:7 |
| Praise thou the | Lord, — | O my | soul. 8 |
| World | with - out | end. A- | *men.* |

## BENEDIC ANIMA MEA.

TRINITY TO 8TH SUNDAY AFTER. FITZHERBERT & HAYES.

TREBLE.
SECOND.
TENOR.
BASS.

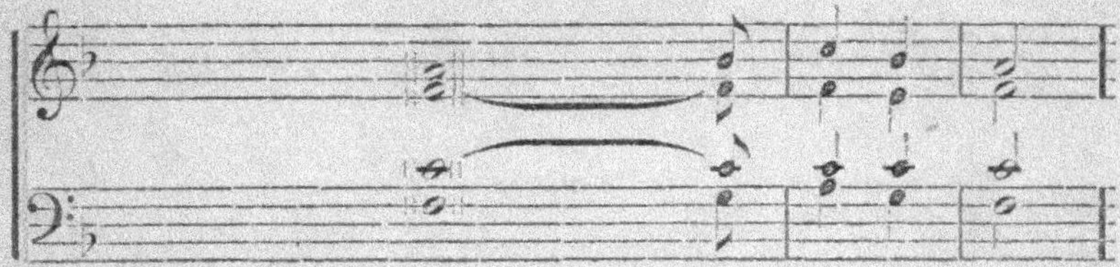

| | | | |
|---|---|---|---|
| 1 Praise the Lord............ | O | my | soul: |
| 3 Who forgiv-............ eth..... | all | thy | sins, |
| 5 O praise the Lord ye angels of his, ye that............ ex-.... | cel | in | strength: |
| 8 Glory be to the Father,............ and..... | to | the | Son, |

| | | | | |
|---|---|---|---|---|
| And all that is within me............ | praise his | ho - ly | name. | 2 |
| And ............ | healeth all | thine in- | firmities. | 4 |
| Ye that fulfill his commandment, and hearken un-........ | to the | voice of his | word. | 6 |
| And ............ | to the | Ho - ly | Ghost. | 9 |

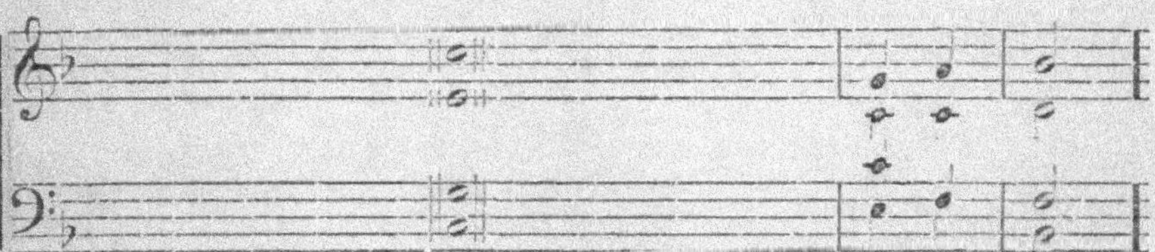

| | | | |
|---|---|---|---|
| 2 Praise the Lord,............ | O | my | soul: |
| 4 Who saveth thy............ | life from de- | | struction: |
| {6 O praise the Lord, all............ | ye | His | hosts: |
| {7 O speak good of the Lord, all ye works of His, in all places of............ | His | do- | minion: |
| 9 As it was in the beginning, is now, and............ | ev - | er | shall be, |

| | | | | | | |
|---|---|---|---|---|---|---|
| And for-............ | get | not | all | his | benefits. | 3 |
| And crowneth thee with............ | mercy and | | lov - | ing | kindness. | 5 |
| Ye servants of............ | His | that | do | His | pleasure.:‖: | 7 |
| Praise thou the............ | Lord | — | O | my | soul. | 8 |
| World ............ | with - | out | end. | *A-* | *men.* | |

## BENEDIC ANIMA MEA.

9TH TO 16TH SUNDAY AFTER TRINITY. A. CORFE.

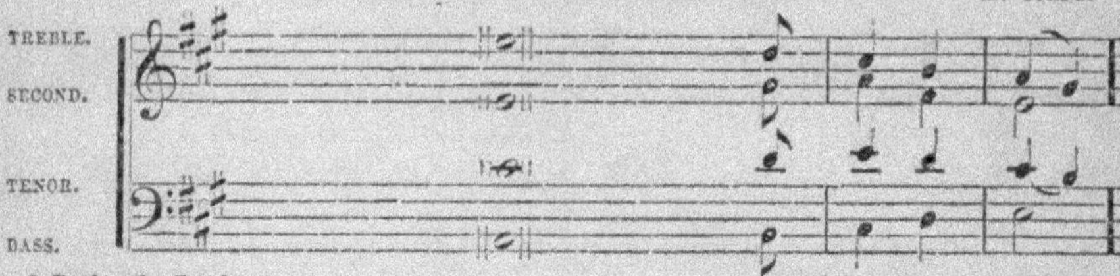


1 Praise the Lord................................................. | O my | soul :
3 Who forgiv-...................................................... eth..... | all thy | sins,
5 O praise the Lord ye angels of his, ye that............................ ex-..... | cel in | strength :
8 Glory be to the Father,.............................. ..........., and..... | to the | Son,

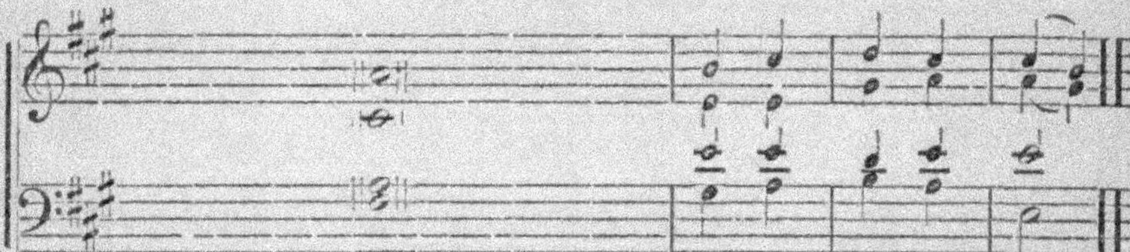

And all that is within me........................................ | praise his | ho - ly | name. 2
And................................................................ | healeth all | thine in- | firmities. 4
Ye that fulfill his commandment, and hearken un-......... | to the | voice of his | word. 6
And................................................................ | to the | Ho - ly | Ghost. 9

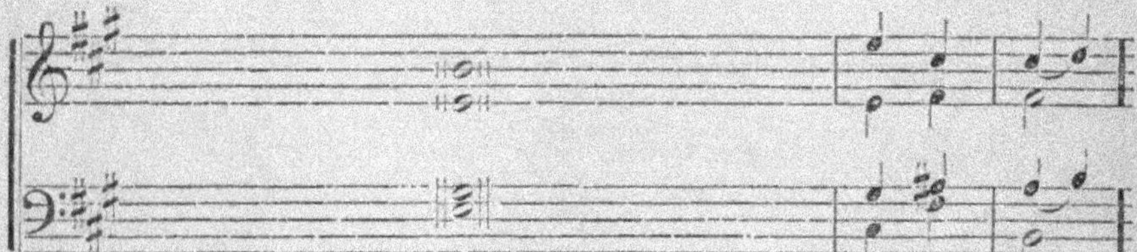

2 Praise the Lord,................................................. | O my | soul :
4 Who saveth thy................................................... | life from de- | struction :
{6 O praise the Lord, all........................................ | ye His | hosts :
{7 O speak good of the Lord, all ye works of His, in all places of............ | His do- | minion :
9 As it was in the beginning, is now, and............................ | ev - er | shall be,

And for-............................................................ | get not | all his | benefits. 3
And crowneth thee with......................................... | mercy and | lov - ing | kindness. 5
Ye servants of...................................................... | His, that | do His | pleasure.:‖:7
Praise thou the..................................................... | Lord, — | O my | soul. 8
World................................................................ | with - out | end. A- | *men.*

## BENEDIC ANIMA MEA.

17TH TO 27TH SUNDAY AFTER TRINITY. DR. BECKWITH.

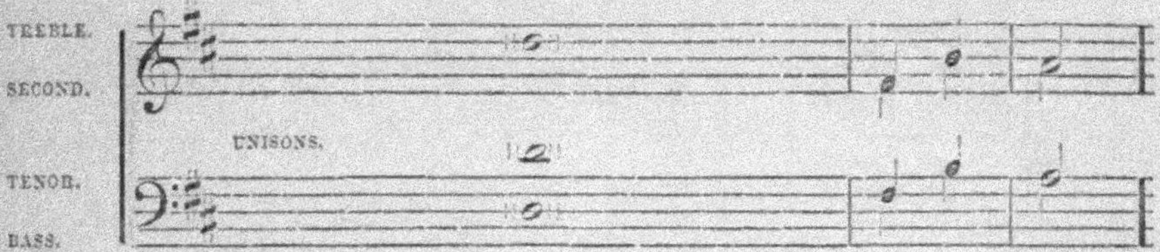


| | | | |
|---|---|---|---|
| 1 Praise the Lord,...... | O | my | soul: |
| 3 Who forgiveth...... | all | thy | sins, |
| 5 O praise the Lord ye angels of his, ye that ex-...... | cel | in | strength: |
| 8 Glory be to the Father, and ...... | to | the | Son, |

| | | | | |
|---|---|---|---|---|
| And all that is within me...... | praise his | ho - ly | name. | 2 |
| And ...... | healeth all | thine in- | firmities. | 4 |
| Ye that fulfill his commandment, and hearken un-...... | to the | voice of his | word. | 6 |
| And ...... | to the | Ho - ly | Ghost. | 9 |

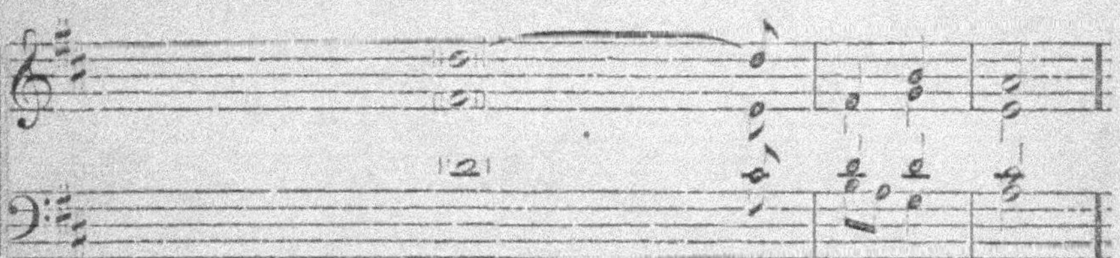

| | | | |
|---|---|---|---|
| 2 Praise the Lord...... | O | my | soul: |
| 4 Who saveth...... thy...... | life from | de- | struction: |
| {6 O praise the Lord,...... all...... | ye | His | hosts: |
| {7 O speak good of the Lord, all ye works of His, in all places...... of...... | His | do- | minion: |
| 9 As it was in the beginning, is now,...... and...... | ev - | er | shall be, |

| | | | | |
|---|---|---|---|---|
| And for-...... | get not | all his | benefits. | 3 |
| And crowneth thee with...... | mercy and | lov - ing | kindness. | 5 |
| Ye servants of...... | His that | do His | pleasure.:‖:7 | |
| Praise thou the...... | Lord — | O my | soul. | 8 |
| World ...... | with - out | end. *A-* | *men.* | |

## BURIAL OF

TREBLE.
SECOND.
TENOR.
BASS.

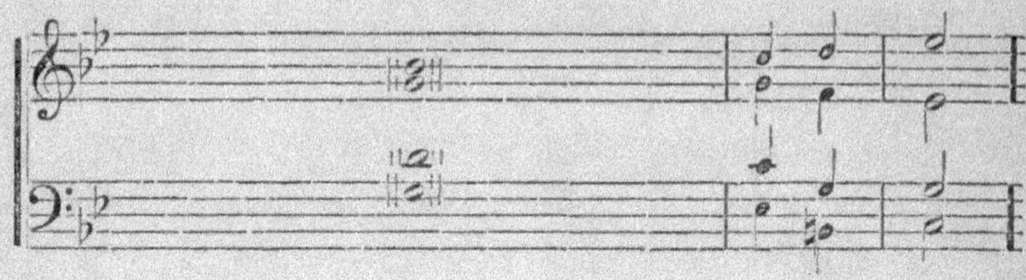

| | | |
|---|---|---|
| 1 Lord, let me know my end, and the | number of | my days: |
| 3 For man walketh in a vain shadow, and disquieteth him- | self in | vain: |
| 5 Deliver me from | all mine of- | fenses: |
| 7 Hear my prayer, O Lord; and with thine ears con- | sider my | calling: |
| 9 O spare me a little, that I may re- | cover my | strength: |
| 11 Before the mountains were brought forth, or ever the earth and the | world were | made: |
| 13 For a thousand years in thy sight are | but as | yesterday: |
| 15 In the morning it is green, and | grow - eth | up: |
| 17 Thou hast set our mis- | deeds be- | fore thee: |
| 19 The days of our age are threescore years and ten; and though men be so strong that they come to fourscore years, yet is their strength then but | labor and | sorrow: |
| 21 Glory be to the Father, and | to the | Son, |

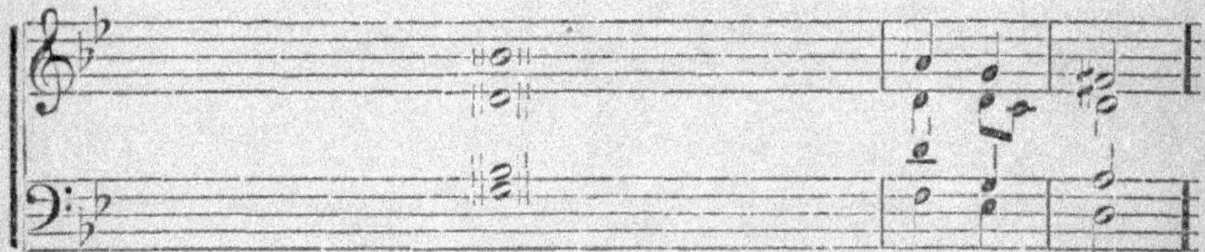

| | | |
|---|---|---|
| 2 Behold, thou hast made my days as it were a span long; and mine age is even as nothing in re- | spect of | Thee: |
| 4 And now, Lord, | what is my | hope? |
| 6 When thou with rebukes dost chasten man for sin, thou makest his beauty to consume away, like as it were a moth | fretting a | garment: |
| 8 For I am a stranger with Thee, | and a | sojourner: |
| 10 Lord, thou hast | been our | refuge: |
| 12 Thou turnest man | to de- | struction: |
| 14 As soon as thou scatterest them, they are | even as | asleep: |
| 16 For we consume away in | thy dis- | pleasure: |
| 18 For when thou art angry all our | days are | gone: |
| 20 So teach us to | number our | days: |
| 22 As it was in the beginning, is now, and | ev - er | shall be: |

## THE DEAD.

NOVELLO.

| | | | | |
|---|---|---|---|---|
| That I may be certified how | long I | have to | live. | 2 |
| He heapeth up riches, and can not | tell - | who shall | gather them. | 4 |
| And make me not a re- | buke un- | to the | foolish. | 6 |
| Hold not thy | peace - | at my | tears. | 8 |
| Before I go hence | and be | no more | seen. | 10 |
| Thou art God from ever- | lasting and | world without | end. | 12 |
| Seeing that it is past | as a | watch in the | night. | 14 |
| But in the evening it is cut | down, dried | up, and | withered. | 16 |
| And our secret | sins in the | light of thy | countenance. | 18 |
| So soon passeth it a- | way and | we are | gone. | 20 |
| and | to the | Ho - ly | Ghost. | 22 |

PURCELL, 1687.

| | | | | |
|---|---|---|---|---|
| And verily every man living is, | al - to- | geth - er | vanity. | 3 |
| Truly my | hope is | even in | Thee. | 5 |
| Every man | there - fore | is but | vanity. | 7 |
| As | all my | fa - thers | were. | 9 |
| From one gene- | ra - tion | to an- | other. | 11 |
| Again thou sayest, come a- | gain ye | children of | men. | 13 |
| And fade away | sudden-ly | like the | grass. | 15 |
| And are afraid at thy | wrath - ful | in - dig- | nation. | 17 |
| We bring our years to an end as it | were a | tale that is | told. | 19 |
| That we may ap- | ply our | hearts unto | wisdom. | 21 |
| World | with - out | end. A- | men. | |

## PSALM 1. C. M.

OLD 98TH. RAVENSCROFT, 1621.

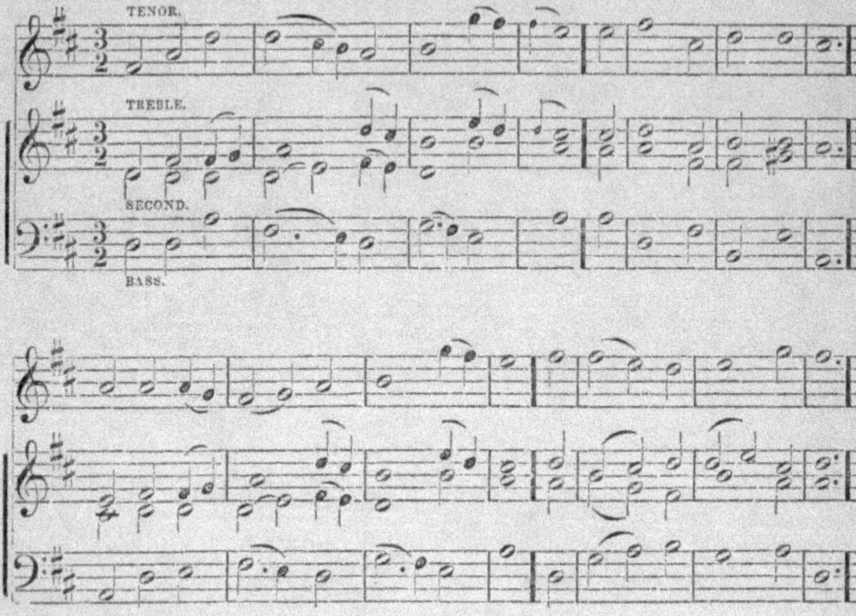


Verses 2, 4, 6, and Gloria.

# SELECTIONS FROM THE PSALMS OF DAVID.

## IN METER.

---

### PSALM 1. C. M.

From the i Psalm of David.

1 How blest is he who ne'er consents
By ill advice to walk,
Nor stands in sinners' ways, nor sits
Where men profanely talk;

2 But makes the perfect law of God
His business and delight;
Devoutly reads therein by day,
And meditates by night.

3 Like some fair tree, which, fed by streams,
With timely fruit does bend,
He still shall flourish, and success
All his designs attend.

4 Ungodly men and their attempts,
No lasting root shall find;
Untimely blasted and dispersed
Like chaff before the wind.

5 Their guilt shall strike the wicked dumb
Before their Judge's face;
No formal hypocrite shall then
Among the saints have place.

6 For God approves the just man's ways;
To happiness they tend;
But sinners, and the paths they tread,
Shall both in ruin end.

---

To Father, Son, and Holy Ghost,
The God whom we adore,
Be glory, as it was, is now,
And shall be evermore.

## PSALM 2. C. M.

ST. DAVID'S. RAVENSCROFT, 1621.

## PSALM 3. C. M.

TIVERTON. GRIGG.

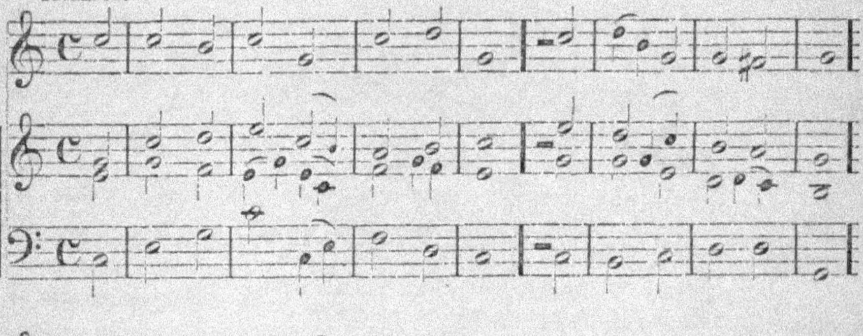

## PSALM 2. C. M.

From the ii Psalm of David.

1 Thus God declares his sovereign will:
"The King that I ordain,
Whose throne is fixed on Sion's hill,
Shall there securely reign."

2 Attend, O earth, while I declare
God's uncontrolled decree:
"Thou art my Son; this day, my heir,
Have I begotten thee.

3 "Ask, and receive thy full demands;
Thine shall the heathen be;
The utmost limit of the lands
Shall be possessed by thee."

4 Learn then, ye princes; and give ear,
Ye judges of the earth;
Worship the Lord with holy fear;
Rejoice with awful mirth.

5 Appease the Son with due respect,
Your timely homage pay;
Lest he revenge the bold neglect,
Incensed by your delay.

6 If but in part his anger rise,
Who can endure the flame?
Then blest are they, whose hope relies
On his most holy Name.

## PSALM 3. C. M.

From the iii Psalm of David.

1 Thou, gracious God, art my defense;
On thee my hopes rely;
Thou art my glory, and shalt yet
Lift up my head on high.

2 Since whensoe'er, in my distress,
To God I made my prayer,
He heard me from his holy hill;
Why should I now despair?

3 Guarded by him I lay me down
My sweet repose to take;
For I through him securely sleep,
Through him in safety wake.

4 Salvation to the Lord belongs;
He only can defend:
His blessings he extends to all
That on his power depend.

---

To Father, Son and Holy Ghost,
The God whom we adore,
Be glory, as it was, is now,
And shall be ever more.

## PSALMS 4 & 5. C. M.

ABRIDGE. I. SMITH.

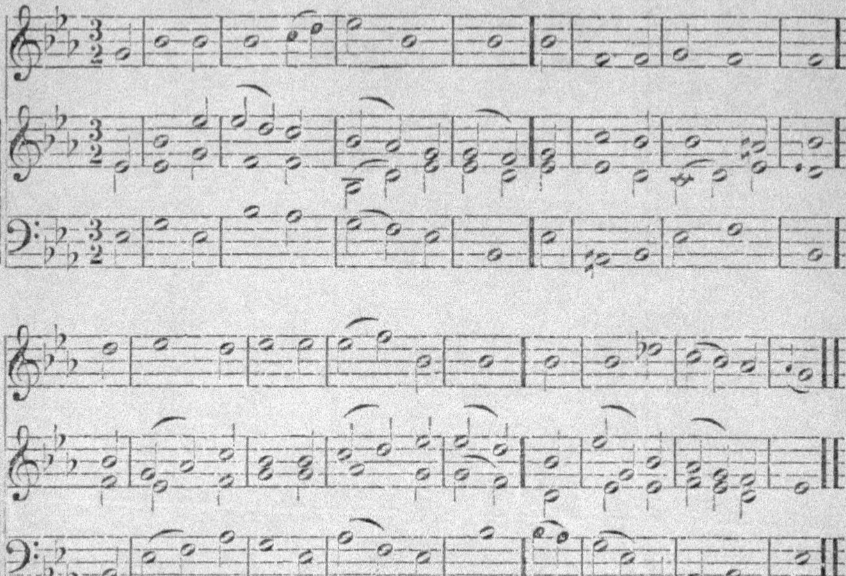

## PSALM 6. S. M.

AYLESBURY. DR. GREENE.

## PSALM 4. C. M.

From the iv Psalm of David.

1 Consider that the righteous man
Is God's peculiar choice;
And when to him I make my prayer
He always hears my voice.

2 Then stand in awe of his commands,
Flee every thing that 's ill,
Commune in private with your hearts,
And bend them to his will.

3 The sacrifice of righteousness
Present to God on high;
And let your hope, securely fixed,
On him alone rely.

4 While worldly minds impatient grow
More prosp'rous times to see;
Still let the glories of thy face
Shine brightly, Lord, on me.

5 So shall my heart o'erflow with joy,
More lasting and more true
Than theirs, who stores of corn and wine
Successively renew.

6 Then down in peace I 'll lay my head,
And take my needful rest;
No other guard, O Lord, I crave,
Of thy defense possessed.

---

To Father, Son, and Holy Ghost,
The God whom we adore,
Be glory, as it was, is now,
And shall be evermore.

## PSALM 5. C. M.

From the v Psalm of David.

1 Regard my words, O gracious Lord,
Accept my secret prayer,
To thee alone, my King, my God,
Will I for help repair.

2 Thou in the morn my voice shalt hear,
And with the dawning day,
To thee devoutly I 'll look up,
To thee devoutly pray.

3 Lord, I within thy house will come,
In thy abundant grace;
And I will worship in thy fear,
Toward thy most holy place.

4 Let those, O Lord, who trust in thee,
With shouts their joy proclaim:
Let them rejoice whom thou preservest,
And all that love thy name.

5 To righteous men, the righteous Lord
His blessing will extend;
And with his favor all his saints,
As with a shield, defend.

---

To Father, Son, and Holy Ghost,
The God whom we adore,
Be glory, as it was, is now,
And shall be evermore.

## PSALM 6. S. M.

From the vi Psalm of David.

1 In mercy, not in wrath,
Rebuke me, gracious God!
Lest, if thy whole displeasure rise,
I sink beneath thy rod.

2 Touched by thy quick'ning power,
My load of guilt I feel:
The wounds thy Spirit hath unclosed,
O let that Spirit heal.

3 In trouble and in gloom,
Must I for ever mourn?
And wilt thou not, at length, O God,
In pitying love return?

4 O come, ere life expire,
Send down thy power to save;
For who shall sing thy name in death,
Or praise thee in the grave?

5 Why should I doubt thy grace,
Or yield to dread despair?
Thou wilt fulfill thy promised word,
And grant me all my prayer.

---

To God, the Father, Son,
And spirit, glory be,
As 't was, and is, and shall be so
To all eternity.

## PSALM 7. C. M.

OLD 98TH. RAVENSCROFT, 1621.

## PSALM 7. C. M.

From the viii Psalm of David.

1 O THOU to whom all creatures bow
Within this earthly frame;
Through all the world how great art thou!
How glorious is thy name!

2 In heaven thy wond'rous acts are sung,
Nor fully reckoned there;
And yet thou mak'st the infant tongue
Thy boundless praise declare.

3 When heaven, thy beauteous work on high,
Employs my wondering sight—
The moon, that nightly rules the sky,
With stars of feebler light;-

4 Oh! what is man, that, Lord, thou lovest,
To keep him in thy mind?
Or what his offspring, that thou provest
To them so wondrous kind?

5 Him next in power thou didst create
To thy celestial train;
Ordained, with dignity and state,
O'er all thy works to reign.

6 They jointly own his powerful sway,
The beasts that prey or graze;
The bird that wings its airy way;
The fish that cuts the seas.

7 O thou, to whom all creatures bow,
Within this earthly frame;
Through all the world, how great art thou,
How glorious is thy name!

---

To Father, Son, and Holy Ghost,
The God whom we adore,
Be glory, as it was, is now,
And shall be evermore.

## PSALM 8. C. M.

BROOMSGROVE.

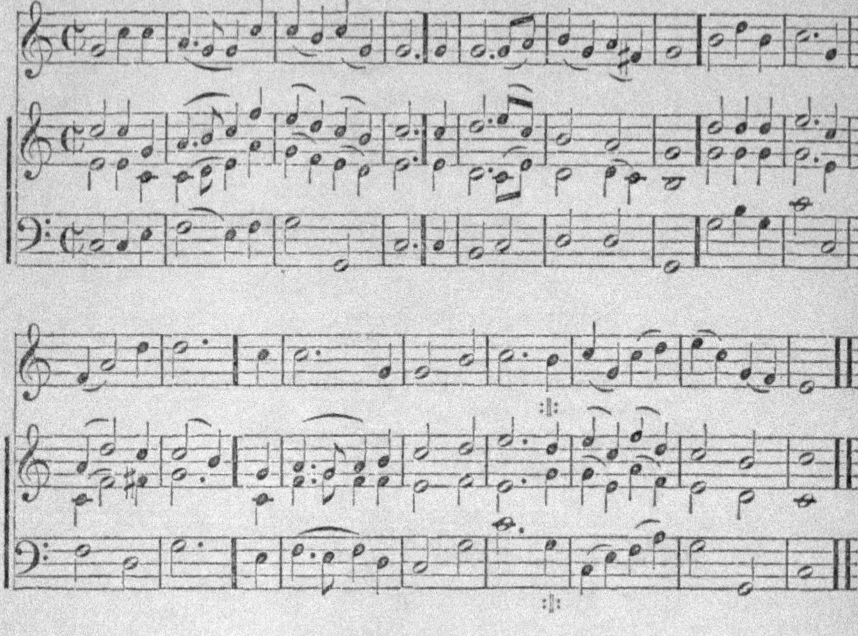

## PSALM 9. C. M.

ST. STEPHENS. W. JONES.

## PSALM 8. C. M.

From the ix Psalm of David.

1 To celebrate thy praise, O Lord,
I will my heart prepare;
To all the listening world, thy works,
Thy wond'rous works, declare.

2 The thought of them shall to my soul
Exalted pleasures bring;
While to thy name, O thou Most High,
Triumphant praise I sing.

3 The Lord for ever lives, who has
His righteous throne prepared,
Impartial justice to dispense,
To punish or reward.

4 All those who have his goodness proved,
Will in his truth confide;
Whose mercy ne'er forsook the man
That on his help relied.

5 Sing praises, therefore, to the Lord,
From Sion, his abode;
Proclaim his deeds, till all the world
Confess no other God.

---

To Father, Son, and Holy Ghost,
The God whom we adore,
Be glory, as it was, is now,
And shall be evermore.

## PSALM 9. C. M.

From the xi Psalm of David.

1 The Lord a holy temple hath,
And righteous throne above;
Whence he surveys the sons of men,
And how their counsels move.

2 If God the righteous, whom he loves,
For trial does correct,
What must the sons of violence,
Whom he abhors, expect?

3 Snares, fire, and brimstone on their heads,
Shall in one tempest shower;
This dreadful mixture his revenge
Into their cup shall pour.

4 The righteous Lord will righteous deeds
With signal favor grace;
And to the upright man disclose
The brightness of his face.

---

To Father, Son, and Holy Ghost,
The God whom we adore,
Be glory, as it was, is now,
And shall be evermore.

## PSALM 10. C. M.

Marlay. Weyman.

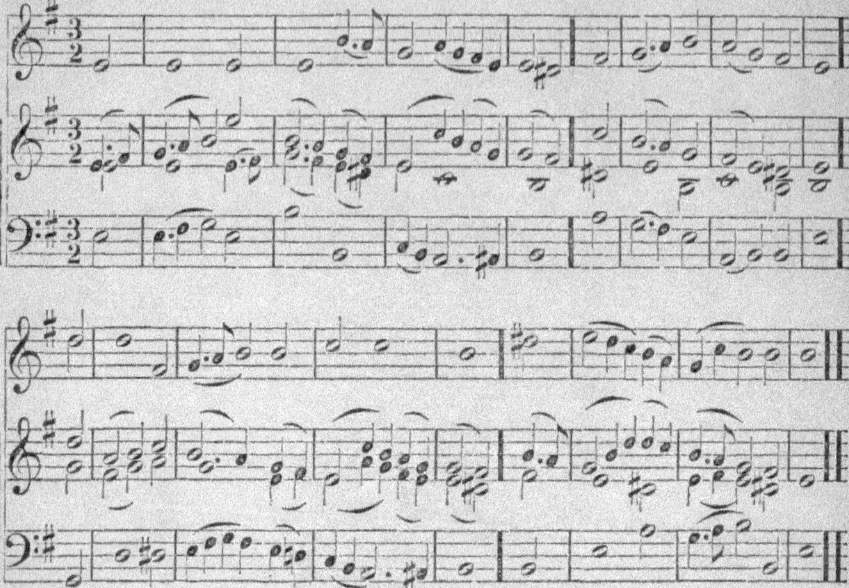

## PSALM 11. L. M.

Rochester. Ions.

## PSALM 10. C. M.

From the xiii Psalm of David.

1 How long wilt thou forget me, Lord,
Must I for ever mourn?
How long wilt thou withdraw from me,
Oh! never to return!

2 O hear, and to my longing eyes
Restore thy wonted light;
Dawn on my spirit, lest I sleep
In death's most gloomy night.

3 Since I have always placed my trust
Beneath thy mercy's wing,
Thy saving health will come, and then
My heart with joy shall spring.

4 Then shall my song, with praise inspired,
To thee, my God, ascend,
Who to thy servant, in distress,
Such bounty didst extend.

---

To Father, Son, and Holy Ghost,
The God whom we adore,
Be glory, as it was, is now,
And shall be evermore.

## PSALM 11. L. M.

From the xiv Psalm of David.

1 The Lord looked down from heaven's high tower,
And all the sons of men did view,
To see if any owned his power,
If any truth or justice knew;

2 But all he saw were gone aside,
All were degenerate grown, and base;
None took religion for their guide,
Not one of all the sinful race.

3 How will they tremble then for fear,
When his just wrath shall them o'ertake,
For, to the righteous God is near,
And never will their cause forsake.

4 Oh! that from Sion he'd employ
His might, and burst the oppressive band;
Then shouts of universal joy
Should loudly echo through the land.

---

To Father, Son, and Holy Ghost,
The God whom earth and heaven adore,
Be glory, as it was of old,
Is now, and shall be evermore.

## PSALM 12. C. M.

St. Catharine's. Jos. Garnett.

## PSALM 13. C. M.

Consolation. T. Adams.

## PSALM 12. C. M.

From the xv Psalm of David.

1 Lord, who 's the happy man that may
To thy blest courts repair,
Not, stranger-like, to visit them,
But to inhabit there?

2 'T is he who walketh uprightly,
Whom righteousness directs;
Whose generous tongue disdains to speak
The thing his heart rejects.

3 Who never did a slander forge,
His neighbor's fame to wound;
Nor hearken to a false report
By malice whispered round.

4 Who vice, in all its pomp and power,
Can treat with just neglect;
And piety, though clothed in rags,
Religiously respect.

5 Who to his plighted vows and trust
Has ever firmly stood;
And, though he promise to his loss,
He makes his promise good.

6 Whose soul in usury disdains
His treasure to employ;
Whom no rewards can ever bribe
The guiltless to destroy.

7 The man who, by this righteous course,
Has happiness ensured,
When earth's foundation shakes, shall stand,
By Providence secured.

---

To Father, Son, and Holy Ghost,
The God whom we adore,
Be glory, as it was, is now,
And shall be evermore.

## PSALM 13. C. M.

From the xvi Psalm of David.

1 My grateful soul shall bless the Lord,
Whose precepts give me light;
And private counsel still afford
In sorrow's dismal night.

2 I strive each action to approve
To his all-seeing eye;
No danger shall my hopes remove,
Because he still is nigh.

3 Therefore my heart all grief defies,
My glory does rejoice;
My flesh shall rest, in hope to rise,
Waked by his powerful voice.

4 Thou, Lord, when I resign my breath,
My soul from hell shalt free;
Nor let thy holy one in death,
The least corruption see.

5 Thou shalt the paths of life display
Which to thy presence lead;
Where pleasures dwell without allay,
And joys that never fade.

---

*To Father, Son, and Holy Ghost, etc.*

## PSALM 14, Part i. L. M.

MENDON. GERMAN AIR.

## PSALM 14, Part ii. L. M.

WARRINGTON. R. HARRISON.

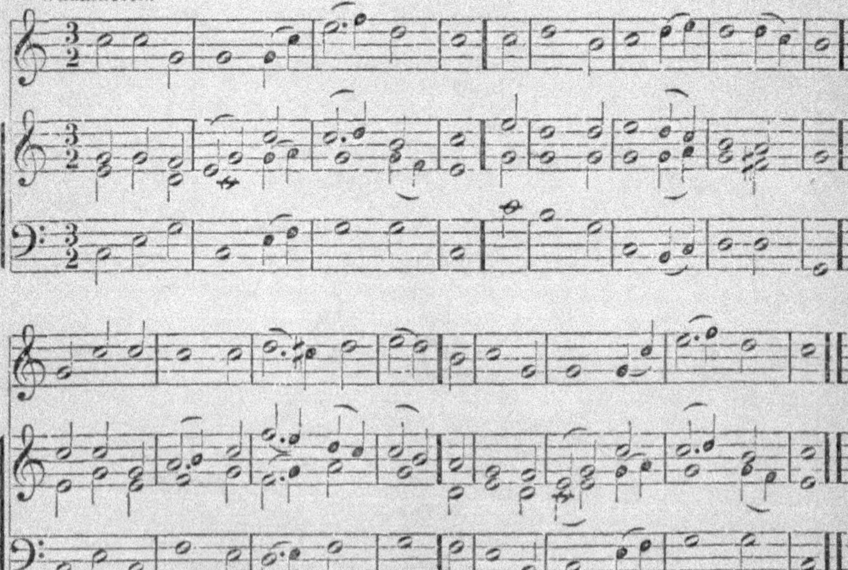

## PSALM 14.

From the xviii Psalm of David.

### PART I. L. M.

1 No change of time shall ever shock
  My firm affection, Lord, to thee;
For thou hast always been my rock,
  A fortress and defense to me.

2 Thou my deliverer art, my God;
  My trust is in thy mighty power;
Thou art my shield from foes abroad,
  At home my safeguard and my tower.

3 To thee I will address my prayer,
  To whom all praise we justly owe;
So shall I, by thy watchful care,
  Be guarded safe from every foe.

---

To Father, Son, and Holy Ghost,
  The God whom earth and heaven adore,
Be glory, as it was of old,
  Is now, and shall be ever more.

### PART II. L. M.

1 Thou suit'st, O Lord, thy righteous ways
  To various paths of human kind;
They who for mercy merit praise,
  With thee shall wond'rous mercy find.

2 Thou to the just shall justice show;
  The pure thy purity shall see;
Such as perversely choose to go,
  Shall meet with due returns from thee.

3 That he the humble soul will save,
  And crush the haughty's boasted might;
In me the Lord an instance gave,
  Whose darkness he has turned to light.

4 Who then deserves to be adored,
  But God, on whom my hopes depend?
Or who, except the mighty Lord,
  Can with resistless power defend?

5 Let the eternal Lord be praised,
  The rock on whose defense I rest!
To highest heavens his name be raised,
  Who me with his salvation blessed!

6 My God, to celebrate thy fame,
  My grateful voice to heaven I'll raise;
And nations, strangers to thy name,
  Shall learn to sing thy glorious praise.

---

*To Father, Son, and Holy Ghost, etc.*

## PSALM 15. C. M.

NOTTINGHAM. PART 1 & 2. JER. CLARKE.

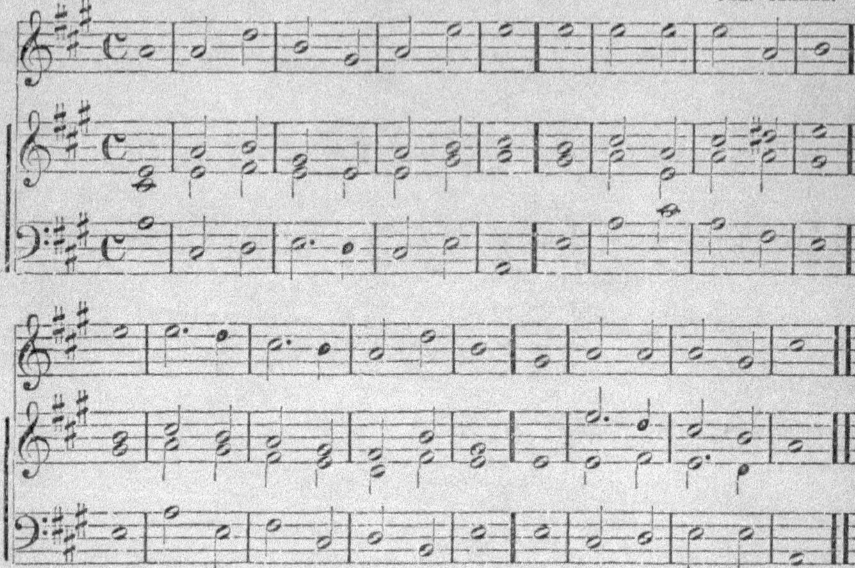

## PSALM. 16. S. M.

CAMBRIDGE. R. HARRISON.

## PSALM 15.

From the xix Psalm of David.

### PART I. C. M.

1 The heavens declare thy glory, Lord,
Which that alone can fill;
The firmament and stars express
Their great Creator's skill.

2 The dawn of each returning day
Fresh beams of knowledge brings;
And from the dark returns of night
Divine instruction springs.

3 Their powerful language to no realm
Or region is confined;
'T is nature's voice, and understood
Alike by all mankind.

4 Their doctrine does its sacred sense
Through earth's extent display;
Its bright contents the circling sun
Does round the world convey.

5 From east to west, from west to east,
His ceaseless course he goes;
And through his progress, cheerful light
And vital warmth bestows.

---

To Father, Son, and Holy Ghost,
The God whom we adore,
Be glory, as it was, is now,
And shall be evermore.

### PART II. C. M.

1 God's perfect law converts the soul,
Reclaims from false desires;
With sacred wisdom his sure word
The ignorant inspires.

2 The statutes of the Lord are just,
And bring sincere delight;
His pure commands in search of truth
Assist the feeblest sight.

3 His perfect worship here is fixed,
On sure foundations laid;
His equal laws are in the scales
Of truth and justice weighed;

4 Of more esteem than golden mines,
Or gold refined with skill;
More sweet than honey, or the drops
That from the comb distill.

5 My trusty counselors they are,
And friendly warnings give:
Divine rewards attend on those
Who by thy precepts live.

6 But what frail man observes how oft
He does from virtue fall?
O cleanse me from my secret faults,
Thou God that know'st them all!

7 Let no presumptuous sin, O Lord,
Dominion have o'er me;
That, by thy grace preserved, I may
The great transgression flee.

8 So shall my prayer and praises be
With thy acceptance blest;
And I, secure on thy defense,
My strength and Saviour, rest.

---

To Father, Son, and Holy Ghost,
The God whom we adore,
Be glory, as it was, is now,
And shall be evermore.

## PSALM 16. S. M.

From the xx Psalm of David.

1 May Jacob's God defend
And hear us in distress;
Our succor from his temple send,
Our cause from Sion bless!

2 May he accept our vow,
Our sacrifice receive,
Our heart's devout request allow,
Our holy wishes give.

3 O Lord, thy saving grace
We joyfully declare;
Our banner in thy name we raise—
"The Lord fulfill our prayer!"

4 Now know we that the Lord
His chosen will defend;
From heaven will strength divine afford,
And will their prayer attend.

5 Some earthly succor trust,
But we in God's right hand:
Lo! while they fall, so vain their boast,
We rise, and upright stand.

6 Still save us, Lord; and still
Thy servants deign to bless:
Hear King of heaven, in times of ill,
The prayers that we address.

---

To God, the Father, Son,
And Spirit, glory be,
As 't was, and is, and shall be so,
To all eternity.

## PSALM 17, Part i & ii. C. M.

ELOI.

## PSALM 17. C. M.

From the xxii Psalm of David.

### PART I.

1 My God, my God, why leavest thou me,
When I with anguish faint?
O! why so far from me removed,
And from my loud complaint?

2 Lo! I am treated like a worm,
Like none of human birth;
Not only by the great reviled,
But made the rabble's mirth.

3 With laughter, all the gazing crowd
My agonies survey;
They shoot the lip, they shake the head,
And thus deriding say:

4 "In God he trusted, boasting oft,
That he was Heaven's delight;
Let God come down to save him now,
And own his favorite."

5 Withdraw not, then, so far from me,
When trouble is so nigh;
O send me help! thy help, on which
Alone I can rely.

---

To Father, Son, and Holy Ghost,
The God whom we adore,
Be glory, as it was, is now,
And shall be evermore.

### PART II. C. M.

1 Like water is my life poured out,
My joints are out of frame;
My heart dissolves within my breast,
Like wax before the flame:

2 My strength is like a potsherd dried,
My tongue is parched with drought;
And to the dismal shades of death
My fainting soul is brought.

3 Like dogs, to compass me, my foes
In wicked counsel meet;
They pierced my inoffensive hands,
They pierced my harmless feet.

4 My body 's racked, till all my bones
Distinctly may be told;
Yet such a spectacle of woe
As pastime they behold.

5 As spoil, my garments they divide,
Lots for my vesture cast:—
Therefore, O leave me not, my God,
But to my succor haste.

---

*To Father, Son, and Holy Ghost, etc.*

## PSALM 17, Part iii. — PSALM 18, C. M.

ST. MATHEW'S. DR. CROFT.

## PSALM 17. C. M.

### PART III.

1 LORD, to my brethren I'll declare
  The triumphs of thy name;
In presence of assembled saints,
  Thy glory thus proclaim:

2 "Ye worshipers of Jacob's God,
  All you of Israel's line,
Oh! praise the Lord, and to your praise
  Sincere obedience join.

3 "He ne'er disdained on low distress
  To cast a gracious eye;
Nor turned from misery his face,
  But hears its humble cry."

4 Thus in thy sacred courts will I
  My cheerful thanks express;
In presence of thy saints perform
  The vows of my distress.

5 The meek companions of my grief
  Shall find my table spread;
And all that seek the Lord, shall be
  With joys immortal fed.

6 Then shall the glad converted world
  To God their homage pay:
And scattered nations of the earth
  One sovereign Lord obey.

7 'T is his supreme prerogative
  O'er all mankind to reign;
'T is just that he should rule the world,
  Who does the world sustain.

8 The rich who are with plenty fed
  His bounty must confess;
The sons of want, by him relieved,
  Their generous patron bless.

9 With humble worship to his throne
  They all for aid resort;
That power, which first their being gave,
  Alone can them support.

10 Then shall a chosen, spotless race,
  Devoted to his name,
To their adoring sons his truth
  And glorious acts proclaim.

---

To Father, Son, and Holy Ghost,
  The God whom we adore,
Be glory, as it was, is now,
  And shall be evermore.

## PSALM 18. C. M.

From the xxiii Psalm of David.

1 THE Lord himself, the mighty Lord,
  Vouchsafes to be my guide;
The shepherd, by whose constant care
  My wants are all supplied.

2 In tender grass he makes me feed,
  And gently there repose;
Then leads me to cool shades, and where
  Refreshing water flows.

3 He does my wandering soul reclaim,
  And, to his endless praise,
Instruct with humble zeal to walk
  In his most righteous ways.

4 I pass the gloomy vale of death,
  From fear and danger free;
For there his aiding rod and staff
  Defend and comfort me.

5 Since God does thus his wondrous love
  Through all my life extend,
That life to him I will devote,
  And in his temple spend.

---

To Father, Son, and Holy Ghost,
  The God whom we adore,
Be glory, as it was, is now,
  And shall be evermore.

## PSALM 19. C. M.

ABRIDGE. I. SMITH.

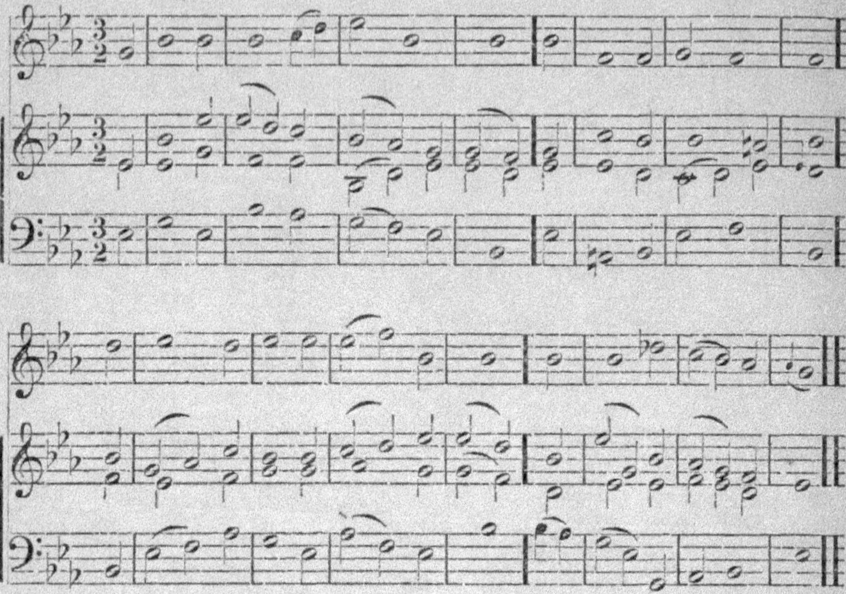

## PSALM 20. S. M.

DURHAM. I. SMITH.

## PSALM 19. C. M.

From the xxiv Psalm of David.

1 The spacious earth is all the Lord's,
The Lord's her fulness is;
The world, and they that dwell therein,
By sovereign right are his.

2 He framed and fixed it on the seas;
And his almighty hand
Upon inconstant floods has made
The stable fabric stand.

3 But for himself, this Lord of all
One chosen seat designed;
Oh! who shall to that sacred hill
Deserved admittance find?

4 The man whose hands and heart are pure,
Whose thoughts from pride are free;
Who honest poverty prefers
To gainful perjury.

5 This, this is he, on whom the Lord
Shall shower his blessings down;
Whom God, his Savior, shall vouchsafe
With righteousness to crown.

6 Such is the race of saints, by whom
The sacred courts are trod;
And such the proselytes that seek
Thy face, O Jacob's God.

7 Erect your heads, eternal gates;
Unfold, to entertain
The King of Glory; see! he comes
With his celestial train.

8 Who is the King of Glory? who?
The Lord for strength renowned;
In battle mighty: o'er his foes
Eternal victor crowned.

9 Erect your heads, ye gates; unfold
In state to entertain
The King of Glory; see! he comes
With all his shining train.

10 Who is the King of Glory? who?
The Lord of hosts renowned;
Of glory he alone is King,
Who is with glory crowned.

---

To Father, Son, and Holy Ghost,
The God whom we adore,
Be glory, as it was, is now,
And shall be evermore.

## PSALM 20. S. M.

From the xxv Psalm of David.

1 To God, in whom I trust,
I lift my heart and voice;
Oh! let me not be put to shame,
Nor let my foes rejoice.

2 Those who on thee rely,
Let no disgrace attend;
Be that the shameful lot of such
As willfully offend.

3 To me thy truth impart,
And lead me in thy way;
For thou art he that brings me help
On thee I wait all day.

4 Thy mercies and thy love,
O Lord, recall to mind;
And graciously continue still,
As thou wert ever kind.

5 Let all my youthful crimes
Be blotted out by thee;
And, for thy wondrous goodness' sake,
In mercy think on me.

6 His mercy and his truth
The righteous Lord displays,
In bringing wandering sinners home,
And teaching them his ways.

7 He those in justice guides
Who his direction seek;
And in his sacred paths shall lead
The humble and the meek.

8 Through all the ways of God
Both truth and mercy shine,
To such as, with religious hearts,
To his blest will incline.

9 Since mercy is the grace
That most exalts thy fame,
Forgive my heinous sin, O Lord,
And so advance thy name.

10 Whoe'er, with humble fear,
To God his duty pays,
Shall find the Lord a faithful guide,
In all his righteous ways.

11 For God to all his saints
His secret will imparts,
And does his gracious covenant write
In their obedient hearts.

12 To Israel's chosen race
Continue ever kind;
And, in the midst of all their wants,
Let them thy succor find.

---

To God the Father, Son,
And Spirit, glory be,
As 't was, and is, and shall be so,
To all eternity.

## PSALMS 21 & 22. C. M.

IRISH. I. SMITH.

## PSALM 23. C. M.

HARMONY. COOMBS.

### PSALM 21. C. M.

From the xxvi Psalm of David.*

1 Judge me, O Lord, for I the paths
Of righteousness have trod;
I shall not fail, who all my trust
Repose on thee, my God.

2 I'll wash my hands in innocence,
And round thine altar go;
Pour the glad hymn of triumph thence,
And thence thy wonders show.

3 My thanks I'll publish there, and tell
How thy renown excels;
That seat affords me most delight,
In which thine honor dwells.

---

To Father, Son, and Holy Ghost,
The God whom we adore,
Be glory, as it was, is now,
And shall be evermore.

### PSALM 22. C. M.

From the xxvii Psalm of David.

1 Whom should I fear, since God to me
Is saving health and light?
Since strongly he my life supports,
What can my soul affright?

2 Henceforth, within his house to dwell
I earnestly desire;
His wondrous beauty there to view,
And of his will inquire.

3 For there I may with comfort rest,
In times of deep distress;
And safe, as on a rock, abide
In that secure recess.

4 When us to seek, thy glorious face
Thou kindly dost advise;
"Thy glorious face I'll always seek,"
My grateful heart replies.

5 Then hide not thou thy face, O Lord,
Nor me in wrath reject;
My God and Saviour, leave not him
Thou didst so oft protect.

6 Though all of nearest earthly ties
Me, in my woe, forsake,
Yet thou, whose love excels them all,
Wilt care and pity take.

7 Instruct me in thy paths, O Lord,
My ways directly guide;
Lest sinful men, who watch my steps,
Should see me tread aside.

8 I trusted that my future life
Should with thy love be crowned;
Or else my fainting soul had sunk,
With sorrow compassed round.

9 God's time with patient faith expect,
Who will inspire thy breast
With inward strength; do thou thy part,
And leave to him the rest.

---

To Father, Son, and Holy Ghost,
The God whom we adore,
Be glory, as it was, is now,
And shall be evermore.

### PSALM 23. C. M.

From the xxviii Psalm of David.

1 Adored for ever be the Lord;
His praise I will resound,
From whom the cries of my distress
A gracious answer found.

2 He is my strength and shield; my heart
Has trusted in his name;
And now relieved, my heart, with joy,
His praises shall proclaim.

3 The Lord, the everlasting God,
Is my defense and rock,
The saving health, the saving strength,
Of his anointed flock.

4 O save and bless thy people, Lord,
Thy heritage preserve;
Feed, strengthen, and support their hearts,
That they may never swerve.

---

To Father, Son, and Holy Ghost,
The God whom we adore,
Be glory, as it was, is now,
And shall be evermore.

---

* Extract from the Journal of the General Convention, 1832:

"*Resolved*, As the sense and declaration of this Convention, that so much of the rubrics in the form of consecration of a church or chapel as requires the singing of 'Psalm 26, verses 6, 7, and 8,' will hereafter be duly complied with by singing verses 2 and 3, in the selection from the 26th Psalm, included in the Psalms in metre authorized by these resolutions to be set forth."

## PSALM 24. L. M.

PARK STREET. VENUA.

## PSALM 25. C. M.

MANCHESTER. DR. WAINWRIGHT.

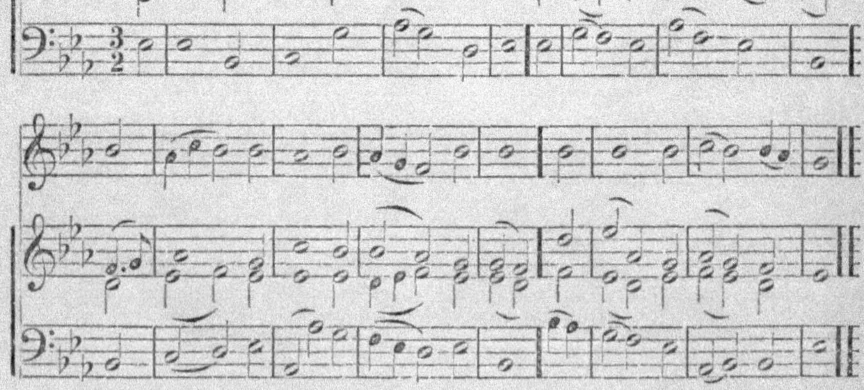

### PSALM 24. L. M.

From the xxix Psalm of David.

1 Ye that in might and power excel,
Your grateful sacrifice prepare;
God's glorious actions loudly tell,
His wondrous power to all declare.

2 To his great name fresh altars raise;
Devoutly due respect afford;
Him in his holy temple praise,
Where he's with solemn state adored.

3 'Tis he that, with amazing noise,
The watery clouds in sunder breaks;
The ocean trembles at his voice,
When he from heaven in thunder speaks.

4 How full of power his voice appears!
With what majestic terror crowned!
Which from their roots tall cedars tears!
And strews their scattered branches round.

5 God rules the angry floods on high;
His boundless sway shall never cease;
His saints with strength he will supply,
And bless his own with constant peace.

To Father, Son, and Holy Ghost,
The God whom earth and heaven adore,
Be glory, as it was of old,
Is now, and shall be evermore.

### PSALM 25. C. M.

From the xxx Psalm of David.

1 In my distress to God I cried,
Who kindly did relieve,
And from the grave's expecting mouth
My hopeless life retrieve.

2 O to his courts, ye saints of his,
With songs of praise repair;
With me commemorate his truth,
And providential care.

3 His wrath has but a moment's reign,
His favor no decay;
The night of grief is recompensed
With joy's returning day.

4 Therefore, O Lord, I'll gladly sing
Thy praise in grateful verse;
And as thy favors endless are,
Thy endless praise rehearse.

*To Father, Son, and Holy Ghost, etc.*

## PSALM 26. S. M.

DURHAM. I. SMITH.

## PSALM 27. L. M.

BEREA.

### PSALM 26. S. M.

From the xxxi Psalm of David.

1 DEFEND me, Lord, from shame,
For still I trust in thee;
As just and righteous is thy Name,
From danger set me free.

2 Bow down thy gracious ear,
And speedy succor send;
Do thou my steadfast rock appear,
To shelter and defend.

3 To thee, the God of truth,
My life, and all that 's mine,
(For thou preserv'st me from my youth,)
I willingly resign.

4 My hope, my steadfast trust,
I on thy help repose:
That thou, my God, art good and just,
My soul with comfort knows.

5 Whate'er events betide,
Thy wisdom times them all;
Then, Lord, thy servant safely hide
From those that seek his fall.

6 The brightness of thy face
To me, O Lord, disclose;
And, as thy mercies still increase,
Preserve me from my foes.

7 How great thy mercies are
To such as fear thy Name,
Which thou, for those that trust thy care,
Dost to the world proclaim!

8 O all ye saints, the Lord
With eager love pursue;
Who to the just will help afford,
And give the proud their due.

9 Ye that on God rely,
Courageously proceed;
For he will still your hearts supply
With strength in time of need.

---

To God the Father, Son,
And Spirit, glory be,
As 't was, and is, and shall be so,
To all eternity.

### PSALM 27. L. M.

From the xxxii Psalm of David.

1 HE 's blest, whose sins have pardon gained,
No more in judgment to appear;
Whose guilt remission has obtained,
And whose repentance is sincere.

2 No sooner I my wound disclosed,
The guilt that tortured me within,
But thy forgiveness interposed,
And mercy's healing balm poured in.

3 Sorrows on sorrows multiplied,
The hardened sinner shall confound;
But them who in his truth confide,
Blessings of mercy shall surround.

4 His saints, that have performed his laws,
Their life in triumph shall employ;
Let them, as they alone have cause,
In grateful raptures shout for joy.

---

To Father, Son, and Holy Ghost,
The God whom earth and heaven adore,
Be glory, as it was of old,
Is now, and shall be evermore.

## PSALM 23, Part i & ii. C. M.

ST. STEPHENS. JACKSON.

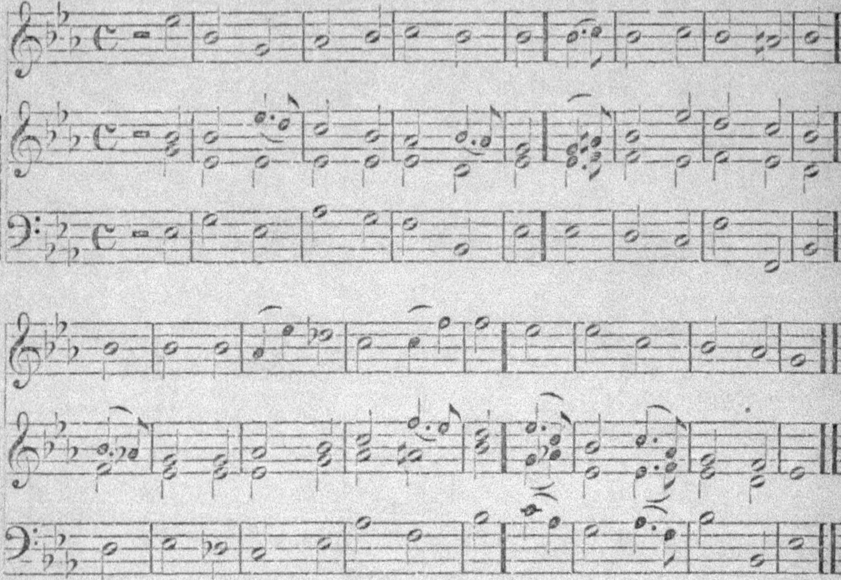

## PSALM 29, Part i. C. M.

WILTSHIRE. SIR G. SMART.

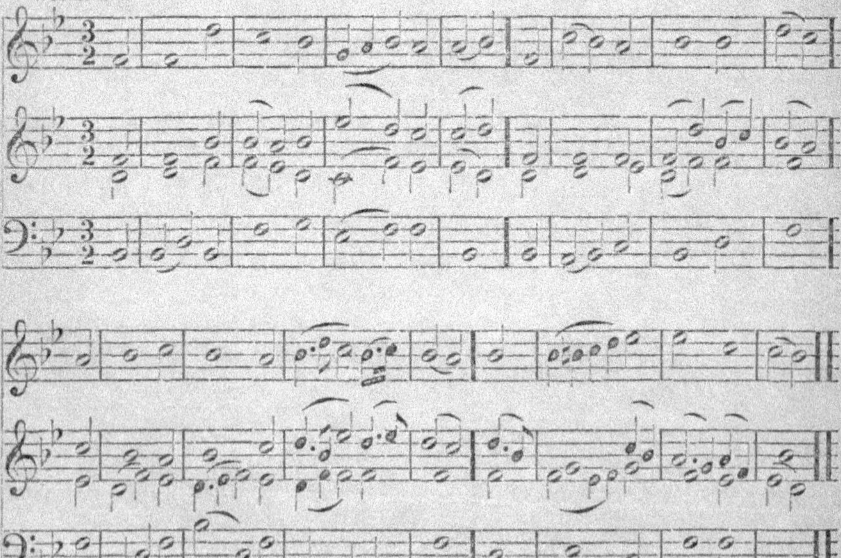

## PSALM 28.

From the xxxiii Psalm of David.

### PART I. C. M.

1 LET all the just to God, with joy,
Their cheerful voices raise;
For well the righteous it becomes
To sing glad songs of praise.

2 Let harps, and psalteries, and lutes,
In joyful concert meet;
And new-made songs of loud applause
The harmony complete.

3 For faithful is the word of God;
His works with truth abound;
He justice loves; and all the earth
Is with his goodness crowned.

4 By his almighty word, at first,
The heavenly arch was rear'd;
And all the beauteous hosts of light
At his command appeared.

5 Let earth and all that dwell therein,
Before him trembling stand;
For, when he spake the word, 't was made,
'T was fixed at his command.

### PART II. C. M.

1 WHATE'ER the mighty Lord decrees,
Shall stand for ever sure;
The settled purpose of his heart
To ages shall endure.

2 How happy then are they, to whom
The Lord for God is known!
Whom he from all the world besides,
Has chosen for his own.

3 Our soul on God with patience waits;
Our help and shield is he;
Then, Lord, let still our hearts rejoice,
Because we trust in thee.

4 The riches of thy mercy, Lord
Do thou to us extend;
Since we, for all we want or wish,
On thee alone depend.

---

To Father, Son, and Holy Ghost,
The God whom we adore,
Be glory, as it was, is now,
And shall be evermore.

## PSALM 29.

From the xxxiv Psalm of David.

### PART I. C. M.

1 THROUGH all the changing scenes of life,
In trouble and in joy,
The praises of my God shall still
My heart and tongue employ.

2 Of his deliverance I will boast,
Till all that are distrest,
From my example comfort take,
And charm their griefs to rest.

3 O magnify the Lord with me,
With me exalt his name:
When in distress to him I called,
He to my rescue came.

4 The Angel of the Lord encamps
Around the good and just;
Deliverance he affords to all
Who on his succor trust.

5 O make but trial of his love,
Experience will decide;
How blest they are, and only they,
Who in his truth confide.

6 Fear him, ye saints; and you will then
Have nothing else to fear;
Make you his service your delight
Your wants shall be his care.

---

To Father, Son, and Holy Ghost,
The God whom we adore,
Be glory, as it was, is now,
And shall be evermore.

## PSALM 29, Part ii. C. M.

WINTRINGHAM. WAINWRIGHT.

## PSALM 29.

### PART II. C. M.

1 Approach, ye children of the Lord,
And my instruction hear;
I'll teach you the true discipline
Of his religious fear.

2 Let him who length of life desires,
And prosperous days would see;
From slandering language keep his tongue,
His lips from falsehood free;

3 The crooked paths of vice decline,
And virtue's ways pursue;
Establish peace, where 't is begun;
And where 't is lost, renew.

4 The Lord from heaven beholds the just
With favorable eyes:
And, when distressed, his gracious ear,
Is open to their cries;

5 But turns his wrathful look on those
Whom mercy can't reclaim,
To cut them off and from the earth
Blot out their evil name.

6 Deliverance to his saints he gives,
When his relief they crave;
He 's nigh to heal the broken heart,
And contrite spirit save.

7 Great troubles may afflict the just,
Yet God will save them still;
The righteous he will keep from harm,
And guard from every ill.

8 The wicked, from their wickedness,
Their ruin shall derive;
While righteous men whom they detest,
Shall them and theirs survive.

9 For God preserves the souls of those
Who on his truth depend;
To them, and their posterity,
His blessing shall descend.

---

To Father, Son, and Holy Ghost,
The God whom we adore,
Be glory, as it was, is now,
And shall be evermore.

## PSALM 30. L. M.

St. Peters. Harwood.

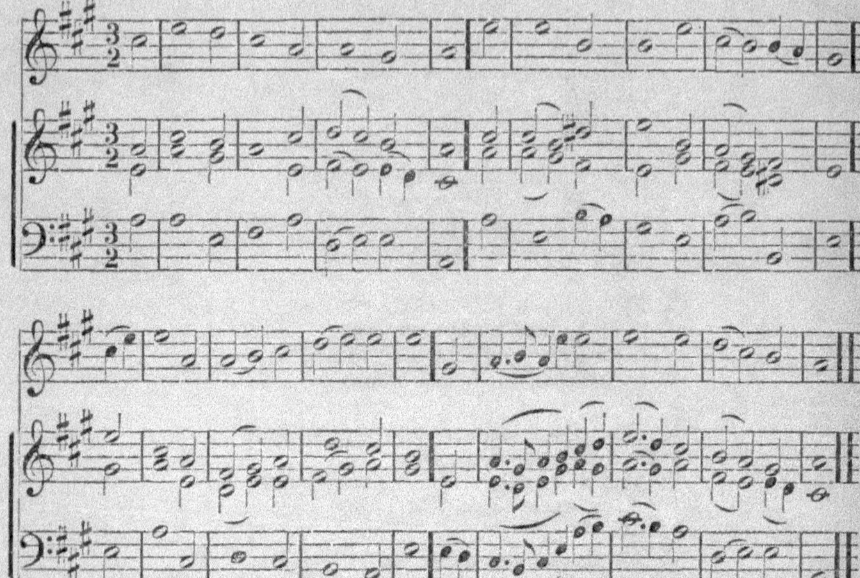

## PSALM 31, Part i. II 2.

Newcourt. H. Bond.

### PSALM 30. L. M.

From the xxxvi Psalm of David.

1 O Lord, thy mercy, my sure hope,
The highest orb of heaven transcends;
Thy sacred truth's unmeasured scope
Beyond the spreading sky extends.

2 Thy justice like the hills remains,
Unfathomed depths thy judgments are;
Thy providence the world sustains,
The whole creation is thy care.

3 Since of thy goodness all partake,
With what assurance should the just
Thy sheltering wings their refuge make,
And saints to thy protection trust!

4 Such guests shall to thy courts be led,
To banquet on thy love's repast,
And drink, as from a fountain's head
Of joys that shall for ever last.

5 With thee the springs of life remain,
Thy presence is eternal day;
O let thy saints thy favor gain,
To upright hearts thy truth display.

---

To Father, Son, and Holy Ghost,
The God whom earth and heaven adore,
Be glory, as it was of old,
Is now, and shall be evermore.

### PSALM 31.

From the xxxvii Psalm of David.

PART I. H 2.

1 Though wicked men grow rich or great,
Yet let not their successful state
Thy anger or thy envy raise;
For they, cut down like tender grass,
Or like young flowers away shall pass,
Whose blooming beauty soon decays.

2 Depend on God, and him obey;
So thou within the land shalt stay
Secure from danger and from want:
Make his commands thy chief delight;
And he, thy duty to requite,
Shall all thy earnest wishes grant.

3 In all thy ways trust thou the Lord,
And he will needful help afford,
To perfect every just design:
He 'll make like light, serene and clear,
Thy clouded innocence appear,
And as a midday sun to shine.

4 With quiet mind on God depend,
And patiently for him attend,
Nor envy the success of crime;
For God will sinful men destroy;
While they his presence shall enjoy,
Who trust on him and wait his time.

---

To Father, Son, and Holy Ghost,
The God whom heaven's triumphant host,
And suffering saints on earth adore;
Be glory as in ages past,
As now it is, and so shall last
When time itself shall be no more.

## PSALM 31, Part ii & iii. II 2.

JENNINGS. JENNINGS.

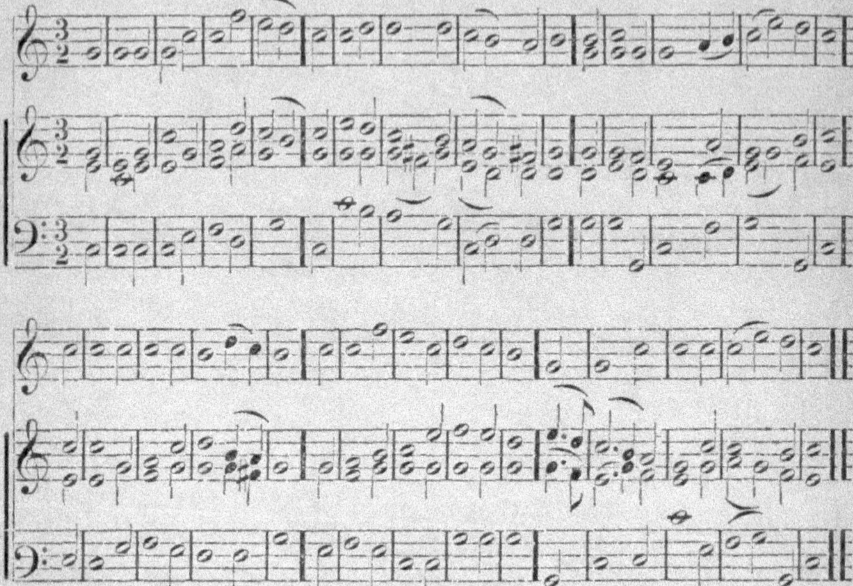

## PSALM 32. C. M.

CAROLINA. COOMBS.

## PSALM 31.

### PART II. II 2.

1 The good man's way is God's delight:
He orders all the steps aright,
Of him that moves by his command;
Though he sometimes may be distressed,
Yet shall he ne'er be quite oppressed,
For God upholds him with his hand.

2 With caution shun each wicked deed,
In virtue's ways with zeal proceed,
And so prolong your happy days:
For God, who judgment loves, does still
Preserve his saints secure from ill,
While soon the wicked race decays.

3 The upright shall possess the land,
His portion shall for ages stand;
His mouth with wisdom is supplied,
His tongue by rules of judgment moves,
His heart the law of God approves;
Therefore his footsteps never slide.

### PART III. II 2.

1 The wicked I in power have seen,
And like a bay-tree fresh and green,
That spreads its pleasant branches round:
But he was gone as swift as thought;
And, though in every place I sought,
No sign or track of him I found.

2 Observe the perfect man with care,
And mark all such as upright are;
Their roughest days in peace shall end:
While on the latter end of those
Who dare God's sacred will oppose,
A common ruin shall attend.

3 God to the just will aid afford,
Their only safeguard is the Lord,
Their strength in time of need is he:
Because on him they still depend,
The Lord will timely succor send,
And from the wicked set them free.

---

To Father, Son, and Holy Ghost,
The God whom heaven's triumphant host,
And suffering saints on earth adore;
Be glory as in ages past,
As now it is, and so shall last
When time itself shall be no more.

## PSALM 32. C. M.

From the xxxviii Psalm of David.

1 Thy chastening wrath, O Lord restrain,
Though I deserve it all;
Nor let on me the heavy storm
Of thy displeasure fall.

2 My sins, which to a deluge swell,
My sinking head o'erflow,
And for my feeble strength to bear,
Too vast a burden grow.

3 But, Lord, before thy searching eyes,
All my desires appear;
The groanings of my burdened soul
Have reached thine open ear.

4 Forsake me not, O Lord, my God
Nor far from me depart;
Make haste to my relief, O thou
Who my salvation art.

---

To Father, Son, and Holy Ghost,
The God whom we adore,
Be glory, as it was, is now,
And shall be ever more.

## PSALM 33. C. M.

ST. MARGARET'S. JOS. GARNETT.

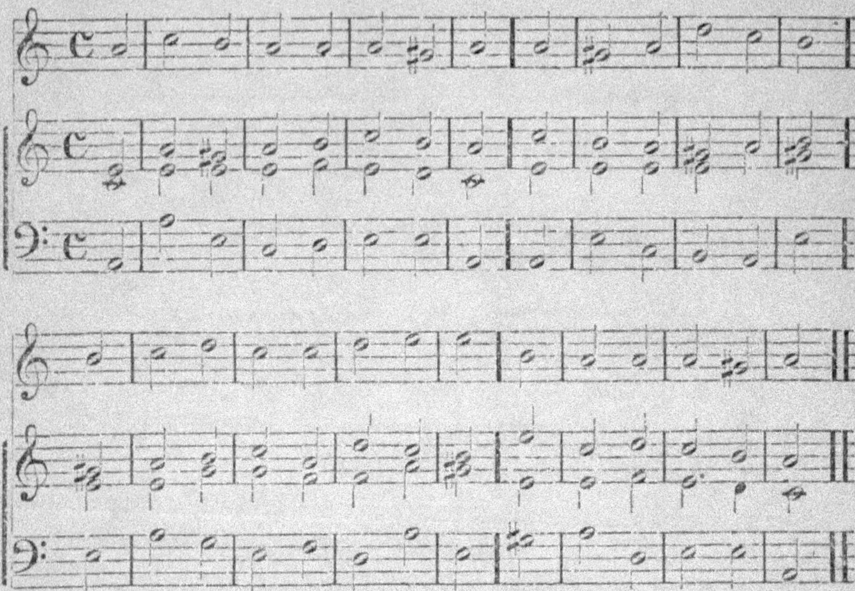

## PSALM 34. L. M.

ROCHESTER. IONS.

## PSALM 33. C. M.

From the xxxix Psalm of David.

1 LORD, let me know my term of days,
How soon my life will end:
The numerous train of ills disclose,
Which this frail state attend.

2 My life, thou know'st, is but a span,
A cipher sums my years:
And every man, in best estate,
But vanity appears.

3 Man, like a shadow, vainly walks,
With fruitless cares oppressed;
He heaps up wealth, but can not tell
By whom 'twill be possessed.

4 Why then should I on worthless toys,
With anxious cares attend?
On thee alone my steadfast hope
Shall ever, Lord, depend.

5 Lord, hear my cry, accept my tears,
And listen to my prayer;
Who sojourn like a stranger here,
As all my fathers were.

6 O spare me yet a little time;
My wasted strength restore,
Before I vanish quite from hence,
And shall be seen no more.

---

To Father, Son, and Holy Ghost,
The God whom we adore,
Be glory, as it was, is now,
And shall be evermore.

## PSALM 34. L. M.

From the xl Psalm of David.

1 I WAITED meekly for the Lord,
Till He vouchsafed a kind reply;
Who did his gracious ear afford,
And heard from heaven my humble cry.

2 The wonders he for me has wrought
Shall fill my mouth with songs of praise;
And others, to his worship brought,
To hope of like deliverance raise.

3 For blessings shall that man reward,
Who on the Almighty Lord relies;
Who treats the proud with disregard,
And hates the hypocrite's disguise.

4 Who can the wondrous works recount
Which thou, O God, for us hast wrought;
The treasures of thy love surmount,
The power of numbers, speech and thought.

5 I've learned that thou hast not desired
Offerings and sacrifice alone;
Nor blood of guiltless beasts required
For man's transgression to atone.

6 I therefore come—come to fulfill
The oracles thy books impart;
'Tis my delight to do thy will,
Thy law is written in my heart.

7 In full assemblies I have told
Thy truth and righteousness at large;
Nor did, thou know'st, my lips withhold
From uttering what thou gavest in charge

8 Nor kept within my breast confined
Thy faithfulness and saving grace;
But preached thy love, for all designed,
That all might that and truth embrace.

9 Then let those mercies I declared
To others, Lord, extend to me;
Thy loving-kindness my reward,
Thy truth my safe protection be.

---

To Father, Son, and Holy Ghost,
The God whom earth and heaven adore,
Be glory, as it was of old,
Is now, and shall be evermore.

## PSALM 35. C. M.

CONSOLATION. T. ADAMS.

## PSALM 36. C. M.

KENT. MORNINGTON.

### PSALM 35. C. M.

From the xli Psalm of David.

1 Happy the man whose tender care
Relieves the poor distressed!
When troubles compass him around,
The Lord shall give him rest.

2 The Lord his life with blessings crowned,
In safety shall prolong;
And disappoint the will of those
That seek to do him wrong.

3 If he, in languishing estate,
Oppressed with sickness lie;
The Lord will easy make his bed,
And inward strength supply.

4 Secure of this, to thee, my God,
I thus my prayer addressed;
"Lord, for thy mercy, heal my soul,
Though I have much transgressed."

5 Thy tender care secures my life
From danger and disgrace;
And thou vouchsafest to set me still
Before thy glorious face.

6 Let, therefore, Israel's Lord and God
From age to age be blessed;
And all the people's glad applause
With loud amens expressed.

---

To Father, Son, and Holy Ghost,
The God whom we adore,
Be glory, as it was, is now,
And shall be evermore.

### PSALM 36. C. M.

From the xlii Psalm of David.

1 As pants the hart for cooling streams,
When heated in the chase;
So longs my soul, O God, for thee,
And thy refreshing grace.

2 For thee, my God, the living God,
My thirsty soul doth pine;
Oh! when shall I behold thy face,
Thou Majesty Divine?

3 Why restless, why cast down, my soul?
Trust God; who will employ
His aid for thee, and change these sighs
To thankful hymns of joy.

4 God of my strength, how long shall I,
Like one forgotten, mourn;
Forlorn, forsaken, and exposed
To my oppressor's scorn?

5 My heart is pierced, as with a sword,
While thus my foes upbraid:
"Vain boaster, where is now thy God?
And where his promised aid?"

6 Why restless, why cast down my soul?
Hope still; and thou shalt sing
The praise of him who is thy God,
Thy health's eternal spring.

---

To Father, Son, and Holy Ghost,
The God whom we adore,
Be glory, as it was, is now,
And shall be evermore.

## PSALM 37. 11. 5.

BLEST SHADE. DR. CALCOTT.

### PSALM 37. II 5.

From the xlii Psalm of David.

1 As pants the wearied hart for cooling springs,
That sinks exhausted in the summer's chase,
So pants my soul for thee, great King of kings,
So thirsts to reach thy sacred dwelling place.

2 Why throb, my heart? why sink, my saddening soul?
Why droop to earth, with various woes oppressed?
My years shall yet in blissful circles roll,
And peace be yet an inmate of this breast.

3 Lord, thy sure mercies, ever in my sight,
My heart shall gladden through the tedious day;
And mid the dark and gloomy shades of night,
To thee, my God, I'll tune the grateful lay.

4 Why faint, my soul? why doubt Jehovah's aid?
Thy God the God of mercy still shall prove;
Within his courts thy thanks shall yet be paid:
Unquestioned be his faithfulness and love.

---

To God the Father, and to God the Son,
To God the Holy Spirit, Three in One,
Be praise from all on earth and all in heaven,
As was, and is, and ever shall be given.

## PSALM 38. L. M.

BRENTFORD.

## PSALM 39. C. M.

ABRIDGE. I. SMITH.

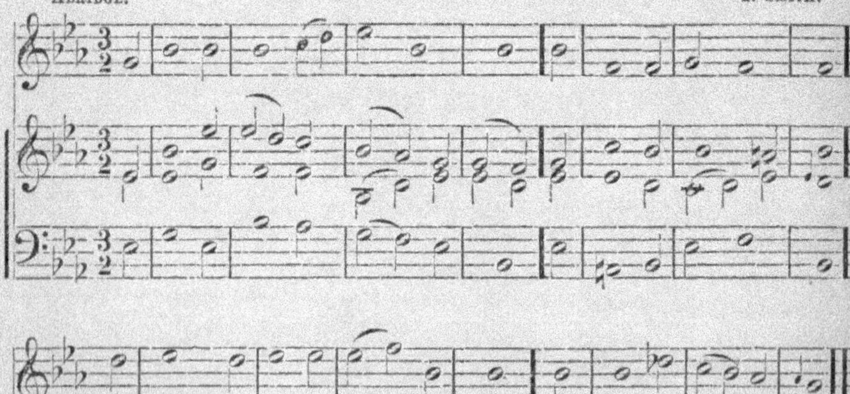

### PSALM 38. L. M.

From the xliii Psalm of David.

1 Let me with light and truth be blest;
Be these my guides to lead the way,
Till on thy holy hill I rest,
And in thy sacred temple pray.

2 Then will I there fresh altars raise
To God, who is my only joy;
And well-tuned harps, with songs of praise,
Shall all my grateful hours employ.

3 Why then cast down, my soul? and why
So much oppressed with anxious care?
On God, thy God, for aid rely,
Who will thy ruined state repair.

---

To Father, Son, and Holy Ghost,
The God whom earth and heaven adore,
Be glory, as it was of old,
Is now, and shall be evermore.

### PSALM 39. C. M.

From the xlv Psalm of David.

1 While I the King's loud praise rehearse,
Indited by my heart,
My tongue is like the pen of him
That writes with ready art.

2 How matchless is thy form, O King!
Thy mouth with grace o'erflows;
Because fresh blessings God on thee
Eternally bestows.

3 Gird on thy sword, most mighty Prince;
And clad in rich array,
With glorious ornaments of power,
Majestic pomp display.

4 Ride on in state, and still protect
The meek, the just, and true;
While thy right hand, with swift revenge,
Does all thy foes pursue.

5 How sharp thy weapons are to them
That dare thy power despise!
Down, down they fall, while through their heart
The piercing arrow flies.

6 But thy firm throne, O God, is fixed,
For ever to endure;
Thy scepter's sway shall always last,
By righteous laws secure.

7 Because thy heart, by justice led,
Did upright ways approve,
And hated still the crooked paths,
Where wandering sinners rove:

8 Therefore did God, thy God, on thee
The oil of gladness shed;
And has above thy fellows round,
Advanced thy lofty head.

---

To Father, Son, and Holy Ghost,
The God whom we adore,
Be glory, as it was, is now,
And shall be evermore.

## PSALM 40. II 2.

MONMOUTH. DAVIS.

## PSALM 41. L. M.

SHEFFIED. R. TAYLOR.

## PSALM 40. H 2.

From the xlvi Psalm of David.

1 God is our refuge in distress,
A present help when dangers press;
In him, undaunted, we 'll confide,
Though earth were from her center tossed,
And mountains in the ocean lost,
Torn piece-meal by the roaring tide.

2 A gentler stream with gladness still
The city of our Lord shall fill,
The royal seat of God most high;
God dwells in Sion, whose fair towers
Shall mock the assaults of earthly powers,
While his almighty aid is nigh.

3 Submit to God's almighty sway,
For him the heathen shall obey,
And earth her sovereign Lord confess;
The God of hosts conducts our arms,
Our tower of refuge in alarms
As to our fathers, in distress.

---

To Father, Son, and Holy Ghost,
The God whom heaven's triumphant host
And suffering saints on earth adore;
Be glory as in ages past,
As now it is, and so shall last,
When time itself shall be no more.

## PSALM 41. L. M.

From the xlvii Psalm of David.

1 O all ye people, clap your hands,
And with triumphant voices sing;
No force the mighty power withstands,
Of God, the universal King.

2 He shall assaulting foes repel,
And with success our battles fight;
Shall fix the place where we must dwell,
The pride of Jacob, his delight.

3 God is gone up, our Lord and King,
With shouts of joy and trumpet's sound;
To him repeated praises sing,
And let the cheerful song rebound.

4 Your utmost skill in praise be shown,
For him who all the world commands,
Who sits upon his righteous throne,
And spreads his sway o'er heathen lands.

---

To Father, Son, and Holy Ghost,
The God whom earth and heaven adore,
Be glory, as it was of old,
Is now, and shall be evermore.

## PSALM 42. C. M.

HARMONY. COOMBS.

## PSALM 43, Part i. H 2.

NEWCOURT. H. BOND.

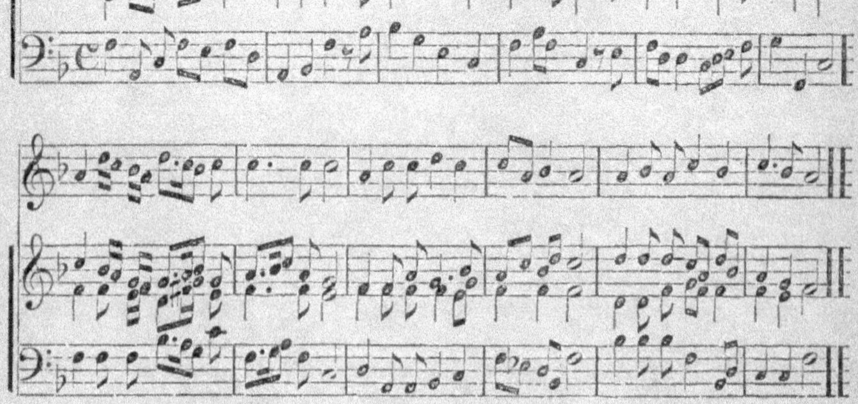

## PSALM 42. C. M.

From the xlviii Psalm of David.

1 The Lord, the only God, is great,
And greatly to be praised
In Sion, on whose happy mount
His sacred throne is raised.

2 In Sion we have seen performed
A work that was foretold,
In pledge that God, for times to come,
His city will uphold.

3 Let Sion's mount with joy resound;
Her daughters all be taught
In songs his judgment to extol,
Who this deliverance wrought.

4 Compass her walls in solemn pomp,
Your eyes quite round her cast;
Count all her towers, and see if there
You find one stone displaced.

5 Her forts and palaces survey,
Observe their order well;
That to the ages yet to come
His wonders you may tell.

6 This God is ours, and will be ours,
While we in him confide;
Who, as he has preserved us now,
Till death will be our guide.

---

To Father, Son, and Holy Ghost,
The God whom we adore,
Be glory, as it was, is now,
And shall be evermore.

## PSALM 43.

From the l Psalm of David.

### PART I. H 2.

1 The Lord hath spoke, the mighty God
Hath sent his summons all abroad,
From dawning light till day declines;
The listening earth his voice hath heard,
And he from Sion hath appeared,
Where beauty in perfection shines.

2 Our God shall come, and keep no more
Misconstrued silence, as before,
But wasting flames before him send;
Around shall tempests fiercely rage,
While he does heaven and earth engage,
His just tribunal to attend.

3 Assemble all my saints to me,
(Thus runs the great divine decree,)
That in my lasting covenant live,
And offerings bring with constant care;
The heavens his justice shall declare,
For God himself shall sentence give.

---

To Father, Son, and Holy Ghost,
The God whom heaven's triumphant host
And suffering saints on earth adore;
Be glory as in ages past,
As now it is, and so shall last,
When time itself shall be no more.

## PSALM 43, Part ii. II 2.

JENNINGS. JENNINGS.

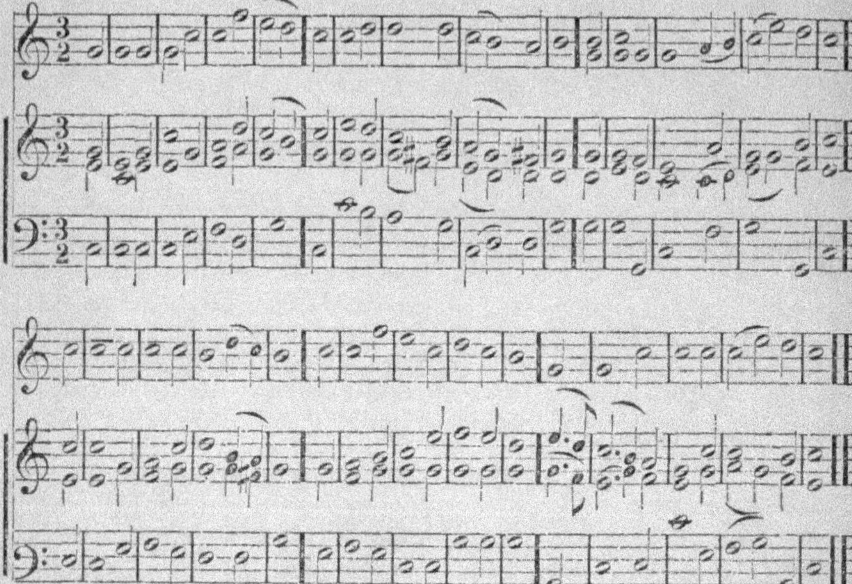

## PSALM 44. S. M.

ALNWICK. J. GARNETT.

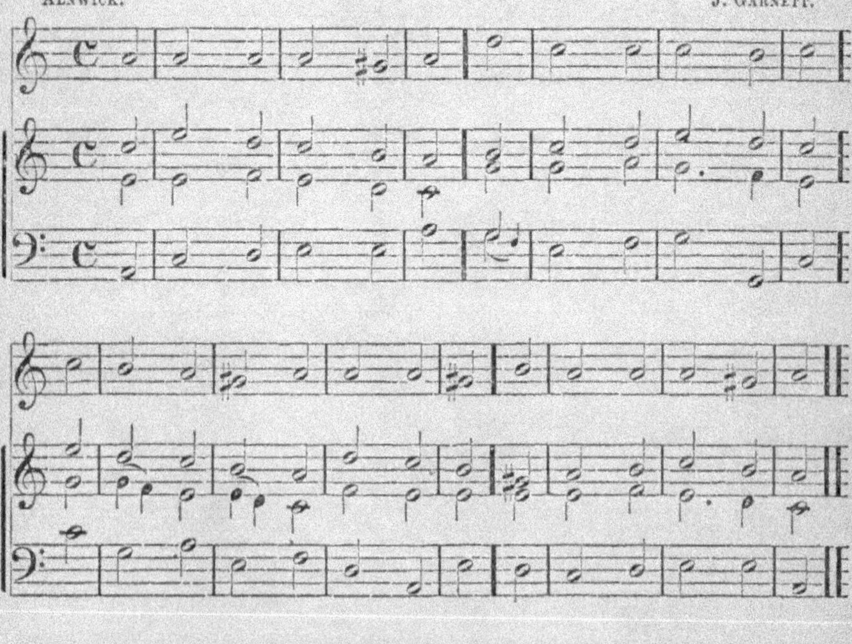

## PSALM 43.

PART II. II 2.

1 ATTEND, my people; Israel, hear;
Thy strong accuser I'll appear;
Thy God, thine only God, am I;
'T is not of offerings I complain,
Which, daily in my temple slain,
My sacred altar did supply.

2 The sacrifices I require
Are hearts which love and zeal inspire,
And vows which strictest care made good;
In time of trouble call on me,
And I will set thee safe and free,
And thou shalt praise thy gracious God.

3 Consider this, ye thoughtless men!
My vengeance shall not fall in vain,
And none will dare your cause to own;
Who praises me due honor gives,
And to the man that justly lives
My strong salvation shall be shown.

---

To Father, Son, and Holy Ghost,
The God whom heaven's triumphant host
And suffering saints on earth adore;
Be glory as in ages past,
As now it is, and so shall last,
When time itself shall be no more.

## PSALM 44. S. M.

From the li Psalm of David.

1 HAVE mercy, Lord, on me,
As thou wert ever kind;
Let me, oppressed with loads of guilt,
Thy wonted mercy find.

2 Wash off my foul offense,
And cleanse me from my sin;
For I confess my crime, and see
How great my guilt has been.

3 Against thee, Lord, alone,
And only in thy sight
Have I transgressed; and, though condemned,
Must own thy judgment right.

4 In guilt each part was formed
Of all this sinful frame;
In guilt I was conceived, and born
The heir of sin and shame.

5 Yet, Lord, thy searching eye
Does inward truth require;
And secretly, with wisdom's laws,
My soul thou wilt inspire.

12

6 With hyssop purge me, Lord,
And so I clean shall be;
I shall with snow in whiteness vie,
When purified by thee.

7 Make me to hear with joy
Thy kind forgiving voice;
That so the bones which thou hast broke
May with fresh strength rejoice.

8 Blot out my crying sins,
Nor me in anger view;
Create in me a heart that's clean,
An upright mind renew.

9 Withdraw not thou thy help,
Nor cast me from thy sight;
Nor let thy Holy Spirit take
His everlasting flight.

10 The joy thy favor gives,
Let me, O Lord, regain,
And thy free Spirit's firm support
My fainting soul sustain.

11 So I thy righteous ways
To sinners will impart;
While my advice shall wicked men
To thy just laws convert.

12 Could sacrifice atone,
Whole flocks and herds should die;
But on such off'rings thou disdain'st
To cast a gracious eye.

13 A broken spirit is
By God most highly prized;
By him a broken, contrite heart
Shall never be despised.

14 Let Sion favor find,
Of thy good will assured;
And thy own city flourish long,
By lofty walls secured.

15 The just shall then attend,
And pleasing tribute pay;
And sacrifice of choicest kind
Upon thine altar lay.

---

To God, the Father, Son,
And Spirit, glory be,
As 't was, and is, and shall be so,
To all eternity.

## PSALM 45. C. M.

RICHMOND. DR. HAWEIS.

## PSALM 46. C. M.

ST. NICHOLAS, (new) W. H. HAVERGALL.

## PSALM 45. C. M.

From the lv Psalm of David.

1 Give ear, thou Judge of all the earth,
And listen when I pray;
Nor from thy humble suppliant turn
Thy glorious face away.

2 My heart is pained: the shades of death
Their terrors round me spread;
While fearful tremblings seize my breast,
Horrors o'erwhelm my head.

3 And thus I breathe my heavy sigh
To him who hears above:
"O that my soul on wings could fly,
And emulate the dove!

4 "Swift I'd escape, and flee afar,
Some secret place to find;
Hide from the world's distracting care,
And rest my weary mind:

5 "I'd wing my everlasting flight,
Bidding the world farewell,
From sin and strife, to realms of light,
Where peace and quiet dwell."

6 Thus will I call on God, who still
Shall in my aid appear;
At morn, at noon, at night I'll pray,
And he my voice shall hear.

---

To Father, Son, and Holy Ghost,
The God whom we adore,
Be glory, as it was, is now,
And shall be evermore.

## PSALM 46. C. M.

From the lvi Psalm of David.

1 Lord, though at times surprised by fear,
On danger's first alarm,
Yet still for succor I depend
On thy almighty arm.

2 God's faithful promise I shall praise,
On which I now rely;
In God I trust, and, trusting him,
The arm of flesh defy.

3 I'll trust God's word, and so despise
The force that man can raise;
To thee, O God, my vows are due,
To thee I'll render praise.

4 Thou hast retrieved my soul from death,
And thou wilt still secure
The life thou hast so oft preserved
And make my footsteps sure:

5 That thus protected by thy power,
I may this light enjoy;
And in the service of my God
My lengthened days employ.

---

To Father, Son and Holy Ghost,
The God whom we adore,
Be glory, as it was, is now,
And shall be evermore.

## PSALM 47. L. M.

ANTIGUA.

## PSALM 48. L. M.

ROCHESTER. IONS.

### PSALM 47. L. M.

From the lvii Psalm of David.

1 O God, my heart is fixed, 't is bent,
Its thankful tribute to present;
And, with my heart, my voice I'll raise
To thee, my God, in songs of praise.

2 Awake, my glory; harp and lute,
No longer let your strings be mute:
And I, my tuneful part to take,
Will with the early dawn awake.

3 Thy praises, Lord, I will resound
To all the listening nations round:
Thy mercy highest heaven transcends,
Thy truth beyond the clouds extends.

4 Be thou, O God, exalted high;
And as thy glory fills the sky,
So let it be on earth displayed,
'Till thou art here, as there, obeyed.

---

To Father, Son, and Holy Ghost,
The God whom earth and heaven adore,
Be glory, as it was of old,
Is now, and shall be evermore.

### PSALM 48. L. M.

From the lxii Psalm of David.

1 My soul, for help on God rely,
On him alone thy trust repose;
My rock and health will strength supply,
To bear the shock of all my foes.

2 God does his saving health dispense,
And flowing blessings daily send:
He is my fortress and defense,
On him my soul shall still depend.

3 In him, ye people, always trust:
Before his throne pour out your hearts:
For God, the merciful and just,
His timely aid to us imparts.

4 The Lord has oft his will expressed,
And I this truth have fully known;
To be of boundless power possessed,
Belongs of right to God alone.

5 Though mercy is his darling grace,
In which he chiefly takes delight,
Yet will he all the human race
According to their works requite.

---

To Father, Son, and Holy Ghost,
The God whom earth and heaven adore,
Be glory, as it was of old,
Is now, and shall be evermore.

## PSALM 49. II 2.

MARTIN'S LANE. DR. ARNE.

## PSALM 50, Part i. L. M.

NEW SABBATH. PHILLIPS.

## PSALM 49. II 2.

From the lxiii Psalm of David.

1 O God, my gracious God, to thee
My morning prayers shall offered be;
For thee my thirsty soul does pant;
My fainting flesh implores thy grace,
As in a dry and barren place,
Where I refreshing waters want.

2 Oh! to my longing eyes once more,
That view of glorious power restore,
Which thy majestic house displays;
Because to me thy wondrous love
Than life itself does dearer prove,
My lips shall always speak thy praise.

3 My life, while I that life enjoy,
In blessing God I will employ,
With lifted hands adore his name;
As with its choicest food supplied,
My soul shall be full satisfied
While I with joy his praise proclaim.

4 When down I lie, sweet sleep to find,
Thou, Lord, art present to my mind;
And when awake in dead of night,
Because thou still doth succor bring,
Beneath the shadow of thy wing
I rest with safety and delight.

---

To Father, Son, and Holy Ghost,
The God whom heaven's triumphant host
And suffering saints on earth adore;
Be glory as in ages past,
As now it is, and so shall last,
When time itself shall be no more.

## PSALM 50.

From the lxv Psalm of David.

PART I. L. M.

1 For thee, O God, our constant praise
In Sion waits, thy chosen seat;
Our promised altars there we'll raise,
And all our zealous vows complete.

2 Thou, who to every humble prayer
Dost always bend thy listening ear,
To thee shall all mankind repair,
And at thy gracious throne appear.

3 Our sins, though numberless, in vain
To stop thy flowing mercy try;
While thou o'erlookest the guilty stain,
And washest out the crimson dye.

4 Blest is the man who, near thee placed,
Within thy sacred dwelling lives;
'T is there abundantly we taste
The vast delights thy temple gives.

---

To Father, Son, and Holy Ghost,
The God whom earth and heaven adore,
Be glory, as it was of old,
Is now, and shall be evermore.

## PSALM 50, Part ii. L. M.

BOWEN. HAYDN.

## PSALM 51, Part i & ii. C. M.

ST. NICHOLAS, (new) W. H. HAVERGALL.

### PSALM 50.

PART II. L. M.

1 LORD, from thy unexhausted store,
Thy rain relieves the thirsty ground,
Makes lands that barren were before,
With corn and useful fruits abound.

2 On rising ridges down it pours,
And every furrowed valley fills;
Thou mak'st them soft with gentle showers,
In which a blest increase distills.

3 Thy goodness does the circling year
With fresh returns of plenty crown;
And where thy glorious paths appear,
The fruitful clouds drop fatness down.

4 They drop on barren deserts, changed
By them to pastures fresh and green;
The hills about in order ranged,
In beauteous robes of joy are seen.

5 Large flocks, with fleecy wool, adorn
The cheerful downs; the valleys bring
A plenteous crop of full eared corn,
And seem, for joy, to shout and sing.

---

To Father, Son, and Holy Ghost,
The God whom earth and heaven adore,
Be glory, as it was of old,
Is now, and shall be evermore.

### PSALM 51.

From the lxvi Psalm of David.

PART I. C. M.

1 LET all the lands, with shouts of joy,
To God their voices raise;
Sing psalms in honor of his name,
And spread his glorious praise.

2 And let them say, How dreadful, Lord,
In all thy works art thou!
To thy great power thy stubborn foes
Shall all be forced to bow.

3 Through all the earth, the nations round
Shall thee, their God, confess;
And, with glad hymns, their awful dread
Of thy great name express.

4 O come, behold the works of God,
And then with me you 'll own,
That he to all the sons of men
Has wondrous judgment shown.

5 O all ye nations bless our God,
And loudly speak his praise;
Who keeps our souls alive, and still
Confirms our steadfast ways.

PART II. C. M.

1 MY offerings to God's house I'll bring,
And there my vows will pay,
Which I with solemn zeal did make
In trouble's dismal day.

2 O come, all ye that fear the Lord,
Attend with heedful care,
While I what God for me has done,
With grateful joy declare.

3 As I before his aid implored,
So now I praise his name;
But if my heart to sin incline,
My prayer will God disclaim.

4 But God to me, whene'er I cried,
His gracious ear did bend,
And to the voice of my request
With constant love attend.

5 Then blessed for ever be my God,
Who never, when I pray,
Withholds his mercy from my soul,
Nor turns his face away.

---

To Father, Son, and Holy Ghost,
The God whom we adore,
Be glory, as it was, is now,
And shall be evermore.

## PSALM 52, S. M.

KIDDERMEISTER. BAXTER.

## PSALM 52. S. M.

From the lxvii Psalm of David.

1 To bless thy chosen race,
In mercy Lord incline:
And cause the brightness of thy face
On all thy saints to shine:

2 That so thy wondrous way
May through the world be known;
While distant lands their tribute pay,
And thy salvation own.

3 Let differing nations join
To celebrate thy fame;
Let all the world, O Lord, combine
To praise thy glorious Name.

4 O let them shout and sing,
With joy and pious mirth;
For thou, the righteous Judge and King
Shalt govern all the earth.

5 Let different nations join
To celebrate thy fame;
Let all the world, O Lord, combine
To praise thy glorious Name.

6 Then God upon our land
Shall constant blessings shower;
And all the world in awe shall stand
Of his resistless power.

---

To God the Father, Son,
And Spirit, glory be,
As 'twas, and is, and shall be so,
To all eternity.

## PSALM 53. L. M.

WARRINGTON. R. HARRISON.

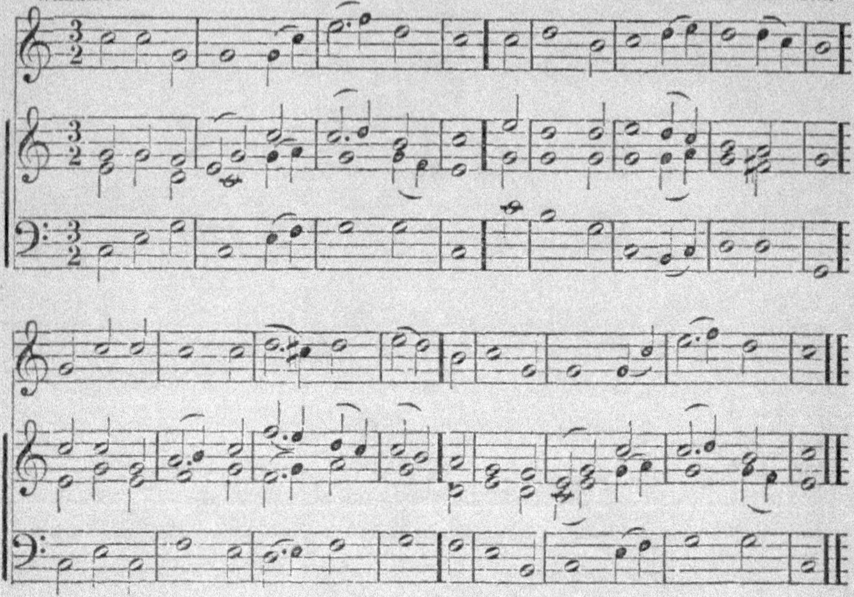

## PSALM 54. Part i. L. M.

SAMPSON'S SONG. R. TAYLOR.

### PSALM 53. L. M.

From the lxviii Psalm of David.

1 The servants of Jehovah's will
His favor's gentle beams enjoy;
Their upright hearts let gladness fill,
And cheerful songs their tongues employ.

2 To him your voice in anthems raise,
Jehovah's awful name he bears;
In him rejoice, extol his praise,
Who rides upon high-rolling spheres.

3 His chariots numberless; his powers
Are heavenly hosts, that wait his will;
His presence now fills Sion's towers,
As once it honored Sinai's hill.

4 Ascending high, in triumph thou
Captivity hast captive led,
And on thy people didst bestow
Thy gifts and graces freely shed.

5 E'en rebels shall partake thy grace,
And humble proselytes repair
To worship at thy dwelling-place,
And all the world pay homage there.

6 For benefits each day bestowed,
Be daily his great name adored,
Who is our Saviour and our God,
Of life and death the sovereign Lord.

---

To Father, Son, and Holy Ghost,
The God whom earth and heaven adore,
Be glory, as it was of old,
Is now, and shall be evermore.

### PSALM 54.

From the lxix Psalm of David.

PART I. L. M.

1 Save me, O God, from waves that roll
And press to overwhelm my soul;
With painful steps in mire I tread,
And deluges o'erflow my head.

2 O Lord, to thee I will repair
For help, with humble, timely prayer;
Relieve me from thy mercy's store;
Display thy truth's preserving power.

3 From threatening dangers me relieve,
And from the mire my feet retrieve;
From all my foes in safety keep,
And snatch me from the raging deep.

4 Lord, hear the humble prayer I make
For thy transcending goodness' sake;
Relieve thy supplicant once more
From thy abounding mercy's store.

5 Reproach and grief have broke my heart;
I looked for some to take my part,
To pity, or relieve my pain;
But looked, alas! for both in vain.

6 With hunger pined, for food I call,
Instead of food they gave me gall;
And when with thirst my spirits sink,
They give me vinegar to drink.

7 For new afflictions they procured
For him who had thy stripes endured;
And made the wounds thy scourge had torn
To bleed afresh with sharper scorn.

---

*To Father, Son, and Holy Ghost, etc.*

## PSALM 54, Part ii. L. M.

BEREA.

## PSALM 55. C. M.

ST. THOMAS. T. IONS.

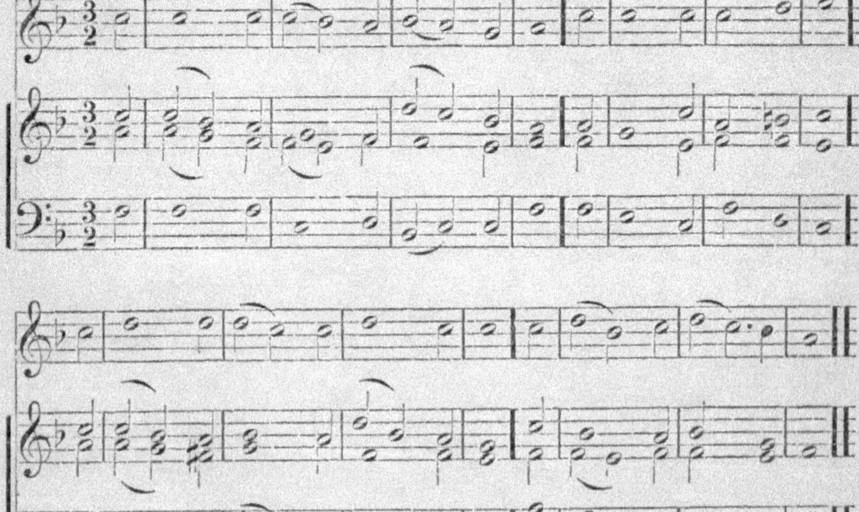

## PSALM 54.

### PART II. L. M.

1 My soul, howe'er distressed and poor,
Thy strong salvation shall restore;
Thy power with songs I'll then proclaim,
And celebrate with thanks thy name.

2 Our God shall this more highly prize
Than herds or flocks in sacrifice;
Which humble saints with joy shall see,
And hope for like redress with me.

3 For God regards the poor's complaint,
And frees the captive from restraint;
Let heaven, earth, sea, their voices raise,
And all the world resound his praise.

---

To Father, Son, and Holy Ghost,
The God whom earth and heaven adore,
Be glory, as it was of old,
Is now, and shall be evermore.

## PSALM 55. C. M.

From the lxxi Psalm of David.

1 In thee I put my steadfast trust,
Defend me, Lord, from shame;
Incline thine ear, and save my soul,
For righteous is thy name.

2 Be thou my strong abiding-place,
To which I may resort;
Thy promise, Lord, is my defense,
Thou art my rock and fort.

3 My steadfast and unchanging hope
Shall on thy power depend;
And I in grateful songs of praise
My time to come will spend.

4 Thy righteous acts and saving health
My mouth shall still declare;
Unable yet to count them all,
Though summed with utmost care.

5 While God vouchsafes me his support,
I'll in his strength go on;
All other righteousness disclaim,
And mention his alone.

6 Thou, Lord, hast taught me from my youth,
To praise thy glorious name;
And ever since, thy wondrous works
Have been my constant theme.

7 Therefore, with psaltery and harp,
Thy truth, O Lord, I'll praise;
To thee, the God of Jacob's race,
My voice in anthems raise.

8 Then joy shall fill my mouth, and song
Employ my cheerful voice;
My grateful soul, by thee redeemed,
Shall in thy strength rejoice.

---

To Father, Son, and Holy Ghost,
The God whom we adore,
Be glory, as it was, is now,
And shall be evermore.

## PSALM 56. C. M.

WINTRINGHAM. WAINWRIGHT.

## PSALM 56. C. M.

From the lxxii Psalm of David.

1 Lo! hills and mountains shall bring forth
The happy fruits of peace;
Which all the lands shall own to be
The work of righteousness:

2 While David's Son our needy race
Shall rule with gentle sway;
And from their humble neck shall take
Oppressive yokes away.

3 In every heart thy awful fear
Shall then be rooted fast,
As long as sun and moon endure,
Or time itself shall last.

4 He shall descend like rain, that cheers
The meadow's second birth;
Or like warm showers, whose gentle drops
Refresh the thirsty earth.

5 In his blest days the just and good
Shall spring up all around;
The happy land shall every where
With endless peace abound.

6 His uncontrolled dominion shall
From sea to sea extend;
Begin at proud Euphrates' stream,
At nature's limits end.

7 To him the savage nations round
Shall bow their servile heads;
His vanquished foes shall lick the dust,
Where he his conquests spreads.

8 The kings of Tarshish and the isles
Shall costly presents bring;
From spicy Sheba gifts shall come,
And wealthy Saba's king.

9 To him shall every king on earth
His humble homage pay;
And differing nations gladly join
To own his righteous sway.

10 For he shall set the needy free,
When they for succor cry;
Shall save the helpless and the poor,
And all their wants supply.

11 For him shall constant prayer be made,
Through all his prosperous days;
His just dominion shall afford
A lasting theme of praise.

12 The memory of his glorious name
Through endless years shall run;
His spotless fame shall shine as bright,
And lasting as the sun.

13 In him the nations of the world
Shall be completely blessed,
And his unbounded happiness
By every tongue confessed.

14 Then blessed be God, the mighty Lord,
The God whom Israel fears;
Who only wondrous in his works
Beyond compare, appears.

15 Let earth be with his glory filled,
For ever bless his name;
While to his praise the listening world
Their glad assent proclaim.

---

To Father, Son, and Holy Ghost,
The God whom we adore,
Be glory, as it was, is now,
And shall be evermore.

## PSALM 57, L. M.

ROCKINGHAM. MILLER.

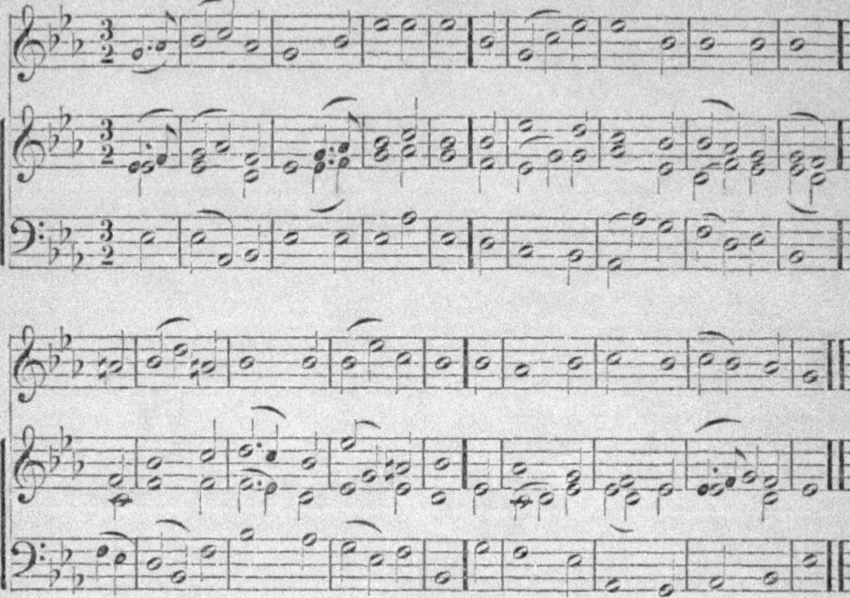

## PSALM 58. C. M.

ST. THOMAS. T. IONS.

### PSALM 57. L. M.

From the lxxiii Psalm of David.

1 Thy presence, Lord, hath me supplied,
Thou my right hand support dost give:
Thou first shalt with thy counsel guide,
And then to glory me receive.

2 Whom then in heaven, but thee alone,
Have I, whose favor I require?
Throughout the spacious earth there's none,
Compared with thee, that I desire.

3 My trembling flesh and aching heart
May often fail to succor me:
But God shall inward strength impart,
And my eternal portion be.

4 For they that far from thee remove
Shall into sudden ruin fall;
If after other gods they rove,
Thy vengeance shall destroy them all.

5 But as for me, 't is good and just
That I should still to God repair;
In him I always put my trust,
And will his wondrous works declare.

To Father, Son, and Holy Ghost,
The God whom earth and heaven adore,
Be glory, as it was of old,
Is now, and shall be evermore.

### PSALM 58. C. M.

From the lxxiv Psalm of David.

1 Thine is the cheerful day, O Lord;
Thine the return of night;
Thou hast prepared the glorious sun
And every feebler light.

2 By thee the borders of the earth
In perfect order stand:
The summer's warmth and winter's cold
Attend on thy command.

---

To Father, Son, and Holy Ghost,
The God whom we adore,
Be glory, as it was, is now,
And shall be evermore.

## PSALM 59. IV 1.

ST. MICHAEL'S. HANDEL.

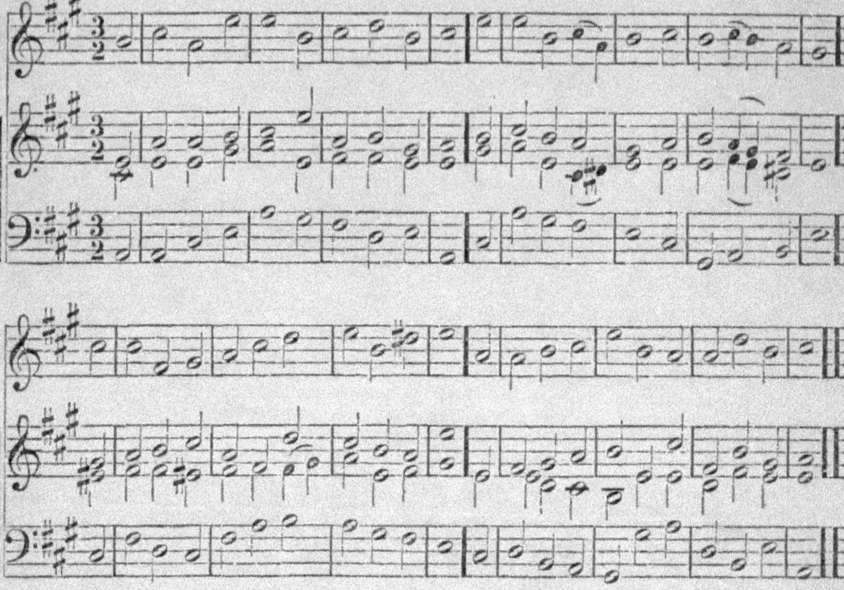

## PSALM 60. C. M.

ST. NICHOLAS, (new.) W. H. HAVERGALL.

### PSALM 59. IV 1.

From the lxxvi Psalm of David.

1 The name of our God
In Israel is known;
His mansion beloved
Is Sion alone:
There broke he the arrows
The enemy hurled,
And honored his mountain
Above all the world.

2 The pride of thy foes
Is turned to thy praise;
Their fierceness o'erruled
Thy providence sways;
Their sin overflowing
Thy power will restrain;
Thy arm on the wicked
New glory will gain.

3 Ye nations, to God
Vow homage sincere;
Devote to him gifts,
Love, worship, and fear;
Before him, ye mighty,
Your spirits repress:
Ye high, and ye humble,
His wonders confess.

---

By angels in heaven
Of every degree,
And saints upon earth
All praise be addressed;
To God in three persons,
One God ever blessed,
As it has been, now is,
And ever shall be.

### PSALM 60. C. M.

From the lxxviii Psalm of David.

1 Hear O my people, to my law
Devout attention lend;
Let the instruction of my mouth
Deep in your hearts descend.

2 My tongue shall oracles proclaim
Which ancient times have known;
The truths which our forefathers' care
To us has handed down.

3 We will not hide them from our sons,
Our offspring shall be taught
The praises of the Lord, whose strength
Has works of wonder wrought.

4 For Jacob he his law ordained,
His league with Israel made;
With charge to be from age to age
From race to race conveyed;

5 That generations yet to come
Should to their unborn heirs
Religiously transmit the same,
And they again to theirs.

6 To teach them that in God alone
Their hope securely stands;
That they should ne'er his works forget
But keep his just commands.

---

To Father, Son, and Holy Ghost,
The God whom we adore,
Be glory, as it was, is now,
And shall be evermore.

## PSALM 61. L. M.

NAZARETH. WEBBE.

## PSALM 62. C. M.

ST. STEPHENS. W. JONES.

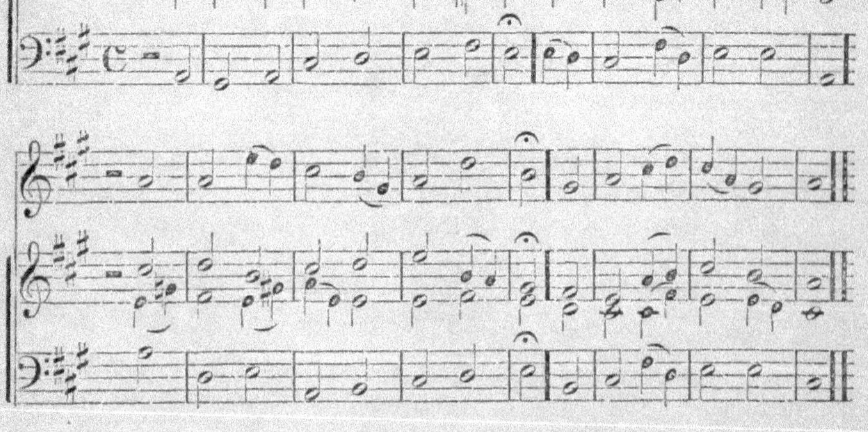

### PSALM 61. L. M.

From the lxxx Psalm of David.

1 O THOU whom heavenly hosts obey
How long shall thy fierce anger burn?
How long thy suffering people pray,
And to their prayers have no return?

2 Thou brought'st a vine from Egypt's land;
And, casting out the heathen race,
Didst plant it with thine own right hand,
And firmly fix it in their place.

3 Before it thou preparedst the way,
And made it take a lasting root;
Which, blessed with thy indulgent ray,
O'er all the land did widely shoot.

4 The hills were covered with its shade,
Its goodly boughs did cedars seem;
Its branches to the sea were spread,
And reached to proud Euphrates' stream.

5 To thee, O God of hosts, we pray,
Thy wonted goodness Lord, renew;
From heaven, thy throne, this vine survey,
And her sad state with pity view.

6 Behold the vineyard made by thee,
Which thy right hand did guard so long;
And keep that branch from danger free,
Which for thyself thou madest so strong.

7 Do thou convert us, Lord, do thou
The luster of thy face display;
And all the ills we suffer now,
Like scattered clouds, shall pass away.

---

To Father, Son, and Holy Ghost,
The God whom earth and heaven adore,
Be glory as it was of old,
Is now, and shall be evermore.

### PSALM 62. C. M.

From the lxxxi Psalm of David.

1 To God, our never-failing strength,
With loud applauses sing:
And jointly make a cheerful noise
To Jacob's awful King.

2 Compose a hymn of praise, and touch
Your instruments of joy;
Let psalteries and tuneful harps
Your grateful skill employ.

3 Let trumpets at the festival
Their joyful voices raise,
To celebrate the appointed time,
The solemn day of praise.

4 For this a statute was of old,
Which Jacob's God decreed
To be with pious care observed
By Israel's chosen seed.

---

To Father, Son, and Holy Ghost,
The God whom we adore,
Be glory, as it was, is now,
And shall be evermore.

## PSALM 63. C. M.

BEDFORD. WHEALL.

## PSALM 64. C. M.

MATLACK. NOVELLO.

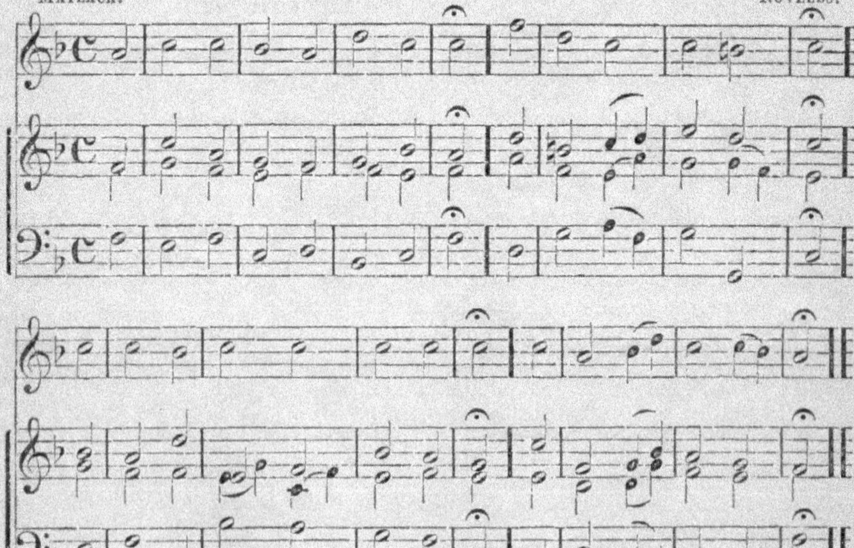

## PSALM 63. C. M.

From the lxxxiv Psalm of David.

1 O God of hosts, the mighty Lord,
How lovely is the place
Where thou, enthroned in glory, show'st
The brightness of thy face!

2 My longing soul faints with desire
To view thy blest abode;
My panting heart and flesh cry out
For thee, the living God.

3 The birds, more happy far than I,
Around thy temple throng;
Securely there they build, and there
Securely hatch their young.

4 O Lord of hosts, my King and God,
How highly blessed are they,
Who in thy temple always dwell,
And there thy praise display!

5 Thrice happy they, whose choice has thee
Their sure protection made,
Who long to tread the sacred ways
That to thy dwelling lead.

6 Who pass through parched and thirsty vales,
Yet no refreshment want;
Their pools are filled with rain, which thou
At their request dost grant.

7 Thus they proceed from strength to strength,
And still approach more near;
Till all on Sion's holy mount
Before their God appear.

8 Within thy courts one single day
'Tis better to attend,
Than, Lord, in any other place
A thousand days to spend.

9 Much rather in God's house will I
The meanest office take,
Than in the wealthy tents of sin
My pompous dwelling make.

10 For God, who is our Sun and Shield,
Will grace and glory give;
And no good thing will he withhold
From them that justly live.

11 Thou, God, whom heavenly hosts obey,
How highly blessed is he,
Whose hope and trust, securely placed,
Are still reposed on thee.

14

To Father, Son, and Holy Ghost,
The God whom we adore,
Be glory, as it was, is now,
And shall be evermore.

## PSALM 64. C. M.

From the lxxxv Psalm of David.

1 O God our Saviour, all our hearts
To thy obedience turn;
That, quenched with our repenting tears
Thy wrath no more may burn.

2 For why shouldst thou be angry still,
And wrath so long retain?
Revive us, Lord, and let thy saints
Thy wonted comfort gain.

3 Thy gracious favor, Lord, display,
Which we have long implored;
And, for thy wondrous mercy's sake,
Thy wonted aid afford.

4 God's answer patiently I'll wait:
For he with glad success,
If they no more to folly turn,
His mourning saints will bless.

5 To all that fear God's holy Name
His sure salvation's near;
His glory in our happy land
For ever shall appear.

6 For mercy now with truth is joined;
And righteousness with peace,
Like kind companions absent long,
With friendly arms embrace.

7 Truth from the earth shall spring, while heaven
Shall streams of justice pour;
And God, from whom all goodness flows,
Shall endless plenty shower.

8 Before him righteousness shall march,
And his just paths prepare;
While we his holy steps pursue
With constant zeal and care.

---

To Father, Son, and Holy Ghost,
The God whom we adore,
Be glory, as it was, is now,
And shall be evermore.

## PSALM 65. C. M.

CAROLINA. COOMBS.

## PSALM 66. II 3.

GLOUCESTER. B. MILGROVE.

## PSALM 65. C. M.

From the lxxxvi Psalm of David.

1 To my complaint, O Lord my God,
Thy gracious ear incline;
Hear me, distressed and destitute
Of all relief but thine.

2 Do thou, O God, preserve my soul,
That does thy name adore;
Thy servant keep, and him whose trust
Relies on thee, restore.

3 To me, who daily thee invoke,
Thy mercy, Lord, extend;
Refresh thy servant's soul, whose hopes
On thee alone depend.

4 Thou, Lord, art good; nor only good,
But prompt to pardon too;
Of plenteous mercy to all those
Who for thy mercy sue.

5 To my repeated humble prayer,
O Lord, attentive be;
When troubled, I on thee will call,
For thou wilt answer me.

6 Among the gods there's none like thee,
O Lord, alone divine!
To thee as much inferior they,
As are their works to thine.

7 Therefore their great Creator, thee
The nations shall adore;
Their long misguided prayers and praise
To thy blest name restore.

8 All shall confess thee great, and great
The wonders thou hast done;
Confess thee God, the God supreme,
Confess thee God alone.

9 Teach me thy way, O Lord, and I
From truth shall ne'er depart;
In reverence to thy sacred name
Devoutly fix my heart.

10 Thee will I praise, O Lord my God,
Praise thee with heart sincere;
And to thy everlasting name
Eternal trophies rear.

11 Thy boundless mercy shown to me
Transcends my power to tell;
For thou hast oft redeemed my soul
From lowest deeps of hell.

12 And thou thy constant goodness didst
To my assistance bring;
Of patience, mercy, and of truth,
Thou everlasting spring.

---

To Father, Son, and Holy Ghost.
The God whom we adore,
Be glory, as it was, is now,
And shall be evermore.

## PSALM 66. II 3.

From the lxxxvii Psalm of David.

1 God's temple crowns the holy mount,
The Lord there condescends to dwell;
His Sion's gates, in his account,
Our Israel's fairest tents excel;
Yea, glorious things of thee we sing,
O city of th' Almighty King!

2 Of honored Sion, we aver
Illustrious throngs from her proceed;
Th' Almighty shall establish her,
And shall enroll her holy seed;
Yea, for his people he shall count
The children of his favored mount.

3 He'll Sion find with numbers filled,
Who celebrate his matchless praise;
Who, here in hallelujahs skilled,
In heaven their harps and hymns shall raise;
O Sion, seat of Israel's King,
Be mine to drink thy living spring.

---

To God the Father, God the Son,
And God the Spirit, Three in One,
Be glory in the highest given,
By all in earth and all in heaven,
As was through ages heretofore,
Is now, and shall be evermore.

## PSALM 67. L. M.

NEWRY. WEYMAN.

## PSALM 68. L. M.

WARRINGTON. R. HARRISON.

## PSALM 67. L. M.

From the lxxxviii Psalm of David.

1 God of my life, O Lord most high,
To thee by day and night I cry;
Vouchsafe my mournful voice to hear;
To my distress incline thine ear.

2 Like those whose strength and hopes are fled,
They number me among the dead;
Like those who, shrouded in the grave,
From thee no more remembrance have.

3 Wilt thou by miracle revive
The dead whom thou forsook'st alive?
Shall the mute grave thy love confess,
A mouldering tomb thy faithfulness?

4 To thee, O Lord, I cry forlorn,
My prayer prevents the early morn:
Why hast, thou, Lord, my soul forsook,
Nor once vouchsafed a gracious look?

5 Companions dear, and friends beloved,
Far from my sight thou hast removed;
God of my life, O Lord most high,
Vouchsafe to hear my mournful cry.

---

To Father, Son, and Holy Ghost,
The God whom earth and heaven adore,
Be glory, as it was of old,
Is now, and shall be evermore.

## PSALM 68. L. M.

From the lxxxix Psalm of David.

1 Thy mercies, Lord, shall be my song,
My song on them shall ever dwell;
To ages yet unborn, my tongue
Thy never-failing truth shall tell.

2 I have affirmed, and still maintain
Thy mercy shall for ever last;
Thy truth, that does the heavens sustain,
Like them, shall stand for ever fast.

3 Thus spak'st thou by the prophet's voice:
"With David I a league have made;
To him, my servant, and my choice,
By solemn oath this grant conveyed:

4 "While earth, and seas, and skies endure,
Thy seed shall in my sight remain;
To them thy throne I will ensure,
They shall to endless ages reign."

5 For such stupendous truth and love,
Both heaven and earth just praises owe,
By choirs of angels sung above,
And by assembled saints below.

6 What seraph of celestial birth
To vie with Israel's God shall dare?
Or who among the gods of earth
With our almighty Lord compare?

7 With reverence and religious dread,
His saints should to his temple press;
His fear through all their hearts should spread,
Who his Almighty name confess.

8 Lord God of armies, who can boast,
Of strength or power like thine renowned?
Of such a numerous, faithful host,
As that which does thy throne surround?

9 Thou dost the lawless sea control,
And change the prospect of the deep;
Thou mak'st the sleeping billows roll;
Thou mak'st the rolling billows sleep.

10 In thee the sovereign right remains
Of earth and heaven; thee, Lord, alone
The world, and all that it contains,
Their Maker and Preserver own.

11 Thine arm is mighty, strong thy hand
Yet, Lord, thou dost with justice reign;
Possessed of absolute command,
Thou truth and mercy dost maintain.

12 Happy, thrice happy, they who hear
Thy sacred trumpet's joyful sound;
Who may at festivals appear,
With thy most glorious presence crowned.

13 Thy saints shall always be o'erjoyed,
Who on thy sacred name rely;
And, in thy righteousness employed,
Above their foes be raised on high.

14 For in thy strength they shall advance,
Whose conquests from thy favor spring;
The Lord of hosts is our defense,
And Israel's God our Israel's King.

---

To Father, Son, and Holy Ghost,
The God whom earth and heaven adore,
Be glory, as it was of old,
Is now, and shall be evermore.

## PSALM 69, Part i & ii. C. M.

ST. MATHEW'S. DR. CROFT.

## PSALM 69.

From the xc Psalm of David.

PART I. C. M.

1 O Lord, the Saviour and defense
Of us thy chosen race,
From age to age thou still hast been
Our sure abiding place.

2 Before thou brought'st the mountains forth,
Or the earth and world didst frame,
Thou always wast the mighty God,
And ever art the same.

3 Thou turnest man, O Lord, to dust,
Of which he first was made:
And when thou speak'st the word "Return,"
'T is instantly obeyed.

4 For in thy sight a thousand years
Are like a day that 's past;
Or like a watch in dead of night,
Whose hours unminded waste.

5 Thou sweep'st us off as with a flood,
We vanish hence like dreams:
At first we grow like grass that feels
The sun's reviving beams;

6 But howsoever fresh and fair
Its morning beauty shows,
'T is all cut down and withered quite
Before the evening close.

7 We by thine anger are consumed,
And by thy wrath dismayed;
Our public crimes and secret sins
Before thy sight are laid.

8 Beneath thine anger's sad effects
Our drooping days we spend;
Our unregarded years break off,
Like tales that quickly end.

9 Our term of time is seventy years,
An age that few survive:
But if, with more than common strength,
To eighty we arrive—

10 Yet then our boasted strength decays,
To sorrow turned and pain:
So soon the slender thread is cut,
And we no more remain.

---

To Father, Son, and Holy Ghost,
The God whom we adore,
Be glory, as it was, is now,
And shall be evermore.

PART II. C. M.

1 But who thine anger's dread effects
Does, as he ought, revere?
And yet thy wrath does fall or rise,
As more or less we fear.

2 So teach us, Lord, the uncertain sum
Of our short days to mind,
That to true wisdom all our hearts
May ever be inclined.

3 O to thy servants, Lord, return,
And speedily relent!
As we of our misdeeds, do thou
Of our just doom repent.

4 To satisfy and cheer our souls,
Thy early mercy send;
That we may all our days to come
In joy and comfort spend.

5. To all thy servants, Lord, let this
Thy wondrous work be known;
And to our offspring yet unborn,
Thy glorious power be shown.

6 Let thy bright rays upon us shine,
Give thou our work success;
The glorious work we have in hand
Do thou vouchsafe to bless.

---

*To Father, Son, and Holy Ghost, etc.*

## PSALM 70, Part i. II 2.

JENNINGS. JENNINGS.

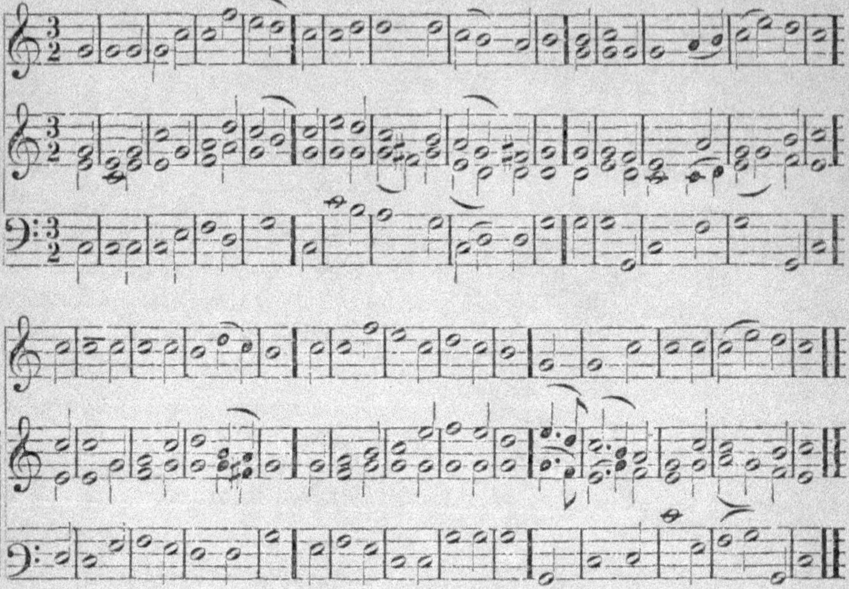

## PSALM 70, Part ii. III 3.

ALSEN. F. L. ABEL.

## PSALM 70.

From the xci Psalm of David.

### PART I. II 2.

1 He that has God his guardian made,
Shall, under the Almighty's shade,
Secure and undisturbed abide:
Thus to my soul of him I'll say,
He is my fortress and my stay,
My God, in whom I will confide.

2 His tender love and watchful care
Shall free thee from the fowler's snare,
And from the noisome pestilence;
He over thee his wings shall spread,
And cover thy unguarded head;
His truth shall be thy strong defense.

3 No terrors, that surprise by night,
Shall thy undaunted courage fright,
Nor deadly shafts that fly by day;
Nor plague of unknown rise, that kills
In darkness, nor infectious ills,
That in the burning noon-tide slay.

4 Because with well-placed confidence
Thou mak'st the Lord thy sure defense,
Thy refuge, even God most high;
Therefore, no ill on thee shall come,
Nor to thy heaven-protected home
Shall overwhelming plagues draw nigh.

To Father, Son, and Holy Ghost,
The God whom heaven's triumphant host
And suffering saints on earth adore;
Be glory, as in ages past,
As now it is, and so shall last,
When time itself shall be no more.

### PART II. III 3.

1 God shall charge his angel legions
Watch and ward o'er thee to keep;
Though thou walk through hostile regions,
Though in desert wilds thou sleep.

2 On the lion vainly roaring,
On his young, thy foot shall tread;
And the dragon's den exploring,
Thou shalt bruise the serpent's head.

3 Since, with pure and firm affection,
Thou on God hast set thy love,
With the wings of his protection
He will shield thee from above.

4 Thou shalt call on him in trouble,
He will hearken, he will save;
Here for grief reward thee double,
Crown with life beyond the grave.

---

Praise the Father, earth and heaven,
Praise the Son, the Spirit praise,
As it was, and is, be given
Glory through eternal days.

## PSALM 71. C. M.

ST. CATHARINE'S. JOS. GARNETT.

## PSALM 72. L. M.

STONEFIELD. STANLEY.

### PSALM 71. C. M.

From the xcii Psalm of David.

1 How good and pleasant must it be
To thank the Lord most high;
And with repeated hymns of praise
His Name to magnify!

2 With every morning's early dawn
His goodness to relate:
And of his constant truth each night,
The glad effects repeat!

3 To ten-stringed instruments we'll sing,
With tuneful psalteries joined;
And to the harp with solemn sounds,
For sacred use designed.

4 For through thy wondrous works, O Lord,
Thou mak'st my heart rejoice;
The thoughts of them shall make me glad,
And shout with cheerful voice.

5 How wondrous are thy works, O Lord!
How deep are thy decrees!
Whose winding tracks, in secret laid,
No careless sinner sees.

6 He little thinks, when wicked men,
Like grass, look fresh and gay,
How soon their short-lived splendor must
For ever pass away.

7 But thou, my God, art still most high;
And all thy lofty foes,
Who thought they might securely sin,
Shall be o'erwhelmed with woes.

8 But righteous men, like rising palms,
Shall grow and flourish still;
Thy flock shall spread, like cedars choice,
On Lebanon's high hill.

9 These, planted in the house of God,
Within his courts shall thrive;
Their vigor and their luster both
Shall in old age revive.

10 Thus will the Lord his justice show;
And God, my strong defense,
Shall due rewards to all the world
Impartially dispense.

---

To Father, Son, and Holy Ghost,
The God whom we adore,
Be glory, as it was, is now,
And shall be evermore.

### PSALM 72. L. M.

From the xciii Psalm of David.

1 With glory clad, with strength arrayed,
The Lord that o'er all nature reigns,
The world's foundation strongly laid,
And the vast fabric still sustains.

2 How surely stablished is thy throne!
Which shall no change or period see;
For thou, O Lord, and thou alone,
Art God from all eternity.

3 The floods, O Lord, lift up their voice,
And toss the troubled waves on high;
But God above can still their noise,
And make the angry sea comply.

4 Thy promise, Lord, is ever sure,
And they that in thy house would dwell,
That happy station to secure,
Must still in holiness excel.

---

To Father, Son, and Holy Ghost,
The God whom earth and heaven adore,
Be glory, as it was of old,
Is now, and shall be evermore.

## PSALM 73. Part i & ii. C. M.

ST. ASAPH'S. NOVELLO.

## PSALM 74. L. M.

PARK STREET. VENUA.

## PSALM 73.

From the xciv Psalm of David.

### PART I. C. M.

1 Say ye, the Lord shall not regard,
Shall not your sins discern?
Take heed, ye foolish and unwise;
When will ye wisdom learn?

2 Can he be deaf who formed the ear,
Or blind, who framed the eye?
Shall earth's great Judge not punish those
Who his known will defy?

3 He fathoms all the hearts of men,
To him their thoughts lie bare;
His eye surveys them all, and sees
How vain their counsels are.

---

To Father, Son, and Holy Ghost,
The God whom we adore,
Be glory, as it was, is now,
And shall be evermore.

### PART II. C. M.

1 Blessed is the man whom thou, O Lord,
In kindness dost chastise,
And by thy sacred rules to walk
Dost lovingly advise.

2 This man shall rest and safety find,
In seasons of distress;
While God prepares a pit for those
That stubbornly transgress.

3 For God will never from his saints
His favor wholly take;
His own possession and his lot
He will not quite forsake.

4 The world shall yet confess thee just
In all that thou hast done;
And those that choose thy upright ways
Shall in those paths go on.

5 Long since had I in silence slept,
But that the Lord was near,
To stay me when I slipped; when sad,
My troubled heart to cheer.

6 My soul's defense is firmly placed
In God the Lord most high:
He is my rock, to which I may
For refuge always fly.

---

*To Father, Son, and Holy Ghost, etc.*

## PSALM 74. L. M.

From the xcv Psalm of David.

1 O come, loud anthems let us sing,
Loud thanks to our almighty King;
For we our voices high should raise,
When our salvation's rock we praise.

2 Into his presence let us haste,
To thank him for his favors past;
To him address, in joyful songs,
The praise that to his Name belongs:

3 For God the Lord, enthroned in state,
Is, with unrivaled glory, great;
A King superior far to all
Whom gods the heathen falsely call.

4 The depths of earth are in his hand,
Her secret wealth at his command;
The strength of hills that reach the skies,
Subjected to his empire lies.

5 The rolling ocean's vast abyss
By the same sovereign right is his;
'T was made by his almighty hand,
That formed and fixed the solid land.

6 O let us to his courts repair,
And bow with adoration there;
Down on our knees devoutly all
Before the Lord, our Maker, fall.

7 For he 's our God, our shepherd he,
His flock and pasture sheep are we;
O then, ye faithful flock, to-day,
His warning hear, his voice obey.

---

To Father, Son, and Holy Ghost,
The God whom earth and heaven adore,
Be glory, as it was of old,
Is now, and shall be evermore.

## PSALM 75. II 8.

GUERNSEY.

## PSALM 76. L. M.

MENDON. GERMAN AIR.

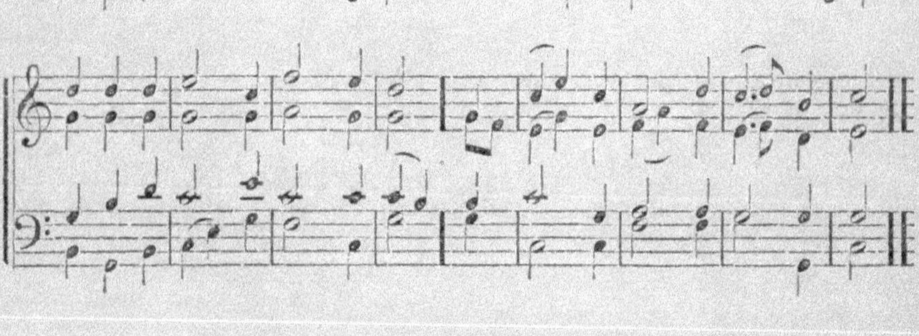

## PSALM 75. H 8.

From the xcvi Psalm of David.

1 Sing to the Lord a new-made song;
Let earth in one assembled throng,
Her common patron's praise resound;
Sing to the Lord, and bless his name,
From day to day his praise proclaim,
Who us has with salvation crowned;
To heathen lands his fame rehearse,
His wonders to the universe.

2 He 's great, and greatly to be praised;
In majesty and glory raised
Above all other deities;
For pageantry and idols all
Are they whom gods the heathen call;
He only rules who made the skies;
With majesty and honor crowned,
Glory and strength his throne surround.

3 Be glory then to him restored
By all who have false gods adored;
Ascribe due honor to his name;
Peace-offerings on his altar lay,
Before his throne your homage pay,
Which he, and he alone, can claim;
To worship at his sacred court,
Let all the trembling world resort.

4 Proclaim aloud, Jehovah reigns,
Whose power the universe sustains,
And banished justice will restore;
Let therefore heaven new joys confess,
And heavenly mirth let earth express,
Its loud applause the ocean roar,
Its mute inhabitants rejoice,
And for this triumph find a voice.

5 For joy let fertile valleys sing,
The cheerful groves their tribute bring,
And tuneful harmonies awake;
Behold! in truth and justice clad,
God comes to judge the world he made,
And to himself its throne to take;
He's come to judge the world, he 's come
With justice to reward and doom.

---

By all in earth and all in heaven
Be everlasting glory given,
To God the Father, God the Son,
And God the Spirit; equal Three
In undivided Unity,
Ere time had yet its course begun;
As was, and is, be highest praise,
As still shall be through endless days.

## PSALM 76. L. M.

From the xcvii Psalm of David.

1 Jehovah reigns, let all the earth
In his just government rejoice;
Let all the lands, with sacred mirth,
In his applause unite their voice.

2 Darkness and clouds of awful shade
His dazzling glory shroud in state;
Judgment and righteousness are made
The habitation of his seat.

3 For thou, O God, art seated high,
Above earth's potentates enthroned;
Thou, Lord, unrivaled in the sky,
Supreme by all the gods art owned.

4 Ye who to serve this Lord aspire,
Abhor what 's ill, and truth esteem;
He 'll keep his servants' souls entire,
And them from wicked hands redeem.

5 For seeds are sown of glorious light,
A future harvest for the just;
And gladness for the heart that 's right,
To recompense its pious trust.

6 Rejoice, ye righteous, in the Lord;
Memorials of his holiness
Deep in your faithful breasts record,
And with your thankful tongues confess.

---

To Father, Son, and Holy Ghost,
The God whom earth and heaven adore,
Be glory, as it was of old,
Is now, and shall be evermore.

## PSALM 77. C. M.

OLD 98TH. RAVENSCROFT, 1621.

## PSALM 77. C. M.

From the xcviii Psalm of David.

1 SING to the Lord a new-made song,
Who wondrous things has done;
With his right hand and holy arm,
The conquest he has won.

2 The Lord has through th' astonished world
Displayed his saving might,
And made his righteous acts appear
In all the heathen's sight.

3 Of Israel's house his love and truth
Have ever mindful been;
Wide earth's remotest parts the power
Of Israel's God have seen.

4 Let, therefore, earth's inhabitants
Their cheerful voices raise,
And all with universal joy
Resound their Maker's praise.

5 With harp and hymn's soft melody,
Into the concert bring
The trumpet and shrill cornet's sound,
Before th' Almighty King.

6 Let the loud ocean roar her joy,
With all that seas contain;
The earth and her inhabitants
Join concert with the main.

7 Let floods and torrents clap their hands,
With joy their homage pay;
Let echoing vales, from hill to hill,
Redoubled shouts convey:

8 To welcome down the world's great Judge,
Who does with justice come,
And with impartial equity,
Both to reward and doom.

---

To Father, Son, and Holy Ghost,
The God whom we adore,
Be Glory, as it was, is now,
And shall be evermore.

## PSALM 78. C. M.

BEXLEY. NOVELLO.

## PSALM 79, L. M.

OLD HUNDRED. UNKNOWN. *

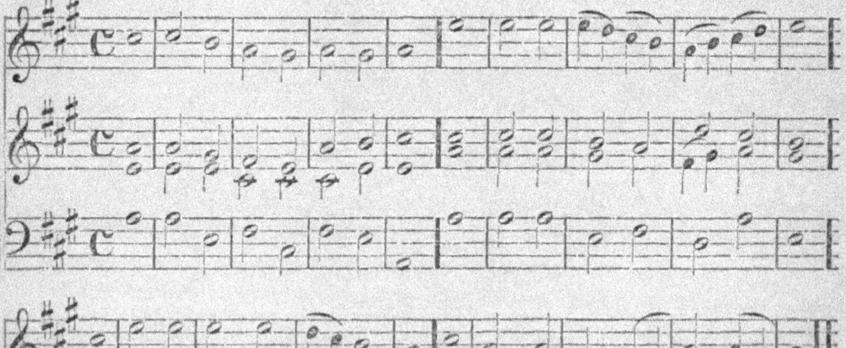

* Attributed to Claude Goudimel. of Lyons, about 1565.

### PSALM 78. C. M.

From the xcix Psalm of David.

1 Jehovah reigns; let therefore all
The guilty nations quake;
On cherubs' wings he sits enthroned;
Let earth's foundations shake.

2 On Sion's hill he keeps his court,
His palace makes her towers;
And thence his sovereignty extends
Supreme o'er earthly powers.

3 Let therefore all with praise address
His great and dreadful name;
And with his unresisted might
His holiness proclaim.

4 For truth and justice, in his reign,
Of strength and power take place;
His judgments are with righteousness
Dispensed to Jacob's race.

5 Therefore exalt the Lord our God,
Before his footstool fall;
And with his unresisted might
His holiness extoll.

6 With worship at his sacred courts
Exalt our God and Lord;
For he, who only holy is,
Alone should be adored.

---

To Father, Son, and Holy Ghost,
The God whom we adore,
Be glory, as it was, is now,
And shall be evermore.

### PSALM 79. L. M.

From the c Psalm of David.

1 With one consent let all the earth
To God their cheerful voices raise;
Glad homage pay with awful mirth,
And sing before him songs of praise.

2 Convinced that he is God alone,
From whom both we and all proceed;
We, whom he chooses for his own,
The flock that he vouchsafes to feed.

3 O enter then his temple gate,
Thence to his courts devoutly press;
And still your grateful hymns repeat,
And still his name with praises bless.

4 For he's the Lord, supremely good,
His mercy is for ever sure;
His truth, which always firmly stood,
To endless ages shall endure.

---

To Father, Son, and Holy Ghost
The God whom earth and heaven adore,
Be glory, as it was of old,
Is now, and shall be evermore.

## PSALM 80, Part i. C. M

CAROLINA. COOMBS.

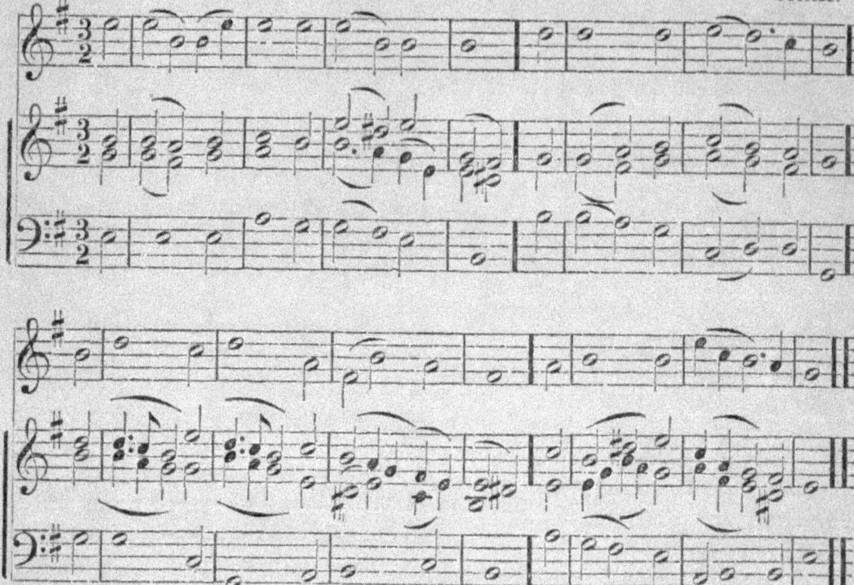

## PSALM 80, Parts ii & iii. C. M.

TIVERTON. GRIGG.

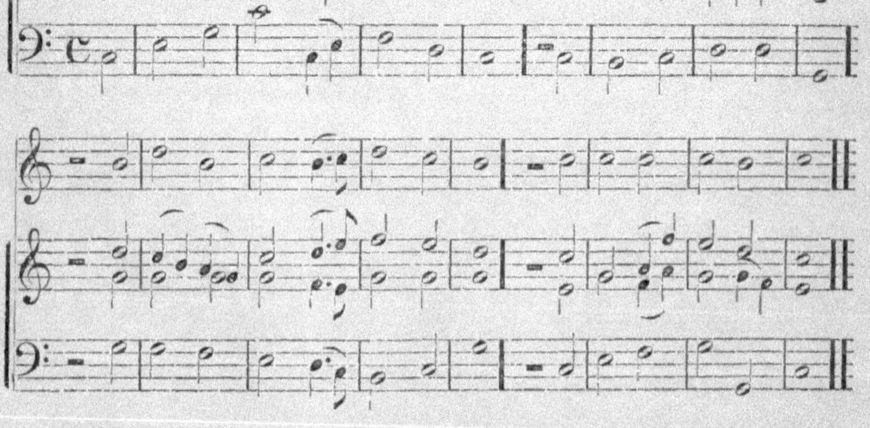

## PSALM 80.

From the cii Psalm of David.

### PART I. C. M.

1 When I pour out my soul in prayer,
Do thou, O Lord, attend;
To thy eternal throne of grace
Let my sad cry ascend.

2 O hide not thou thy glorious face
In times of deep distress;
Incline thine ear, and, when I call,
My sorrows soon redress.

3 My days, just hastening to their end,
Are like an evening shade;
My beauty does, like withered grass,
With waning luster fade.

4 But thine eternal state, O Lord,
No length of time shall waste;
The memory of thy wondrous works
From age to age shall last.

---

To Father, Son, and Holy Ghost,
The God whom we adore,
Be glory, as it was, is now,
And shall be evermore.

### PART II. C. M.

1 God shall arise, and Sion view
With an unclouded face:
For now her time is come, his own
Appointed day of grace.

2 The name and glory of the Lord
All heathen kings shall fear,
When he shall Sion build again,
And in full state appear.

3 For God, from his abode on high,
His gracious beams displayed;
The Lord from heaven, his lofty throne,
Hath all the earth surveyed.

4 That they, in Sion, where he dwells,
Might celebrate his fame,
And through the holy city sing,
Loud praises to his Name.

---

To Father, Son, and Holy Ghost,
The God whom we adore,
Be glory, as it was, is now,
And shall be evermore.

### PART III. C. M.

1 The strong foundations of the earth
Of old by thee were laid;
Thy hands, O Lord, the arch of heaven
With wondrous skill have made.

2 While thou for ever shalt endure,
They soon shall pass away;
And, like a garment often worn,
Shall tarnish and decay.

3 Like that, when thou ordain'st their change,
To thy command they bend;
But thou continuest still the same,
Nor have thy years an end.

4 Thou to the children of thy saints
Shall lasting quiet give;
Whose happy race securely fixed,
Shall in thy presence live.

---

To Father, Son, and Holy Ghost,
The God whom we adore,
Be glory, as it was, is now.
And shall be evermore.

## PSALM 81. L. M.

St. Peter's. Harwood.

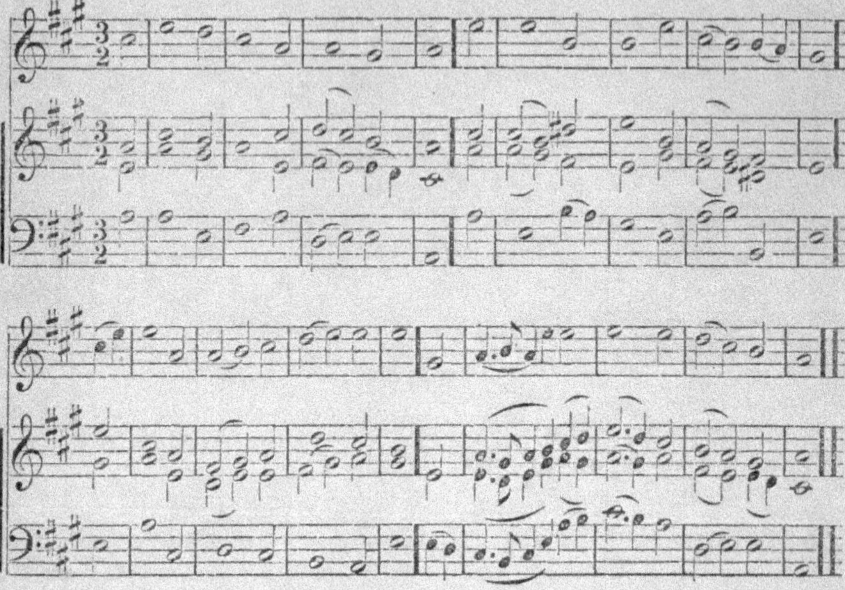

## PSALM 82. S. M.

Warrington. Mornington.

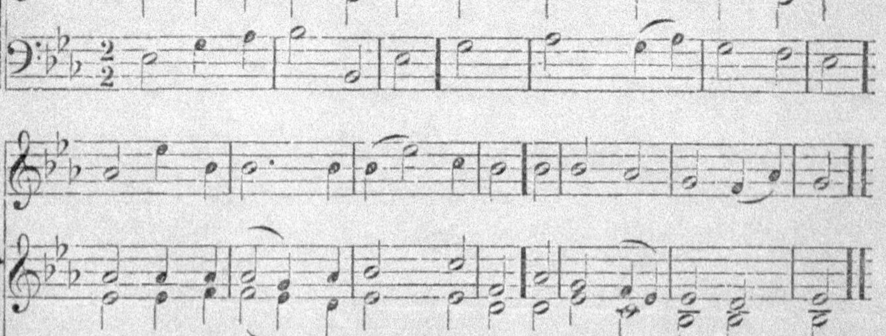

## PSALM 81. L. M.

From the ciii Psalm of David.

1 My soul, inspired with sacred love,
God's holy name for ever bless;
Of all his favors mindful prove,
And still thy grateful thanks express.

2 'Tis he that all thy sins forgives,
And, after sickness, makes thee sound;
From danger he thy life retrieves,
By him with grace and mercy crowned.

3 He with good things thy mouth supplies,
Thy vigor, eagle-like, restores;
He to the sufferer promptly flies,
Who, wronged, his righteous help implores.

4 The Lord abounds with tender love
And unexampled acts of grace;
His wakened wrath doth slowly move,
His willing mercy flies apace.

5 God will not always harshly chide,
But with his anger quickly part;
And loves his punishment to guide
More by his love than our desert.

6 As high as heaven its arch extends
Above this little spot of clay,
So much his boundless love transcends
The small respects that we can pay.

7 As far as 't is from east to west,
So far hath he our sins removed;
Who, with a father's tender breast,
Has such as fear him always loved.

8 For God, who all our frame surveys,
Considers that we are but clay;
How fresh soe'er we seem, our days
Like grass or flowers must fade away.

9 While they are nipped with sudden blasts,
Nor can we find their former place,
God's faithful mercy ever lasts
To those that fear him and their race.

10 This shall attend on such as still
Proceed in his appointed way;
And who not only know his will,
But to it just obedience pay.

11 The Lord, the universal King,
In heaven has fixed his lofty throne;
To him, ye angels, praises sing,
In whose great strength his power is shown.

12 Ye that his just commands obey,
And hear and do his sacred will,
Ye hosts of his, this tribute pay,
Who still what he ordains fulfill.

13 Let every creature jointly bless
The might Lord; and thou, my heart,
With grateful joy thy thanks express,
And in this concert bear thy part.

---

To Father, Son, and Holy Ghost,
The God whom earth and heaven adore,
Be glory, as it was of old,
Is now, and shall be evermore.

## PSALM 82. S. M.

From the ciii Psalm of David.

1 O bless the Lord, my soul,
His grace to thee proclaim;
And all that is within me, join
To bless his holy name.

2 O bless the Lord, my soul,
His mercies bear in mind;
Forget not all his benefits,
Who is to thee so kind.

3 He pardons all thy sins,
Prolongs thy feeble breath;
He healeth thine infirmities,
And ransoms thee from death.

4 He feeds thee with his love,
Upholds thee with his truth;
And, like the eagle's, he renews
The vigor of thy youth.

5 Then bless the Lord, my soul,
His grace, his love proclaim;
Let all that is within me, join
To bless his holy name.

---

To God the Father, Son,
And Spirit, glory be,
As 'twas, and is, and shall be so,
To all eternity.

## PSALM 83. Part i. L. M.

DUKE STREET. HATTON.

## PSALM 83, Part ii. L. M.

BEREA.

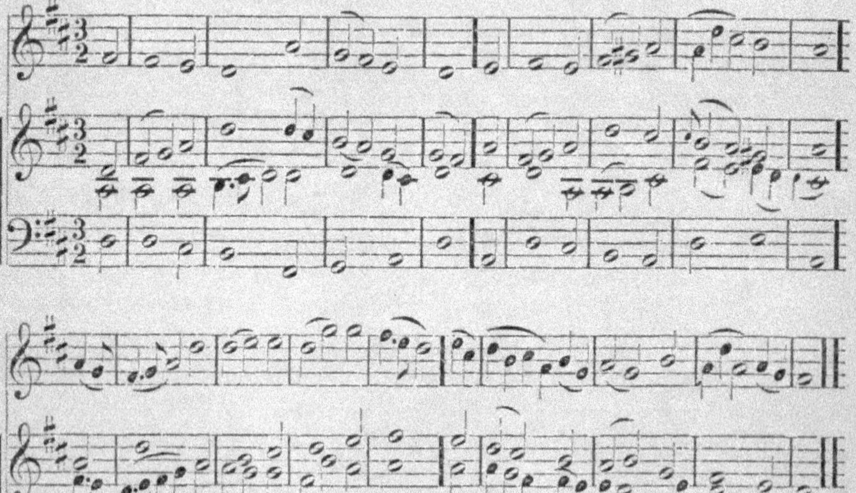

## PSALM 83.

From the civ Psalm of David.

### PART I. L. M.

1 Bless God, my soul; thou, Lord, alone
Possessest empire without bounds,
With honor thou art crowned, thy throne
Eternal majesty surrounds.

2 With light thou dost thyself enrobe,
And glory for a garment take;
Heaven's curtain stretch beyond the globe,
Thy canopy of state to make.

3 God builds on liquid air, and forms
His palace chambers in the skies;
The clouds his chariots are, and storms
The swift-winged steeds with which he flies.

4 As bright as flame, as swift as wind,
His ministers heaven's palace fill;
They have their sundry tasks assigned,
All prompt to do their sovereign's will.

5 In praising God while he prolongs
My breath, I will that breath employ;
And join devotion to my songs,
Sincere, as in him is my joy.

---

To Father, Son, and Holy Ghost,
The God whom earth and heaven adore,
Be glory, as it was of old,
Is now, and shall be evermore.

### PART II. L. M.

1 How various, Lord, thy works are found,
For which thy wisdom we adore!
The earth is with thy treasure crowned,
Till nature's hand can grasp no more.

2 All creatures, both of sea and land,
In sense of common want agree;
All wait on thy dispensing hand,
And have their daily alms from thee.

3 They gather what thy stores disperse,
Without their trouble to provide;
Thou op'st thy hand, the universe,
The craving world, is all supplied.

4 Thou for a moment hid'st thy face,
The numerous ranks of creatures mourn;
Thou tak'st their breath, all nature's race
Decay, and to their dust return.

5 Again thou send'st thy spirit forth,
Inspiring vital energies;
Nature 's restored; replenished earth,
Joyous, her new creation sees.

6 Thus through successive ages stands
Firm fixed thy providential care;
Pleased with the work of thine own hands,
Thou dost the wastes of time repair.

---

To Father, Son, and Holy Ghost,
The God whom earth and heaven adore,
Be glory, as it was of old,
Is now, and shall be evermore.

## PSALM 84. II 3.

GLOUCESTER. B. MILGROVE.

## PSALM 85. C. M.

NEW CAMBRIDGE. DR. RANDALL.

### PSALM 84. II 3.

From the civ Psalm of David.

1 How manifold thy works, O Lord,
In wisdom, power, and goodness wrought!
The earth is with thy riches stored,
And ocean with thy wonders fraught:
Unfathomed caves beneath the deep
For thee their hidden treasures keep.

2 By thee alone the living live—
Hide but thy face, their comforts fly;
They gather what thy seasons give—
Take thou away their breath, they die;
But send again thy Spirit forth,
And life renews the gladdened earth.

3 Joy in his works Jehovah takes,
Yet to destruction they return;
He looks upon the earth, it quakes—
Touches the mountains, and they burn:
But God for ever is the same;
Glory to his eternal name!

---

To God the Father, God the Son,
And God the Spirit, Three in One,
Be glory in the highest given,
By all in earth and all in heaven,
As was through ages heretofore,
Is now, and shall be evermore.

### PSALM 85. C. M.

From the cv Psalm of David.

1 O RENDER thanks, and bless the Lord,
Invoke his sacred name;
Acquaint the nations with his deeds,
His matchless deeds proclaim.

2 Sing to his praise in lofty hymns,
His wondrous works rehearse;
Make them the theme of your discourse,
And subject of your verse.

3 Rejoice in his almighty name,
Alone to be adored;
And let their hearts o'erflow with joy,
That humbly seek the Lord.

4 Seek ye the Lord, his saving strength
Devoutly still implore;
And, where he 's ever present, seek
His face for evermore.

5 The wonders that his hands have wrought
Keep thankfully in mind;
The righteous statutes of his mouth,
And laws to us assigned.

---

To Father, Son, and Holy Ghost,
The God whom we adore,
Be glory, as it was, is now,
And shall be evermore.

## PSALM 86. L. M.

DUKE STREET. HATTON.

## PSALM 87. Part i. III 1.

KENMERE.

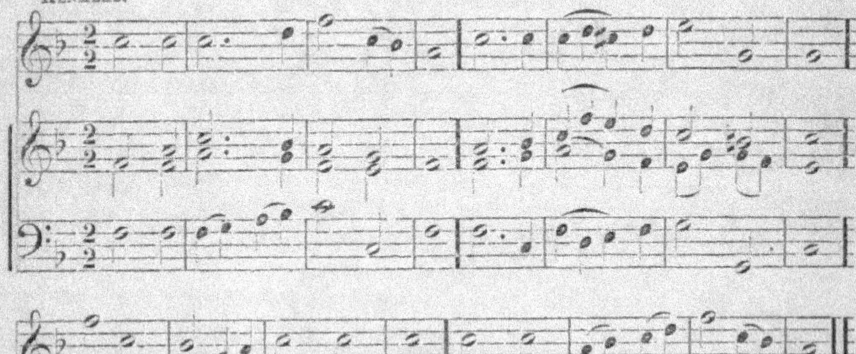

### PSALM 86. L. M.

From the cvi Psalm of David.

1 O RENDER thanks to God above,
The fountain of eternal love;
Whose mercy firm through ages past
Has stood, and shall for ever last.

2 Who can his mighty deeds express,
Not only vast, but numberless?
What mortal eloquence can raise
His tribute of immortal praise?

3 Happy are they, and only they,
Who from thy judgments never stray;
Who know what's right; nor only so,
But always practice what they know.

4 Extend to me that favor, Lord,
Thou to thy chosen dost afford;
When thou return'st to set them free,
Let thy salvation visit me.

5 O may I worthy prove to see
Thy saints in full prosperity;
That I the joyful choir may join,
And count thy people's triumph mine.

6 Let Israel's God be ever blessed,
His name eternally confessed;
Let all his saints, with full accord,
Sing loud amens—praise ye the Lord.

---

To Father, Son, and Holy Ghost,
The God whom earth and heaven adore,
Be glory, as it was of old,
Is now, and shall be evermore.

### PSALM 87.

From the cvii Psalm of David.

PART I. III 1.

1 MAGNIFY Jehovah's name;
For his mercies ever sure,
From eternity the same,
To eternity endure.

2 Let his ransomed flock rejoice,
Gathered out of every land,
As the people of his choice,
Plucked from the destroyer's hand.

3 In the wilderness astray,
In the lonely wastes they roam,
Hungry, fainting by the way,
Far from refuge, shelter, home.

4 To the Lord their God they cry;
He inclines a gracious ear,
Sends deliv'rance from on high,
Rescues them from all their fear.

5 Them to pleasant lands he brings,
Where the vine and olive grow;
Where, from verdant hills, the springs
Through luxuriant valleys flow.

6 O that men would praise the Lord,
For his goodness to their race;
For the wonders of his word,
And the riches of his grace!

---

Holy Father, Holy Son,
Holy Spirit, Three in One,
Glory, as of old, to thee,
Now and evermore shall be.

## PSALM 87, Part ii. C. M.

ST. NICHOLAS. W. H. HAVERGALL.

## PSALM 88. C. M.

BROOMSGROVE.

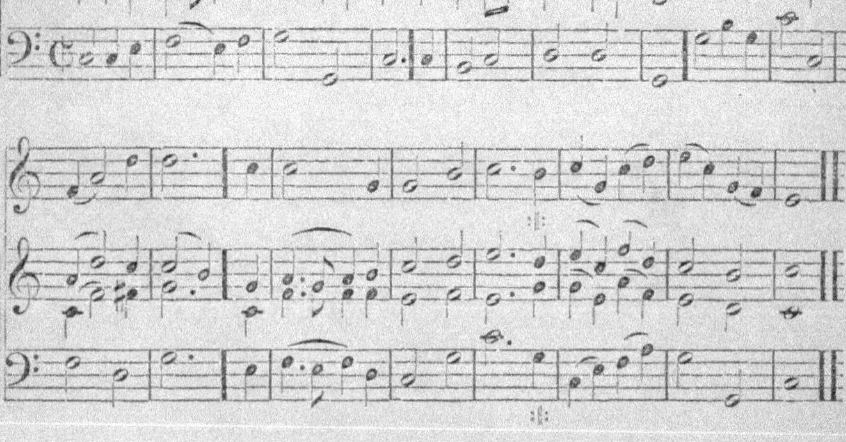

## PSALM 87

From the cvii Psalm of David.

PART II. C. M.

1 Thy wondrous power, Almighty Lord,
That rules the boisterous sea,
The bold adventurers record,
Who tempt that dangerous way.

2 At thy command the winds arise,
And swell the towering waves;
While they astonished mount the skies,
And sink in gaping graves.

3 Dismayed they climb the watery hills,
Dismayed they plunge again;
Each like a tottering drunkard reels,
And finds his courage vain.

4 Then to the Lord they raise their cries,
He hears their loud request,
He calms the fierce tempestuous skies
And lays the floods to rest.

5 Rejoicing, they forget their fears,
They see the storm allayed;
The wished-for haven now appears;
There, let their vows be paid!

6 O that the sons of men would praise
The goodness of the Lord!
And those who see his wondrous ways
His wondrous love record!

---

To Father, Son, and Holy Ghost,
The God whom we adore,
Be glory, as it was, is now,
And shall be evermore.

## PSALM 88. C. M.

From the cviii Psalm of David.

1 O God, my heart is fully bent
To magnify thy Name;
My tongue with cheerful songs of praise
Shall celebrate thy fame.

2 Awake, my lute, not thou, my harp,
Thy warbling notes delay;
While I with early hymns of joy
Prevent the dawning day.

3 To all the listening tribes, O Lord,
Thy wonders I will tell,
And to those nations sing thy praise
That round about us dwell;

4 Because thy mercy's boundless hight
The highest heaven transcends;
And far beyond the aspiring clouds
Thy faithful truth extends.

5 Be thou, O God, exalted high
Above the starry frame;
And let the world, with one consent,
Confess thy glorious Name.

---

To Father, Son, and Holy Ghost,
The God whom we adore,
Be glory, as it was, is now,
And shall be evermore.

## PSALM 89. II 2.

CALCOTT. DR. CALCOTT.

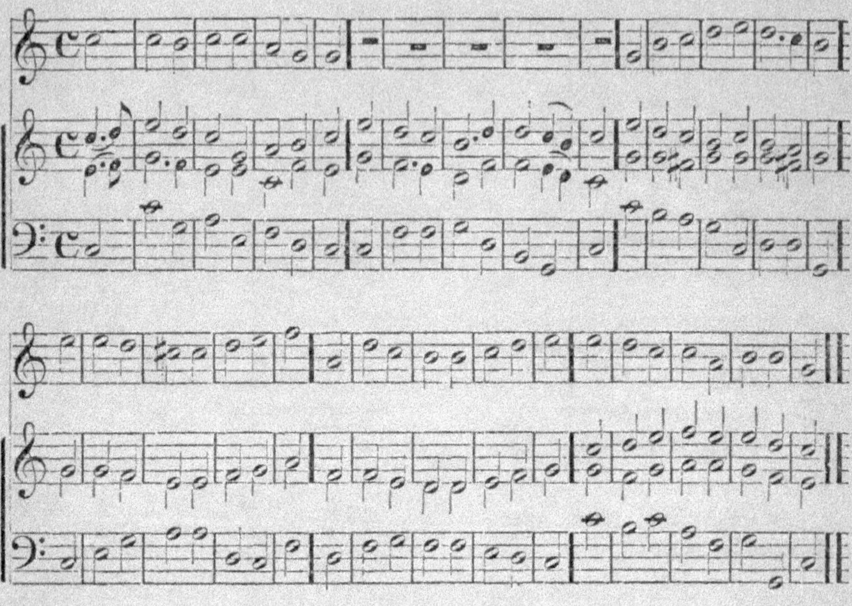

## PSALM 90. L. M.

DUKE STREET. HATTON.

## PSALM 89. H 2.

From the cx Psalm of David.

1 The Lord unto my Lord thus spake:
"Till I thy foes thy footstool make,
Sit thou in state at my right hand;
Supreme in Sion thou shalt be,
And all thy proud opposers see
Subjected to thy just command.

2 "Thee, in thy power's triumphant day,
The willing people shall obey;
And when thy rising beams they view,
Shall all (redeemed from error's night)
Appear more numerous and bright
Than crystal drops of morning dew."

3 The Lord hath sworn, nor sworn in vain,
That, like Melchisedec's, thy reign
And priesthood shall no period see;
Anointed Prince! thou, bending low,
Shall drink where darkest torrents flow,
Then raise thy head in victory!

---

To Father, Son, and Holy Ghost,
The God whom heaven's triumphant host
And suffering saints on earth adore;
Be glory as in ages past,
As now it is, and so shall last,
When time itself shall be no more.

## PSALM 90. L. M.

From the cxi Psalm of David.

1 Praise ye the Lord! our God to praise
My soul her utmost power shall raise;
With private friends, and in the throng
Of saints, his praise shall be my song.

2 His works, for greatness though renowned,
His wondrous works with ease are found
By those who seek for them aright,
And in the pious search delight.

3 His works are all of matchless fame,
And universal glory claim;
His truth, confirmed through ages past,
Shall to eternal ages last.

4 By precepts he hath us enjoined
To keep his wondrous works in mind;
And to posterity record
That good and gracious is our Lord.

5 His bounty, like a flowing tide,
Has all his servants' wants supplied;
And he will ever keep in mind
His covenant with our fathers signed.

6 Just are the dealings of his hands,
Immutable are his commands,
By truth and equity sustained,
And for eternal rules ordained.

7 He set his saints from bondage free,
And then established his decree,
For ever to remain the same:
Holy and reverend is his name.

8 Who wisdom's sacred prize would win,
Must with the fear of God begin;
Immortal praise and heavenly skill
Have they who know and do his will.

---

To Father, Son, and Holy Ghost,
The God whom earth and heaven adore,
Be glory, as it was of old,
Is now, and shall be evermore.

## PSALM 91. L. M.

BOWEN. HAYDN.

## PSALM 92. II 2.

OLD 113TH. DR. MILLER.

### PSALM 91. L. M.

From the cxii Psalm of David.

1 That man is blessed who stands in awe
Of God, and loves his sacred law;
His seed on earth shall be renowned,
And with successive honors crowned.

2 The soul that 's filled with virtue's light
Shines brightest in affliction's night;
To pity the distressed inclined,
As well as just to all mankind.

3 His liberal favors he extends,
To some he gives, to others lends;
Yet what his charity impairs,
He saves by prudence in affairs.

4 Beset with threatening dangers round,
Unmoved shall he maintain his ground;
The sweet remembrance of the just
Shall flourish when he sleeps in dust.

---

To Father, Son, and Holy Ghost,
The God whom earth and heaven adore,
Be glory, as it was of old,
Is now, and shall be evermore.

### PSALM 92. II 2.

From the cxiii Psalm of David.

1 Ye saints and servants of the Lord,
The triumphs of his Name record;
His sacred Name for ever bless:
Where'er the circling sun displays
His rising beams or setting rays,
Due praise to his great Name address.

2 God through the world extends his sway;
The regions of eternal day
But shadows of his glories are:
With him whose majesty excels,
Who made the heaven in which he dwells,
Let no created power compare.

3 Though 't is beneath his state to view
In highest heaven what angels do,
Yet he to earth vouchsafes his care;
He takes the needy from his cell,
Advancing him in courts to dwell,
Companion to the greatest there.

---

To Father, Son, and Holy Ghost,
The God whom heaven's triumphant host,
And suffering saints on earth adore;
Be glory as in ages past,
As now it is, and so shall last
When time itself shall be no more.

## PSALM 93. C. M.

ST ALBAN'S. CROFT.

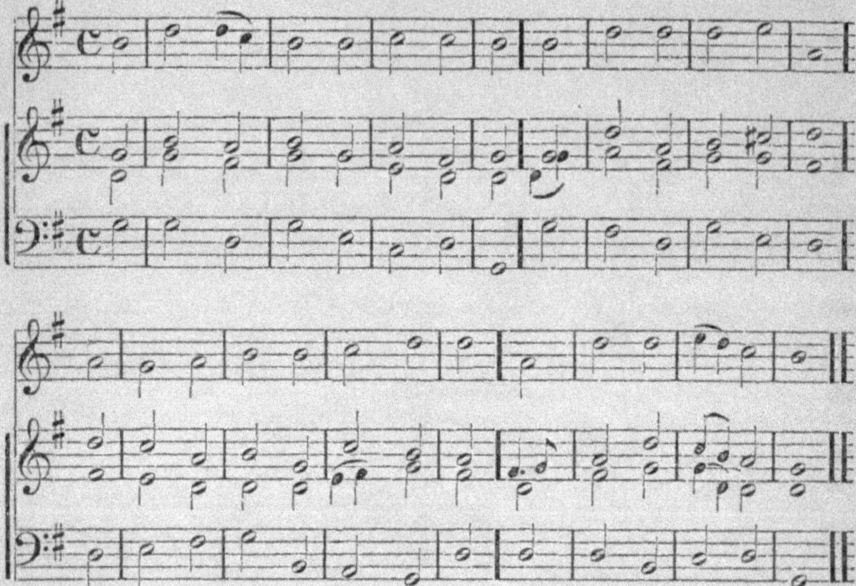

## PSALM 94. C. M.

MARTYRDOM. R. BINFIELD.

## PSALM 93. C. M.

From the cxv Psalm of David.

1 Lord, not to us, we claim no share,
But to thy sacred Name
Give glory for thy mercy's sake,
And truth's eternal fame.

2 Why should the heathen cry, "Where's now
The God whom ye adore?"
Convince them that in heaven thou art,
And uncontrolled thy power.

3 O Israel, make the Lord your trust,
Who is your help and shield;
Priests, Levites, trust in him alone,
Who only help can yield.

4 Let all who truly fear the Lord,
On him they fear rely;
Who them in danger can defend,
And all their wants supply.

5 Of us he oft has mindful been,
And Israel's house will bless;
Priests, Levites, Proselytes, e'en all
Who his great Name confess.

6 On you, and on your heirs, he will
Increase of blessings bring:
Thrice happy you, who favorites are
Of this almighty King!

7 Heaven's highest orb of glory he
His empire's seat designed;
And gave this lower globe of earth
A portion to mankind.

8 They who in death and silence sleep,
To him no praise afford;
But we will bless for evermore
Our everliving Lord.

---

To Father, Son, and Holy Ghost,
The God whom we adore,
Be glory, as it was, is now,
And shall be evermore.

## PSALM 94. C. M.

From the cxvi Psalm of David.

1 My soul with grateful thoughts of love
Entirely is possessed,
Because the Lord vouchsafed to hear
The voice of my request.

2 Since he has now his ear inclined,
I never will despair;
But still in all the straits of life
To him address my prayer.

3 With deadly sorrows compassed round,
With pains of hell oppressed;
When troubles seized my aching heart,
And anguish racked my breast;

4 On God's almighty name I called,
And thus to him I prayed;
"Lord, I beseech thee save my soul,
With sorrows quite dismayed."

5 How just and merciful is God,
How gracious is the Lord!
Who saves the harmless, and to me
Does timely help afford.

6 Then, free from pensive cares, my soul
Resume thy wonted rest;
For God has wondrously to thee
His bounteous love expressed.

7 When death alarmed me, he removed
My dangers and my fears;
My feet from falling he secured,
And dried my eyes from tears.

8 Therefore my life's remaining years,
Which God to me shall lend,
Will I, in praises to his Name,
And in his service spend.

9 In God I trusted, and of him
Did boast in greatest fear;
Though in my trouble I exclaimed,
All men are insincere.

10 O what return to God shall I
For all his goodness make?
I'll praise his Name, and with glad zeal
The cup of blessing take.

11 I'll pay my vows among his saints,
Whose blood (howe'er despised
By wicked men) in God's account
Is always highly prized.

12 To thee I'll offerings bring of praise;
And while I bless thy Name,
The just performance of my vows
To all thy saints proclaim.

13 They in Jerusalem shall meet,
And in thy house shall join
To bless thy name with one consent,
And mix their songs with mine.

---

To Father, Son, and Holy Ghost,
The God whom we adore,
Be glory, as it was, is now,
And shall be evermore.

## PSALMS 95 & 96. C. M.

NOTTINGHAM. JER. CLARKE.

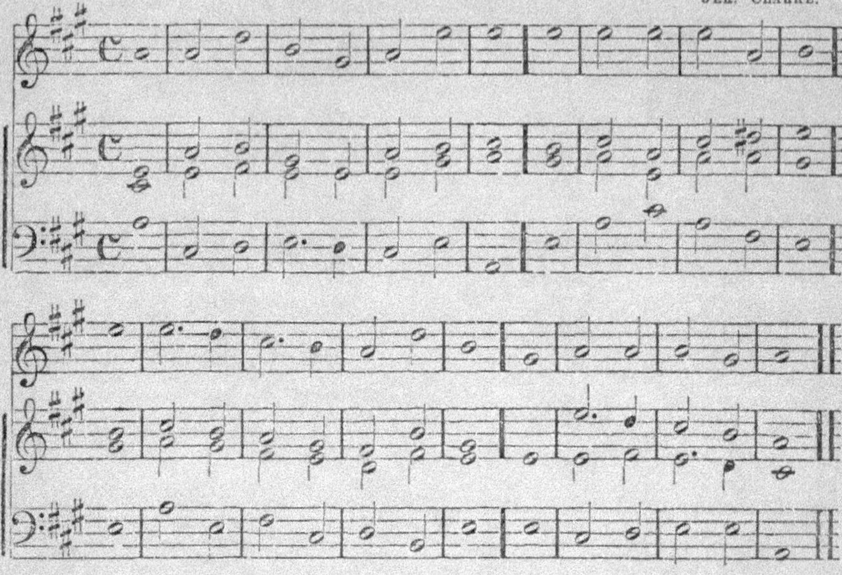

## PSALM 97, Part i. C. M.

ST. STEPHENS. W. JONES.

## PSALM 95. C. M.

From the cxvii Psalm of David.

1 WITH cheerful notes let all the earth
To heaven their voices raise;
Let all, inspired with godly mirth,
Sing solemn hymns of praise.

2 God's tender mercy knows no bound,
His truth shall ne'er decay;
Then let the willing nations round
Their grateful tribute pay.

---

To Father, Son, and Holy Ghost,
The God whom we adore,
Be glory, as it was, is now,
And shall be evermore.

## PSALM 96. C. M.

From the cxviii Psalm of David.

1 O PRAISE the Lord, for he is good,
His mercies ne'er decay;
That his kind favors ever last,
Let thankful Israel say.

2 Their sense of his eternal love
Let Aaron's house express;
And that it never fails, let all
That fear the Lord confess.

3 Far better 'tis to trust in God,
And have the Lord our friend,
Than on the greatest human power
For safety to depend.

4 The Lord has been my help; the praise
To him alone belongs;
He is my Saviour and my strength,
He only claims my songs.

5 Joy fills the dwelling of the just,
Whom God has saved from harm;
For wondrous things are brought to pass
By his Almighty arm.

6 He, by his own resistless power,
Has endless honor won;
The saving strength of his right hand
Amazing works has done.

7 God will not suffer me to fall,
But still prolongs my days;
That, by declaring all his works,
I may advance his praise.

8 When God had sorely me chastised
'Till quite of hopes bereaved,
His mercy from the gates of death
My fainting life reprieved.

9 Then open wide the temple gates
To which the just repair,
That I may enter in and praise
My great deliverer there.

10 Within those gates of God's abode
To which the righteous press,
Since thou hast heard and set me safe
Thy holy Name I'll bless.

11 That which the builders once refused
Is now the corner-stone;
This is the wondrous work of God,
The work of God alone.

12 This day is God's; let all the land
Exalt their cheerful voice:
"Lord we beseech thee, save us now
And make us still rejoice."

13 Him that approaches in God's name
Let all the assembly bless;—
"We that belong to God's own house
Have wished you good success."

14 God is the Lord, through whom we all,
Both light and comfort find;
Fast to the altar's horns with cords
The chosen victim bind.

15 Thou art my Lord, O God, and still
I'll praise thy holy Name,
Because thou only art my God,
I'll celebrate thy fame.

16 O then with me give thanks to God,
Who still does gracious prove;
And let the tribute of our praise
Be endless as his love.

---

To Father, Son, and Holy Ghost,
The God whom we adore,
Be glory, as it was, is now,
And shall be evermore.

## PSALM 97.

From the cxix Psalm of David.

### PART I. ALEPH. C. M.

1 How blessed are they who always keep
The pure and perfect way;
Who never from the sacred paths
Of God's commandments stray!

2 How blessed, who to his righteous laws
Have still obedient been;
And have, with fervent, humble zeal,
His favor sought to win!

3 Such men their utmost caution use
To shun each wicked deed;
But in the path which he directs
With constant care proceed.

4 Thou strictly hast enjoined us, Lord,
To learn thy sacred will;
And all our diligence employ
Thy statutes to fulfill.

5 O then that thy most holy will
Might o'er my ways preside;
And I the course of all my life
By thy direction guide!

6 Then with assurance should I walk,
From all confusion free;
Convinced, with joy, that all my ways
With thy commands agree.

7 My upright heart shall my glad mouth
With cheerful praises fill,
When, by thy righteous judgments taught
I shall have learned thy will.

8 So to thy sacred laws shall I
Entire observance pay:
O then, forsake me not, my God,
Nor cast me quite away!

---

*To Father, Son, and Holy Ghost, etc.*

## PSALM 97, Part ii. C. M.

MANCHESTER. DR. WAINWRIGHT.

## PSALM 97, Part iii. C. M

MARTYRDOM. R. BINFIELD.

## PSALM 97.

### PART II. BETH. C. M.

1 How shall the young preserve their ways
From all pollution free?
By making still their course of life
With thy commands agree.

2 With hearty zeal for thee I seek,
To thee for succor pray;
O suffer not my careless steps
From thy right paths to stray.

3 Safe in my heart, and closely hid,
Thy word, my treasure, lies,
To succor me with timely aid
When sinful thoughts arise.

4 Secured by that, my grateful soul
Shall ever bless thy name;
O teach me then by thy just laws
My future life to frame.

5 My lips, unlocked by pious zeal,
To others have declared
How well the judgments of thy mouth
Deserve our best regard.

6 While in the way of thy commands
More solid joy I found,
Than had I been with vast increase
Of envied riches crowned.

7 Therefore thy just and upright laws
Shall always fill my mind;
And those sound rules which thou prescrib'st,
Entire respect shall find.

8 To keep thy statutes undefaced
Shall be my constant joy,
The strict remembrance of thy word
Shall all my thoughts employ.

---

To Father, Son, and Holy Ghost,
The God whom we adore,
Be glory, as it was, is now,
And shall be evermore.

### PART III. GIMEL. C. M.

1 Be gracious to thy servant, Lord;
Do thou my life defend,
That I, according to thy word,
My time to come may spend.

2 Enlighten both my eyes and mind,
That so I may discern
The wondrous things which they behold,
Who thy just precepts learn.

3 My fainting soul is almost pined
With earnest longing spent,
While always on the eager search
Of thy just will intent.

4 Thy sharp rebuke shall crush the proud,
Whom still thy curse pursues;
Since they to walk in thy right ways
Presumptuously refuse.

5 But far from me do thou, O Lord,
Contempt and shame remove;
For I thy sacred laws affect
With undissembled love.

6 For thy commands have always been
My comfort and delight;
By them I learn with prudent care
To guide my steps aright.

---

To Father, Son, and Holy Ghost,
The God whom we adore,
Be glory, as it was, is now,
And shall be evermore.

## PSALM 97, Part iv. C. M.

COVENTRY. DR. HOWARD.

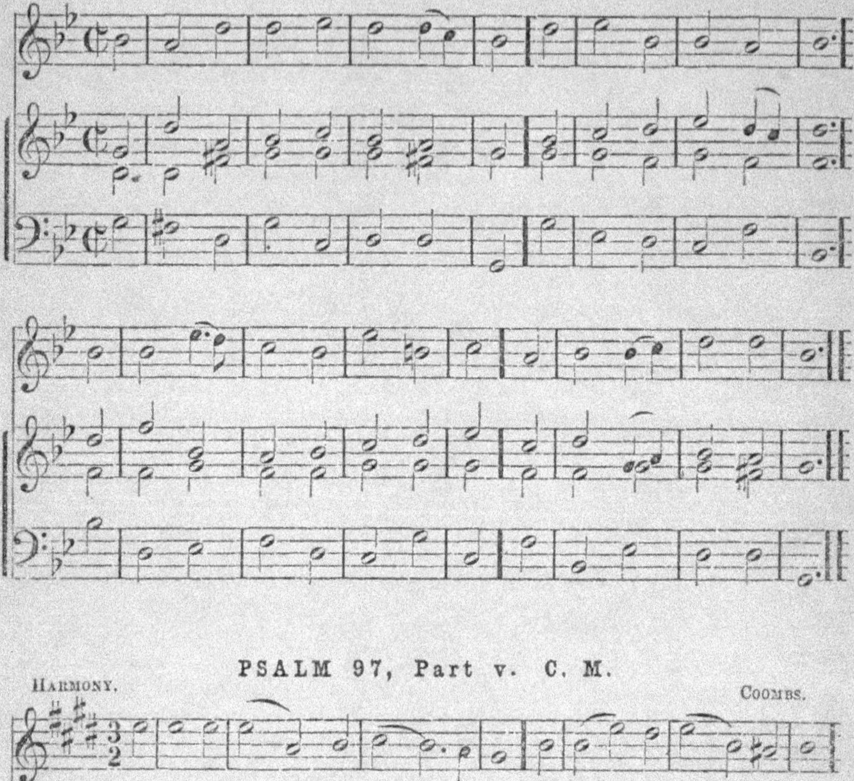

## PSALM 97, Part v. C. M.

HARMONY. COOMBS.

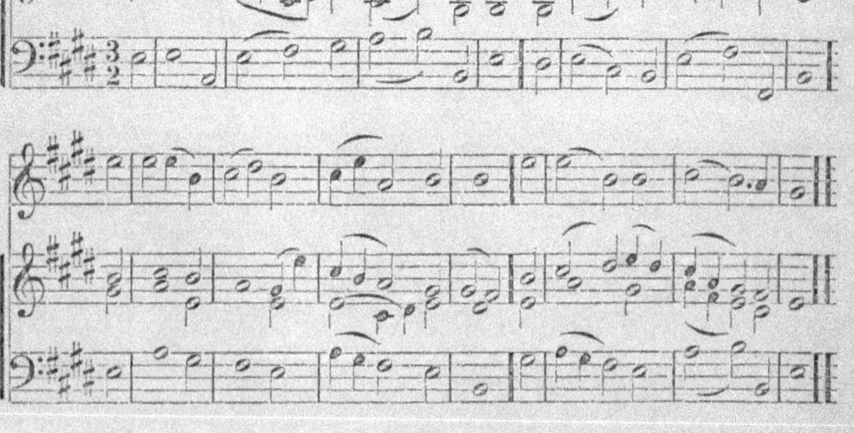

## PSALM 97.

### PART IV. DALETH. C. M.

1 My soul, oppressed with deadly care,
Close to the dust doth cleave;
Revive me, Lord, and let me now
Thy promised aid receive.

2 To thee I still declared my ways,
And thou inclinedst thine ear;
O teach me, then, my future life
By thy just laws to steer.

3 If thou wilt make me know thy laws,
And by their guidance walk,
The wondrous works which thou hast done
Shall be my constant talk.

4 But see, my soul within me sinks,
Pressed down with weighty care;
Do thou, according to thy word,
My wasted strength repair.

5 Far, far from me be all false ways
And lying arts removed;
But kindly grant I still may keep
The path by thee approved.

6 Thy faithful ways, thou God of truth,
My happy choice I've made;
Thy judgments, as my rule of life,
Before me always laid.

7 My care has been to make my life
With thy commands agree;
O then preserve thy servant, Lord,
From shame and ruin free.

8 So in the way of thy commands
Shall I with pleasure run;
And, with a heart enlarged with joy,
Successfully go on.

---

To Father, Son, and Holy Ghost,
The God whom we adore,
Be glory, as it was, is now,
And shall be evermore.

### PART V. HE. C. M.

1 Instruct me in thy statutes, Lord,
Thy righteous paths display;
And I from them, through all my life,
Will never go astray.

2 If thou true wisdom from above
Wilt graciously impart,
To keep thy perfect laws I will
Devote my zealous heart.

3 Direct me in the sacred ways
To which thy precepts lead;
Because my chief delight has been
Thy righteous paths to tread.

4 Do thou to thy most just commands
Incline my willing heart;
Let no desire of worldly wealth
From thee my thoughts divert.

5 From those vain objects turn mine eyes,
Which this false world displays;
But give me lively power and strength
To keep thy righteous ways.

6 Confirm the promise of thy word,
And give thy servant aid,
Who to transgress thy sacred laws
Is awfully afraid.

7 The censure and reproach I fear
In mercy, Lord, remove;
For all the judgments thou ordain'st
Are full of grace and love.

8 Thou know'st how after thy commands
My longing heart does pant;
O then make haste to raise me up,
And promised succor grant.

---

To Father, Son, and Holy Ghost,
The God whom we adore,
Be glory, as it was, is now,
And shall be evermore.

## PSALM 97. Part vi & vii. C. M.

LANCASTER. DR. HOWARD.

## PSALM 97, Part viii. C. M.

MANCHESTER. DR. WAINWRIGHT.

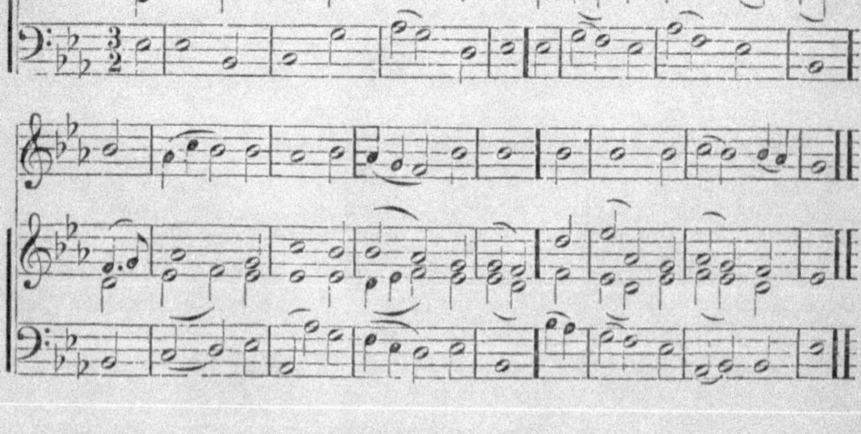

## PSALM 97.

### PART VI. VAU. C. M.

1 Thy constant blessing, Lord, bestow,
To cheer my drooping heart;
To me, according to thy word,
Thy saving health impart.

2 So shall I, whosoe'er upbraids,
This ready answer make:
"In God I trust, who never will
His faithful promise break."

3 Then let not quite the word of truth
Be from my mouth removed,
Since still my ground of steadfast hope
Thy judgments, Lord, have proved.

4 So I to keep thy righteous laws
Will all my study bend;
And constantly my time to come
In their observance spend.

5 My soul shall gladly walk at large,
From all oppression free,
Since I resolve to make my life
With thy commands agree.

6 My longing heart and ravished soul
Shall both o'erflow with joy,
When in thy loved commandments I
My happy hours employ.

7 Then will I to thy holy laws
Lift up my willing hands;
My care and business then shall be
To study thy commands.

---

To Father, Son, and Holy Ghost,
The God whom we adore,
Be glory, as it was, is now,
And shall be evermore.

### PART VII. ZAIN. C. M.

1 According to thy promised grace,
Thy favor, Lord, extend;
Make good to me the word on which
Thy servant's hopes depend.

2 That only comfort in distress
Did all my griefs control;
Thy word, when troubles hemmed me round,
Revived my fainting soul.

3 Thy judgments, then, of ancient date
I quickly called to mind,
Till, ravished with such thoughts, my soul
Did speedy comfort find.

4 Thy name, that cheered my heart by day,
Has filled my thoughts by night;
I then resolved by thy just laws
To guide my steps aright.

5 That peace of mind which has my soul
In deep distress sustained,
By strict obedience to thy will
I happily obtained.

---

To Father, Son, and Holy Ghost,
The God whom we adore,
Be glory, as it was, is now,
And shall be evermore.

### PART VIII. CHETH. C. M.

1 O Lord my God, my portion thou
And sure possession art;
Thy words I steadfastly resolve
To treasure in my heart.

2 With all the strength of warm desire
I did thy grace implore;
Disclose, according to thy word,
Thy mercy's boundless store.

3 With deep reflection and strict care
On all my ways I thought;
And so, reclaimed to thy just paths
My wandering steps I brought.

4 Prolonging not the time, my soul
Resolved, without delay,
To watch, that I might never more
From thy commandments stray.

5 To such as fear thy holy name
Myself I closely join—
To all who their obedient wills
To thy commands resign.

6 O'er all the earth thy mercy, Lord,
Abundantly is shed;
O grant that I may truly learn
Thy sacred paths to tread.

---

To Father, Son, and Holy Ghost,
The God whom we adore,
Be glory, as it was, is now,
And shall be evermore.

## PSALM 97. Part ix & x. C. M.

ST. GREGORY. WAINWRIGHT.

## PSALM 97, Part xi. C. M.

MARLAY. WEYMAN.

## PSALM 97.

### PART IX. TETH. C. M.

1 With me, thy servant, thou hast dealt
Most graciously, O Lord;
Repeated benefits bestowed,
According to thy word.

2 Teach me the sacred skill by which
Right judgment is attained,
Who in belief of thy commands
Have steadfastly remained.

3 Before affliction stopped my course,
My footsteps went astray;
But I have since been disciplined
Thy precepts to obey.

4 Thou art, O Lord, supremely good,
And all thou dost is so;
On me, thy statutes to discern,
Thy saving skill bestow.

5 'T is good for me that I have felt
Affliction's chastening rod,
That I may duly learn and keep
The statutes of my God.

6 The law that from thy mouth proceeds,
Of more esteem I hold
Than richest mines, than thousand mines
Of silver and of gold.

---

To Father, Son, and Holy Ghost,
The God whom we adore,
Be glory, as it was, is now,
And shall be evermore.

### PART X. JOD. C. M.

1 To me, who am the workmanship,
Of thy almighty hands,
The heavenly understanding give
To learn thy just commands.

2 My preservation, to thy saints
Strong comfort will afford,
To see success attend my hopes,
Who trusted in thy word.

3 That right thy judgments are, I now
By sure experience see:
And that in faithfulness, O Lord,
Thou hast afflicted me.

4 O let thy tender mercy now
Afford me needful aid;
According to thy promise, Lord,
To me, thy servant, made.

5 To me thy saving grace restore,
That I again may live;
Whose soul can relish no delight
But what thy precepts give.

6 In thy blest statutes let my heart
Continue always sound;
That guilt and shame, the sinner's lot,
May never me confound.

---

To Father, Son, and Holy Ghost,
The God whom we adore,
Be glory, as it was, is now,
And shall be evermore.

### PART XI. CAPH. C. M.

1 My soul, with long expectance, faints
To see thy saving grace;
Yet still on thy unerring word
My confidence I place.

2 My very eyes consume and fail
With waiting for thy word;
O when wilt thou thy kind relief
And promised aid afford?

3 Thy wonted kindness, Lord, restore
My drooping heart to cheer;
That by thy righteous statutes, I
My life's whole course may steer.

---

To Father, Son, and Holy Ghost,
The God whom we adore,
Be glory, as it was, is now,
And shall be evermore.

## PSALM 97, Part xii & xiii. C. M.

ST. GREGORY. WAINWRIGHT.

## PSALM 97. Part xiv & xv. C. M.

MATLACK. NOVELLO.

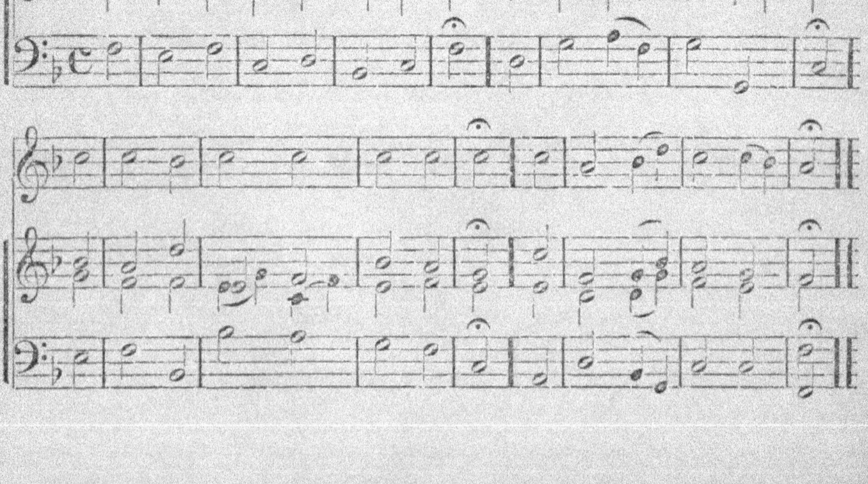

## PSALM 97.

### PART XII. LAMED. C. M.

1 For ever and for ever, Lord,
Unchanged thou dost remain;
Thy word, established in the heavens,
Does all their orbs sustain.

2 Through circling ages, Lord, thy truth,
Immovable shall stand,
As doth the earth, which thou uphold'st
By thine almighty hand.

3 All things the course by thee ordained
E'en to this day fulfill;
They are the faithful subjects all,
And servants of thy will.

4 Unless thy sacred law had been
My comfort and delight,
I must have fainted, and expired
In dark affliction's night.

5 Thy precepts, therefore, from my thoughts
Shall never, Lord, depart;
For thou by them hast to new life
Restored my dying heart.

6 I've seen an end of what we call
Perfection here below;
But thy commandments, like thyself,
No change or period know.

To Father, Son, and Holy Ghost,
The God whom we adore,
Be glory, as it was, is now,
And shall be evermore.

### PART XIII. MEM. C. M.

1 The love that to thy laws I bear
No language can display;
They with fresh wonder entertain
My raptured thoughts all day.

2 My feet with care I have refrained
From every sinful way,
That to thy sacred word I might
Entire obedience pay.

3 I have not from thy judgments strayed,
By vain desires misled;
For, Lord, thou hast instructed me
Thy righteous paths to tread.

4 How sweet are all thy words to me;
O what divine repast!
How much more grateful to my soul
Than honey to my taste!

5 Taught by thy sacred precepts, I
With heavenly skill am blest;
Through which the treach'rous ways of sin
I utterly detest.

To Father, Son, and Holy Ghost,
The God whom we adore,
Be glory, as it was, is now,
And shall be evermore.

### PART XIV. NUN. C. M.

1 Thy word is to my feet a lamp,
The way of truth to show;
A watch-light to point out the path
In which I ought to go.

2 I've vowed, and from my covenant, Lord,
Will never start aside,
That in thy righteous judgments I
Will steadfastly abide.

3 Let still my sacrifice of praise
With thee acceptance find;
And in thy righteous judgments, Lord,
Instruct my willing mind.

4 Thy testimonies I have made
My heritage and choice;
For they, when other comforts fail,
My drooping heart rejoice.

5 My heart with early zeal began
Thy statutes to obey;
And, till my course of life is done,
Shall keep thine upright way.

*To Father, Son, and Holy Ghost, etc.*

### PART XV. SAMECH. C. M.

1 Deceitful thoughts and practices
I utterly detest;
But to thy law affection bear,
Too great to be expressed.

2 My hiding-place, my refuge-tower,
And shield art thou, O Lord;
I firmly anchor all my hopes
On thy unerring word.

3 Away from me, ye wicked men,
Approach to my abode;
For firmly I resolve to keep
The precepts of my God.

4 According to thy gracious word
From danger set me free;
Nor make me of those hopes ashamed,
That I repose on thee.

*To Father, Son, and Holy Ghost, etc.*

## PSALM 97. Part xvi. C. M.

St. Mary's. Croft or Blow.

## PSALM 97, Part xvii & xviii. C. M.

St. Alban's. Croft.

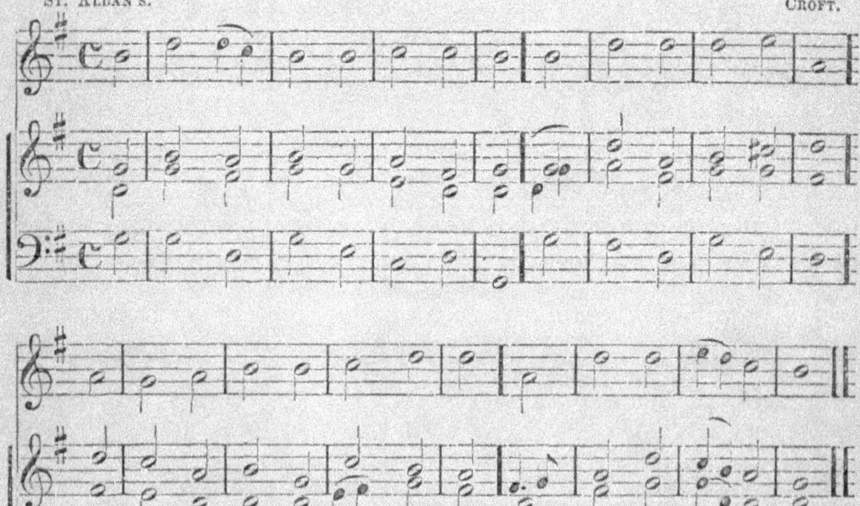

## PSALM 97.

### PART XVI. AIN. C. M.

1 MINE eyes, alas! begin to fail,
In long expectance held;
Till thy salvation they behold
And righteous word fulfilled.

2 To me, thy servant in distress,
Thy wonted grace display,
And discipline my willing heart
Thy statutes to obey.

3 On me, devoted to thy fear,
Thy sacred skill bestow,
That of thy testimonies I
The full extent may know.

4 Thy laws and precepts I account
In all respects divine;
They teach me to discern the right,
And all false ways decline.

---

To Father, Son, and Holy Ghost,
The God whom we adore,
Be glory, as it was, is now,
And shall be evermore.

### PART XVII. PE. C. M.

1 THE wonders which thy laws contain
No words can represent;
Therefore to learn and practice them
My zealous heart is bent.

2 The very entrance to thy word
Celestial light displays,
And knowledge of true happiness
To simplest minds conveys.

3 With eager hopes I waiting stood,
And fainting with desire,
That of thy wise commands I might
The sacred skill acquire.

4 With favor, Lord, look down on me,
Who thy relief implore,
As thou art wont to visit those
Who thy blest name adore.

5 Directed by thy heavenly word
Let all my footsteps be;
Nor wickedness of any kind
Dominion have o'er me.

6 On me, devoted to thy fear,
Lord, make thy face to shine;
Thy statutes, both to know and keep,
My heart with zeal incline.

---

To Father, Son, and Holy Ghost,
The God whom we adore,
Be glory, as it was, is now,
And shall be evermore.

### PART XVIII. TSADDI. C. M.

1 THOU art the righteous Judge, in whom
Wronged innocence may trust;
And, like thyself, thy judgments, Lord,
In all respects are just.

2 Most just and true those statutes were
Which thou didst first decree;
And all with faithfulness performed
Succeeding times shall see.

3 Lord! each neglected word of thine,
Howe'er by men despised,
Is pure, and for eternal truth
By me, thy servant, prized.

4 Thy righteousness shall then endure
When time itself is past;
Thy law is truth itself, that truth
Which shall for ever last.

5 Though trouble, anguish, doubts and dread,
To compass me unite;
Beset with danger, still I make
Thy precepts my delight.

6 Eternal and unerring rules
Thy testimonies give;
Teach me the wisdom that will make
My soul for ever live.

---

To Father, Son, and Holy Ghost,
The God whom we adore,
Be glory, as it was, is now,
And shall be evermore.

## PSALM 97, Part xix & xx. C. M.

COVENTRY. DR. HOWARD.

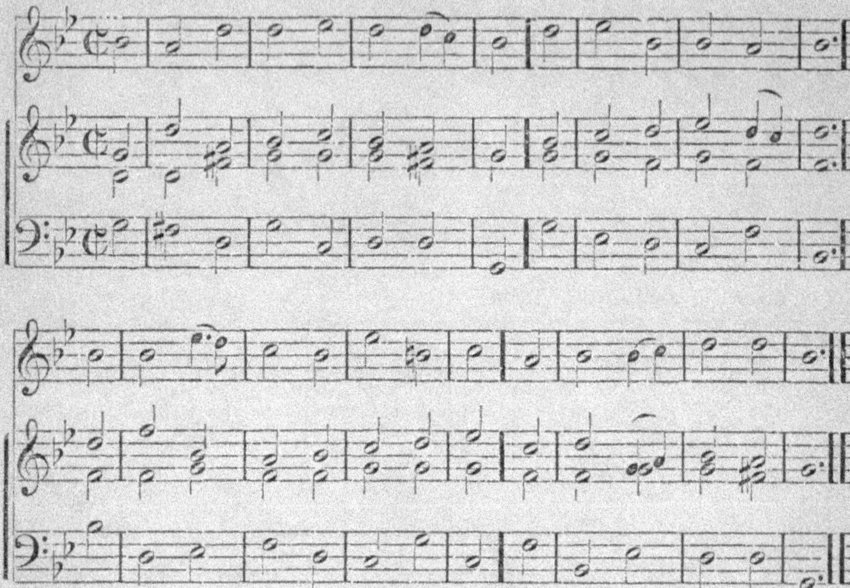

## PSALM 97, Part xxi. C. M.

CONSOLATION. T. ADAMS.

## PSALM 97.

### PART XIX. KOPH. C. M.

1 With my whole heart to God I called—
Lord, hear my earnest cry;
And I thy statutes to perform
Will all my care apply.

2 Again more fervently I prayed—
O save me, that I may
Thy testimonies fully know,
And steadfastly obey.

3 My earlier prayer the dawning day
Prevented, while I cried
To him upon whose faithful word
My hope alone relied.

4 Lord, hear my supplicating voice,
And wonted favor show;
O quicken me, and so approve
Thy judgments ever true.

5 Concerning thy divine commands
My soul has known, of old,
That they were true, and shall their truth
To endless ages hold.

---

To Father, Son, and Holy Ghost,
The God whom we adore,
Be glory, as it was, is now,
And shall be evermore.

## PSALM 97.

### PART XX. RESCH. C. M.

1 Consider my affliction, Lord,
And me from bondage draw;
Think on thy servant in distress,
Who ne'er forgets thy law.

2 Defend my cause, and me to save
Thy timely aid afford;
With beams of mercy quicken me,
According to thy word.

3 From hardened sinners thou removest
Salvation far away;
'T is just thou should withdraw from them
Who from thy statutes stray.

4 Since great thy tender mercies are
To all who thee adore;
According to thy judgments, Lord,
My fainting hopes restore.

5 Consider, O my gracious God,
How I thy precepts love;
O therefore quicken me with beams
Of mercy from above.

6 As from the birth of time, thy truth
Has held through ages past,
So shall thy righteous judgments firm
To endless ages last.

---

To Father, Son, and Holy Ghost,
The God whom we adore,
Be glory, as it was, is now,
And shall be evermore.

### PART XXI. SCHIN. C. M.

1 Thy sacred word my joyful breast
With heavenly rapture warms;
Nor conquest, nor the spoils of war,
Have such transporting charms.

2 Perfidious practices and lies
I utterly detest;
But to thy laws affection bear
Too vast to be expressed.

3 Seven times a day, with grateful voice,
Thy praises I resound,
Because I find thy judgments all
With truth and justice crowned.

4 Secure, substantial peace have they
Who truly love thy law;
No smiling mischief them can tempt,
Nor frowning danger awe.

5 For thy salvation I have hoped,
And though so long delayed,
With cheerful zeal and anxious care
All thy commands obeyed.

6 Thy testimonies I have kept,
And constantly obeyed;
Because the love I bore to them
Thy service easy made.

7 From strict observance of thy laws
I never yet withdrew;
Convinced that my most secret ways
Are open to thy view.

---

To Father, Son, and Holy Ghost,
The God whom we adore,
Be glory, as it was, is now,
And shall be evermore.

## PSALM 97, Part xxii. C. M

ST. ASAPH'S. NOVELLO.

## PSALM 98. C. M.

BYZANTIUM. JACKSON.

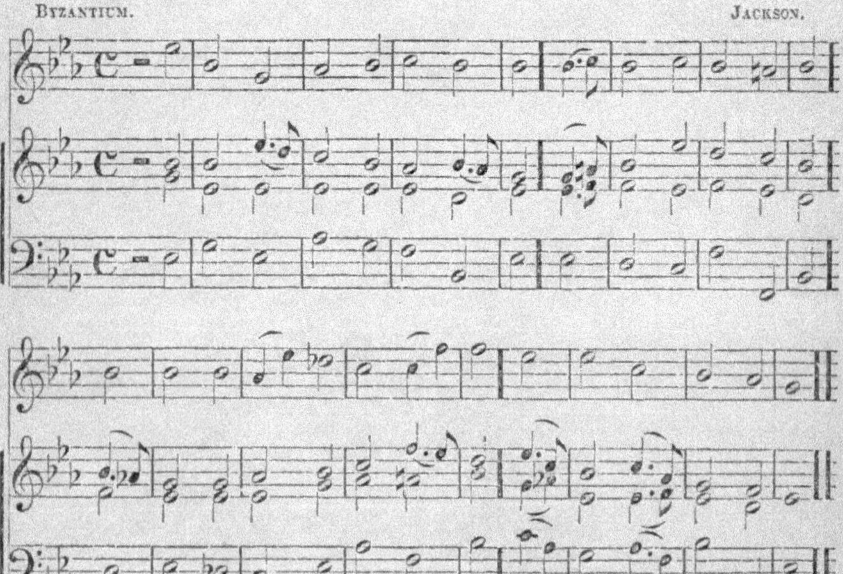

### PSALM 97.

PART XXII. TAU. C. M.

1 To my request and earnest cry
Attend, O gracious Lord;
Inspire my heart with heavenly skill,
According to thy word.

2 Let my repeated prayer at last
Before thy throne appear;
According to thy plighted word,
For my relief draw near.

3 Then shall my grateful lips return
The tribute of their praise,
When thou thy counsels hast revealed,
And taught me thy just ways.

4 My tongue the praises of thy word
Shall thankfully resound;
For thy commands are right, thy laws
With truth and justice crowned.

5 Let thy almighty arm appear,
And bring me timely aid;
For I the laws thou hast ordained,
My heart's free choice have made.

6 My soul has waited long to see
Thy saving grace restored;
Nor comfort knew, but what thy laws,
Thy heavenly laws, afford.

7 Prolong my life, that I may sing
My great Restorer's praise;
Whose justice, from the depths of woe,
My fainting soul shall raise.

8 Though like a sheep that 's lost I 've strayed,
And from thy ways declined,
Do thou, O Lord, thy servant seek,
Who keeps thy laws in mind.

---

To Father, Son, and Holy Ghost,
The God whom we adore,
Be glory, as it was, is now,
And shall be evermore.

### PSALM 98. C. M.

From the cxxi Psalm of David.

1 To Sion's hill I lift my eyes,
From thence expecting aid;
From Sion's hill and Sion's God,
Who heaven and earth has made.

2 He will not let thy foot be moved,
Thy guardian will not sleep;
Behold, the God who slumbers not
Will favored Israel keep.

3 Sheltered beneath th' Almighty's wings,
Thou shalt securely rest,
Where neither sun nor moon shall thee
By day or night molest.

4 From common accidents of life
The Lord shall guard thee still;
'T is even he that shall preserve
Thy soul from every ill.

5 At home, abroad, in peace, in war,
Thy God shall thee defend;
Conduct thee through life's pilgrimage,
Safe to thy journey's end.

---

To Father, Son, and Holy Ghost,
The God whom we adore,
Be glory, as it was, is now,
And shall be evermore.

## PSALM 99. C. M.

RICHMOND. DR. HAWEIS.

## PSALM 100. C. M.

LANCASTER. DR. HOWARD.

### PSALM 99. C. M.

From the cxxii Psalm of David.

1 O 'TWAS a joyful sound to hear
Our tribes devoutly say:
Up, Israel; to the temple haste,
And keep your festal day!

2 At Salem's courts we must appear,
With our assembled powers,
In strong and beauteous order ranged,
Like her united towers.

3 'T is thither, by divine command,
The tribes of God repair,
Before his ark, to celebrate
His name with praise and prayer.

4 O, ever pray for Salem's peace;
For they shall prosp'rous be,
Thou holy city of our God,
Who bear true love to thee.

5 May peace within thy sacred walls
A constant guest be found;
With plenty and prosperity
Thy palaces be crowned.

6 For my dear brethren's sake, and friends
No less than brethren dear,
I'll pray—May peace in Salem's towers
A constant guest appear.

7 But most of all, I'll seek thy good,
And ever wish thee well,
For Sion and the temple's sake,
Where God vouchsafes to dwell.

---

To Father, Son, and Holy Ghost,
The God whom we adore,
Be glory, as it was, is now,
And shall be evermore.

### PSALM 100. C. M.

From the cxxiv Psalm of David.

1 HAD not the Lord, may Israel say,
On Israel's side engaged,
The foe had quickly swallowed us,
So furiously he raged.

2 Had not the Lord himself vouchsafed
To check his fierce control,
The adversary's dreary flood
Had overwhelmed our soul.

3 But praised be our eternal Lord,
Who left us not his prey;
The snare is broke, his rage disarmed,
And we again are free.

4 Secure in God's almighty name
Our confidence remains;
The God who made both heaven and earth,
Of both sole monarch reigns.

---

To Father, Son, and Holy Ghost,
The God whom we adore,
Be glory, as it was, is now,
And shall be evermore.

## PSALM 101. C. M.

TIVERTON. GRIGG.

## PSALMS 102 & 103. C. M.

BEDFORD. WHEALL.

### PSALM 101. C. M.

From the cxxv Psalm of David.

1 Who place on Sion's God their trust,
Like Sion's rock shall stand;
Like her immovably be fixed
By his almighty hand.

2 Look how the hills on every side
Jerusalem enclose;
So stands the Lord around his saints
To guard them from their foes.

3 Be good, O righteous God, to those
Who righteous deeds affect;
The heart that innocence retains,
Let innocence protect.

4 All those who walk in crooked paths,
The Lord shall soon destroy;
Cut off the unjust, but crown the saint
With lasting peace and joy.

---

To Father, Son, and Holy Ghost,
The God whom we adore,
Be glory, as it was, is now,
And shall be evermore.

### PSALM 102. C. M.

From the cxxvii Psalm of David.

1 We build with fruitless cost, unless
The Lord the pile sustain;
Unless the Lord the city keep,
The watchman wakes in vain.

2 In vain we rise before the day,
And late to rest repair,
Allow no respite to our toil,
And eat the bread of care.

3 Supplies of life, with ease to them,
He on his saints bestows;
He crowns their labors with success,
Their nights with safe repose.

---

To Father, Son, and Holy Ghost,
The God whom we adore,
Be glory, as it was, is now,
And shall be evermore.

### PSALM 103. C. M.

From the cxxviii Psalm of David.

1 The man is blest that fears the Lord,
Nor only worship pays,
But keeps his steps confined with care
To his appointed ways.

2 He shall upon the sweet returns
Of his own labor feed;
Without dependence live, and see
His wishes all succeed.

3 Who fears the Lord shall prosper thus;
Him Sion's God shall bless,
And grant him all his days to see
Jerusalem's success.

---

To Father, Son, and Holy Ghost,
The God whom we adore,
Be glory, as it was, is now,
And shall be evermore.

## PSALM 104. S. M.

AYLESBURY. DR. GREENE.

## PSALM 105. III 1.

STOEL. T. WALKER.

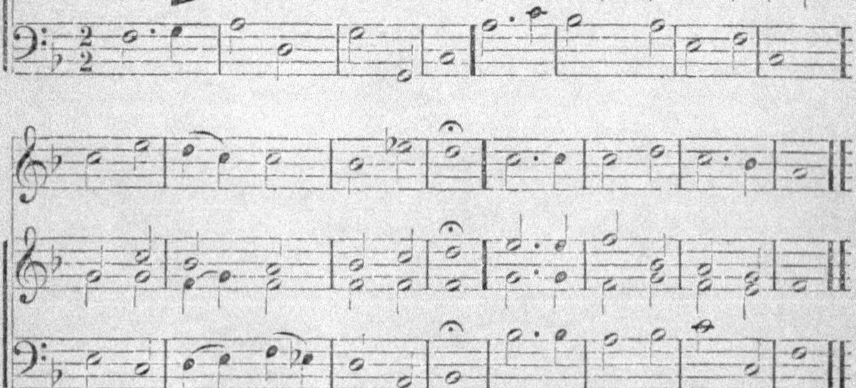

### PSALM 104. S. M.

From the cxxx Psalm of David.

1 From lowest depths of woe
To God I sent my cry;
Lord, hear my supplicating voice,
And graciously reply.

2 Should'st thou severely judge,
Who can their trial bear?
But thou forgiv'st, lest we despond,
And quite renounce thy fear.

3 My soul with patience waits
For thee, the living Lord;
My hopes are on thy promise built,
Thy never-failing word.

4 My longing eyes look out
For thy enlivening ray,
More duly than the morning watch
To spy the dawning day.

5 Let Israel trust in God,
No bounds his mercy knows;
The plenteous source and spring from whence
Eternal succor flows:

6 Whose friendly streams to us
Supplies in want convey;
A healing spring, a spring to cleanse
And wash our guilt away.

---

To God the Father, Son,
And Spirit, glory be,
As 't was, and is, and shall be so
To all eternity.

### PSALM 105. III 1.

From the cxxxi Psalm of David.

1 Lord, for ever at thy side
Let my place and portion be:
Strip me of the robe of pride,
Clothe me with humility.

2 Meekly may my soul receive
All thy Spirit hath revealed;
Thou hast spoken—I believe,
Though the oracle be sealed.

3 Humble as a little child,
Weaned from the mother's breast,
By no subtleties beguiled,
On thy faithful word I rest.

4 Israel! now and evermore
In the Lord Jehovah trust;
Him, in all his ways adore,
Wise, and wonderful, and just.

---

Holy Father, Holy Son,
Holy Spirit, Three in One!
Glory, as of old, to Thee,
Now and evermore shall be.

## PSALM 106. C. M.

LANCASTER. DR. HOWARD.

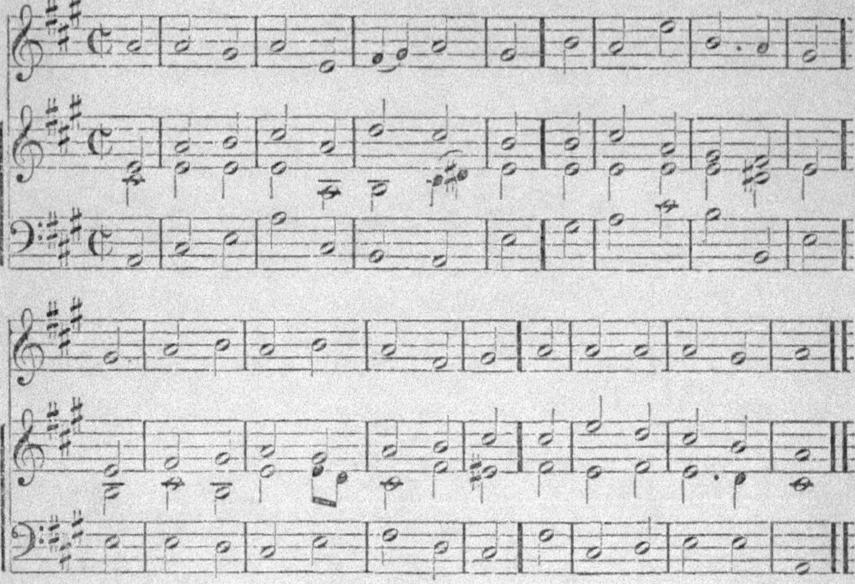

## PSALM 107. C. M.

ST. CATHARINE'S. JOS. GARNETT.

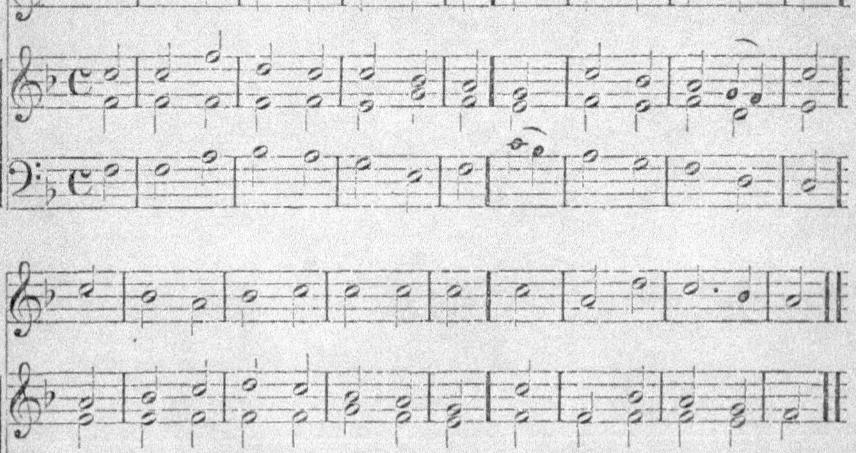

### PSALM 106. C. M.

From the cxxxii Psalm of David.

1 O WITH due reverence let us all
To God's abode repair;
And, prostrate at his footstool fall,
Pour out our humble prayer.

2 Arise, O Lord, and now possess
Thy constant place of rest;
Be that, not only with thy ark,
But with thy presence blest.

3 Clothe thou thy priests with righteousness,
Make thou thy saints rejoice;
And, for thy servant David's sake
Hear thy Anointed's voice.

4 Fair Sion does, in God's esteem,
All other seats excell;
His place of everlasting rest,
Where he desires to dwell.

5 Her store th' Almighty will increase,
Her poor with plenty bless;
Her saints shall shout for joy, her priests
His saving health confess.

---

To Father, Son, and Holy Ghost,
The God whom we adore,
Be glory, as it was, is now,
And shall be evermore.

### PSALM 107. C. M.

From the cxxxiii Psalm of David.

1 How vast must their advantage be,
How great their pleasure prove,
Who live like brethren, and consent
In offices of love!

2 True love is like the precious oil,
Which, poured on Aaron's head,
Ran down his beard, and o'er his robes
Its costly fragrance shed.

3 'Tis like refreshing dew, which does
On Herman's top distill;
Or like the early drops that fall
On Sion's favored hill.

4 For Sion in the chosen seat
Where the Almighty King
The promised blessing has ordained,
And life's eternal spring.

---

To Father, Son, and Holy Ghost,
The God whom we adore,
Be glory, as it was, is now,
And shall be evermore.

## PSALM 108. C. M.

LOUGHTON. C. WESLEY.

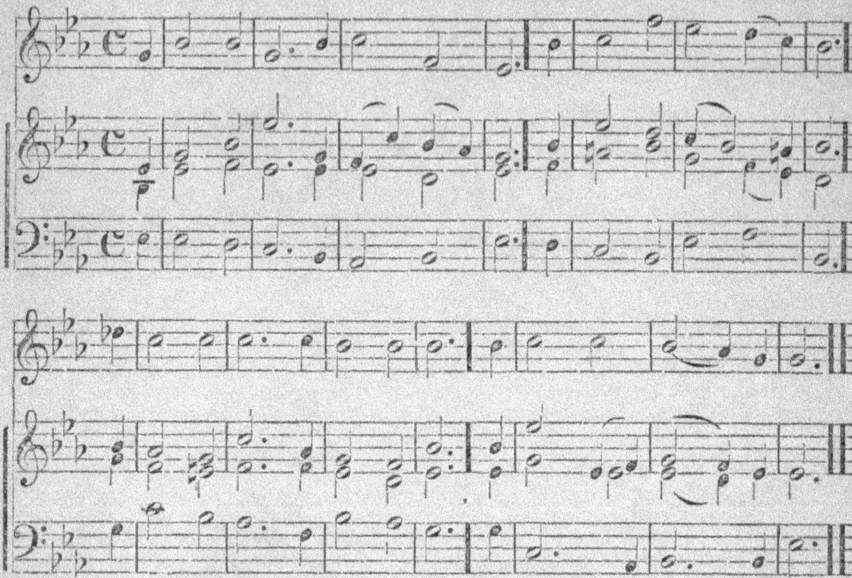

## PSALM 109. C. M.

BYZANTIUM. JACKSON.

### PSALM 108. C. M.

From the cxxxiv Psalm of David.

1 Bless God, ye servants, that attend
Upon his solemn state;
That in his temple's hallowed courts
With humble reverence wait.

2 Within his house lift up your hands,
And bless his holy Name;
From Sion bless thy Israel, Lord,
Who earth and heaven did'st frame.

---

To Father, Son, and Holy Ghost,
The God whom we adore,
Be glory, as it was, is now,
And shall be evermore.

### PSALM 109. C. M.

From the cxxxv Psalm of David.

1 O praise the Lord with one consent,
And magnify his Name;
Let all the servants of the Lord
His worthy praise proclaim.

2 Praise him, all ye that in his house
Attend with constant care;
With those that to his outmost courts
With humble zeal repair.

3 For God his own peculiar choice
The sons of Jacob makes;
And Israel's offspring for his own
Most valued treasure takes.

4 That God is great, we often have
By glad experience found:
And seen how he, with wondrous power,
Above all gods is crowned.

5 For he, with unresisted strength,
Performs his sovereign will,
In heaven and earth, and watery stores
That earth's deep caverns fill.

6 Their just returns of thanks to God
Let grateful Israel pay;
Nor let anointed Aaron's race
To bless the Lord delay.

7 Their sense of his unbounded love
Let Levi's house express;
And let all those who fear the Lord,
His name for ever bless.

8 Let all, with thanks, his wondrous works
In Sion's courts proclaim;
Let them in Salem, where he dwells,
Exalt his holy Name.

---

To Father, Son, and Holy Ghost,
The God whom we adore,
Be glory, as it was, is now,
And shall be evermore.

## PSALM 110. II 4.

ST. PHILLIPS. LEVESQUE.

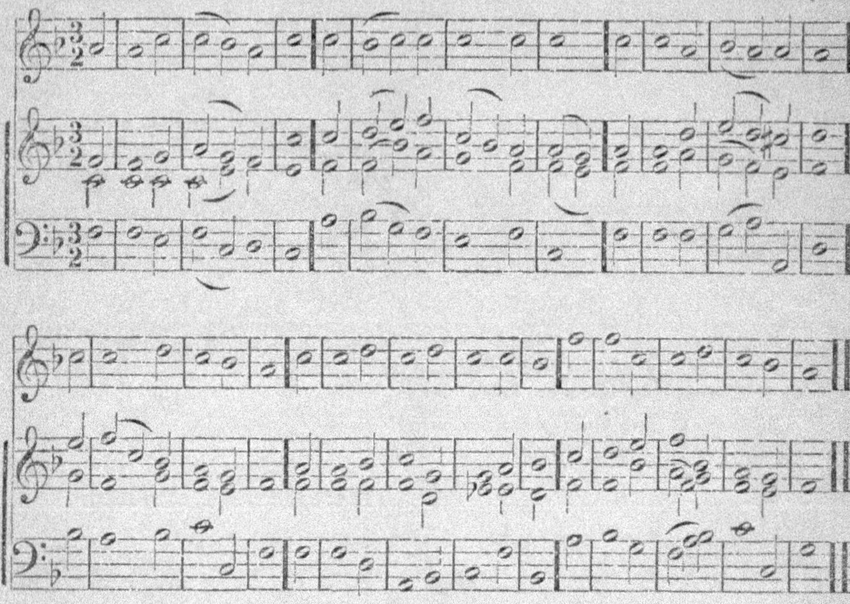

## PSALM 111. L. M.

BABYLON STREAMS. RAVENSCROFT, 1621.

## PSALM 110. H 4.

From the cxxxvi Psalm of David.

1 To God the mighty Lord,
Your joyful thanks repeat;
To him due praise afford,
As good as he is great:
For God does prove
Our constant friend;
His boundless love
Shall never end.

2 To him, whose wondrous power
All other gods obey,
Whom earthly kings adore,
Your grateful homage pay:
For God, etc.

3 By his almighty hand
Amazing works are wrought;
The heavens by his command
Were to perfection brought:
For God, etc.

4 He spread the ocean round
About the spacious land;
And bade the rising ground
Above the waters stand:
For God, etc.

5 By him the heavens display
Their numerous hosts of light,
The sun to rule by day,
The moon and stars by night:
For God, etc.

6 He in our depth of woes,
On us with favor thought;
And from our cruel foes
In peace and safety brought:
For God, etc.

7 He does the food supply
On which all creatures live;
To God who reigns on high,
Eternal praises give:
For God will prove
Our constant friend;
His boundless love
Shall never end.

---

To God, the Father, Son,
And Spirit, ever blessed,
Eternal Three in One,
All worship be addressed,
As heretofore
It was, is now,
And shall be so
For evermore.

## PSALM 111. L. M.

From the cxxxvii Psalm of David.

1 When we, our weary limbs to rest,
Sat down by proud Euphrates' stream,
We wept, with doleful thoughts opprest,
And Sion was our mournful theme.

2 Our harps that, when with joy we sung,
Were wont their tuneful parts to bear,
With silent strings neglected hung
On willow trees that withered there.

3 O Salem, our once happy seat,
When I of thee forgetful prove,
Let then my trembling hand forget
The speaking strings with art to move.

4 If I to mention thee forbear,
Perpetual silence be my doom;
Or if my chiefest joy compare
With thee, Jerusalem, my home!

---

To Father, Son, and Holy Ghost,
The God whom earth and heaven adore,
Be glory, as it was of old,
Is now, and shall be evermore.

## PSALM 112. C. M.

BEXLEY. NOVELLO.

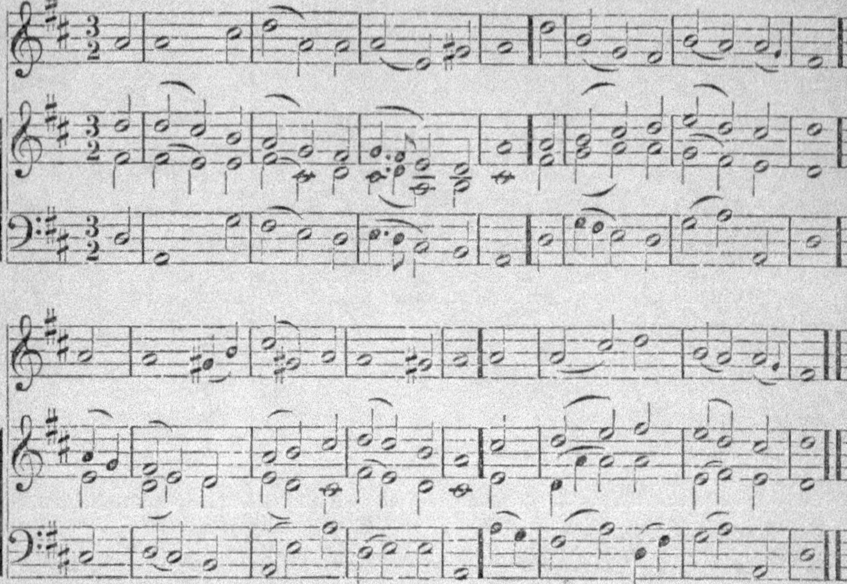

## PSALM 113. L. M.

BOWEN. HAYDN.

## PSALM 112. C. M.

From the cxxxviii Psalm of David.

1 WITH my whole heart, my God and King,
Thy praise I will proclaim;
Before the mighty I will sing,
And bless thy holy name.

2 I'll worship at thy sacred seat,
And, with thy love inspired,
The praises of thy truth repeat,
O'er all thy works admired.

3 Thou graciously inclinedst thine ear,
When I to thee did cry;
And, when my soul was pressed with fear,
Didst inward strength supply.

4 For God, although enthroned on high,
Does thence the poor respect;
The proud, far off, his scornful eye
Beholds with just neglect.

5 Though I with troubles am oppressed,
He shall my foes disarm,
Relieve my soul when most distressed,
And keep me safe from harm.

6 The Lord, whose mercies ever last,
Shall fix my happy state;
And, mindful of his favors past,
Shall his own work complete.

---

To Father, Son, and Holy Ghost,
The God whom we adore,
Be glory, as it was, is now,
And shall be evermore.

## PSALM 113. L. M.

From the cxxxix Psalm of David.

1 THOU, Lord, by strictest search hast known
My rising up and lying down;
My secret thoughts are known to thee,
Known long before conceived by me.

2 Thine eye my bed and path surveys,
My public haunts and private ways;
Thou know'st what 't is my lips would vent,
My yet unuttered words' intent.

3 Surrounded by thy power I stand,
On every side I find thy hand;
O skill for human reach too high!
Too dazzling bright for mortal eye!

4 From thy all-seeing spirit, Lord,
What hiding-place does earth afford?
O where can I thy influence shun,
Or whither from thy presence run?

5 If up to heaven I take my flight,
'T is there thou dwell'st enthroned in light;
If to the world unseen, my God,
There also hast thou thine abode.

6 If I the morning's wings could gain,
And fly beyond the western main;
E'en there, in earth's remotest land,
I still should find thy guiding hand.

7 Or should I try to shun thy sight
Beneath the sable wings of night;
One glance from thee, one piercing ray,
Would kindle darkness into day.

8 The vail of night is no disguise,
No screen from thy all-searching eyes;
Through midnight shades thou find'st thy way,
As in the blazing noon of day.

9 Thou know'st the texture of my heart,
My reins, and every vital part;
I'll praise thee, from whose hands I came,
A work of such a wondrous frame.

10 Let me acknowledge, too, O God,
That since this maze of life I trod,
Thy thoughts of love to me surmount
The power of numbers to recount.

11 Far sooner could I reckon o'er
The sands upon the ocean's shore;
Each morn, revising what I've done,
I find th' account but new begun.

12 Search, try, O God, my thoughts and heart,
If mischief lurk in any part;
Correct me where I go astray,
And guide me in thy perfect way.

---

To Father, Son, and Holy Ghost,
The God whom earth and heaven adore,
Be glory, as it was of old,
Is now, and shall be evermore.

## PSALM 114. C. M.

KENT. MORNINGTON.

## PSALM 115. C. M.

ST. MARY'S. CROFT OR BLOW.

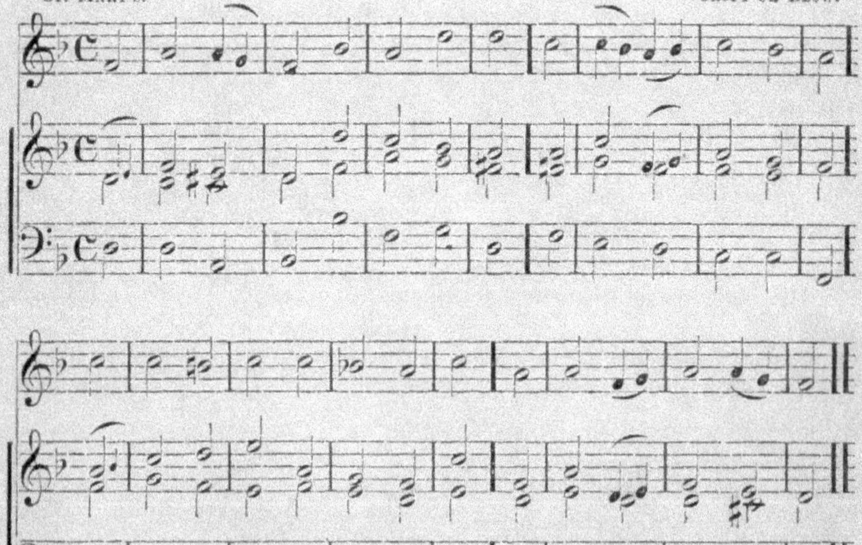

## PSALM 114. C. M.

From the cxli Psalm of David.

1 Lord, in thy sight, O let my prayer
Like morning incense rise;
My lifted hands accepted be
As evening sacrifice.

2 From hasty language curb my tongue,
And let a constant guard
Still keep the portal of my lips
With wary silence barred.

3 From wicked men's designs and deeds
My heart and hands restrain;
Nor let me share their evil works,
Or their unrighteous gain.

4 Let upright men reprove my faults,
And I shall think them kind;
Like healing oil upon my head
I their reproof shall find.

---

To Father, Son, and Holy Ghost,
The God whom we adore,
Be glory, as it was, is now,
And shall be evermore.

## PSALM 115. C. M.

From the cxliii Psalm of David.

1 Lord, hear my prayer, and to my cry
Thy wonted audience lend;
In thy accustomed faith and truth
A gracious answer send.

2 Nor at thy strict tribunal bring
Thy servant to be tried;
For in thy sight no living man
Can e'er be justified.

3 To thee my hands in humble prayer
I fervently stretch out;
My soul for thy refreshment thirsts,
Like land oppressed with drought.

4 Hear me with speed, my spirit fails;
Thy face no longer hide,
Lest I become forlorn, like them
That in the grave reside.

5 Thy kindness early let me hear,
Whose trust on thee depends;
Teach me the way where I should go,
My soul to thee ascends.

6 Do thou, O Lord, from all my foes
Preserve and set me free;
A safe retreat, a hiding-place,
My soul implores from thee.

7 Thou art my God, thy righteous will
Instruct me to obey;
Let thy good Spirit lead and keep
My soul in thy right way.

8 O, for the sake of thy great Name,
Revive my drooping heart;
For thy truth's sake, to me distressed
Thy saving health impart.

---

To Father, Son, and Holy Ghost,
The God whom we adore,
Be glory, as it was, is now,
And shall be evermore.

## PSALM 116. L. M.

ROCKINGHAM. MILLER.

## PSALM 117, Part i & ii. C. M.

LOUGHTON. C. WESLEY.

## PSALM 116. L. M.

From the cxliv Psalm of David.

1 Lord, what's in man that thou should'st love,
Or him such tender care to take?
What in his offspring could thee move
Such great account of him to make?

2 The life of man does quickly fade,
His thoughts but empty are and vain,
His days are like a flying shade,
Of whose short stay no signs remain.

3 To thee, almighty King of kings,
In new-made hymns my voice I'll raise;
And instruments of many strings
Shall help me to adore and praise.

---

To Father, Son, and Holy Ghost,
The God whom earth and heaven adore,
Be glory, as it was of old,
Is now, and shall be evermore.

## PSALM 117.

From the cxlv Psalm of David.

### PART I. C. M.

1 Thee I will bless, my God and King,
Thy endless praise proclaim;
This tribute daily I will bring,
And ever bless thy name.

2 Thou, Lord, beyond compare, art great,
And highly to be praised;
Thy majesty, with boundless hight,
Above our knowledge raised.

3 Renowned for mighty acts, thy fame
To future time extends;
From age to age thy glorious name
Successively descends.

4 While I thy glory and renown,
And wondrous works express;
The world with me thy might shall own,
And thy great power confess.

5 The praise that to thy love belongs
They shall with joy proclaim;
Thy truth of all their grateful songs
Shall be the constant theme.

6 The Lord is good; fresh acts of grace
His pity still supplies;
His anger moves with slowest pace,
His willing mercy flies.

7 Thy love through earth extends its fame,
To all thy works expressed;



These show thy praise, while thy great name
Is by thy servant blessed.

8 They, with a glorious prospect fired,
Shall of thy kingdom speak;
And thy great power, by all admired,
Their lofty subject make.

9 God's mighty works of ancient date
Shall thus to all be known;
And thus his kingdom's glorious state
In all its splendor shown.

10 His steadfast throne, from changes free,
Shall stand for ever fast;
His boundless sway no end shall see,
But time itself outlast.

---

To Father, Son, and Holy Ghost,
The God whom we adore,
Be glory, as it was, is now,
And shall be evermore.

### PART II. C. M.

1 The Lord does them support that fall,
And makes the prostrate rise;
For his kind aid all creatures call,
Who timely food supplies.

2 Whate'er their various wants require
With open hands he gives;
And so fulfills the just desire
Of every thing that lives.

3 How holy is the Lord, how just,
How righteous all his ways!
How nigh to him, who with firm trust,
For his assistance prays.

4 He grants the full desire of those
Who him with fear adore;
And will their troubles soon compose
When they his aid implore.

5 The Lord preserves all those with care
Whom grateful love employs;
But sinners, who his vengeance dare,
In justice he destroys.

6 My time to come, in praises spent,
Shall still advance his fame;
And all mankind, with one consent,
For ever bless his name.

---

To Father, Son, and Holy Ghost,
The God whom we adore,
Be glory, as it was, is now,
And shall be evermore.

## PSALM 118. III 3.

HAYDN'S HYMN. HAYDN.

## PSALM 119. C. M.

NEW CAMBRIDGE. DR. RANDALL.

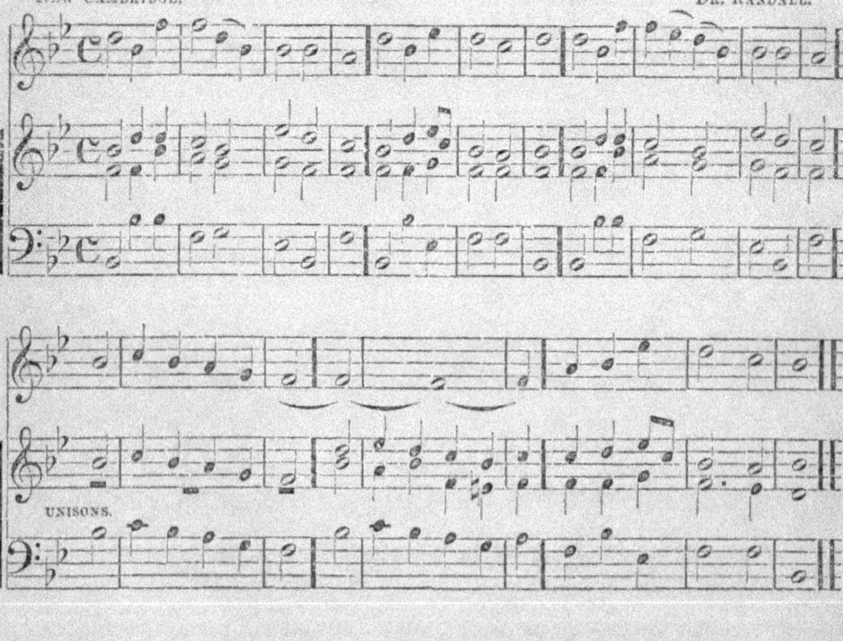

## PSALM 118. III 3.

From the cxlv Psalm of David.

1 God, my King, thy might confessing,
Ever will I bless thy Name;
Day by day thy throne addressing,
Still will I thy praise proclaim.

2 Honor great our God befitteth;
Who his majesty can reach?
Age to age his works transmitteth,
Age to age his power shall teach.

3 They shall talk of all thy glory,
On thy might and greatness dwell,
Speak of thy dread acts the story,
And thy deeds of wonder tell.

4 Nor shall fail from memory's treasure
Works by love and mercy wrought;
Works of love surpassing measure,
Works of mercy passing thought.

5 Full of kindness and compassion,
Slow to anger, vast in love,
God is good to all creation;
All his works his goodness prove.

6 All thy works, O Lord, shall bless thee,
Thee shall all thy saints adore;
King supreme shall they confess thee,
And proclaim thy sovereign power.

7 They thy might, all might excelling,
Shall to all mankind make known;
And the brightness of thy dwelling,
And the glories of thy throne.

8 Ever, God of endless praises,
Shall thy royal might remain;
Evermore thy brightness blazes,
Ever lasts thy righteous reign.

9 Them that fall the Lord protecteth,
He sustains the bowed and bent:
Every eye from thee expecteth,
Fixed on thee, its nourishment.

10 Thou to all, great God of nature,
Giv'st in season due their food;
Spread'st thy hand, and every creature
Satisfiest still with good.

11 God is just in all he doeth,
Kind is he in all his ways;
He his ready presence showeth,
When a faithful servant prays.

12 Who sincerely seek and fear him,
He to them their wish will give;
When they call, the Lord will hear them,
He will hear them, and relieve.

13 From Jehovah all who prize him
Shall his saving health enjoy:
All the wicked who despise him,
He will in their sin destroy.

14 Still, Jehovah, thee confessing,
Shall my tongue thy praise proclaim;
And may all mankind with blessing
Ever hail thy holy Name.

---

Praise the Father, earth and heaven,
Praise the Son, the Spirit praise,
As it was, and is, be given
Glory through eternal days.

## PSALM 119. C. M.

From the cxlvi Psalm of David.

1 O praise the Lord, and thou my soul,
For ever bless his Name:
His wondrous love while life shall last,
My constant praise shall claim.

2 On princes, on the sons of men,
Let none for aid rely;
They can not help, they turn to dust,
And all their counsels die.

3 Then happy he, who Jacob's God
For his protector takes;
Who still with well-placed hope, the Lord
His constant refuge makes.

4 The Lord, who made both heaven and earth,
And all that they contain
Will never quit his steadfast truth
Nor make his promise vain.

5 The poor, oppressed, from all their wrongs
Are eased by his decree;
He gives the hungry needful food,
And sets the prisoners free.

6 By him the blind receive their sight,
The weak and fall'n he rears;
With kind regard and tender love
He for the righteous cares.

7 The strangers he preserves from harm,
The orphan kindly treats;
Defends the widow, and the wiles
Of wicked men defeats.

8 The God that does in Sion dwell
Is our eternal King:
From age to age his reign endures
Let all his praises sing.

---

To Father, Son, and Holy Ghost,
The God whom we adore,
Be glory, as it was, is now,
And shall be evermore.

## PSALM. 120. II 2.

MARTIN'S LANE. DR. ARNE.

## PSALM 121, Part i. C. M.

ST. THOMAS. T. IONS.

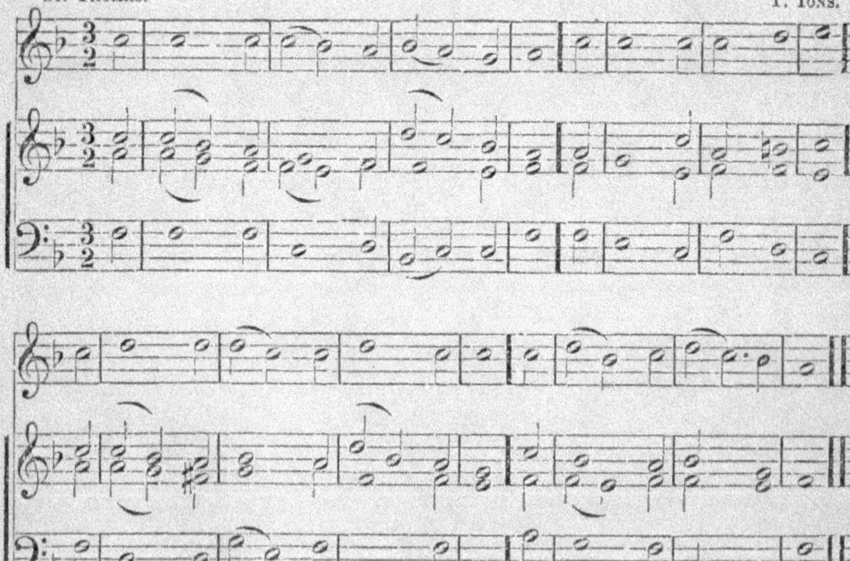

## PSALM 120. II 2.

From the cxlvi Psalm of David.

1 I'LL praise my Maker with my breath,
And when my voice is lost in death,
Praise shall employ my nobler powers;
My days of praise shall ne'er be past,
While life, and thought, and being last,
Or immortality endures.

2 Why should I place in man my trust?
E'en princes die and turn to dust,
Vain is the help of flesh and blood;
Their breath departs, their pomp and power,
And thoughts, all vanish in an hour,
Nor can they make their promise good.

3 Happy the man whose hopes rely
On Israel's God; he made the sky,
And earth, and seas, with all their train;
He saves th' oppressed, he feeds the poor;
His truth for ever stands secure,
And none shall find his promise vain.

4 The Lord gives eyesight to the blind,
The Lord supports the sinking mind;
He sends the righteous strength and peace;
He helps the stranger in distress,
The widow and the fatherless,
And to the prisoner grants release.

5 God shall the wicked overturn,
On them his wrath shall ever burn,
Sinners shall perish in their ways;
Sion! the God thy sons adore,
He, he is King for evermore;
The Lord thy God for ever praise.

---

To Father, Son, and Holy Ghost,
The God whom heaven's triumphant host
And suffering saints on earth adore;
Be glory as in ages past,
As now it is, and so shall last,
When time itself shall be no more.

## PSALM 121.

From the cxlvii Psalm of David.

### PART I. C. M.

1 O PRAISE the Lord with hymns of joy,
And celebrate his fame;
For pleasant, good, and comely 'tis
To praise his holy name.

2 His holy city God will build,
Though leveled with the ground;
Bring back his people, though dispersed,
Through all the nations round.

3 He kindly heals the broken hearts,
And all their wounds does close;
He tells the numbers of the stars,
Their several names he knows.

4 Great is the Lord, and great his power,
His wisdom has no bound;
The meek he raises, and throws down
The wicked to the ground.

5 To God the Lord a hymn of praise
With grateful voices sing;
To songs of triumph tune the harp,
And strike each warbling string.

6 He covers heaven with clouds, and thence
Refreshing rain bestows;
And on the mountains, through his care,
The grass in plenty grows.

7 His care the beasts that loosely range
With timely food supplies;
He feeds the raven's tender brood,
And stops their hungry cries.

8 The Lord to him that fears his name
His tender love extends;
To him that on his boundless grace
With steadfast hope depends.

9 Let Sion and Jerusalem
To God their praise address;
Whose strength secures their lasting gates,
Who does their children bless.

---

To Father, Son, and Holy Ghost.
The God whom we adore,
Be glory, as it was, is now,
And shall be evermore.

## PSALM 121, Part ii. L. M.

MENDON. GERMAN AIR.

## PSALM 122. II 4.

DARWELL. DARWELL.

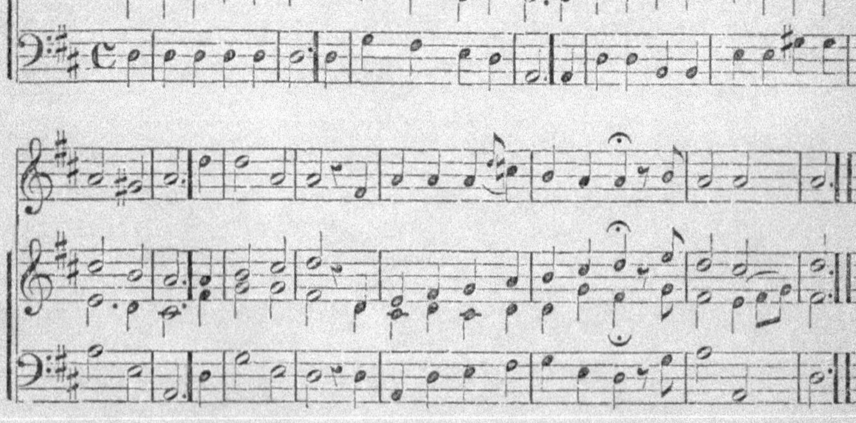

## PSALM 121.

### PART II. L. M.

1 JEHOVAH speaks ; swift from the skies
To earth the sovereign mandate flies ;
The elements confess their Lord,
With prompt obedience to his word :

2 The thick descending flakes of snow
O'er earth a fleecy mantle throw ;
And glittering frost o'er all the plains
Binds nature fast in icy chains.

3 He speaks : the ice and snow obey,
And nature's fetters melt away ;
Softly the vernal breezes blow,
And murmuring waters freely flow.

4 But nobler works his grace record :
To Israel he reveals his word ;
To them, his chosen flock, alone,
He makes his sacred precepts known.

5 Such bliss no heathen nation shares,
His oracles are only theirs :
Let Israel then their voices raise,
And bless their God in songs of praise.

---

To Father, Son, and Holy Ghost,
The God whom earth and heaven adore,
Be glory, as it was of old,
Is now, and shall be evermore.

## PSALM 122. II 4.

From the cxlviii Psalm of David.

1 YE boundless realms of joy,
Exalt your Maker's fame ;
His praise your songs employ
Above the starry frame :
Your voices raise,
Ye Cherubim
And Seraphim,
To sing his praise.

2 Thou moon, that rulest the night,
And sun, that guidest the day,
Ye glittering stars of light,
To him your homage pay :
His praise declare,
Ye heavens above,
And clouds that move
In liquid air.

3 Let them adore the Lord,
And praise his holy Name,
By whose almighty word
They all from nothing came :
And all shall last,
From changes free ;
His firm decree
Stands ever fast.

4 Let earth her tribute pay :
Praise him, ye dreadful whales,
And fish that through the sea
Glide swift with glittering scales ;
Fire, hail, and snow,
And misty air,
And winds that where
He bids them blow.

5 By hills and mountains, all
In grateful concert joined ;
By cedars stately tall,
And trees for fruit designed,
By every beast,
And creeping thing,
And fowl of wing,
His name be blest.

6 Let all of highest birth,
With those of humble name,
And judges of the earth,
His matchless praise proclaim :
In this design,
Let youths with maids,
And hoary heads
With children join.

7 United zeal be shown
His wondrous fame to raise,
Whose glorious Name alone
Deserves our endless praise :
Earth's utmost ends
His power obey ;
His glorious sway
The sky transcends.

8 His chosen saints to grace,
He sets them up on high ;
And favors Israel's race,
Who still to him are nigh ;
O therefore raise
Your grateful voice,
And still rejoice
The Lord to praise !

---

To God the Father, Son,
And Spirit, ever blessed,
Eternal Three in One,
All worship be addressed,
As heretofore,
It was, is now,
And shall be so
For evermore.

## PSALM 123. IV 1.

ST. MICHAEL'S. HANDEL.

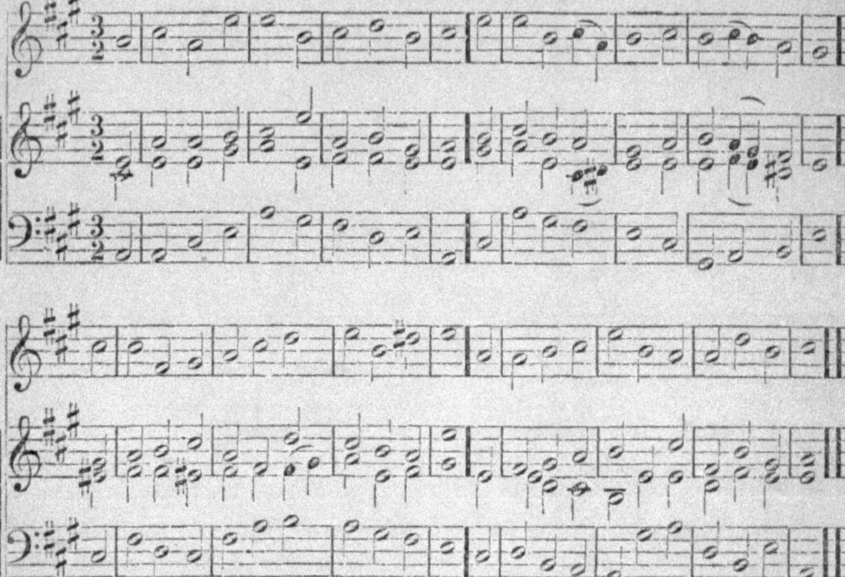

## PSALM 124. L. M.

LAUDATE. JOSH. GARNETT.

### PSALM 123. IV 1.

From the cxlix Psalm of David.

1 O PRAISE ye the Lord,
Prepare your glad voice,
His praise in the great
Assembly to sing:
In their great Creator
Let Israel rejoice;
And children of Sion
Be glad in their King.

2 Let them his great name
Extol in their songs,
With hearts well attuned,
His praises express;
Who always takes pleasure
To hear their glad tongues,
And waits with salvation
The humble to bless.

3 With glory adorned,
His people shall sing
To God, who their heads
With safety doth shield;
Such honor and triumph
His favor shall bring;
O therefore, for ever
All praise to him yield!

---

By angels in heaven
Of every degree,
And saints upon earth,
All praise be addressed.
To God in three persons,
One God ever blessed,
As it has been, now is,
And ever shall be.

### PSALM 124. L. M.

From the cl Psalm of David.

1 O PRAISE the Lord in that blest place,
From whence his goodness largely flows;
Praise him in heaven, where he his face,
Unvailed, in perfect glory shows.

2 Praise him for all the mighty acts,
Which he, in our behalf, has done;
His kindness this return exacts,
With which our praise should equal run.

3 Let the shrill trumpet's warlike voice
Make rocks and hills his praise rebound;
Praise him with harp's melodious noise,
And gentle psaltery's silver sound.

4 Let them who joyful hymns compose,
To cymbals set their songs of praise;
To well-tuned cymbals, and to those
That loudly sound on solemn days.

5 Let all that vital breath enjoy,
The breath he does to them afford,
In just returns of praise employ:
Let every creature praise the Lord!

---

To Father, Son, and Holy Ghost,
The God whom earth and heaven adore,
Be glory, as it was of old,
Is now, and shall be evermore.

# TABLE,

## TO FIND HYMNS SUITED TO PARTICULAR SUBJECTS AND OCCASIONS.

# HYMNS.

## HYMN 1. C. M.

LIVERPOOL. WAINWRIGHT.

## HYMN 2. C. M.

MANSFIELD.

## I.—THE HOLY SCRIPTURES.

### HYMN 1. C. M.

WATTS.

1 GREAT God! with wonder and with praise
On all thy works I look;
But still thy wisdom, power, and grace,
Shine brightest in thy book.

2 The stars that in their courses roll,
Have much instruction given;
But thy good word informs my soul
How I may soar to heaven.

3 The fields provide me food, and show
The goodness of the Lord;
But fruits of life and glory grow
In thy most holy word.

4 Here are my choicest treasures hid,
Here my best comfort lies;
Here my desires are satisfied,
And here my hopes arise.

5 Lord, make me understand thy law,
Show what my faults have been;
And from thy gospel let me draw
Pardon for all my sin.

6 Here would I learn how Christ has died
To save my soul from hell;
Not all the books on earth beside,
Such heavenly wonders tell.

7 Then let me love my Bible more,
And take a fresh delight
By day to read these wonders o'er,
And meditate by night.

---

To Father, Son, and Holy Ghost,
The God whom we adore,
Be glory, as it was, is now,
And shall be evermore.

### HYMN 2. C. M.

STEELE.

1 FATHER of mercies! in thy word
What endless glory shines!
For ever be thy name adored,
For these celestial lines.

2 Here may the wretched sons of want
Exhaustless riches find;
Riches above what earth can grant,
And lasting as the mind.

3 Here the fair tree of knowledge grows,
And yields a free repast;
Sublimer sweets than nature knows,
Invite the longing taste.

4 Here the Redeemer's welcome voice
Spreads heavenly peace around;
And life and everlasting joys,
Attend the blissful sound.

5 O may these heavenly pages be
My ever dear delight;
And still new beauties may I see,
And still increasing light.

6 Divine Instructor, gracious Lord!
Be thou for ever near;
Teach me to love thy sacred word,
And view my Saviour there.

---

To Father, Son, and Holy Ghost,
The God whom we adore,
Be glory, as it was, is now,
And shall be evermore.

## HYMNS 3 & 4. C. M.

HAVENS.

## HYMNS 5 & 6. II 1.

WORCESTER. HARWOOD.

## II.—CREATION.

### HYMN 3. C. M.

BROWN.

1 GREAT first of beings! mighty Lord
Of all this wondrous frame!
Produced by thy creating word,
The world from nothing came.

2 Thy voice sent forth the high command,
'Twas instantly obeyed:
And through thy goodness all things stand,
Which by thy power were made.

3 Lord, for thy glory shine the whole;
They all reflect thy light:
For this, in course the planets roll,
And day succeeds the night.

4 For this, the sun dispenses heat
And beams of cheering day;
And distant stars in order set,
By night thy power display.

5 For this the earth its produce yields;
For this, the waters flow:
And blooming plants adorn the fields,
And trees aspiring grow.

6 Inspired with praise, our minds pursue
This wise and noble end;
That all we think and all we do,
Shall to thine honor tend.

---

To Father, Son, and Holy Ghost,
The God whom we adore,
Be glory, as it was, is now,
And shall be evermore.

### HYMN 4. C. M.

Genesis I. LOGAN.

1 LET heaven arise, let earth appear,
Proclaimed th' Eternal Lord:
The heaven arose, the earth appeared,
At his creating word.

2 But formless was the earth, and void,
Dark, sluggish, and confused;
Till o'er the mass the Spirit moved,
And quickening power diffused.

3 Then spake the Lord Omnipotent
The mandate, "Be there light:"
Light darted forth in vivid rays,
And scattered ancient night.

4 The glorions firmament he spread,
To part the earth and sky;
And fixed the upper elements
Within their spheres on high.

5 He bade the seas together flow;
They left the solid land;
And herbs and plants, and fruitful trees,
Sprung forth at his command.

6 Above, he formed the stars; and placed
Two greater orbs of light;
The radiant sun to rule the day,
The moon to rule the night.

7 To all the varied living tribes
He gave their wondrous birth;
Some formed within the watery deep,
Some, from the teeming earth.

8 Then, chief o'er all his works below,
Man, honored man, was made;
His soul with God's pure image stamped,
With innocence arrayed,

9 Completed now the mighty work,
God his creation viewed;
And pleased with all that he had made,
Pronounced it "very good."

---

*To Father, Son, and Holy Ghost, etc.*

### HYMN 5. H I.

Psalm cxlviii. OGLEVIE.

*Praise from living Creatures.*

1 BEGIN, my soul, the exalted lay,
Let each enraptured thought obey,
And praise the Almighty's name;
Let heaven and earth, and seas and skies,
In one melodious concert rise,
To swell the inspiring theme.

2 Ye angels, catch the thrilling sound,
While all the adoring thrones around
His boundless mercy sing;
Let every listening saint above
Wake all the tuneful soul of love,
And touch the sweetest string.

3 What e'er this living world contains,
That wings the air, or treads the plains,
United praise bestow;
Ye tenants of the ocean wide,
Proclaim him through the mighty tide,
And in the deeps below.

4 Let man, by nobler passions swayed,
The feeling heart, the judging head,
In heavenly praise employ;
Spread His tremendous Name around,
While heaven's broad arch rings back the sound,
The general burst of joy.

---

*To Father, Son, etc., page 271.*

### HYMN 6. H 1.

Psalm cxlviii. OGLEVIE.

*Praise from the Elements and Worlds.*

1 YE fields of light, celestial plains,
Where pure, serene effulgence reigns,
Ye scenes divinely fair,
Your Maker's wondrous power proclaim,
Tell how he formed your shining frame,
And breathed the fluid air.

2 Join all ye stars, the vocal choir;
Thou dazzling orb of liquid fire
The mighty chorus aid;
And, soon as evening vails the plain,
Thou moon, prolong the hallowed strain,
And praise him in the shade.

3 Thou heaven of heavens, his vast abode,
Proclaim the glories of thy God;
Ye worlds declare his might;
He spake the word, and ye were made,
Darkness and dismal chaos fled,
And nature sprung to light.

4 Let every element rejoice;
Ye thunders, burst with awful voice
To him who bids you roll;
His praise in softer notes declare,
Each whispering breeze of yielding air,
And breathe it to the soul.

---

*To Fat'er, Son, etc., page 271.*

## HYMN 7. L. M.

CREATION. THEME FROM MADAN.

### HYMN 7. L. M.

*Psalm* xix. ADDISON.

1 THE spacious firmament on high,
With all the blue ethereal sky,
And spangled heavens, a shining frame,
Their great Original proclaim.

2 The unwearied sun from day to day,
Does his Creator's power display,
And publishes to every land
The work of an Almighty hand.

3 Soon as the evening shades prevail,
The moon takes up the wondrous tale;
And, nightly, to the listening earth,
Repeats the story of her birth;

4 While all the stars that round her burn,
And all the planets in their turn,
Confirm the tidings as they roll,
And spread the truth from pole to pole.

5 What though in solemn silence all
Move round this dark terrestrial ball;
What though no real voice nor sound
Amid their radiant orbs be found;

6 In reason's ear they all rejoice,
And utter forth a glorious voice,
For ever singing as they shine,
"The hand that made us is divine."

---

To Father, Son, and Holy Ghost,
The God whom earth and heaven adore,
Be glory, as it was of old,
Is now, and shall be evermore.

## HYMN 8. S. M.

SEASONS. PLEYEL.

## HYMN 9. II 3.

BRIGHTON.

## III. PROVIDENCE.

### HYMN 8. L. M.

RIPPON.

1 ETERNAL source of every joy!
Well may thy praise our lips employ,
While in thy temple we appear,
To hail thee sovereign of the year.

2 Wide as the wheels of nature roll,
Thy hand supports and guides the whole:
The sun is taught by thee to rise,
And darkness when to vail the skies.

3 The flowery spring at thy command
Perfumes the air, and paints the land;
The summer rays with vigor shine,
To raise the corn, and cheer the vine.

4 Thy hand in autumn richly pours
Through all our coasts redundant stores;
And winters, softened by thy care,
No more the face of horror wear.

5 Seasons, and months, and weeks, and days,
Demand successive songs of praise;
And be the grateful homage paid,
With morning light and evening shade.

6 Here in thy house let incense rise,
And circling sabbaths bless our eyes,
Till to those lofty hights we soar,
Where days and years revolve no more.

To Father, Son, and Holy Ghost,
The God whom earth and heaven adore,
Be glory, as it was of old,
Is now, and shall be evermore.

### HYMN 9. II 3.

Psalm xxiii. ADDISON.

1 THE Lord my pasture shall prepare,
And feed me with a shepherd's care;
His presence shall my wants supply,
And guard me with a watchful eye;
My noonday walks he shall attend,
And all my midnight hours defend.

2 When in the sultry glebe I faint,
Or on the thirsty mountain pant,
To fertile vales and dewy meads
My weary, wandering steps he leads,
Where peaceful rivers, soft and slow,
Amid the verdant landscape flow.

3 Though in the paths of death I tread,
With gloomy horrors overspread;
My steadfast heart shall fear no ill,
For thou, O Lord, art with me still;
Thy friendly crook shall give me aid,
And guide me through the dreadful shade

---

To God the Father, God the Son,
And God the Spirit, Three in One,
Be glory in the highest given,
By all in earth and all in heaven,
As was through ages heretofore,
Is now, and shall be evermore.

## HYMN 10. C. M.

NEWTON. JACKSON.

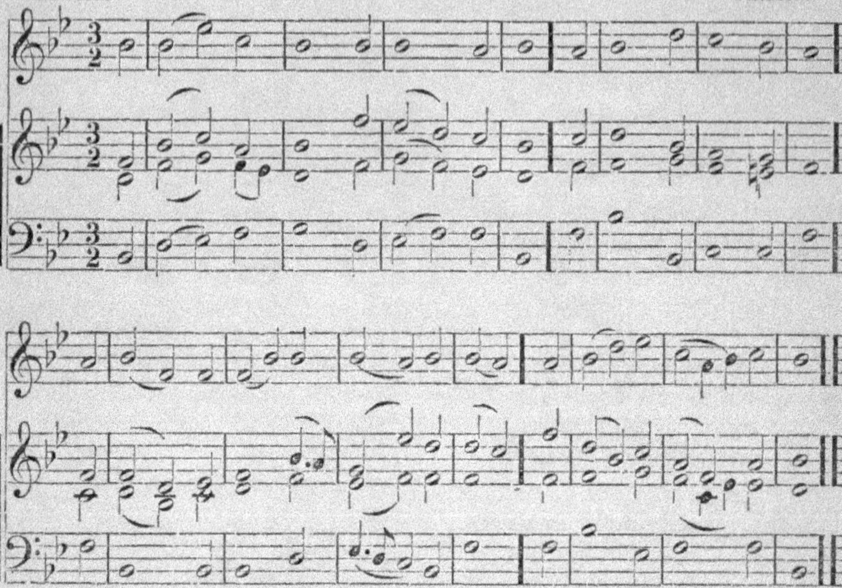

## HYMN 11. III 1.

PLEYEL'S HYMN. PLEYEL.

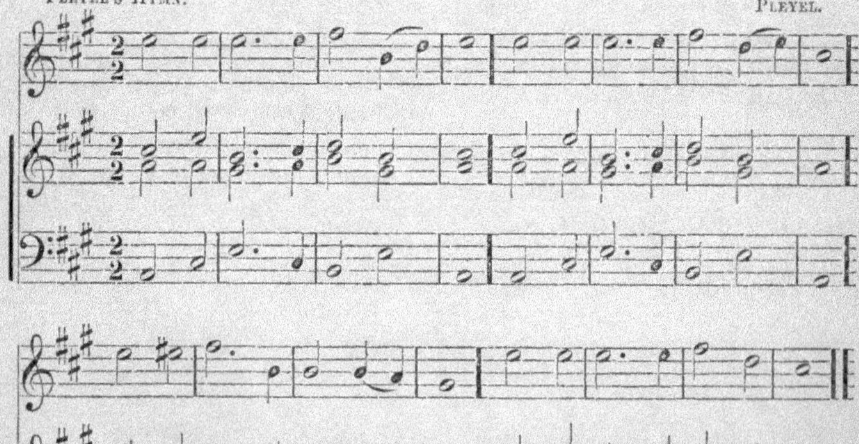

## HYMN 10. C. M.

ADDISON.

1 When all thy mercies, O my God,
My rising soul surveys,
Transported with the view, I 'm lost
In wonder, love, and praise.

2 O how shall words with equal warmth
The gratitude declare,
That glows within my ravished heart!
But thou canst read it there.

3 Thy providence my life sustained,
And all my wants redressed,
When in the silent womb I lay,
And hung upon the breast.

4 To all my weak complaints and cries
Thy mercy lent an ear,
Ere yet my feeble thoughts had learnt
To form themselves in prayer.

5 Unnumbered comforts to my soul
Thy tender care bestowed,
Before my infant heart conceived
From whom those comforts flowed.

6 When in the slippery paths of youth
With heedless steps I ran,
Thine arm, unseen, conveyed me safe,
And led me up to man.

7 Through hidden dangers, toils, and deaths,
It gently cleared my way,
And through the pleasing snares of vice,
More to be feared than they.

8 When worn with sickness, oft hast thou
With health renewed my face;
And, when in sins and sorrows sunk,
Revived my soul with grace.

9 Thy bounteous hand with worldly bliss
Has made my cup run o'er;
And in a kind and faithful friend
Has doubled all my store.

10 Ten thousand thousand precious gifts
My daily thanks employ;
Nor is the least a cheerful heart,
That tastes those gifts with joy.

11 Through every period of my life
Thy goodness I'll pursue;
And after death, in distant worlds,
The glorious theme renew.

12 When nature fails, and day and night
Divide thy works no more,
My ever grateful heart, O Lord,
Thy mercy shall adore.

13 Through all eternity, to thee
A joyful song I'll raise;
But, oh! eternity's too short
To utter all thy praise.

---

To Father, Son, and Holy Ghost,
The God whom we adore,
Be glory, as it was, is now,
And shall be evermore.

## HYMN 11. III 1.

Psalm xxi: 15. RYLAND.

*"My times are in thy hand."*

1 Sovereign Ruler of the skies,
Ever gracious, ever wise;
All our times are in thy hand,
All events at thy command.

2 He that formed us in the womb,
He shall guide us to the tomb;
All our ways shall ever be
Ordered by his wise decree.

3 Times of sickness, times of health,
Blighting want, and cheerful wealth,
All our pleasures, all our pains,
Come, and end, as God ordains.

4 May we always own thy hand,
Still to thee surrendered stand;
Know that thou art God alone,
We and ours are all thy own.

---

Holy Father, Holy Son,
Holy Spirit, Three in One!
Glory, as of old, to thee,
Now, and evermore shall be!

## HYMN 12. C. M.

HAVENS.

## HYMN 13. S. M.

ST. BRIDE'S. DR. HOWARD.

### HYMN 12. C. M.

COWPER.

1 God moves in a mysterious way
His wonders to perform;
He plants his footsteps in the sea,
And rides upon the storm.

2 Deep in unfathomable mines,
With never-failing skill,
He treasures up his bright designs,
And works his gracious will.

3 Ye fearful saints, fresh courage take,
The clouds ye so much dread
Are big with mercy, and shall break
In blessings on your head.

4 Judge not the Lord by feeble sense,
But trust him for his grace;
Behind a frowning providence
He hides a smiling face.

5 His purposes will ripen fast,
Unfolding every hour;
The bud may have a bitter taste,
But sweet will be the flower.

6 Blind unbelief is sure to err,
And scan his work in vain;
God is his own interpreter,
And he will make it plain.

---

To Father, Son, and Holy Ghost,
The God whom we adore,
Be glory, as it was, is now,
And shall be evermore.

## IV.—REDEMPTION.

### HYMN 13. S. M.

Job ix: 2–6. LOGAN.

1 Ah! how shall fallen man
Be just before his God;
If he contend in righteousness,
We sink beneath his rod.

2 If he our ways should mark
With strict inquiring eyes,
Could we for one of thousand faults
A just excuse devise.

3 All-seeing, powerful God!
Who can with thee contend?
Or who that tries the unequal strife,
Shall prosper in the end?

4 The mountains, in thy wrath,
Their ancient seats forsake!
The trembling earth deserts her place,
Her rooted pillars shake!

5 Ah! how shall guilty man
Contend with such a God?
None, none can meet him, and escape,
But through the Saviour's blood.

---

To God the Father, Son,
And Spirit, glory be,
As 't was, and is, and shall be so,
To all eternity.

## HYMN 14. L. M.

ST. PAUL'S. GREENE.

## HYMN 15. L. M.

TRURO. DR. BURNEY.

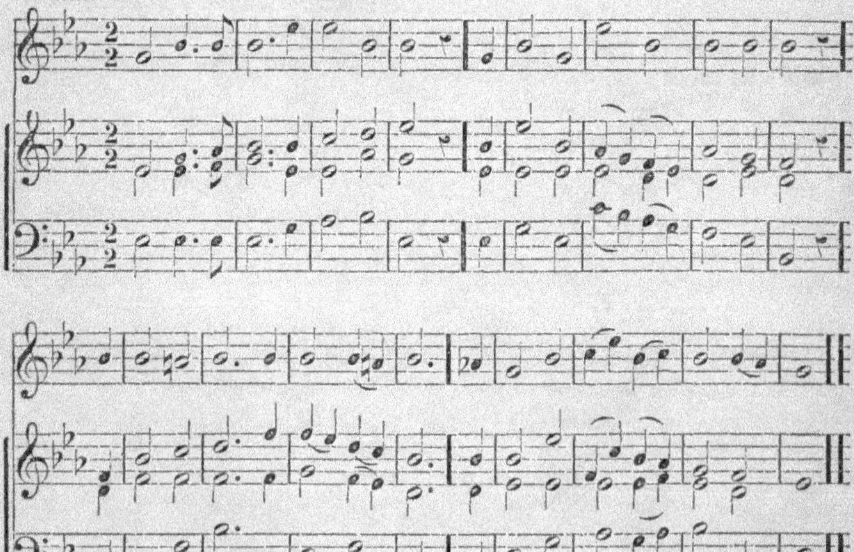

### HYMN 14. L. M.

Job ix: 30-33. ONDERDONK.

1 THOUGH I should seek to wash me clean
In water of the driven snow,
My soul would yet its spot retain,
And sink in conscious guilt and woe.

2 The Spirit, in his power divine,
Would cast my vaunting soul to earth,
Expose the foulness of its sin,
And show the vileness of its worth.

3 Ah! not like erring man is God,
That men to answer him should dare;
Condemned, and into silence awed,
They helpless stand before his bar.

4 There, must a Mediator plead,
Who, God and man, may both embrace;
With God, for man to intercede,
And offer man the purchased grace.

5 And, lo! the Son of God is slain
To be this Mediator crowned;
In him, my soul, be cleansed from stain,
In him thy righteousness be found.

---

To Father, Son, and Holy Ghost,
The God whom earth and heaven adore,
Be glory, as it was of old,
Is now, and shall be evermore.

### HYMN 15. L. M.

ADDISON.

1 ALL glorious God! what hymns of praise
Shall our transported voices raise!
What ardent love and zeal are due,
While heaven stands open to our view!

2 Once we were fallen, and O how low,
Just on the brink of endless woe;
When Jesus, from the realms above,
Borne on the wings of boundless love,

3 Scattered the shades of death and night,
And spread around his heavenly light!
By him what wondrous grace is shown
To souls impoverished and undone.

4 He shows, beyond these mortal shores,
A bright inheritance as ours;
Where saints in light our coming wait,
To share their holy, happy state.

---

To Father, Son, and Holy Ghost,
The God whom earth and heaven adore,
Be glory, as it was of old,
Is now, and shall be evermore.

## HYMN 16. C. M.

ASHLEY. MADAN.

### HYMN 16. C. M.

WATTS.

1 SALVATION! O the joyful sound,
Glad tidings to our ears,
A sovereign balm for every wound
A cordial for our fears.

2 Salvation! buried once in sin,
At hell's dark door we lay;
But now we rise by grace divine,
And see a heavenly day.

3 Salvation! let the echo fly
The spacious earth around;
While all the armies of the sky
Conspire to raise the sound.

4 Salvation! O thou bleeding Lamb,
To thee the praise belongs;
Our hearts shall kindle at thy Name,
Thy Name inspire our songs.

*Chorus, for the end of each verse.*

Glory, honor, praise, and power
Be unto the Lamb for ever;
Jesus Christ is our Redeemer!
Hallelujah, praise the Lord.

## HYMN 17. C. M.

CHRISTMAS. HANDEL.

## HYMN 18. III 3.

ALMA. WEBBE.

### HYMN 17. C. M.

A. STEELE.

1 To our Redeemer's glorious name
Awake the sacred song;
O may his love (immortal flame!)
Tune every heart and tongue.

2 His love, what mortal thought can reach;
What mortal tongue display!
Imagination's utmost stretch
In wonder dies away.

3 He left his radiant throne on high,
Left the bright realms of bliss,
And came to earth to bleed and die!
Was ever love like this?

4 Dear Lord, while we adoring pay
Our humble thanks to thee,
May every heart with rapture say,
"The Saviour died for me."

5 O may the sweet, the blissful theme,
Fill every heart and tongue;
Till strangers love thy charming name,
And join the sacred song.

---

To Father, Son, and Holy Ghost,
The God whom we adore,
Be glory, as it was, is now,
And shall be evermore.

### HYMN 18. III 3.

ROBINSON.

1 SAVIOUR, source of every blessing,
Tune my heart to grateful lays;
Streams of mercy, never ceasing,
Call for ceaseless songs of praise.

2 Teach me some melodious measure,
Sung by raptured saints above;
Fill my soul with sacred pleasure,
While I sing redeeming love.

3 Thou did seek me when a stranger,
Wandering from the fold of God;
Thou, to save my soul from danger,
Did redeem me with thy blood.

4 By thy hand restored, defended,
Safe through life thus far I've come;
Safe, O Lord, when life is ended,
Bring me to my heavenly home.

---

Praise the Father, earth and heaven,
Praise the Son, the Spirit praise,
As it was, and is, be given
Glory through eternal years.

## HYMN 19. C. M.

MANSFIELD.

## HYMN 20. C. M.

WALSAL. PURCELL, 1680.

### HYMN 19. C. M.

Titus iii: 4-7. LOGAN.

1 My grateful soul, for ever praise,
For ever love his name,
Who turned thee from the fatal paths
Of folly, sin, and shame.

2 Vain and presumptuous is the trust
Which in our works we place;
Salvation from a higher source
Flows to our fallen race.

3 'T is from the love of God through Christ
That all our hopes begin;
His mercy saved our souls from death
And washed us from our sin.

4 His Spirit, through the Saviour shed,
His sacred fire imparts,
Removes our dross, and love divine
Enkindles in our hearts.

5 Thus raised from death, we live anew;
And, justified by grace,
We hope in glory to appear,
And see our Father's face.

---

To Father, Son, and Holy Ghost,
The God whom we adore,
Be glory, as it was, is now,
And shall be evermore.

### HYMN 20. C. M.

MRS. STEELE.

1 How helpless guilty nature lies,
Unconscious of its load;
The heart unchanged, can never rise
To happiness and God.

2 The will perverse, the passions blind,
In paths of ruin stray;
Reason debased can never find
The safe, the narrow way.

3 Can aught beneath a power divine
The stubborn will subdue?
'T is thine, Almighty Saviour, thine
To form the heart anew.

4 'T is thine the passions to recall,
And upward bid them rise;
And make the scales of error fall
From reason's darkened eyes.

5 To chase the shades of death away,
And bid the sinner live;
A beam of heaven, a vital ray,
'T is thine alone to give.

6 O change these wretched hearts of ours,
And give them life divine;
Then shall our passions and our powers,
Almighty Lord, be thine.

---

To Father, Son, and Holy Ghost,
The God whom we adore,
Be glory, as it was, is now.
And shall be evermore.

## HYMN 21. C. M.

NEWTON. JACKSON.

## HYMN 22. III 1.

CLARK. CLARK.

### HYMN 21. C. M.

MRS. STEELE.

1 FATHER, to thee my soul I lift,
On thee my hopes depends,
Convinced that every perfect gift
From thee alone descends.

2 Mercy and grace are thine alone,
And power and wisdom too;
Without the Spirit of thy Son
We nothing good can do.

3 Thou all our works in us hast wrought,
Our good is all divine;
The praise of every holy thought
And righteous word is thine.

4 From thee, through Jesus, we receive
The power on thee to call,
In whom we are, and move and live:
Our God is all in all.

---

To Father, Son, and Holy Ghost,
The God whom we adore,
Be glory, as it was, is now,
And shall be evermore.

### HYMN 22. III 1.

C. WESLEY.

1 SING my soul His wondrous love,
Who, from yon bright throne above,
Ever watchful o'er our race,
Still to man extends his grace.

2 Heaven and earth by him were made,
All is by his scepter swayed;
What are we that he should show
So much love to us below!

3 God the merciful and good,
Bought us with the Saviour's blood;
And, to make our safety sure,
Guides us by his Spirit pure.

4 Sing, my soul, adore his name:
Let his glory be thy theme;
Praise him till he calls thee home,
Trust his love for all to come.

---

Holy Father, Holy Son,
Holy Spirit, Three in One!
Glory, as of old, to thee,
Now, and evermore shall be.

## HYMN 23. S. M.

SILVER STREET. SMITH.

## HYMN 24. S. M.

PELHAM. GIARDINI.

UNISONS.

### HYMN 23. S. M.

DODDRIDGE.

1 GRACE! 't is a charming sound!
Harmonious to the ear;
Heaven with the echo shall resound,
And all the earth shall hear.

2 Grace first contrived a way
To save rebellious man,
And all the means that grace display,
Which drew the wondrous plan.

3 Grace guides my wandering feet
To tread the heavenly road,
And new supplies each hour I meet
While pressing on to God.

4 Grace all the work shall crown
Through everlasting days;
It lays in heaven the topmost stone,
And well deserves the praise.

---

To God the Father, Son,
And Spirit, glory be,
As 't was, and is, and shall be so,
To all eternity.

## V.—THE CHURCH.

### HYMN 24. S. M.

MUHLENBURG.

1 LIKE Noah's weary dove,
That soared the earth around,
But not a resting-place above
The cheerless waters found;

2 O cease, my wandering soul,
On restless wing to roam;
All the wide world, to either pole,
Has not for thee a home.

3 Behold the ark of God,
Behold the open door;
Hasten to gain that dear abode,
And rove, my soul, no more.

4 There, safe thou shalt abide,
There, sweet shall be thy rest,
And every longing satisfied,
With full salvation blest.

5 And, when the waves of ire
Again the earth shall fill,
The Ark shall ride the sea of fire,
Then rest on Zion's hill.

---

To God the Father, Son,
And Spirit, glory be,
As 't was, and is, and shall be so,
To all eternity.

## HYMN 25. S. M.

PADDINGTON. REV. B. WOOD.

## HYMN 26. C. M.

WAINWRIGHT. WAINWRIGHT.

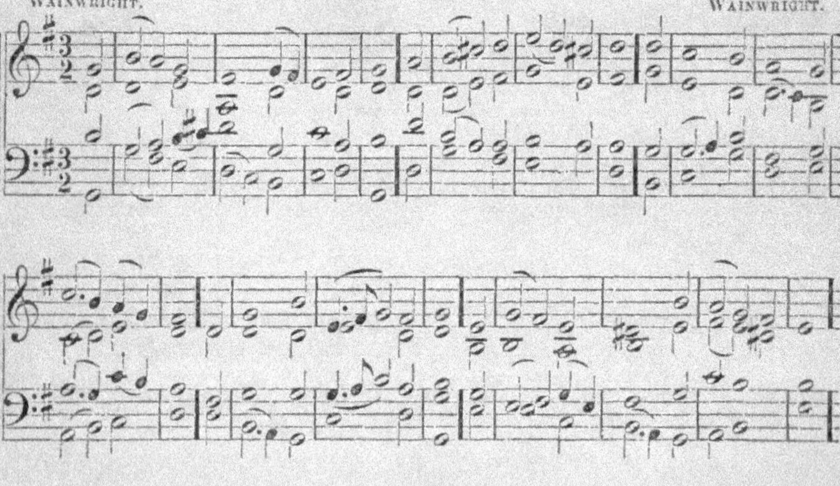

### HYMN 25. S. M.

DWIGHT.

1 I LOVE thy kingdom, Lord,
The house of thine abode,
The Church our blest Redeemer saved
With his own precious blood.

2 I love thy Church, O God!
Her walls before thee stand,
Dear as the apple of thine eye,
And graven on thy hand.

3 If e'er to bless thy sons,
My voice or hands deny,
These hands let useful skill forsake,
This voice in silence die.

4 If e'er my heart forget
Her welfare, or her woe,
Let every joy this heart forsake,
And every grief o'erflow.

5 For her my tears shall fall;
For her my prayers ascend;
To her my cares and toils be given,
Till toils and cares shall end.

6 Beyond my highest joy
I prize her heavenly ways,
Her sweet communion, solemn vows,
Her hymns of love and praise.

7 Jesus, thou Friend divine,
Our Saviour and our King,
Thy hand from every snare and foe
Shall great deliverance bring.

8 Sure as thy truth shall last,
To Zion shall be given
The brightest glories earth can yield,
And brighter bliss of heaven.

To God the Father, Son,
And Spirit, glory be;
As 't was, and is, and shall be so
To all eternity.

### HYMN 26. C. M.

*Heb.* xii : 18, 22-24. WATTS.

1 NOT to the terrors of the Lord,
The tempest, fire, and smoke;
Not to the thunder of that word
Which God on Sinai spoke:

2 But we are come to Sion's hill,
The city of our God;
Where milder words declare his will,
And spread his love abroad.

3 Behold the innumerable host
Of angels clothed in light!
Behold the spirits of the just,
Whose faith is changed to sight.

4 Behold the blessed assembly there
Whose names are writ in heaven;
Hear God, the judge of all, declare
Their sins, through Christ, forgiven!

5 Angels, and living saints, and dead,
But one communion make;
All join in Christ, their vital Head,
And of his love partake.

---

To Father, Son, and Holy Ghost,
The God whom we adore,
Be glory, as it was, is now,
And shall be evermore.

## HYMN 27. S. M.

HANDEL. HANDEL.

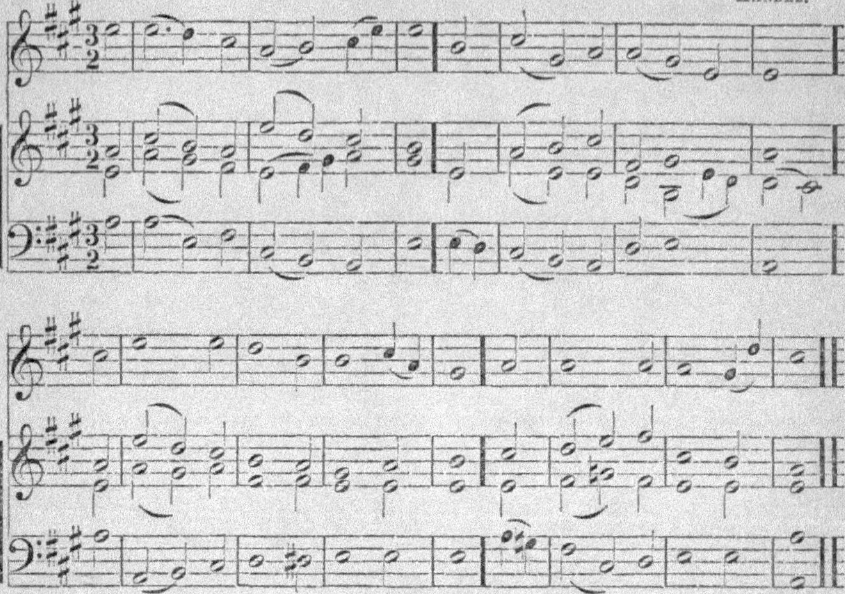

## HYMN 28. II 1.

COLUMBIA RAVENSCROFT.

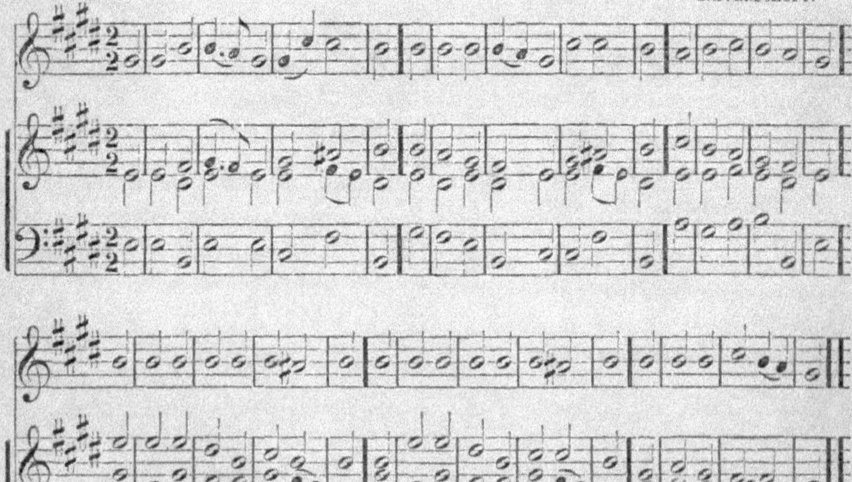

### HYMN 27. S. M.

FAWCETT.

1 Blest is the tie that binds
Our hearts in Christian love;
The fellowship of kindred minds
Is like to that above.

2 Before our Father's throne
We pour united prayers;
Our fears, our hopes, our aims are one,
Our comforts and our cares.

3 We share our mutual woes,
Our mutual burdens bear;
And often for each other flows
The sympathizing tear.

4 When we at death must part,
How keen, how deep the pain;
But we shall still be joined in heart,
And hope to meet again.

5 From sorrow, toil, and pain,
And sin, we shall be free;
And perfect love and friendship reign
Throughout eternity.

---

To God the Father, Son,
And Spirit, glory be,
As 't was, and is, and shall be so,
To all eternity.

### HYMN 28. II 1.

Psalm cxxii.

*The Church in glory.* MERRICK.

1 With joy shall I behold the day
That calls my willing soul away
To dwell among the blest;
For, lo! my great Redeemer's power
Unfolds the everlasting door,
And points me to his rest.

2 E'en now, to my expecting eyes,
The heaven-built towers of Salem rise;
Their glory I survey;
I view her mansions that contain
The angel host, a beauteous train,
And shine with cloudless day.

3 Thither, from earth's remotest end,
Lo! the redeemed of God ascend,
Borne on immortal wing;
There, crowned with everlasting joy,
In ceaseless hymns their tongues employ,
Before th' Almighty King.

4 The King a seat hath there prepared,
High on eternal base upreared,
For his eternal Son;
His palaces with joy abound;
His saints, by him, with glory crowned,
Attend and share his throne.

5 Mother of cities! o'er thy head
Bright peace, with healing wings outspread,
For evermore shall dwell;
Let me, blest seat, my name behold
Among thy citizens enrolled,
And bid the world farewell.

---

To Father, Son, and Holy Ghost,
The God whom heaven's triumphant host,
And saints on earth adore;
Be glory, as in ages past,
As now it is, and so shall last
When time shall be no more.

## HYMN 29. L. M.

TRURO. DR. BURNEY.

## HYMN 30. II 4.

SHAFTSBURY. W. BURNEY.

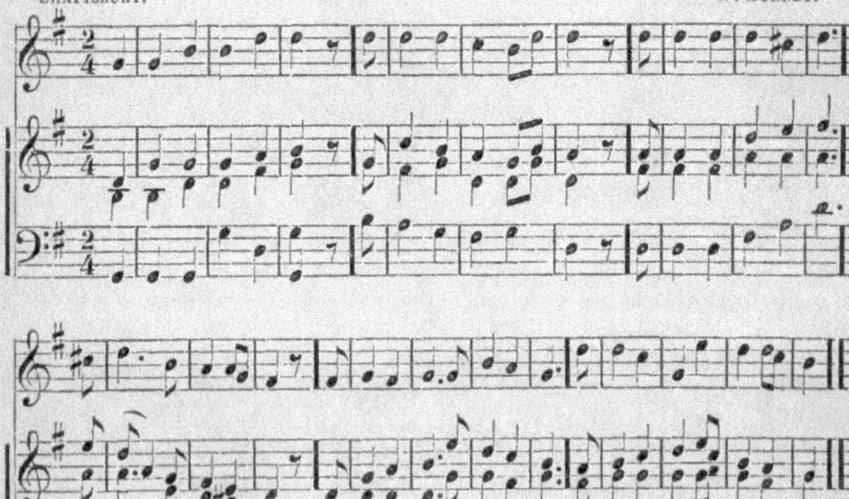

### HYMN 29. L. M.

Isaiah lii: 1, 2. DODDRIDGE.

1 TRIUMPHANT Sion! lift thy head
From dust, and darkness, and the dead:
Though humbled long, awake at length,
And gird thee with thy Saviour's strength.

2 Put all thy beauteous garments on,
And let thy excellence be known:
Decked in the robes of righteousness,
The world thy glories shall confess.

3 No more shall foes unclean invade,
And fill thy hallowed walls with dread;
No more shall hell's insulting host
Their victory and thy sorrows boast.

4 God from on high has heard thy prayer,
His hand thy ruins shall repair:
Nor will thy watchful Monarch cease
To guide thee in eternal peace.

---

To Father, Son, and Holy Ghost,
The God whom earth and heaven adore,
Be glory, as it was of old,
Is now, and shall be evermore.

## VI. FESTIVALS AND FASTS.

THE LORD'S DAY.

### HYMN 30. II 4.

DODDRIDGE.

1 AWAKE, ye saints, awake,
And hail this sacred day;
In loftiest songs of praise
Your joyful homage pay:
Welcome the day that God hath blest,
The type of heaven's eternal rest.

2 On this auspicious morn
The Lord of life arose;
He burst the bars of death,
And vanquished all our foes;
And now he pleads our cause above,
And reaps the fruits of all his love.

3 All hail, triumphant Lord!
Heaven with hosannas rings,
And earth, in humbler strains,
Thy praise responsive sings:
Worthy the Lamb that once was slain,
Through endless years to live and reign.

4 Great King, gird on thy sword,
Ascend thy conquering car;
While justice, truth, and love,
Maintain thy glorious war;
This day let sinners own thy sway,
And rebels cast their arms away.

---

To God the Father, Son,
And Spirit, ever blessed,
Eternal, Three in One,
All worship be addressed;
As heretofore
It was, is now,
And shall be so
For evermore.

## HYMN 31. C. M.

MANSFIELD.

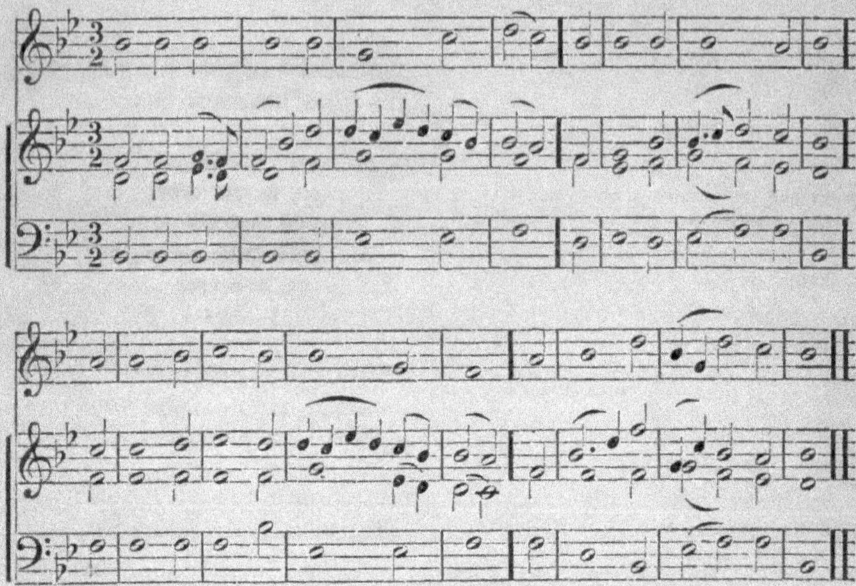

## HYMN 32. S. M.

SILVER STREET. SMITH.

### HYMN 31. C. M.

MONTGOMERY.

1 THIS is the day the Lord hath made,
Let young and old rejoice;
To him be vows and homage paid,
Whose service is our choice.

2 This is the temple of the Lord;
How dreadful is this place!
With meekness let us hear his word,
With reverence seek his face.

3 This is the homage he requires;
The voice of praise and prayer,
The soul's affections, hopes, desires,
Ourselves and all we are.

4 While rich and poor for mercy call,
Propitious from the skies,
The Lord, the Maker of them all,
Accepts the sacrifice.

5 Well pleased, through Jesus Christ, his Son,
From sin he grants release;
According to their faith 'tis done,
He bids them go in peace.

---

To Father, Son, and Holy Ghost,
The God whom we adore,
Be glory, as it was, is now,
And shall be evermore.

### HYMN 32. S. M.

WATTS.

1 WELCOME, sweet day of rest,
That saw the Lord arise;
Welcome to this reviving breast,
And these rejoicing eyes.

2 The King himself comes near
To feast his saints to-day;
Here may we sit, and see him here,
And love, and praise, and pray.

3 One day amid the place
Where Jesus is within,
Is better than ten thousand days
Of pleasure and of sin.

4 My willing soul would stay
In such a frame as this,
Till it is called to soar away
To everlasting bliss.

---

To God the Father, Son,
And Spirit, glory be,
As 'twas, and is, and shall be so,
To all eternity.

## HYMN 33. L. M.

St. Nicholas. Ions.

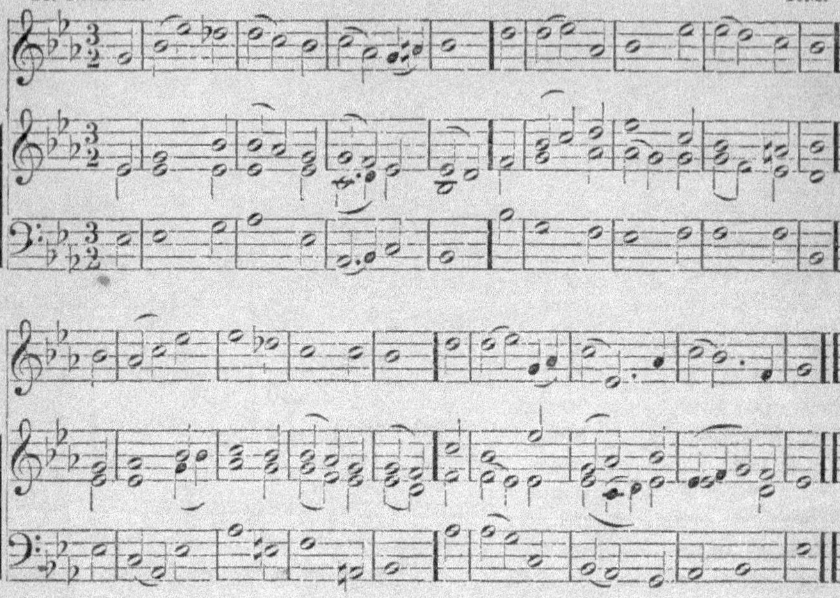

## HYMN 34. II 3.

Eaton. Wyvill.

## HYMN 33. L. M.

STENNETT.

1 ANOTHER six days' work is done,
Another Lord's day has begun;
Return, my soul, enjoy thy rest,
Improve the hours thy God hath blest.

2 This day may our devotions rise
As grateful incense to the skies;
And heaven that sweet repose bestow,
Which none but those who feel it know.

3 This peaceful calm within the breast
Is the sure pledge of heavenly rest,
Which, for the church of God, remains
The end of cares, the end of pains.

4 In holy duties, let the day,
In holy pleasures, pass away;
How sweet a sabbath thus to spend,
In hope of one that ne'er shall end!

---

To Father, Son, and Holy Ghost,
The God whom earth and heaven adore,
Be glory, as it was of old,
Is now, and shall be evermore.

## HYMN 34. II 3.

MRS. STEELE.

1 GREAT God! this sacred day of thine
Demands the soul's collected powers;
Gladly we now to thee resign
These solemn, consecrated hours;
O may our souls, adoring, own
The grace that calls us to thy throne.

2 All-seeing God! thy piercing eye
Can every secret thought explore;
May worldly cares our bosoms fly,
And where thou art, intrude no more;
O may thy grace our spirits move,
And fix our minds on things above.

3 Thy Spirit's powerful aid impart,
And bid thy word, with life divine,
Engage the ear, and warm the heart;
Then shall the day indeed be thine:
Then shall our souls, adoring, own
The grace that calls us to thy throne.

---

To God the Father, God the Son,
And God the Spirit, Three in One,
Be glory in the highest given,
By all on earth, and all in heaven;
As was through ages heretofore,
Is now, and shall be evermore.

## HYMN 35. II 4.

SHAFTSBURY. W. BURNEY.

## HYMN 36. L. M.

ALLENHEAD. T. IONS.

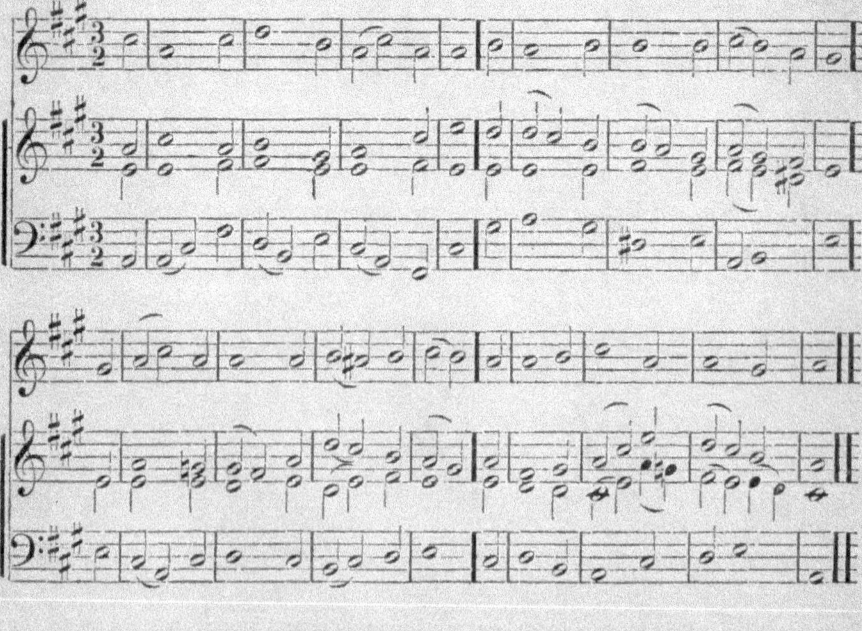

### HYMN 35. II 4.

DODDRIDGE.

1 In loud exalted strains,
The King of glory praise;
O'er heaven and earth he reigns,
Through everlasting days;
But Zion with his presence blest,
Is his delight, his chosen rest.

2 O King of glory! come,
And with thy favor crown
This temple as thy home,
This people as thy own.
Beneath this roof vouchsafe to show
How God can dwell with men below.

3 Now let thine ear attend
Our supplicating cries;
Now let our praise ascend,
Accepted to the skies;
Now let thy gospel's joyful sound
Spread its celestial influence round.

4 Here may the listening throng
Imbibe thy truth and love.
Here Christians join the song
Of seraphim above:
Till all who humbly seek thy face,
Rejoice in thy abounding grace.

---

To God, the Father, Son,
And Spirit, ever blessed,
Eternal Three in One,
All worship be addressed,
As heretofore
It was, is now,
And shall be so
For evermore.

### HYMN 36. L. M.

WATTS.

1 Far from my thoughts, vain world, begone:
Let my religious hours alone:
From flesh and sense I would be free,
And hold communion, Lord, with thee.

2 My heart grows warm with holy fire,
And kindles with a pure desire,
To see thy grace, to taste thy love,
And feel thine influence from above.

3 When I can say that God is mine,
When I can see thy glories shine,
I'll tread the world beneath my feet,
And all that men call rich and great.

4 Send comfort down from thy right hand
To cheer me in this barren land;
And in thy temple let me know
The joys that from thy presence flow.

---

To Father, Son, and Holy Ghost,
The God whom earth and heaven adore,
Be glory, as it was of old,
Is now, and shall be evermore.

## HYMN 37. L. M.

St. Nicholas. | Ions.

## HYMN 38. III 1.

Weldon. | Weldon.

### HYMN 37. L. M.

1 My opening eyes with rapture see
The dawn of thy returning day;
My thoughts, O God, ascend to thee,
While thus my early vows I pay.

2 I yield my heart to thee alone,
Nor would receive another guest;
Eternal King, erect thy throne,
And reign sole monarch in my breast.

3 O bid this trifling world retire,
And drive each carnal thought away,
Nor let me feel one vain desire,
One sinful thought through all the day.

4 Then to thy courts when I repair,
My soul shall rise on joyful wing,
The wonders of thy love declare,
And join the strains which angels sing.

---

To Father, Son, and Holy Ghost,
The God whom earth and heaven adore,
Be glory, as it was of old,
Is now, and shall be evermore.

### HYMN 38. III 1.

MONTGOMERY.

1 To thy temple I repair;
Lord, I love to worship there,
While thy glorious praise is sung,
Touch my lips, unloose my tongue.

2 While the prayers of saints ascend,
God of love, to mine attend;
Hear me, for thy Spirit pleads;
Hear, for Jesus intercedes.

3 While I hearken to thy law,
Fill my soul with humble awe,
Till thy Gospel bring to me
Life and immortality.

4 While thy ministers proclaim
Peace and pardon in thy Name,
Through their voice, by faith, may I
Hear thee speaking from on high.

5 From thy house when I return,
May my heart within me burn;
And at evening let me say,
"I have walked with God to-day."

---

Holy Father, Holy Son,
Holy Spirit, Three in one!
Glory, as of old, to thee,
Now, and evermore shall be!

## HYMN 39. L. M.

St. Nicholas. Ions.

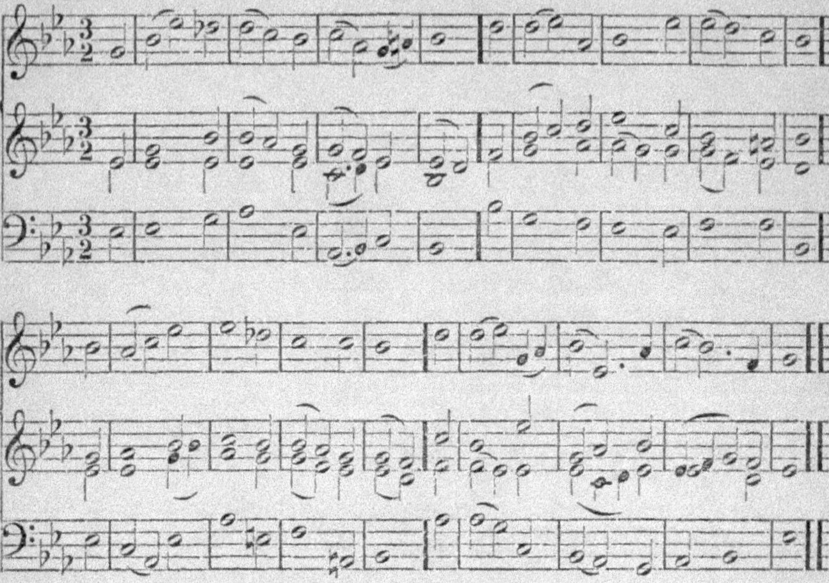

## HYMN 40. III 5.

Benediction. Gregorean.

### HYMN 39. L. M.

*After Sermon.*

1 Almighty Father, bless the word,
Which, through thy grace, we now have heard;
O may the precious seed take root,
Spring up and bear abundant fruit.

2 We praise thee for the means of grace,
Thus in thy courts to seek thy face:
Grant, Lord, that we who worship here
May all, at length, in heaven appear.

---

To Father, Son, and Holy Ghost,
The God whom earth and heaven adore,
Be glory, as it was of old,
Is now, and shall be evermore.

### HYMN 40. III 5.

Burder.

1 Lord, dismiss us with thy blessing,
Fill our hearts with joy and peace;
Let us each, thy love possessing,
Triumph in redeeming grace;
O refresh us,
Traveling through this wilderness.

2 Thanks we give, and adoration,
For the Gospel's joyful sound;
May the fruits of thy salvation
In our hearts and lives abound:
May thy presence
With us evermore be found.

---

Great Jehovah! we adore thee,
God the Father, God the Son,
God the Spirit, joined in glory
On the same eternal throne:
Endless praises
To Jehovah, Three in One.

## HYMN 41. C. M.

MISSIONARY. T. WALKER.

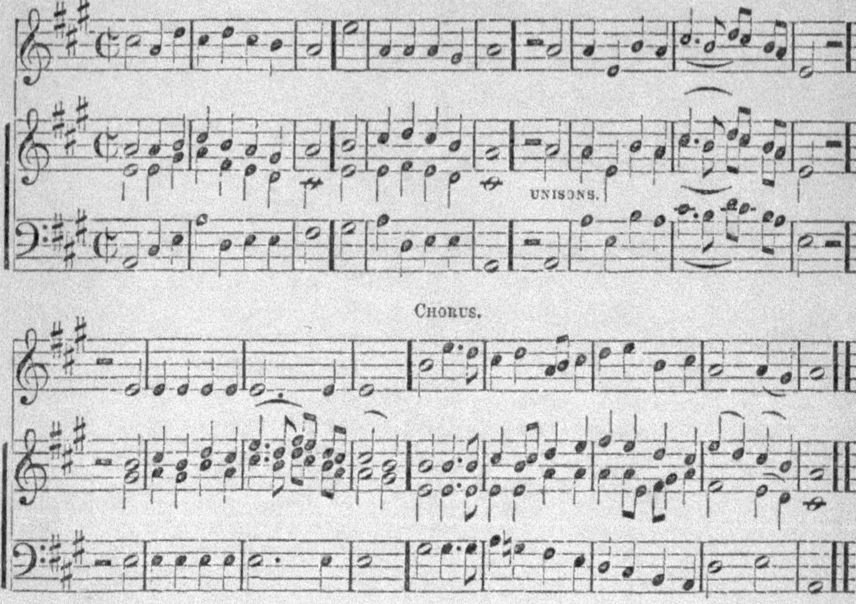


## HYMN 42. III 3.

TUSCANY.

ADVENT.

### HYMN 41. C. M.

DODDRIDGE.

1 Hark! the glad sound, the Saviour comes,
The Saviour promised long;
Let every heart prepare a throne,
And every voice a song.

2 On him the Spirit, largely poured,
Exerts his sacred fire;
Wisdom and might, and zeal and love,
His holy breast inspire.

3 He comes, the prisoners to release,
In Satan's bondage held;
The gates of brass before him burst,
The iron fetters yield.

4 He comes, from thickest films of vice
To clear the mental ray;
And on the eyes oppressed with night,
To pour celestial day.

5 He comes, the broken heart to bind,
The bleeding soul to cure;
And with the treasures of his grace,
T' enrich the humble poor.

6 Our glad hosannas, Prince of peace,
Thy welcome shall proclaim;
And heaven's eternal arches ring
With thy beloved name.

To Father, Son, and Holy Ghost,
The God whom we adore,
Be glory, as it was, is now,
And shall be evermore.

### HYMN 42. III 3.

C. WESLEY.

1 Hail! thou long-expected Jesus,
Born to set thy people free;
From our sins and fears release us,
Let us find our rest in thee.

2 Israel's strength and consolation,
Hope of all the saints, thou art;
Long desired of every nation,
Joy of every waiting heart.

3 Born thy people to deliver,
Born a child, yet God our King;
Born to reign in us for ever,
Now thy gracious kingdom bring.

4 By thine own eternal Spirit,
Rule in all our hearts alone;
By thine all-sufficient merit,
Raise us to thy glorious throne.

---

Praise the Father, earth and heaven,
Praise the Son, the Spirit praise,
As it was, and is, be given
Glory through eternal days.

## HYMN 43. C. M.

BETHLEHEM. DR. MADAN.

## HYMN 44. C. M.

NORTHAMPTON. DR. CROFT.

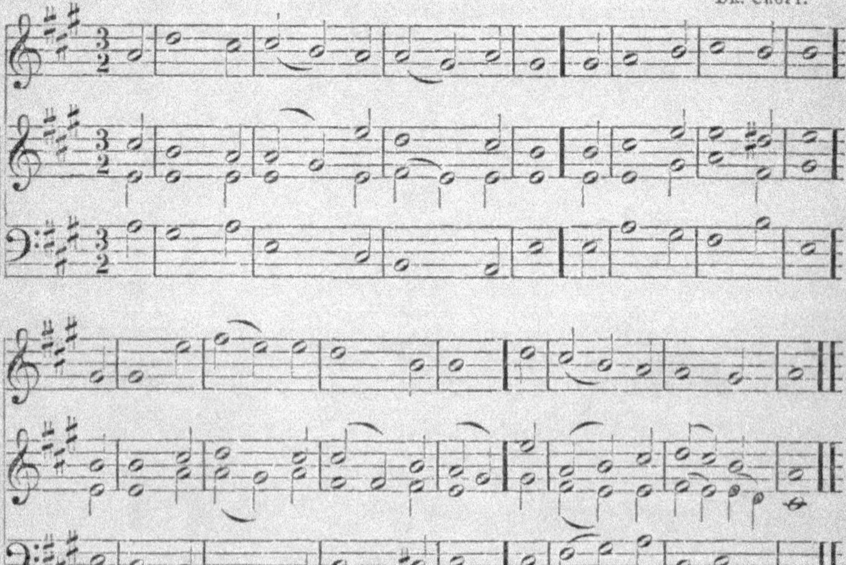

CHRISTMAS.

### HYMN 43. C. M.

Luke ii 8-15. TATE.

1 WHILE shepherds watched their flocks by night,
All seated on the ground,
The angel of the Lord came down,
And glory shone around.

2 "Fear not," said he, for mighty dread
Had seized their troubled minds;
"Glad tidings of great joy I bring
To you, and all mankind.

3 "To you, in David's town, this day
Is born of David's line,
The Saviour, who is Christ the Lord,
And this shall be the sign:

4 "The heavenly babe you there shall find,
To human view displayed,
All meanly wrapt in swathing bands,
And in a manger laid."

5 Thus spake the seraph, and forthwith
Appeared a shining throng
Of angels, praising God, who thus
Addressed their joyful song:

6 "All glory be to God on high,
And to the earth be peace;
Good-will, henceforth, from heaven to men,
Begin and never cease."

---

To Father, Son, and Holy Ghost,
The God whom we adore,
Be glory, as it was, is now,
And shall be evermore.

### HYMN 44. C. M.

1 WHILE angels thus, O Lord, rejoice,
Shall men no anthem raise?
O may we lose these useless tongues,
When we forget to praise.

2 Then let us swell responsive notes,
And join the heavenly throng;
For angels no such love have known
As we, to wake their song.

3 Good-will to sinful dust is shown,
And peace on earth is given;
For, lo! the incarnate Saviour comes,
With news of joy from heaven.

4 Mercy and truth, with sweet accord,
His rising beams adorn;
Let heaven and earth in concert sing,
"The promised child is born!"

5 Glory to God in highest strains,
By highest worlds is paid;
Be glory, then, by us proclaimed,
And by our lives displayed;

6 Till we attain those blissful realms,
Where now our Saviour reigns;
To rival these celestial choirs
In their immortal strains!

---

To Father, Son, and Holy Ghost,
The God whom we adore,
Be glory, as it was, is now,
And shall be evermore.

## HYMN 45. III 1.

HERALD ANGELS. DR. MILLER.

### HYMN 45. III I.

DODDRIDGE.

1 HARK! the herald angels sing
Glory to the the new-born King,
Peace on earth, and mercy mild,
God and sinners reconciled!

2 Joyful all ye nations rise,
Join the triumphs of the skies;
With the angelic hosts proclaim
Christ is born in Bethlehem!

3 Christ, by highest heaven adored,
Christ the everlasting Lord;
Late in time behold him come,
Offspring of the virgin's womb!

4 Vailed in flesh the Godhead see!
Hail the incarnate Deity,
Pleased, as man, with man to dwell,
Jesus, now Emmanuel!

5 Risen with healing in his wings,
Light and life to all he brings;
Hail the Sun of righteousness,
Hail the heaven-born Prince of peace.

---

Holy Father, holy Son,
Holy Spirit, Three in One!
Glory, as of old, to thee,
Now, and evermore shall be.

## HYMN 46.

AVISON. AVISON.

## HYMN 46.

MUHLENBURG.

*Chorus.* Shout the glad tidings, exultingly sing;
Jerusalem triumphs, Messiah is King.

1 ZION! the marvellous story be telling,
The Son of the highest how lowly his birth!
The brightest archangel in glory excelling,
He stoops to redeem thee, he reigns upon earth.

*Chorus.* Shout the glad tidings, exultingly sing;
Jerusalem triumphs, Messiah is King.

2 Tell how he cometh, from nation to nation,
The heart-cheering news let the earth echo round!
How free to the faithful he offers salvation,
How his people with joy everlasting are crowned.

*Chorus.* Shout the glad tidings, exultingly sing;
Jerusalem triumphs, Messiah is King.

3 Mortals! your homage be gratefully bringing,
And sweet let the gladsome hosanna arise;
Ye angels! the full hallelujah be singing,
One chorus resound through the earth and the skies.

*Chorus.* Shout the glad tidings, exultingly sing;
Jerusalem triumphs, Messiah is King.

## HYMNS 47 & 48. C. M.

NORTHAMPTON. DR. CROFT.

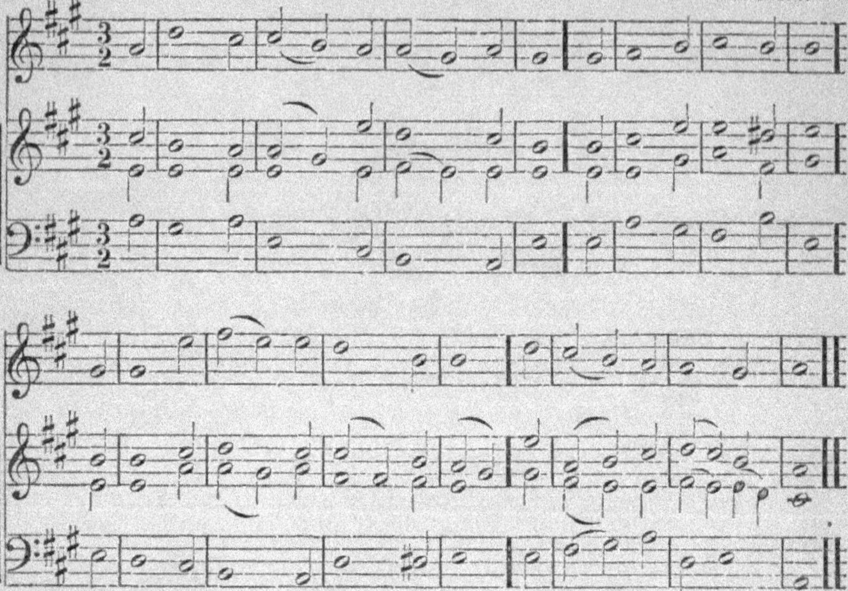

## HYMN 49. C. M.

BEVERLY. M. HOWDON.

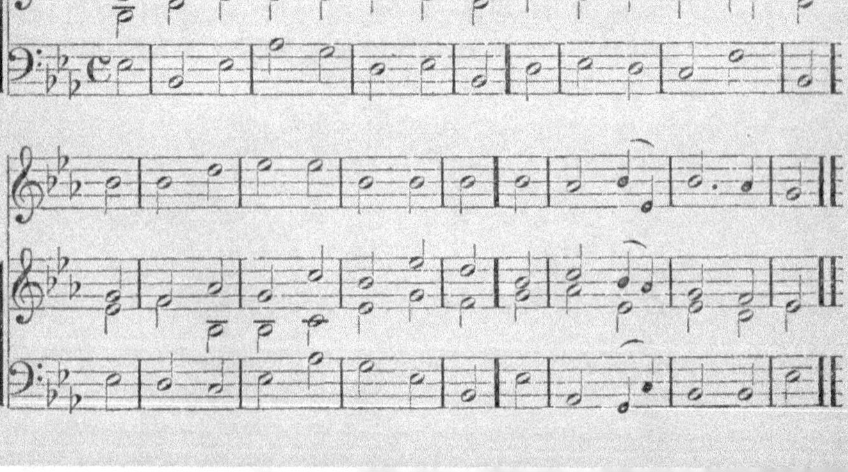

### HYMN 47. C. M.

Isaiah ix: 2-7. LOGAN.

1 THE race that long in darkness pined
Have seen a glorious light;
The people now behold the dawn,
Who dwelt in death and night.

2 To hail thy rising, Sun of life!
The gathering nations come,
Joyous as when the reapers bear
Their harvest treasures home.

3 For thou our burden hast removed,
The oppressor's reign is broke;
Thy fiery conflict with the foe
Has burst his cruel yoke.

4 To us the promised Child is born;
To us the Son is given;
Him shall the tribes of earth obey,
And all the hosts of heaven.

5 His name shall be the Prince of Peace,
For evermore adored,
The Wonderful, the Counselor
The mighty God and Lord.

6 His power increasing still shall spread,
His reign no end shall know:
Justice shall guard his throne above,
And peace abound below.

---

To Father, Son, and Holy Ghost,
The God whom we adore,
Be glory, as it was, is now,
And shall be evermore.

END OF THE YEAR.

### HYMN 48. C. M.

DODDRIDGE.

1 TIME hastens on; ye longing saints
Now raise your voices high;
And magnify that sovereign love
Which shows salvation nigh.

2 As time departs salvation comes;
Each moment brings it near:
Then welcome each declining day,
Welcome each closing year.

3 Not many years their course shall run,
Not many mornings rise,
Ere all its glories stand revealed
To our transported eyes.

---

To Father, Son, and Holy Ghost,
The God whom we adore,
Be glory, as it was, is now,
And shall be evermore.

### HYMN 49. C. M.

St. Luke xiii: 6-9. DODDRIDGE.

1 SEE, in the vineyard of the Lord,
A barren fig-tree stands;
No fruit it yields, no blossom bears,
Though planted by His hands.

2 From year to year the tree He views,
And still no fruit is found;
Then "Cut it down," the Lord commands,
"Why cumbers it the ground?"

3 But lo! the gracious Saviour pleads;
"The barren fig-tree spare,
Another year in mercy wait,
It yet may bloom and bear:

4 "But if my culture prove in vain,
And still no fruit be found,
I plead no more: destroy the tree,
And root it from thy ground."

---

To Father, Son, and Holy Ghost,
The God whom we adore,
Be glory, as it was, is now,
And shall be evermore.

## HYMN 50. L. M.

WANDSWORTH. W. BEALE.

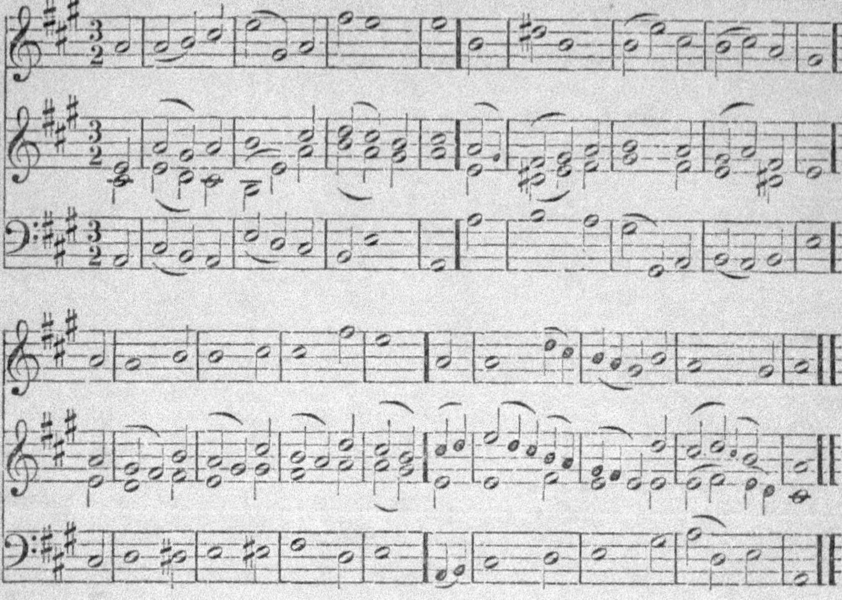

## HYMN 51. C. M.

CROWLE. DR. GREENE.

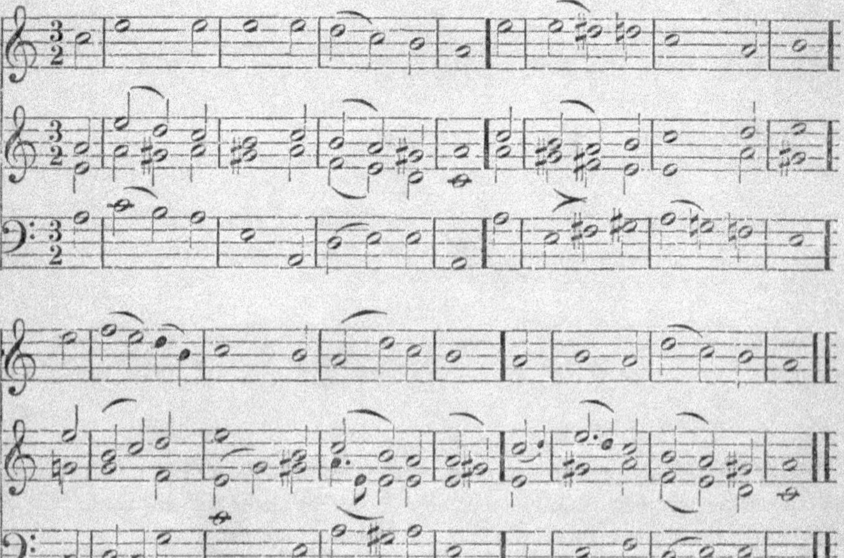

NEW YEAR.

### HYMN 50. L. M.

DODDRIDGE.

1 The God of life, whose constant care
With blessings crowns each opening year,
My scanty span doth still prolong,
And wakes anew mine annual song.

2 How many precious souls are fled
To the vast regions of the dead,
Since to this day the changing sun
Through his last yearly period run!

3 We yet survive; but who can say,
"Or through this year, or month, or day,
I shall retain this vital breath,
Thus far, at least, in league with death?"

4 That breath is thine, eternal God;
'T is thine to fix my soul's abode;
It holds its life from thee alone,
On earth or in the world unknown.

5 To thee our spirits we resign,
Make them and own them still as thine;
So shall they live secure from fear,
Though death shall blast the rising year.

6 Thy children panting to be gone,
May bid the tide of time roll on,
To land them on that happy shore,
Where years and death are known no more.

7 No more fatigue, no more distress,
Nor sin, nor hell, shall reach that place:
No groans, to mingle with the songs
Resounding from immortal tongues.

8 No more alarms from ghostly foes;
No cares to break the long repose:
No midnight shade, no clouded sun,
But sacred, high, eternal noon.

9 O, long-expected year! begin;
Dawn on this world of woe and sin:
Fain would we leave this weary road,
To sleep in death, and rest with God.

---

To Father, Son, and Holy Ghost,
The God whom earth and heaven adore,
Be glory, as it was of old,
Is now, and shall be evermore.

### HYMN 51. C. M.

BP. MIDDLETON.

1 As o'er the past my memory strays,
Why heaves the secret sigh?
'T is that I mourn departed days,
Still unprepared to die.

2 The world and worldly things beloved,
My anxious thoughts employed:
And time unhallowed, unimproved,
Presents a fearful void.

3 Yet, holy Father, wild despair
Chase from my laboring breast;
Thy grace it is which prompts the prayer,
That grace can do the rest.

4 My life's brief remnant all be thine;
And when thy sure decree
Bids me this fleeting breath resign,
O speed my soul to thee.

---

To Father, Son, and Holy Ghost,
The God whom we adore,
Be glory, as it was, is now,
And shall be evermore.

## HYMN 52. S. M.

VIGIL. LEACH.

## HYMN 53. II 5.

WALWORTH. WAINWRIGHT.

EPIPHANY.

### HYMN 52. S. M.

Isaiah lii: 7-10. WATTS.

1 How beauteous are their feet
Who stand on Sion's hill;
Who bring salvation on their tongues,
And words of peace reveal.

2 How charming is their voice;
How sweet their tidings are;
"Sion, behold thy Saviour King,
He reigns and triumphs here."

3 How happy are our ears
That hear this joyful sound,
Which kings and prophets waited for,
And sought, but never found.

4 How blessed are our eyes
That see this heavenly light;
Prophets and kings desired it long,
But died without the sight.

5 The watchmen join their voice,
And tuneful notes employ;
Jerusalem breaks forth in songs,
And deserts learn the joy.

6 The Lord makes bare his arm
Through all the earth abroad;
Let every nation now behold
Their Saviour and their God.

---

To God the Father, Son,
And Spirit, glory be,
As 't was, and is, and shall be so,
To all eternity.

### HYMN 53. II 5.

Isaiah lx, etc. POPE.

1 RISE, crowned with light, imperial Salem, rise!
Exalt thy tow'ring head and lift thine eyes!
See heaven its sparkling portals wide display,
And break upon thee in a flood of day!

2 See a long race thy spacious courts adorn,
See future sons and daughters yet unborn,
In crowding ranks, on every side arise,
Demanding life, impatient for the skies.

3 See barbarous nations at thy gates attend,
Walk in thy light, and in thy temple bend!
See thy bright altars thronged with prostrate kings,
While every land its joyous tribute brings!

4 The seas shall waste, the skies to smoke decay,
Rocks fall to dust, and mountains melt away;
But fixed his word, his saving power remains—
Thy realm shall last, thy own Messiah reigns.

---

To God the Father, and to God the Son,
To God the Holy Spirit, Three in One,
Be praise from all on earth and all in heaven,
As was, and is, and ever shall be given.

## HYMN 54. II 6.

SALUTATION. S. WESLEY.

## HYMN 55. C. M.

MISSIONARY. T. WALKER.

### HYMN 54. II 6.

Psalm lxxii. MONTGOMERY.

1 HAIL to the Lord's Anointed,
Great David's greater Son!
Hail, in the time appointed,
His reign on earth begun!
He comes to break oppression,
To set the captive free;
To take away transgression,
And rule in equity.

2 He comes, with succor speedy,
To those who suffer wrong;
To help the poor and needy,
And bid the weak be strong;
To give them songs for sighing,
Their darkness turn to light,
Whose souls, condemned and dying,
Were precious in his sight.

3 He shall descend like showers
Upon the fruitful earth;
And love and joy, like flowers,
Spring in his path to birth;
Before him, on the mountains,
Shall peace, the herald, go;
And righteousness, in fountains,
From hill to valley flow.

4 To him shall prayer unceasing,
And daily vows, ascend;
His kingdom, still increasing,
A kingdom without end:
The tide of time shall never
His covenant remove;
His name shall stand for ever;
That name to us is love.

---

Eternal praise be given,
And songs of highest worth,
By all the hosts of heaven,
And all the saints on earth,
To God, supreme confessed,
To Christ, his only Son,
And to the Spirit blessed,
Eternal Three in One.

### HYMN 55. C. M.

Isaiah ii: 2-5. LOGAN.

1 O'ER mountain tops the mount of God
In latter days shall rise,
Above the summits of the hills,
And draw the wond'ring eyes.

2 To this the joyful nations round,
All tribes and tongues shall flow;
Up to the mount of God, they'll say,
And to his house we'll go.

3 The beams that shine from Zion's hill
Shall lighten every land;
The King who reigns in Salem's towers
Shall all the world command.

4 Among the nations he shall judge,
His judgments truth shall guide;
His scepter shall protect the just,
And crush the sinner's pride.

5 For peaceful implements shall men
Exchange their swords and spears;
Nor shall they study war again
Throughout those happy years.

6 Come, O ye house of Jacob! come
To worship at his shrine;
And, walking in the light of God,
With holy graces shine.

---

To Father, Son, and Holy Ghost,
The God whom we adore,
Be glory, as it was, is now,
And shall be evermore.

## HYMN 56. III 1.

LITANY. C. MALAN.

## LENT.

### HYMN 56. III 1.

SIR. R. GRANT.

*Litany.*

1 SAVIOUR, when in dust to thee,
Low we bow the adoring knee;
When, repentant, to the skies
Scarce we lift our streaming eyes;
O, by all thy pains and woe,
Suffered once for man below,
Bending from thy throne on high,
Hear our solemn litany.

2 By thy birth and early years,
By thy human griefs and fears,
By thy fasting and distress
In the lonely wilderness:
By thy victory in the hour
Of the subtle tempter's power;
Jesus, look with pitying eye;
Hear our solemn litany.

3 By thine hour of dark despair,
By thine agony of prayer,
By the purple robe of scorn,
By thy wounds—thy crown of thorn,
By thy cross—thy pangs and cries;
By thy perfect sacrifice;
Jesus, look with pitying eye;
Hear our solemn litany.

4 By thy deep expiring groan,
By the sealed sepulchral stone,
By thy triumph o'er the grave,
By thy power from death to save;
Mighty God, ascended Lord,
To thy throne in heaven restored,
Prince and Saviour, hear our cry,
Hear our solemn litany.

---

Holy Father, holy Son,
Holy Spirit, Three in One!
Glory, as of old, to thee,
Now, and evermore shall be!

## HYMN 57. L. M.

St. Luke's. Jer. Clarke.

## HYMNS 58 & 59. C. M.

Darlington. Garnett.

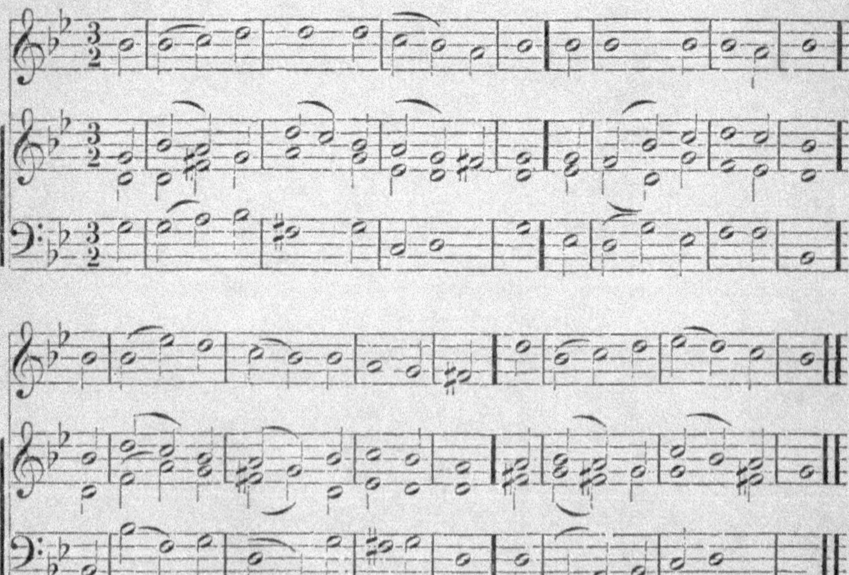

### HYMN 57. L. M.

WATTS.

1 My God, permit me not to be
A stranger to myself and thee:
Amid a thousand thoughts I rove,
Forgetful of my highest love.

2 Why should my passions mix with earth,
And thus debase my heavenly birth?
Why should I cleave to things below,
And all my purest joys forego?

3 Call me away from flesh and sense;
Thy grace, O Lord, can draw me thence:
I would obey the voice divine,
And all inferior joys resign.

---

To Father, Son, and Holy Ghost,
The God whom earth and heaven adore,
Be glory, as it was of old,
Is now, and shall be evermore.

### HYMN 58. C. M.

A. STEELE.

1 ALAS, what hourly dangers rise!
What snares beset my way!
To heaven O let me lift mine eyes,
And hourly watch and pray.

2 How oft my mournful thoughts complain,
And melt in flowing tears!
My weak resistance, ah, how vain!
How strong my foes and fears.

3 O gracious God, in whom I live,
My feeble efforts aid;
Help me to watch, and pray, and strive,
Though trembling and afraid.

4 Increase my faith, increase my hope,
When foes and fears prevail;
And bear my fainting spirit up,
Or soon my strength will fail.

5 Whene'er temptations fright my heart,
Or lure my feet aside,
My God, thy powerful aid impart,
My guardian and my guide.

6 O keep me in thy heavenly way,
And bid the tempter flee;
And let me never, never stray
From happiness and thee.

---

To Father, Son, and Holy Ghost,
The God whom we adore,
Be glory, as it was, is now,
And shall be evermore.

### HYMN 59. C. M.

DODDRIDGE.

1 How oft, alas! this wretched heart
Has wandered from the Lord!
How oft my roving thoughts depart,
Forgetful of his word!

2 Yet sovereign mercy calls, "Return;"
Dear Lord, and may I come?
My vile ingratitude I mourn;
O take the wanderer home.

3 And canst thou, wilt thou yet forgive,
And bid my crimes remove?
And shall a pardoned rebel live,
To speak thy wondrous love?

4 Almighty grace, thy healing power,
How glorious, how divine!
That can to life and bliss restore
So vile a heart as mine.

5 Thy pardoning love, so free, so sweet,
Dear Saviour, I adore;
O keep me at thy sacred feet,
And let me rove no more?

---

To Father, Son, and Holy Ghost,
The God whom we adore,
Be glory, as it was, is now,
And shall be evermore.

## HYMN 60. L. M.

GERMANY. BEETHOVEN.

## HYMN 61. III 4.

CALVARY. STANLEY.

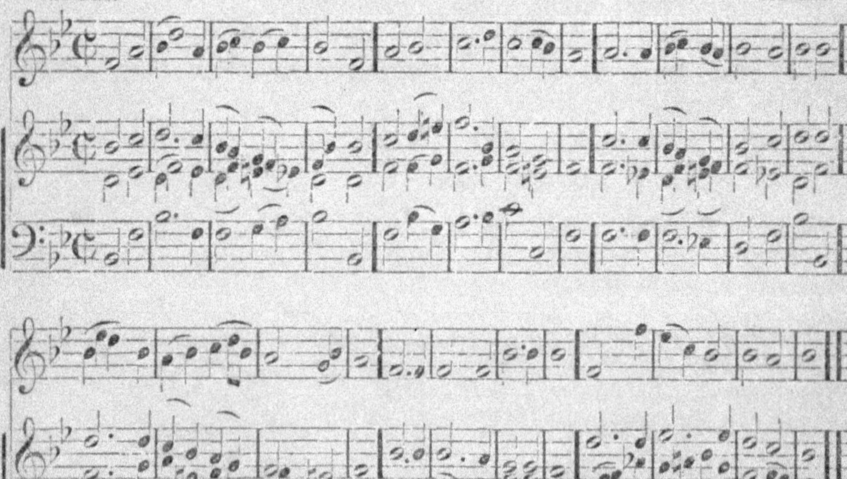

### HYMN 60. L. M.

C. Wesley.

1 O thou, to whose all-searching sight
The darkness shineth as the light,
Search, prove my heart; it looks to thee;
O burst its bonds, and set it free.

2 Wash out its stains, remove its dross,
Bind my affections to the cross;
Hallow each thought; let all within
Be clean, as thou, my Lord, art clean.

3 If in this darksome wild I stray,
Be thou my light, be thou my way;
No foes, no violence I fear,
No harm while thou, my God, art near.

4 When rising floods my soul o'erflow,
When sinks my heart in waves of woe,
Jesus, thy timely aid impart,
And raise my head, and cheer my heart.

5 Saviour! where'er thy steps I see,
Dauntless, untired, I follow thee;
O let thy hand support me still,
And lead me to thy holy hill.

---

To Father, Son, and Holy Ghost,
The God whom earth and heaven adore,
Be glory, as it was of old,
Is now, and shall be evermore.

*See Hymns on Repentance.*

PASSION WEEK AND GOOD FRIDAY.

### HYMN 61. III 4.

Isaiah lxiii: 1-4.

1 Who is this that comes from Edom,
All his raiment stained with blood,
To the captive speaking freedom,
Bringing and bestowing good;
Glorious in the garb he wears,
Glorious in the spoil he bears?

2 'T is the Saviour, now victorious,
Traveling onward in his might;
'T is the Saviour; O how glorious
To his people is the sight!
Satan conquered, and the grave;
Jesus now is strong to save.

3 Why that blood his raiment staining?
'T is the blood of many slain;
Of his foes there 's none remaining,
None, the contest to maintain;
Fallen they are, no more to rise,
All their glory prostrate lies.

4 Mighty Victor, reign for ever,
Wear the crown so dearly won;
Never shall thy people, never,
Cease to sing what thou hast done.
Thou hast fought thy people's foes;
Thou hast healed thy people's woes.

---

To the Father, throned in heaven,
To the Saviour, Christ, his Son,
To the Spirit, praise be given,
Everlasting, Three in One;
As of old, the Trinity
Still is worshiped, still shall be.

## HYMN 62. L. M.

CONTEMPLATION. TATE.

### HYMN 62. L. M.

WATTS.

1 WHEN I survey the wondrous cross,
On which the Prince of Glory died,
My richest gain I count but loss,
And pour contempt on all my pride.

2 Forbid it, Lord, that I should boast,
Save in the cross of Christ my God:
All the vain things that charm me most,
I sacrifice them to thy blood.

3 See! from his head, his hands, his feet,
Sorrow and love flow mingled down:
Did e'er such love and sorrow meet?
Or thorns compose a Saviour's crown?

4 Were the whole realm of nature mine,
That were a tribute far too small;
Love so amazing, so divine,
Demands my life, my soul, my all.

---

To Father, Son, and Holy Ghost,
The God whom earth and heaven adore,
Be glory, as it was of old,
Is now, and shall be evermore.

## HYMN 63. C. M.

CROWLE. DR. GREENE.

## HYMNS 64 & 65. C. M.

BURFORD. PURCELL, 1680.

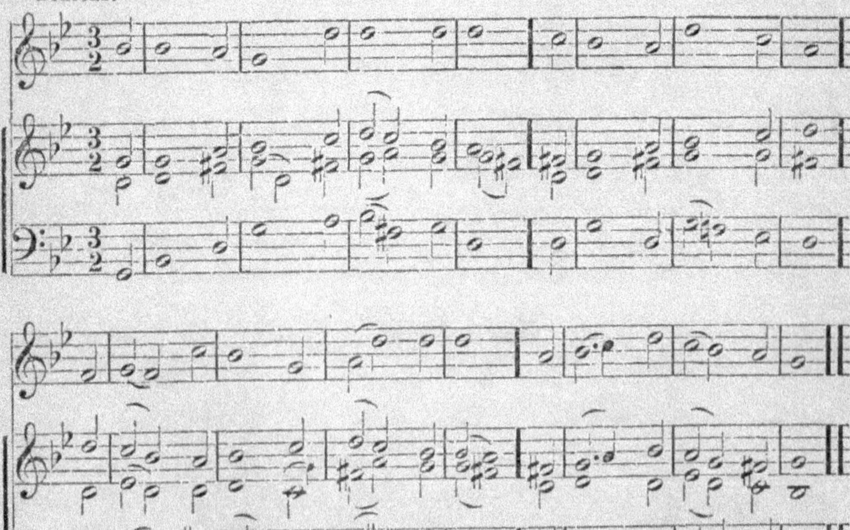

### HYMN 63. C. M.

WESLEY.

1 BEHOLD the Saviour of mankind
Nailed to the shameful tree;
How vast the love that him inclined
To bleed and die for me!

2 Hark, how he groans! while nature shakes,
And earth's strong pillars bend;
The temple's vail in sunder breaks,
The solid marbles rend.

3 'Tis done! the precious ransom's paid;
"Receive my soul!" he cries;
See where he bows his sacred head!
He bows his head and dies.

4 But soon he'll break death's envious chain,
And in full glory shine;
O Lamb of God, was ever pain,
Was ever love like thine!

To Father, Son, and Holy Ghost,
The God whom we adore,
Be glory, as it was, is now,
And shall be evermore.

### HYMN 64. C. M.

NEWTON.

1 MY Saviour hanging on the tree,
In agonies and blood,
Methought once turned his eyes on me,
As near his cross I stood.

2 Sure, never till my latest breath
Can I forget that look;
It seemed to charge me with his death,
Though not a word he spoke.

3 My conscience felt and owned the guilt,
And plunged me in despair;
I saw my sins his blood had spilt,
And helped to nail him there.

4 Alas! I knew not what I did;
But now my tears are vain:
Where shall my trembling soul be hid?
For I the Lord have slain.

5 A second look he gave, which said,
"I freely all forgive;
This blood is for thy ransom paid,
I die that thou may'st live."

6 Thus, while his death my sin displays
In all its blackest hue—
Such is the mystery of grace—
It seals my pardon too.

*To Father, Son, and Holy Ghost, etc.*

### HYMN 65. C. M.

S. WESLEY.

1 FROM whence these direful omens round,
Which heaven and earth amaze?
Wherefore do earthquakes cleave the ground?
Why hides the sun his rays?

2 Well may the earth astonished shake,
And nature sympathize;
The sun as darkest night be black:
Their Maker, Jesus, dies!

3 Behold, fast streaming from the tree,
His all-atoning blood!
Is this the Infinite? 'tis He,
My Saviour and my God!

4 For me these pangs his soul assail,
For me this death is borne;
My sins gave sharpness to the nail,
And pointed every thorn.

5 Let sin no more my soul enslave,
Break, Lord, its tyrant chain;
O save me, whom thou cam'st to save,
Nor bleed, nor die in vain.

*To Father, Son, and Holy Ghost, etc.*

## HYMN 66. L. M.

HARTFORD. BP. WAINWRIGHT.

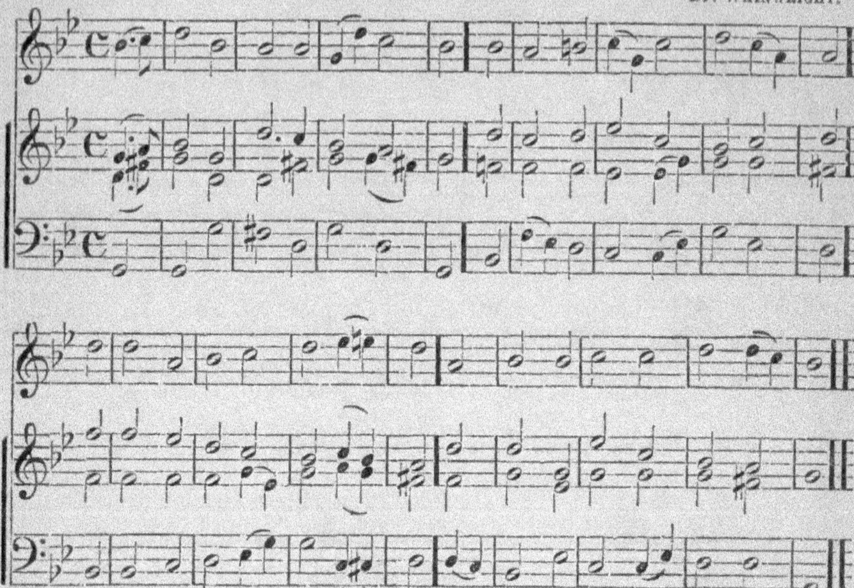

## HYMN 67. L. M.

DARLEY. DARLEY.

### HYMN 66. L. M.

St. John, xix : 30. STENNETT.

1 'Tis finished: so the Saviour cried,
And meekly bowed his head and died:
'T is finished: yes, the work is done,
The battle fought, the victory won.

2 'T is finished: all that heaven decreed,
And all the ancient prophets said,
Is now fulfilled, as long designed,
In me, the Saviour of mankind.

3 'T is finished: Aaron now no more
Must stain his robes with purple gore:
The sacred vail is rent in twain,
And Jewish rites no more remain.

4 'T is finished: this my dying groan,
Shall sins of every kind atone:
Millions shall be redeemed from death,
By this, my last expiring breath.

5 'T is finished: heaven is reconciled,
And all the powers of darkness spoiled:
Peace, love, and happiness, again
Return and dwell with sinful men.

6 'T is finished: let the joyful sound
Be heard through all the nations round.
'T is finished—let the echo fly
Through heaven and hell, through earth and sky.

---

To Father, Son, and Holy Ghost,
The God whom earth and heaven adore,
Be glory, as it was of old,
Is now, and shall be evermore.

### HYMN 67. L. M.

*For the Jews.*

1 High on the bending willows hung,
Israel, still sleeps the tuneful string?
Still mute remains the sullen tongue,
And Zion's song denies to sing?

2 Awake! thy loudest raptures raise;
Let harp and voice unite their strains.
Thy promised King his scepter sways;
Behold, thy own Messiah reigns.

3 By foreign streams no longer roam,
And weeping, think on Jordan's flood;
In every clime behold a home,
In every temple see thy God.

4 No taunting foes the song require;
No strangers mock thy captive chain;
Thy friends provoke the silent lyre,
And brethren ask the holy strain.

5 Then why, on bending willows hung,
Israel, still sleeps the tuneful string?
Why mute remains the sullen tongue,
And Zion's song delays to sing?

---

To Father, Son, and Holy Ghost,
The God whom earth and heaven adore,
Be glory, as it was of old,
Is now, and shall be evermore.

## HYMN 68. C. M.

WAINWRIGHT. WAINWRIGHT.

## HYMN 69. III 1.

CLARK. CLARK.

EASTER.

## HYMN 68. C. M.

1 Cor. v: 8; Rom. vi: 9, 10, 11. TATE.

1 SINCE Christ our Passover is slain,
A sacrifice for all,
Let all with thankful hearts agree
To keep the festival:

2 Not with the leaven, as of old,
Of sin and malice fed;
But with unfeigned sincerity,
And truth's unleavened bread.

3 Christ being raised by power divine,
And rescued from the grave,
Shall die no more; death shall on him
No more dominion have.

4 For that he died, 't was for our sins
He once vouchsafed to die:
But that he lives, he lives to God
For all eternity.

5 So count yourselves as dead to sin,
But graciously restored,
And made, henceforth, alive to God,
Through Jesus Christ our Lord.

---

To Father, Son, and Holy Ghost,
The God whom we adore,
Be glory, as it was, is now,
And shall be evermore.

## HYMN 69. III 1.

C. WESLEY.

1 CHRIST the Lord is risen to-day,
Sons of men and angels say:
Raise your joys and triumphs high,
Sing, ye heavens, and earth reply!

2 Love's redeeming work is done,
Fought the fight, the victory won:
Jesus' agony is o'er,
Darkness vails the earth no more.

3 Vain the stone, the watch, the seal,
Christ has burst the gates of hell;
Death in vain forbids him rise,
Christ hath opened paradise.

4 Soar we now where Christ hath led,
Following our exalted Head;
Made like him, like him we rise,
Ours the cross, the grave, the skies.

---

Holy Father, Holy Son,
Holy Spirit, Three in One!
Glory, as of old, to thee,
Now, and evermore shall be.

## HYMN 70. L. M.

LUTON. BURDER.

## HYMN 71. C. M.

BEVERLY. M. HOWDON.

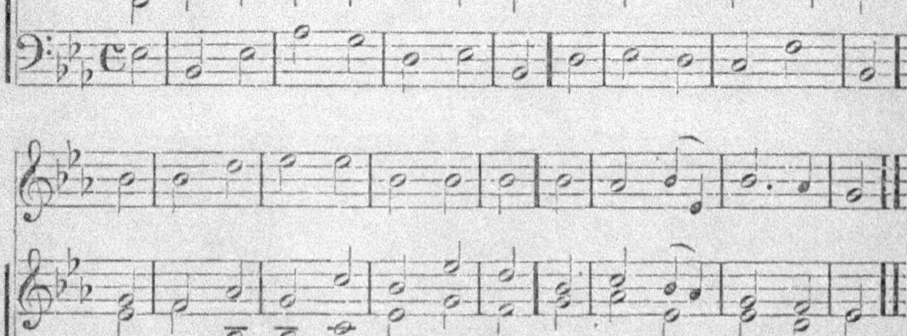

### HYMN 70. L. M.

Col. iii. 1, 2. C. Wesley.

1 Ye faithful souls who Jesus know,
 If risen indeed with him ye are,
Superior to the joys below,
 His resurrection's power declare:

2 Your faith by holy tempers prove,
 By actions show your sins forgiven,
And seek the glorious things above,
 And follow Christ, your head, to heave

3 There your exalted Saviour see,
 Seated at God's right hand again,
In all his Father's majesty,
 In everlasting power to reign.

4 To him continually aspire,
 Contending for your destined place,
And emulate the angel choir,
 And only live to love and praise.

---

To Father, Son, and Holy Ghost,
 The God whom earth and heaven adore,
Be glory, as it was of old,
 Is now, and shall be evermore.

### HYMN 71. C. M.

1 Cor. xv. 20, 21, 22. Col. iii. 1. Tate.

1 Christ from the dead is raised, and made
 The First Fruits of the tomb;
For, as by man came death, by man
 Did resurrection come.

2 For, as in Adam all mankind
 Did guilt and death derive:
So by the righteousness of Christ
 Shall all be made alive.

3 If then ye risen are with Christ,
 Seek only how to get
The things which are above, where Christ
 At God's right hand is set.

---

To Father, Son, and Holy Ghost,
 The God whom we adore,
Be Glory, as it was, is now,
 And shall be evermore.

## HYMN 72. L. M.

ST. LUKE'S. JER. CLARKE.

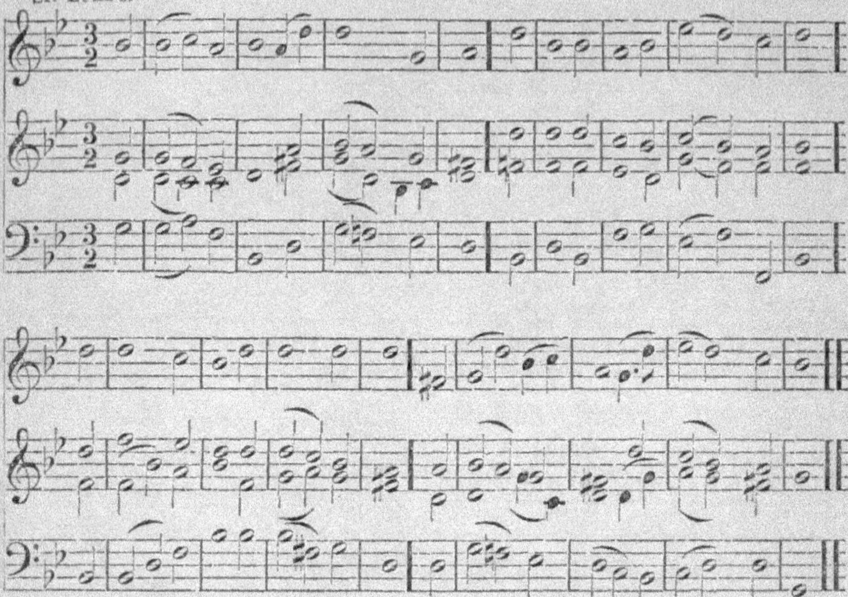

## HYMN 73. L. M.

TRURO. DR. BURNEY.

ASCENSION.

## HYMN 72. L. M.

WATTS.

1 HE dies! the friend of sinners dies!
Lo! Salem's daughters weep around!
A solemn darkness vails the skies!
A sudden trembling shakes the ground!

2 Ye saints, approach! the anguish view
Of him who groans beneath your load;
He gives his precious life for you,
For you he sheds his precious blood.

3 Here's love and grief beyond degree,
The Lord of Glory dies for men;
But lo! what sudden joys we see,
Jesus, the dead, revives again.

4 The rising God forsakes the tomb;
Up to his Father's court he flies;
Cherubic legions guard him home,
And shout him welcome to the skies.

5 Break off your tears, ye saints, and tell
How high our great Deliverer reigns;
Sing how he spoiled the hosts of hell,
And led the tyrant death in chains.

6 Say, "Live for ever, glorious King,
Born to redeem, instruct, and save!"
Then ask, "O death, where is thy sting?
And where thy victory, O grave?"

---

To Father, Son, and Holy Ghost,
The God whom earth and heaven adore,
Be glory, as it was of old,
Is now, and shall be evermore.

## HYMN 73. L. M.

C. WESLEY.

1 OUR Lord is risen from the dead,
Our Jesus is gone up on high;
The powers of hell are captive led,
Dragged to the portals of the sky.

2 There his triumphal chariot waits,
And angels chant the solemn lay:
"Lift up your heads, ye heavenly gates,
Ye everlasting doors give way."

3 Loose all your bars of massy light,
And wide unfold the radiant scene;
He claims those mansions as his right;
Receive the King of Glory in.

4 "Who is the King of Glory, who?"
The Lord that all his foes o'ercame,
The world, sin, death and hell o'erthrew;
And Jesus is the conqueror's name.

5 Lo! his triumphal chariot waits,
And angel's chant the solemn lay,
"Lift up your heads, ye heavenly gates,
Ye everlasting doors, give way."

6 "Who is the King of Glory, who?"
The Lord of boundless power possessed,
The King of saints and angels too,
God over all, for ever blessed.

---

To Father, Son, and Holy Ghost,
The God whom earth and heaven adore,
Be glory, as it was of old,
Is now, and shall be evermore.

## HYMNS 74 & 75. C. M.

BETHLEHEM. DR. MADAN.

## HYMN 76. C. M.

ARLINGTON. DR. ARNE.

WHITSUNDAY.

### HYMN 74. C. M.

WATTS.

1 Come, Holy Ghost, Creator, come,
Inspire these souls of thine;
Till every heart which thou hast made,
Be filled with grace divine.

2 Thou art the Comforter, the gift
Of God, and fire of love;
The everlasting spring of joy,
And unction from above.

3 Thy gifts are manifold, thou writ'st
God's law in each true heart;
The promise of the Father, thou
Dost heavenly speech impart.

4 Enlighten our dark souls, till they
Thy sacred love embrace;
Assist our minds, by nature frail,
With thy celestial grace.

5 Drive far from us the mortal foe,
And give us peace within;
That, by thy guidance blest, we may
Escape the snares of sin.

6 Teach us the Father to confess,
And Son, from death revived,
And thee, with both, O Holy Ghost,
Who art from both derived.

---

To Father, Son, and Holy Ghost,
The God whom we adore,
Be glory, as it was, is now,
And shall be evermore.

### HYMN 75. C. M.

WATTS.

1 Come, Holy Spirit, Heavenly Dove,
With all thy quickening powers;
Kindle a flame of sacred love
In these cold hearts of ours.

2 See how we grovel here below,
Fond of these earthly toys:
Our souls, how heavily they go,
To reach eternal joys.

3 In vain we tune our lifeless songs,
In vain we strive to rise:
Hosannas languish on our tongues,
And our devotion dies.

4 Come, Holy Spirit, Heavenly Dove,
With all thy quickening powers;
Come, shed abroad a Saviour's love,
And that shall kindle ours.

---

To Father, Son, and Holy Ghost,
The God whom we adore,
Be glory, as it was, is now,
And shall be evermore.

### HYMN 76. C. M.

1 He's come, let every knee be bent,
All hearts new joy resume;
Sing, ye redeemed, with one consent,
"The Comforter is come."

2 What greater gift, what greater love,
Could God on man bestow?
Angels for this rejoice above,
Let man rejoice below.

3 Hail, blessed Spirit! may each soul
Thy sacred influence feel;
Do thou each sinful thought control,
And fix our wavering zeal.

4 Thou to the conscience dost convey
Those checks which we should know;
Thy motions point to us the way;
Thou giv'st us strength to go.

---

To Father, Son, and Holy Ghost,
The God whom we adore,
Be glory, as it was, is now,
And shall be evermore.

## HYMN 77. L. M.

HARLEM. HANDEL.

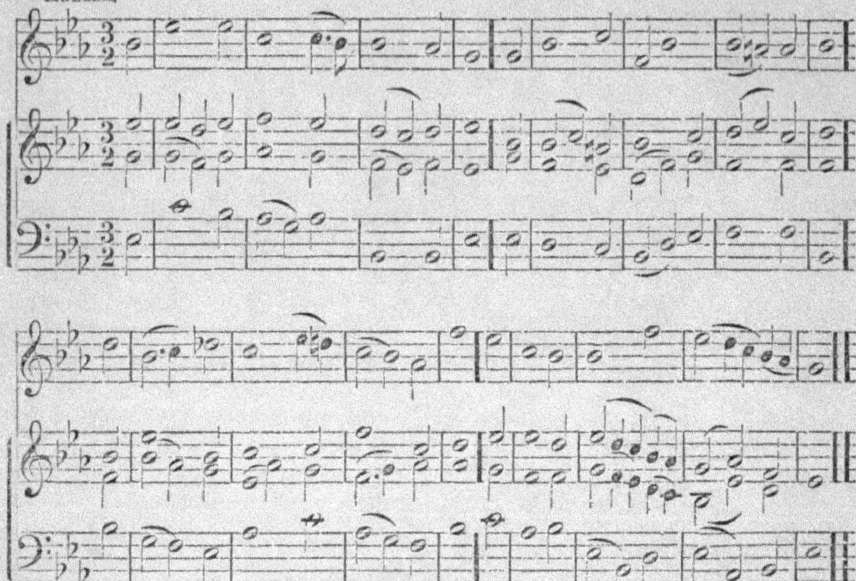

## HYMN 78. L. M.

WANDSWORTH. W. BEALE.

TRINITY SUNDAY.

## HYMN 77. L. M.

J. W. EASTBURN.

1 O HOLY, holy, holy Lord,
Bright in thy deeds and in thy Name,
For ever be thy Name adored,
Thy glories let the world proclaim.

2 O Jesus, Lamb once crucified
To take our load of sins away,
Thine be the hymn that rolls its tide
Along the realms of upper day.

3 O Holy Spirit from above,
In streams of light and glory given,
Thou source of ecstasy and love,
Thy praises ring through earth and heaven!

4 O God triune! to thee we owe
Our every thought, our every song;
And ever may thy praises flow
From saint and seraph's burning tongue!

To Father, Son, and Holy Ghost,
The God whom earth and heaven adore,
Be glory, as it was of old,
Is now, and shall be evermore.

## HYMN 78. L. M.

1 FATHER of all, whose love profound
A ransom for our souls hath found,
Before thy throne we sinners bend;
To us thy pardoning love extend!

2 Almighty Son, incarnate Word,
Our Prophet, Priest, Redeemer, Lord,
Before thy throne we sinners bend;
To us thy saving grace extend!

3 Eternal Spirit, by whose breath
The soul is raised from sin and death,
Before thy throne we sinners bend;
To us thy quickening power extend!

4 Jehovah! Father, Spirit, Son,
Mysterious Godhead, Three in One!
Before thy throne we sinners bend;
Grace, pardon, life, to us extend!

To Father, Son, and Holy Ghost,
The God whom earth and heaven adore,
Be glory, as it was of old,
Is now, and shall be evermore.

## HYMN 79. II 4.

WARSAW. T. CLARK.

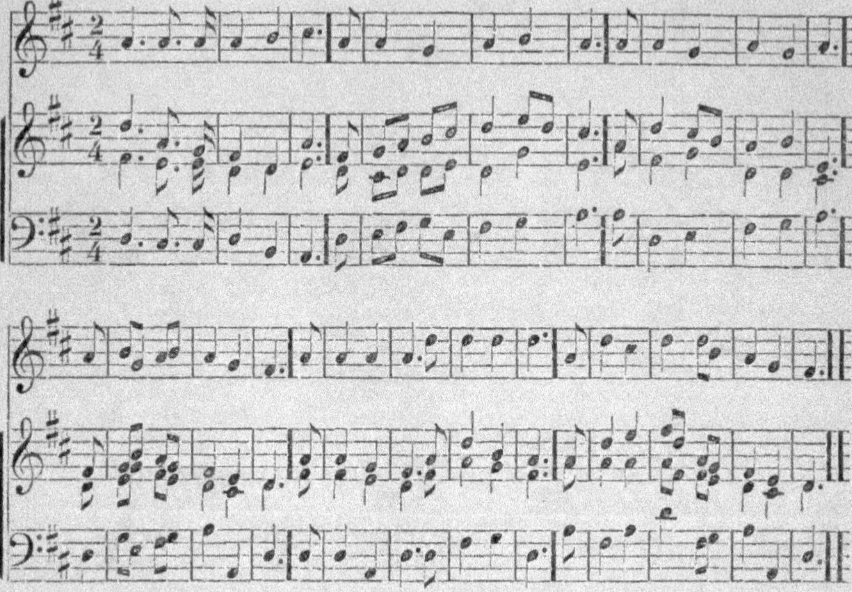

## HYMN 80. C. M.

BURFORD. PURCELL, 1680.

### HYMN 79. H 4.

1 We give immortal praise
To God the Father's love,
For all our comforts here,
And all our hopes above:
He sent his own
Eternal Son,
To die for sins
That man had done.

2 To God the Son belongs
Immortal glory, too,
Who saved us by his blood
From everlasting woe;
And now he lives,
And now he reigns,
And sees the fruit
Of all his pains.

3 To God the Spirit, praise,
And endless worship give,
Whose new-creating power
Makes the dead sinner live:
His work completes
The great design,
And fills the soul
With joy divine.

4 Almighty God! to thee
Be endless honors done;
The sacred Persons three,
The Godhead only one:
Where reason fails
With all her powers,
There faith prevails,
And love adores.

---

To God, the Father, Son,
And Spirit, ever blessed,
Eternal Three in One,
All worship be addressed,
As heretofore
It was, is now,
And shall be so
For evermore.

FAST-DAY.

### HYMN 80. C. M.

STEELE.

1 Almighty Lord! before thy throne
Thy mourning people bend!
'T is on thy pardoning grace alone
Our prostrate hopes depend.

2 Dark judgments, from thy heavy hand,
Thy dreadful power display;
Yet mercy spares our guilty land,
And still we live to pray.

3 How changed, alas! are truths divine,
For error, guilt, and shame!
What impious numbers, bold in sin,
Disgrace the Christian name!

4 O turn us, turn us, mighty Lord;
Convert us by thy grace;
Then shall our hearts obey thy word,
And see again thy face.

5 Then, should oppressing foes invade,
We will not sink in fear;
Secure of all-sufficient aid,
When God, our God, is near.

---

To Father, Son, and Holy Ghost,
The God whom we adore,
Be glory, as it was, is now,
And shall be evermore.

## HYMN 81. III 3.

HAMBURG. MENDELSSOHN.

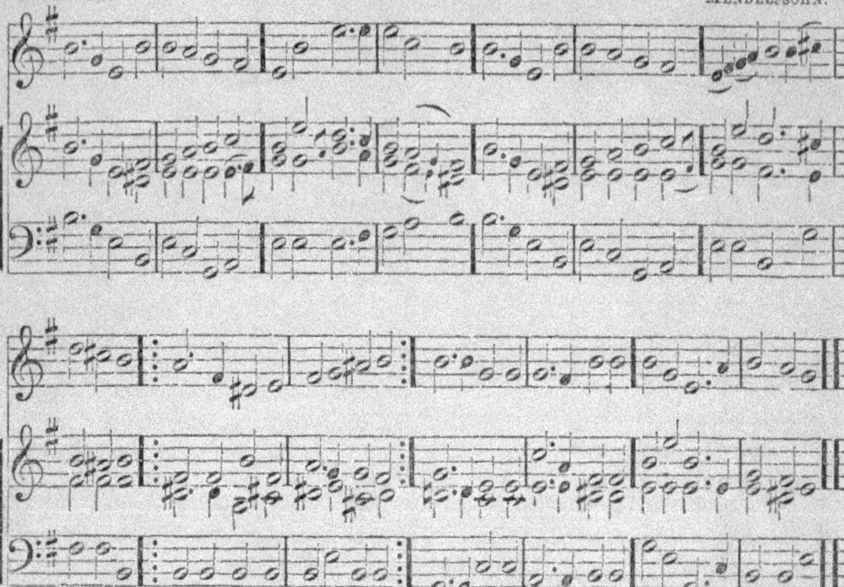

## HYMN 82. L. M.

ALLENHEAD. T. IONS.

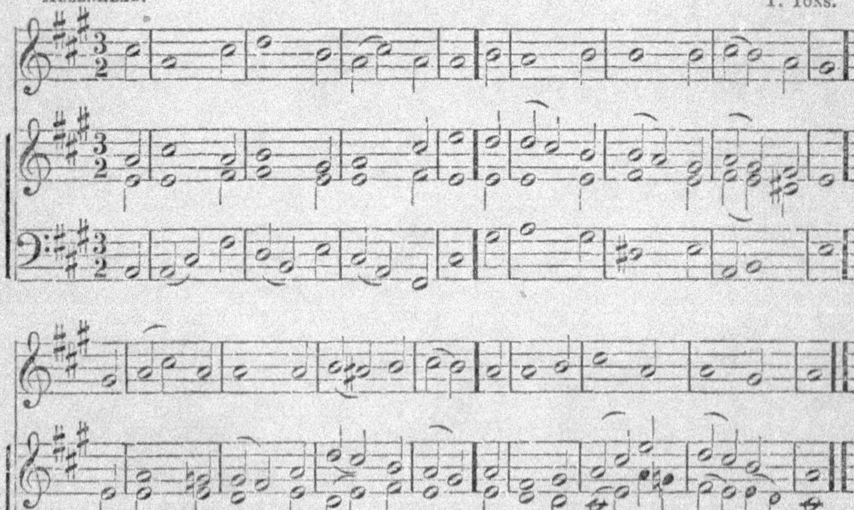

## HYMN 81. III 3.

1 Dread Jehovah! God of nations,
From thy temple in the skies,
Hear thy people's supplications,
Now for their deliverance rise.

2 Lo! with deep contrition turning,
Humbly at thy feet we bend;
Hear us, fasting, praying, mourning,
Hear us, spare us, and defend.

3 Though our sins our hearts confounding,
Long and loud for vengeance call,
Thou hast mercy more abounding,
Jesus' blood can cleanse them all.

4 Let that love vail our transgression,
Let that blood our guilt efface:
Save thy people from oppression,
Save from spoil thy holy place.

---

Praise the Father, earth and heaven,
Praise the Son, the Spirit praise,
As it was, and is, be given
Glory through eternal days.

## HYMN 82. L. M.

*Prayer and Hope of Victory.* Watts.

1 Now may the God of grace and power
Attend his people's humble cry;
Defend them in the needful hour,
And send deliverance from on high.

2 In his salvation is our hope,
And in the name of Israel's God
Our troops shall lift their banners up,
Our navies spread their flags abroad.

3 Some trust in horses trained for war,
And some of chariots make their boasts;
Our surest expectations are
From thee, the Lord of heavenly hosts!

4 Then save us, Lord, from slavish fear,
And let our trust be firm and strong,
Till thy salvation shall appear,
And hymns of peace conclude our song.

---

To Father, Son, and Holy Ghost,
The God whom earth and heaven adore,
Be glory, as it was of old,
Is now, and shall be evermore.

## HYMN 83. Part i & ii. III 2.

SABBATH.

## HYMN 84. C. M.

DORCHESTER. STANLEY.

THANKSGIVING-DAY.

## HYMN 83.

### PART I. III 2.

BARBAULD.

1 PRAISE to God, immortal praise,
For the love that crowns our days;
Bounteous source of every joy,
Let thy praise our tongues employ:
All to thee, our God, we owe,
Source whence all our blessings flow.

2 All the blessings of the fields,
All the stores the garden yields,
Flocks that whiten all the plain,
Yellow sheaves of ripened grain;
Lord, for these our souls shall raise
Grateful vows and solemn praise.

3 Clouds that drop their fattening dews,
Suns that genial warmth diffuse,
All the plenty summer pours,
Autumn's rich o'erflowing stores;
Lord, for these our souls shall raise
Grateful vows and solemn praise.

4 Peace, prosperity, and health,
Private bliss and public wealth,
Knowledge, with its gladdening streams,
Pure religion's holier beams;
Lord, for these our souls shall raise
Grateful vows and solemn praise.

---

Praise the name of God most high,
Praise him, all below the sky,
Praise him, all ye heavenly host,
Father, Son, and Holy Ghost;
As through countless ages past,
Evermore his praise shall last.

### PART II. III 2.

5 YET, should rising whirlwinds tear
From its stem the ripening ear;
Though the sickening flock should fall,
And the herd desert the stall;
Still to thee our souls shall raise
Grateful vows and solemn praise.

6 Should thine altered hand restrain
The early and the latter rain,
Blast each opening bud of joy,
And the rising year destroy;
Still to thee our souls shall raise
Grateful vows and solemn praise.

7 Life and grace, whate'er our woe,
Still to thee, our God, we owe;
Though of earthly hopes bereft,
Yet our hope of heaven is left;
And for these our souls shall raise
Grateful vows and solemn praise.

---

Praise the name of God most high,
Praise him, all below the sky,
Praise him, all ye heavenly host,
Father, Son, and Holy Ghost;
As through countless ages past,
Evermore his praise shall last.

## HYMN 84. C. M.

1 FOUNTAIN of mercy, God of love,
How rich thy bounties are;
The rolling seasons, as they move,
Proclaim thy constant care.

2 When in the bosom of the earth
The sower hid the grain,
Thy goodness marked its secret birth,
And sent the early rain.

3 The spring's sweet influence, Lord, was thine,
The plants in beauty grew;
Thou gav'st the summer's suns to shine,
The mild refreshing dew.

4 These various mercies from above
Matured the swelling grain;
A kindly harvest crowns thy love,
And plenty fills the plain.

5 We own and bless thy gracious sway;
Thy hand all nature hails;
Seed-time nor harvest, night nor day,
Summer nor winter fails.

---

To Father, Son, and Holy Ghost,
The God whom we adore,
Be glory, as it was, is now,
And shall be evermore.

## HYMN 85. L. M.

St. Peter's. Greene.

## HYMN 86. III 3.

Alma. Webbe.

### HYMN 85. L. M.

*For Public Mercies and Deliverances.*

1 Salvation doth to God belong,
His power and grace shall be our song;
From him alone all mercies flow,
His arm alone subdues the foe.

2 Then praise this God, who bows his ear
Propitious to his people's prayer;
And though deliverance he may stay,
Yet answers still in his own day.

3 O may this goodness lead our land,
Still saved by thine Almighty hand,
The tribute of its love to bring
To thee, our Saviour and our King:

4 Till every public temple raise
A song of triumph to thy praise;
And every peaceful, private home,
To thee a temple shall become.

5 Still be it our supreme delight
To walk as in thy glorious sight,
Still in thy precepts and thy fear,
Till life's last hour, to persevere.

---

To Father, Son, and Holy Ghost,
The God whom earth and heaven adore,
Be glory, as it was of old,
Is now, and shall be evermore.

## VII. ORDINANCES AND SPECIAL OCCASIONS.

BAPTISM OF INFANTS.

### HYMN 86. III 3.

Muhlenburg.

1 Saviour, who thy flock art feeding,
With the shepherd's kindest care,
All the feeble gently leading,
While the lambs thy bosom share;

2 Now, *these* little *ones* receiving,
Fold *them* in thy gracious arm;
There, we know, thy word believing
Only there, secure from harm.

3 Never from thy pasture roving,
Let *them* be the Lion's prey;
Let thy tenderness, so loving,
Keep *them* all life's dangerous way:

4 Then, within thy fold eternal,
Let *them* find a resting-place;
Feed in pastures ever vernal,
Drink the rivers of thy grace.

---

Praise the Father, earth and heaven,
Praise the Son, the Spirit praise,
As it was, and is, be given
Glory through eternal days.

## HYMN 87. S. M.

HANDEL. HANDEL.

## HYMN 88. S. M.

SILVER STREET. SMITH.

## HYMN 87. S. M.

DODDRIDGE.

1 THE gentle Saviour calls
Our children to his breast;
He folds them in his gracious arms,
Himself declares them blest.

2 "Let them approach," he cries,
"Nor scorn their humble claim;
The heirs of heaven are such as these,
For such as these I came."

3 Gladly we bring them, Lord,
Devoting them to thee,
Imploring that, as we are thine,
Thine may our offspring be.

---

To God the Father, Son,
And Spirit, glory be,
As 't was, and is, and shall be so,
To all eternity.

BAPTISM OF ADULTS.

## HYMN 88. S. M.

Eph. vi: 10-13. LYRA CATH.

1 SOLDIERS of Christ, arise,
And put your armor on,
Strong in the strength which God supplies
Through his eternal Son.

2 Strong in the Lord of hosts,
And in his mighty power,
Who in the strength of Jesus trusts,
Is more than conqueror.

3 Stand then in his great might,
With all his strength endued;
And take to arm you for the fight,
The panoply of God:

4 That, having all things done,
And all your conflicts past,
Ye may behold your victory won,
And stand complete at last.

---

To God the Father, Son,
And Spirit, glory be,
As 't was, and is, and shall be so,
To all eternity.

## HYMN 89. L. M.

ELLENTHORPE. LINLEY.

## HYMNS 90 & 91. C. M.

WOODSTOCK. DUTTON.

CONFIRMATION.

## HYMN 89. L. M.

DODDRIDGE.

1 O HAPPY day, that stays my choice
On thee, my Saviour and my God!
Well may this glowing heart rejoice,
And tell thy goodness all abroad.

2 O happy bond! that seals my vows
To him who merits all my love;
Let cheerful anthems fill his house,
While to his sacred throne I move.

3 'Tis done, the great transaction's done;
Deign, gracious Lord, to make me thine;
Help me, through grace, to follow on,
Glad to confess thy voice divine.

4 Here rest, my oft divided heart,
Fixed on thy God, thy Saviour rest;
Who with the world would grieve to part,
When called on angels' food to feast?

5 High heaven, that heard the solemn vow,
That vow renewed shall daily hear,
Till in life's latest hour I bow,
And bless in death a bond so dear.

---

To Father, Son, and Holy Ghost,
The God whom earth and heaven adore,
Be glory, as it was of old,
Is now, and shall be evermore.

## HYMN 90. C. M.

BEDDOME.

1 WITNESS, ye men and angels; now
Before the Lord we speak;
To him we make our solemn vow,
A vow we dare not break;

2 That, long as life itself shall last
Ourselves to Christ we yield;
Nor from his cause will we depart,
Or ever quit the field.

3 We trust not in our native strength,
But on his grace rely;
That, with returning wants, the Lord
Will all our need supply.

4 Lord, guide our doubtful feet aright,
And keep us in thy ways;
And, while we turn our vows to prayers,
Turn thou our prayers to praise.

---

To Father, Son, and Holy Ghost,
The God whom we adore,
Be glory, as it was, is now,
And shall be evermore.

## HYMN 91. C. M.

WATTS.

1 YOUTH, when devoted to the Lord,
Is pleasing in his eyes;
A flower, though offered in the bud,
Is no vain sacrifice.

2 'Tis easier far if we begin
To fear the Lord betimes;
For sinners, who grow old in sin,
Are hardened by their crimes.

3 It saves us from a thousand snares
To mind religion young;
Grace will preserve our following years,
And make our virtue strong.

4 To thee, Almighty God, to thee,
Our hearts we now resign;
'T will please us to look back and see
That our whole lives were thine.

---

To Father, Son, and Holy Ghost,
The God whom we adore,
Be glory, as it was, is now,
And shall be evermore.

## HYMN 92. C. M.

WAINWRIGHT. WAINWRIGHT.

## HYMN 92. C. M.

LOGA:

1 O, IN the morn of life, when youth
With vital ardor glows,
And shines in all the fairest charms
That beauty can disclose,—

2 Deep in thy soul, before its powers
Are yet by vice enslaved,
Be thy Creator's glorious Name
And character engraved:

3 Ere yet the shades of sorrow cloud
The sunshine of thy days;
And cares and toils, in endless round,
Encompass all thy ways:

4 Ere yet thy heart the woes of age,
With vain regret deplore,
And sadly muse on former joys,
That now return no more.

5 True wisdom, early sought and gained
In age will give thee rest;
O then, improve the morn of life,
To make its evening blest.

---

To Father, Son, and Holy Ghost,
The God whom we adore,
Be glory, as it was, is now,
And shall be evermore.

## HYMN 93. C. M.

CHRISTMAS. HANDEL.

## HYMN 94. L. M.

ST. PETER'S. GREENE.

THE LORD'S SUPPER.

### HYMN 93. C. M.

*Rev.* v: 9, 12, 13. PATRICK.

1 THOU, God, all glory, honor, power,
Art worthy to receive;
Since all things by thy power were made,
And by thy bounty live.

2 And worthy is the Lamb all power,
Honor, and wealth, to gain,
Glory and strength; who for our sins
A sacrifice was slain.

3 All worthy thou, who hast redeemed,
And ransomed us to God,
From every nation, every coast,
By thy most precious blood.

Blessing and honor, glory, power,
By all in earth and heaven,
To Him that sits upon the throne,
And to the Lamb be given.

---

To Father, Son, and Holy Ghost,
The God whom we adore,
Be glory, as it was, is now,
And shall be evermore.

### HYMN 94. L. M.

DODDRIDGE.

1 MY God, and is thy table spread,
And does thy cup with love o'erflow?
Thither be all thy children led,
And let them thy sweet mercies know.

2 Hail! sacred feast, which Jesus makes,
Rich banquet of his flesh and blood:
Thrice happy he who here partakes
That sacred stream, that heavenly food.

3 Why are its bounties all in vain
Before unwilling hearts displayed?
Was not for you the victim slain?
Are you forbid the children's bread?

4 O let thy table honored be,
And furnished well with joyful guests:
And may each soul salvation see,
That here its holy pledges tastes.

5 Drawn by thy quickening grace, O Lord,
In countless numbers let them come;
And gather from their Father's board,
The bread that lives beyond the tomb.

6 Nor let thy spreading Gospel rest,
Till through the world thy truth has run;
Till with this bread all men be blest,
Who see the light or feel the sun.

---

To Father, Son, and Holy Ghost,
The God whom earth and heaven adore,
Be glory, as it was of old,
Is now, and shall be evermore.

## HYMN 95. C. M.

NORTHAMPTON. DR. CROFT.

## HYMN 96. L. M.

WANDSWORTH. W. BEALE.

### HYMN 95. C. M.

1 And are we now brought near to God,
Who once at distance stood?
And, to effect this glorious change,
Did Jesus shed his blood.

2 O for a song of ardent praise,
To bear our souls above;
What should allay our lively hope,
Or damp our flaming love?

3 Then let us join the heavenly choirs,
To praise our heavenly King;
O may that love which spread this board,
Inspire us while we sing:

4 "Glory to God in highest strains,
And to the earth be peace;
Good-will from heaven to men is come,
And let it never cease."

---

To Father, Son, and Holy Ghost,
The God whom we adore,
Be glory, as it was, is now,
And shall be evermore.

### HYMN 96. L. M.

Steele.

1 To Jesus, our exalted Lord,
That name in heaven and earth adored,
Fain would our hearts and voices raise
A cheerful song of sacred praise.

2 But all the notes which mortals know,
Are weak, and languishing, and low;
Far, far above our humble songs,
The theme demands immortal tongues.

3 Yet, while around his board we meet,
And worship at his sacred feet,
O let our warm affections move,
In glad returns of grateful love.

4 Yes, Lord, we love, and we adore,
But long to know and love thee more;
And, while we taste the bread and wine,
Desire to feed on joys divine.

5 Let faith our feeble senses aid,
To see thy wondrous love displayed;
Thy broken flesh, thy bleeding veins,
Thy dreadful agonizing pains.

6 Let humble, penitential woe
With painful, pleasing anguish flow;
And thy forgiving love impart
Life, hope, and joy to every heart.

---

To Father, Son, and Holy Ghost,
The God whom earth and heaven adore,
Be glory, as it was of old,
Is now, and shall be evermore.

## HYMNS 97 & 98. L. M.

ELLENTHORPE. LINLEY.

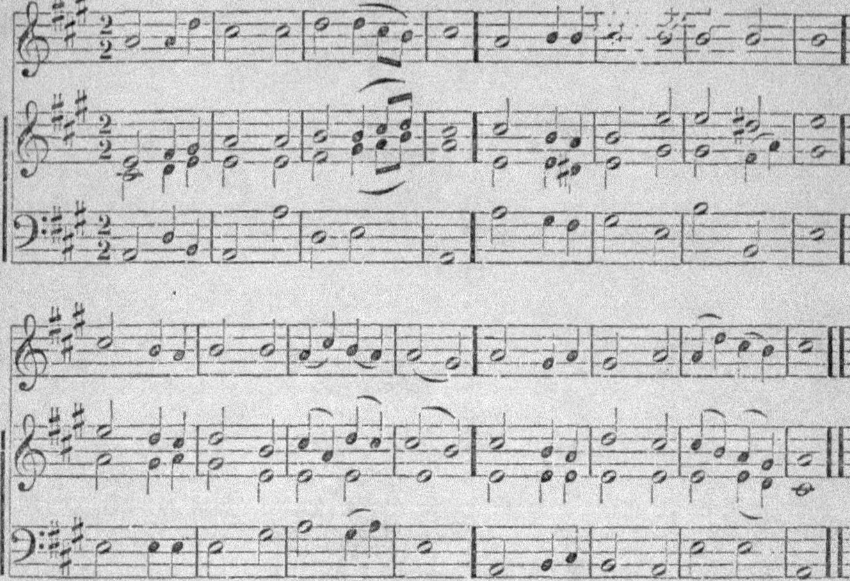

## HYMN 99. L. M.

WINCHELSEA. PRELLEUR.

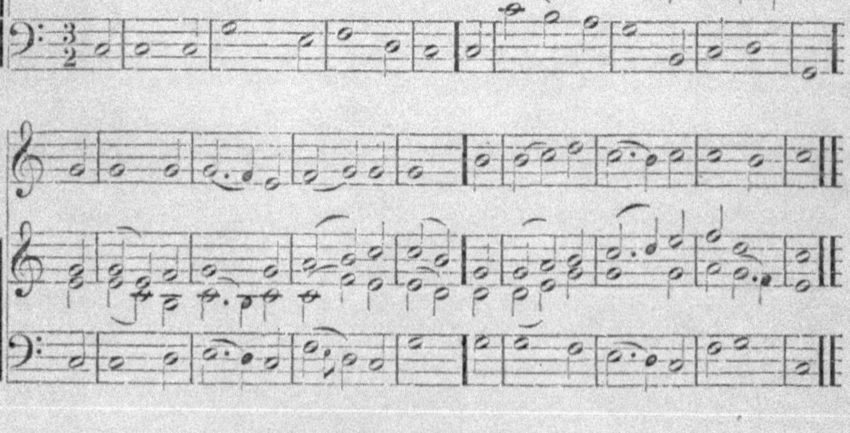

ORDINATION, OR INSTITUTION OF MINISTERS.

### HYMN 97. L. M.

St. Matthew x. LOGAN.

1 Go forth, ye heralds, in my name,
Sweetly the gospel trumpet sound;
The glorious jubilee proclaim,
Where'er the human race is found.

2 The joyful news to all impart,
And teach them where salvation lies;
With care bind up the broken heart,
And wipe the tears from weeping eyes.

3 Be wise as serpents, where you go,
But harmless as the peaceful dove;
And let your heaven-taught conduct show
That ye're commissioned from above.

4 Freely from me ye have received,
Freely, in love, to others give;
Thus shall your doctrines be believed,
And, by your labors, sinners live.

---

To Father, Son, and Holy Ghost,
The God whom earth and heaven adore,
Be glory, as it was of old,
Is now, and shall be evermore.

### HYMN 98. L. M.

St. Mark xvi: 15, etc.; and St. Matthew xxviii: 18, etc. WATTS.

1 "Go, preach my gospel," saith the Lord,
"Bid the whole earth my grace receive;
Explain to them my sacred word,
Bid them believe, obey, and live.

2 "I'll make my great commission known,
And ye shall prove my gospel true,
By all the works that I have done,
And all the wonders ye shall do.

3 "Go heal the sick, go raise the dead,
Go cast out devils in my name;
Nor let my prophets be afraid,
Though Greeks reproach and Jews blaspheme.

4 "While thus ye follow my commands,
I'm with you till the world shall end;
All power is trusted in my hands;
I can destroy, and can defend."

5 He spake, and light shone round his head;
On a bright cloud to heaven he rode;
They to the farthest nations spread
The grace of their ascended God.

---

To Father, Son, and Holy Ghost,
The God whom earth and heaven adore,
Be glory, as it was of old,
Is now, and shall be evermore.

### HYMN 99. L. M.

DODDRIDGE.

1 THE Saviour, when to heaven he rose,
In splendid triumph o'er his foes,
Scattered his gifts on men below,
And wide his royal bounties flow.

2 Hence sprang the *Apostle's* honored name,
Sacred beyond heroic fame;
Hence dictates the *prophetic* sage,
And hence the *evangelic* page.

3 In lower forms, to bless our eyes,
*Pastors* from hence, and *teachers* rise;
Who, though with feebler rays they shine,
Still mark a long extended line.

4 From Christ their varied gifts derive,
And, fed by him, their graces live;
While, guarded by his potent hand,
Amid the rage of hell they stand.

5 So shall the bright Succession run
Through all the courses of the sun;
While unborn churches, by their care,
Shall rise and flourish large and fair.

6 Jesus, our Lord, their hearts shall know,
The spring whence all these blessings flow;
Pastors and people shout his praise,
Through the long round of endless days.

---

To Father, Son, and Holy Ghost,
The God whom earth and heaven adore,
Be glory, as it was of old,
Is now, and shall be evermore.

## HYMN 100. L. M.

MADRID. WHITAKER.

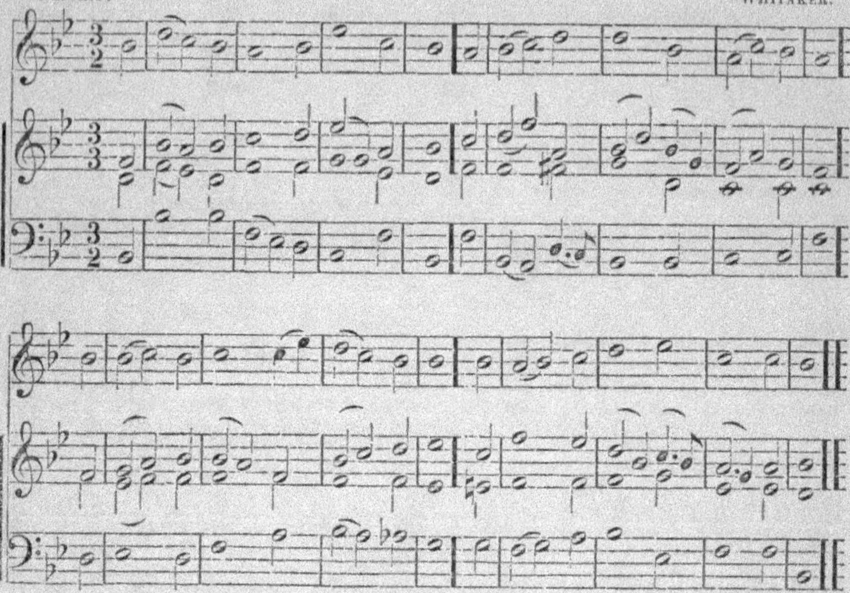

## HYMN 101. L. M.

ZORAH. HANDEL.

### HYMN 100. L. M.

BEDDOME.

1 FATHER of mercies! bow thine ear
Attentive to our earnest prayer;
We plead for those who plead for thee,
Successful pleaders may they be!

2 How great their work, how vast their charge!
Do thou their anxious souls enlarge;
Their best acquirements are our gain,
We share the blessings they obtain.

3 Clothe, then, with energy divine,
Their words, and let those words be thine;
To them thy sacred truth reveal,
Suppress their fear, inflame their zeal.

4 Teach them to sow the precious seed,
Teach them thy chosen flock to feed;
Teach them immortal souls to gain—
Souls that will well reward their pain.

5 Let thronging multitudes around,
Hear from their lips the joyful sound;
In humble strains thy grace implore,
And feel thy new creating power.

6 Let sinners break their massy chains,
Distressed souls forget their pains,
Let light through distant realms be spread,
And Zion rear her drooping head.

To Father, Son, and Holy Ghost,
The God whom earth and heaven adore,
Be glory, as it was of old,
Is now, and shall be evermore.

CONSECRATION OF A CHURCH.

### HYMN 101. L. M.

DODDRIDGE.

1 AND wilt thou, O eternal God,
On earth establish thine abode?
Then look propitious from thy throne,
And take this temple for thine own.

2 These walls we to thine honor raise,
Long may they echo in thy praise;
And thou, descending, fill the place,
With the rich tokens of thy grace.

3 Here may the great Redeemer reign,
With all the graces of his train;
While power divine his word attends,
To conquer foes and cheer his friends.

4 And in the last decisive day,
When God the nations shall survey,
May it before the world appear,
Thousands were born for glory here.

---

To Father, Son, and Holy Ghost,
The God whom earth and heaven adore,
Be glory, as it was of old,
Is now, and shall be evermore.

## HYMN 102 & 103. L. M.

WINCHESTER. CROFT.

## HYMN 104. L. M.

WINCHELSEA. PRELLEUR.

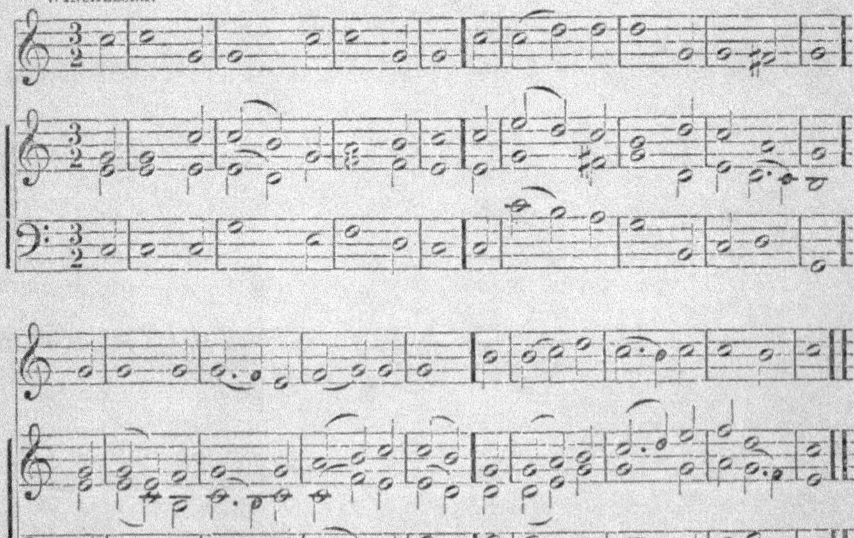

MISSIONS.

### HYMN 102. L. M.

WATTS.

1 JESUS shall reign where'er the sun
Does his successive journeys run;
His kingdom spread from shore to shore,
Till moons shall wax and wane no more.

2 To him shall endless prayer be made,
And praises throng to crown his head:
His name like sweet perfume shall rise
With every morning sacrifice.

3 People and realms, of every tongue,
Dwell on his love with sweetest song;
And infant voices shall proclaim
Their early blessings on his name.

4 Blessings abound where'er he reigns;
The prisoner leaps to burst his chains,
The weary find eternal rest,
And all the sons of want are blest.

5 Where he displays his healing power,
Death and the curse are known no more;
In him the tribes of Adam boast
More blessings than their father lost.

6 Let every creature rise, and bring
Peculiar honors to our King:
Angels descend with songs again,
And earth repeat the loud Amen.

---

To Father, Son, and Holy Ghost,
The God whom earth and heaven adore,
Be glory, as it was of old,
Is now, and shall be evermore.

### HYMN 103. L. M.

Psalm cxvii. WATTS.

1 FROM all that dwell below the skies,
Let the Creator's praise arise;
Jehovah's glorious name be sung
Through every land, by every tongue.

2 Eternal are thy mercies, Lord,
And truth eternal is thy word:
Thy praise shall sound from shore to shore,
Till suns shall rise and set no more.

---

To Father, Son, and Holy Ghost,
The God whom earth and heaven adore,
Be glory, as it was of old,
Is now, and shall be evermore.

### HYMN 104. L. M.

MONTGOMERY.

1 O SPIRIT of the living God,
In all thy plenitude of grace,
Where'er the foot of man hath trod,
Descend on our apostate race.

2 Give tongues of fire and hearts of love,
To preach the reconciling word;
Give power and unction from above,
Where'er the joyful sound is heard.

3 Be darkness, at thy coming, light;
Confusion, order in thy path;
Souls without strength inspire with might·
Bid mercy triumph over wrath.

4 Convert the nations; far and nigh
The triumphs of the cross record,
The name of Jesus glorify,
Till every people call him Lord.

---

*To Father, Son, and Holy Ghost, etc.*

## HYMN 105. II 1.

COLUMBIA. RAVENSCROFT.

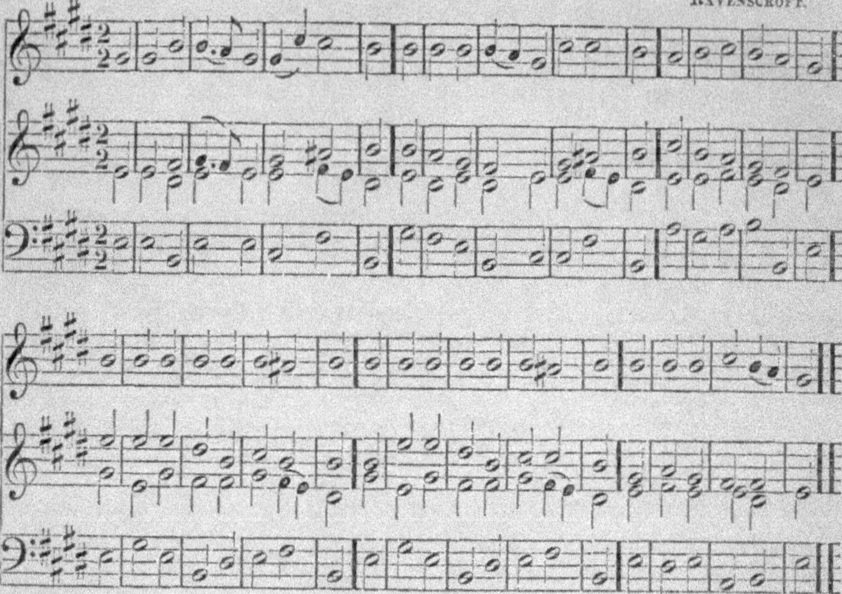

## HYMN 106. C. M.

BEVERLY. M. HOWDON.

## HYMN 105. H 1.

*For Missions to the New Settlements in the United States.* ONDERDONK.

1 When, Lord, to this our western land,
Led by thy providential hand,
Our wand'ring fathers came;
Their ancient homes, their friends in youth,
Sent forth the heralds of thy truth,
To keep them in thy Name.

2 Then, through our solitary coast,
The desert features soon were lost;
Thy temples there arose;
Our shores, as culture made them fair,
Were hallowed by thy rites, by prayer,
And blossomed as the rose.

3 And, O, may we repay this debt
To regions solitary yet,
Within our spreading land;
There brethren, from our common home,
Still westward, like our fathers, roam;
Still guided by thy hand.

4 Saviour, we own this debt of love;
O shed thy Spirit from above,
To move each Christian breast;
Till heralds shall thy truth proclaim,
And temples rise to fix thy name
Through all our desert west.

---

To Father, Son, and Holy Ghost,
The God whom heaven's triumphant host
And saints on earth adore;
Be glory, as in ages past,
As now it is, and so shall last
When time shall be no more.

## HYMN 106. C. M.

Isaiah xxxv: 2. ONDERDONK.

1 On Sion, and on Lebanon,
On Carmel's blooming hight,
On Sharon's fertile plains, once shone
The glory, pure and bright.

2 From thence its mild and cheering ray
Streamed forth from land to land;
And empires now behold its day;
And still its beams expand.

3 Its brightest splendors, darting west,
Our happy shores illume;
Our farther regions, once unblest,
Now like a garden bloom.

4 But, ah! our deserts deep and wild,
See not this heavenly light;
No sacred beams, no radiance mild,
Dispel their dreary night.

5 Thou who didst lighten Sion's hill,
On Carmel who did shine,
Our deserts let thy glory fill,
Thy excellence divine.

6 Like Lebanon, in towering pride,
May all our forests smile;
And may our borders blossom wide,
Like Sharon's fruitful soil.

---

To Father, Son, and Holy Ghost,
The God whom we adore,
Be glory, as it was, is now,
And shall be evermore.

## HYMN 107. II 6.

MISSIONARY HYMN. L. MASON 1824.

## HYMN 108. L. M.

ELLENTHORPE. LINLEY.

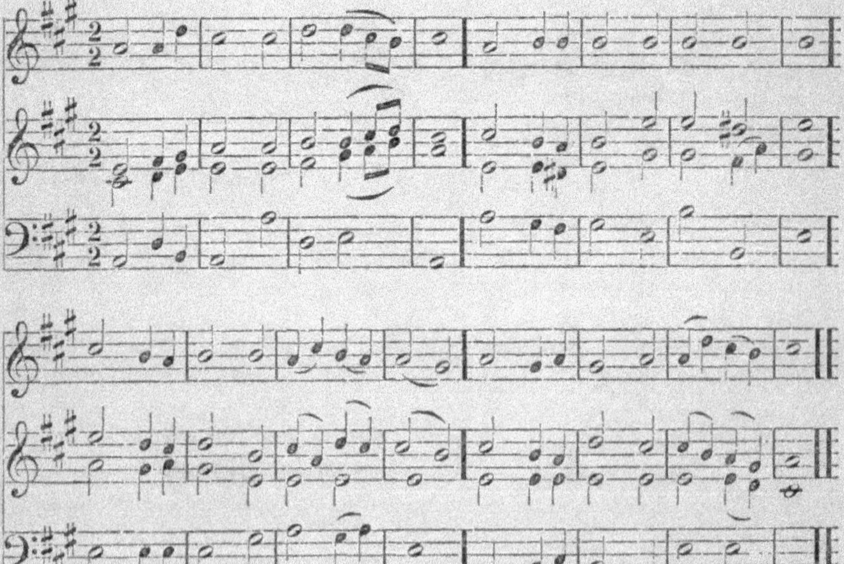

### HYMN 107. II 6.

HEBER.

1 FROM Greenland's icy mountains,
From India's coral strand,
Where Afric's sunny fountains
Roll down their golden sand;
From many an ancient river,
From many a palmy plain,
They call us to deliver
Their land from error's chain.

2 What though the spicy breezes
Blow soft o'er Ceylon's Isle;
Though every prospect pleases,
And only man is vile:
In vain with lavish kindness
The gifts of God are strown;
The heathen in his blindness
Bows down to wood and stone.

3 Shall we, whose souls are lighted
With wisdom from on high,
Shall we, to men benighted,
The lamp of life deny?
Salvation! oh, salvation!
The joyful sound proclaim,
Till each remotest nation
Has learned Messiah's name.

4 Waft, waft, ye winds, his story,
And you, ye waters, roll,
Till, like a sea of glory,
It spreads from pole to pole;
Till o'er our ransomed nature,
The Lamb for sinners slain,
Redeemer, King, Creator,
In bliss returns to reign.

Eternal praise be given,
And songs of highest worth,
By all the hosts of heaven,
And all the saints on earth,
To God, supreme confessed,
To Christ, his only Son,
And to the Spirit blessed,
Eternal Three in One.

### HYMN 108. L. M.

*For the Jews.*

1 DISOWNED of heaven, by man opprest,
Outcasts from Zion's hallowed ground,
Wherefore should Israel's sons, once blest,
Still roam the scorning world around?

2 Lord! visit thy forsaken race;
Back to thy fold the wanderers bring;
Teach them to seek thy slighted grace,
And hail in Christ their promised King.

3 The vail of darkness rend in twain,
Which hides their Shiloh's glorious light;
The severed olive branch again
Firm to its parent stock unite.

4 Hail, glorious day, expected long!
When Jew and Greek one prayer shall pour,
With eager feet one temple throng,
With grateful praise one God adore.

---

To Father, Son, and Holy Ghost,
The God whom earth and heaven adore,
Be glory, as it was of old,
Is now, and shall be evermore.

## HYMN 109. IV 1.

Lyons. Haydn.

## HYMN 110. II 4.

St. Swithins

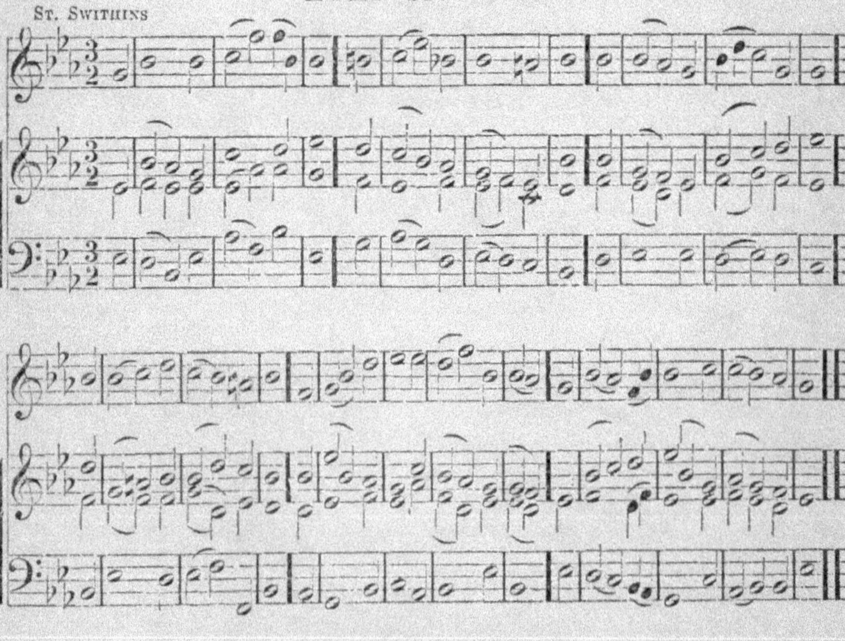

### HYMN 109. IV 1.

Rev. xv : 3, 4. ONDERDONK.

1 How wondrous and great
Thy works, God of praise!
How just, King of saints,
And true are thy ways!
O who shall not fear thee,
And honor thy name!
Thou only art holy,
Thou only supreme!

2 To nations long dark
Thy light shall be shown;
Their worship and vows
Shall come to thy throne;
Thy truth and thy judgments
Shall spread all abroad,
Till earth's every people
Confess thee their God.

---

By angels in heaven
Of every degree,
And saints upon earth,
All praise be addressed
To God in three persons,
One God ever blessed,
As it has been, now is,
And ever shall be.

FOR SUNDAY AND CHARITY SCHOOLS.

### HYMN 110. II 4.

*Children and Congregation.* BEDDOME.

*Children.*

1 COME let our voices join,
In one glad song of praise;
To God, the God of love,
Our grateful hearts we raise:

*Congregation.*

To God alone your praise belongs;
His love demands your earliest songs.

*Children.*

2 Now we are taught to read
The book of life divine;
Where our Redeemer's love
And brightest glories shine:

*Congregation.*

To God alone the praise is due,
Who sends his word to us and you.

*Children.*

3 Within these hallowed walls
Our wandering feet are brought;
Where prayer and praise ascend,
And heavenly truths are taught:

*Congregation.*

To God alone your offerings bring;
Here in his church his praises sing.

*Children.*

4 For blessings such as these,
Our gratitude receive;
Lord, here accept our hearts,
'T is all that we can give:

*Congregation.*

Great God, accept their infant songs:
To thee alone their praise belongs.

*Both.*

5 Lord, bid this work of love
Be crowned with meet success;
May thousands yet unborn,
This institution bless:
Thus shall the praise resound to thee,
Now and through all eternity.

---

To God, the Father, Son,
And Spirit, ever blessed,
Eternal Three in One,
All worship be addressed,
As heretofore
It was, is now,
And shall be so
For evermore.

## HYMN 111. III 1.

WELDON. WELDON.

## HYMN 112. C. M.

WOODSTOCK. DUTTON.

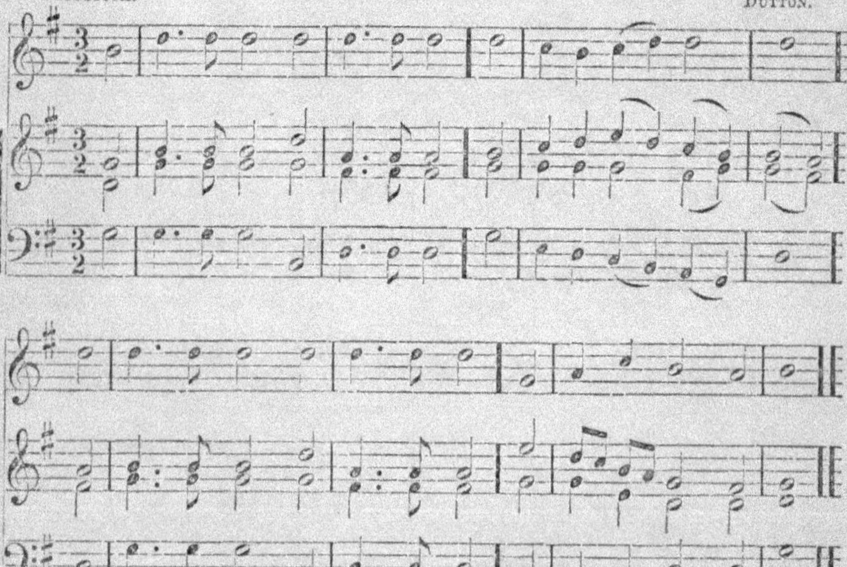

### HYMN 111. III 1.

MONTGOMERY.

1 GLORY to the Father give,
God in whom we move and live;
Children's prayers he deigns to hear;
Children's songs delight his ear.

2 Glory to the Son we bring,
Christ our Prophet, Priest, and King;
Children raise your sweetest strain
To the Lamb, for he was slain.

3 Glory to the Holy Ghost,
He reclaims the sinner lost;
Children's minds may he inspire,
Touch their tongues with holy fire.

4 Glory in the highest be
To the blessed Trinity,
For the gospel from above,
For the word that "God is love!"

### HYMN 112. C. M.

MONTGOMERY.

1 WHEN Jesus left his heavenly throne,
He chose an humble birth;
Like us, unhonored and unknown,
He came to dwell on earth.

2 Like him, may we be found below,
In wisdom's paths of peace;
Like him, in grace and knowledge grow,
As years and strength increase.

3 Sweet were his words, and kind his look,
When mothers round him pressed;
Their infants in his arms he took,
And on his bosom blessed.

4 Safe from the world's alluring harms,
Beneath his watchful eye;
O, thus encircled in his arms,
May we for ever lie.

---

To Father, Son, and Holy Ghost,
The God whom we adore,
Be glory, as it was, is now,
And shall be evermore.

## HYMN 113. L. M.

Nain. T. Wood.

## HYMNS 114 & 115. C. M.

Woodstock. Dutton.

### HYMN 113. L. M.

WATTS.

1 LORD, how delightful 'tis to see
A whole assembly worship thee:
At once they sing, at once they pray;
They hear of heaven, and learn the way.

2 I have been there, and still would go,
'Tis like a little heaven below;
Nor all that earth and sin can say,
Shall tempt me to forget this day.

3 O write upon my memory, Lord,
The text and doctrine of thy word;
That I may break thy laws no more,
But love thee better than before.

4 With thoughts of Christ and things divine,
Fill up this sinful heart of mine;
That hoping pardon through his blood,
I may lie down and wake with God.

---

To Father, Son, and Holy Ghost,
The God whom earth and heaven adore,
Be glory, as it was of old,
Is now, and shall be evermore.

### HYMN 114. C. M.

J. STRAPHAN.

1 MERCY, descending from above,
In softest accents pleads;
O may each tender bosom move,
When mercy intercedes.

2 Children our kind protection claim,
And God will well approve,
When infants learn to lisp his name,
And their Creator love.

3 Delightful work, young souls to win,
And turn the rising race
From the deceitful paths of sin,
To seek their Saviour's face.

4 Almighty God, thine influence shed
To aid this blest design;
The honor of thy name be spread,
And all the glory thine.

---

To Father, Son, and Holy Ghost,
The God whom we adore,
Be glory, as it was, is now,
And shall be evermore.

CHARITABLE OCCASIONS.

### HYMN 115. C. M.

BARBAULD.

1 BLEST is the man whose softening heart
Feels all another's pain;
To whom the supplicating eye
Is never raised in vain:

2 Whose breast responds with generous warmth,
A stranger's woe to feel;
Who weeps in pity o'er the wound
He wants the power to heal.

3 To gentle offices of love
His feet are never slow;
He views, through mercy's melting eye,
A brother in a foe.

4 To him protection shall be shown;
And mercy, from above,
Descend on those who thus fulfill
The Christian law of love.

---

*To Father, Son, and Holy Ghost, etc.*

## HYMN 116. C. M.

WESTHAM. DR. HOWARD.

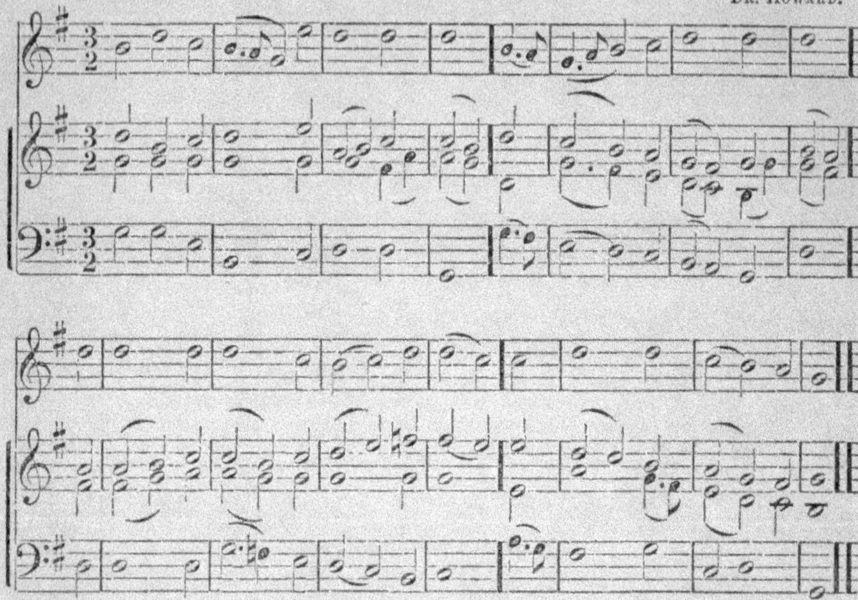

## HYMN 117. III 3.

TUSCANY.

**HYMN 116. C. M.**

DODDRIDGE.

1 RICH are the joys which can not die,
With God laid up in store;
Treasures beyond the changing sky,
Brighter than golden ore.

2 The seeds which piety and love
Have scattered here below,
In the fair fertile fields above
To ample harvests grow.

3 The mite my willing hands can give
At Jesus' feet I lay;
Grace shall the humble gift receive,
Abounding grace repay.

---

To Father, Son, and Holy Ghost,
The God whom we adore,
Be glory, as it was, is now,
And shall be evermore.

**HYMN 117. III 3.**

C. C. MOORE.

1 LORD of life, all praise excelling,
Thou, in glory unconfined,
Deign'st to make thy humble dwelling
With the poor of humble mind.

2 As thy love, through all creation,
Beams like thy diffusive light;
So the high and humble station
Both are equal in thy sight.

3 Thus thy care, for all providing,
Warmed thy faithful prophet's tongue;
Who, the lot of all deciding,
To thy chosen Israel sung:

4 When thy harvest yields thee pleasure,
Thou the golden sheaf shalt bind;
To the poor belongs the treasure
Of the scattered ears behind:

*Chorus.*
These thy God ordains to bless,
The widow and the fatherless.

5 When thine olive-plants increasing,
Pour their plenty o'er thy plain,
Grateful, thou shalt take the blessing,
But not search the bough again:
*Chorus.* These, etc.

6 When thy favoured vintage flowing,
Gladdens thine autumnal scene,
Own the bounteous hand bestowing,
But thy vines the poor shall glean.
*Chorus.* These, etc.

7 Still we read thy word declaring
Mercy, Lord, thine own decree;
Mercy, every sorrow sharing,
Warms the heart resembling thee.

8 Still the orphan and the stranger,
Still the widow owns thy care;
Screened by thee in every danger,
Heard by thee in every prayer.
*Hallelujah. Amen.*

---

Praise the Father, earth and heaven,
Praise the Son, the Spirit praise,
As it was, and is, be given
Glory through eternal days.

## HYMN 118. L. M.

WAREHAM. KNAPP.

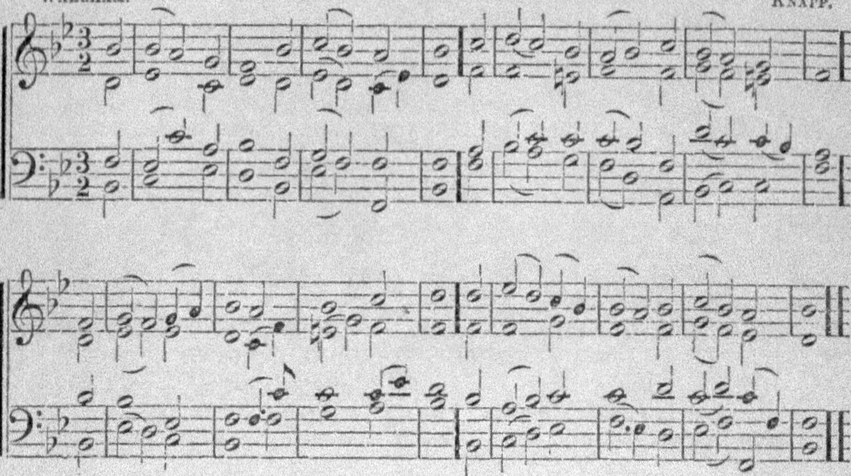

## HYMN 119. IV 5.

MARINER. BEETHOVEN.

TO BE USED AT SEA.

### HYMN 118 L. M.

WATTS.

1 GOD of the seas! thine awful voice
Bids all the rolling waves rejoice;
And one soft word of thy command
Can sink them silent on the sand.

2 The smallest fish that swims the seas,
Sportful to thee a tribute pays;
And largest monsters of the deep,
At thy command, or rage or sleep.

3 Thus in thy glorious power adored!
Among the watery nations, Lord;
Yet men who trace the dangerous waves,
Forget the mighty God who saves!

---

To Father, Son, and Holy Ghost,
The God whom earth and heaven adore,
Be glory, as it was of old,
Is now, and shall be evermore.

### HYMN 119. IV 5.

HEBER.

"*Save, Lord, or we perish.*"—Matthew viii: 25.

1 WHEN through the torn sail the wild tempest is streaming,
When o'er the dark wave the red lightning is gleaming,
Nor hope lends a ray the poor seaman to cherish,
We fly to our Maker, "Save, Lord! or we perish."

2 O Jesus! once rocked on the breast of the billow,
Aroused by the shriek of despair from thy pillow,
Now seated in glory, the mariner cherish,
Who cries in his anguish, "Save, Lord! or we perish."

3 And, oh! when the whirlwind of passion is raging,
When sin in our hearts its wild warfare is waging,
Then send down thy Spirit thy ransomed to cherish,
Rebuke the destroyer; "Save, Lord! or we perish."

---

All glory and praise to the Father be given,
The Son and the Spirit, from earth and from heaven;
As was, and is now, be supreme adoration,
And ever shall be to the God of salvation.

## HYMN 120. L. M.

CHARMOUTH. WAINWRIGHT.

## HYMN 121. L. M.

NAIN. T. WOOD.

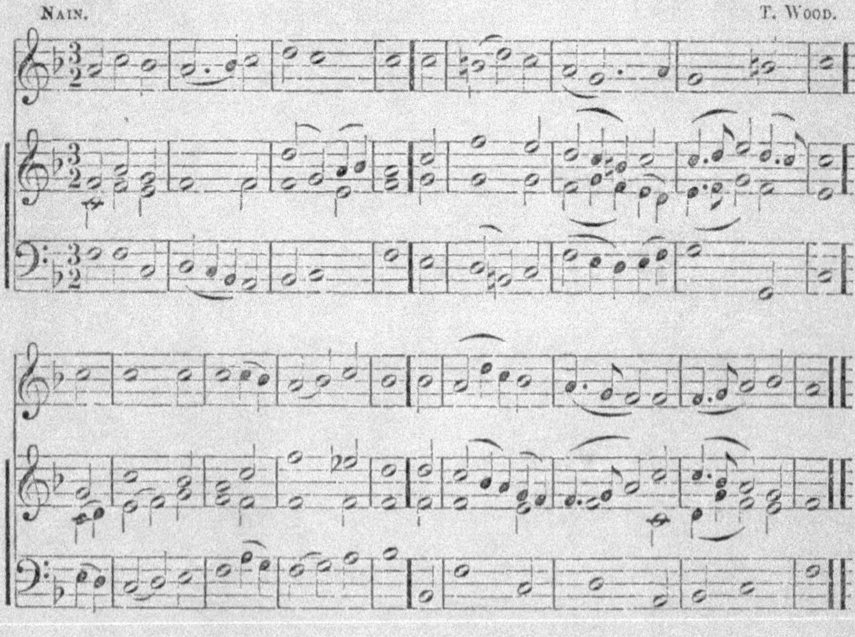

### HYMN 120. C. M.

*Which may be used at Sea or on Land.* ADDISON.

1 LORD! for the just thou dost provide,
Thou art their sure defense;
Eternal wisdom is their guide,
Their help, Omnipotence.

2 Though they through foreign lands should roam,
And breathe the tainted air
In burning climates, far from home,
Yet thou, their God, art there.

3 Thy goodness sweetens every soil,
Makes every country please;
Thou on the snowy hills dost smile,
And smooth'st the rugged seas!

4 When waves on waves to heaven upreared,
Defied the pilot's art;
When terror in each face appeared,
And sorrow in each heart;

5 To thee I raised my humble prayer,
To snatch me from the grave;
I found thine ear not slow to hear,
Nor short thine arm to save.

6 Thou gav'st the word, the winds did cease,
The storms obeyed thy will;
The raging sea was hushed in peace,
And every wave was still.

7 For this my life, in every state,
A life of praise shall be;
And death, when death shall be my fate,
Shall join my soul to thee.

---

To Father, Son, and Holy Ghost,
The God whom we adore,
Be glory, as it was, is now,
And shall be evermore.

FOR THE SICK.

### HYMN 121. L. M.

1 WHEN dangers, woes, or death are nigh,
Past mercies teach me where to fly;
Thine arm, Almighty God, can aid,
When sickness grieves, and pains invade.

2 To all the various helps of art,
Kindly thy healing power impart;
Bethesda's bath refused to save
Unless an angel blessed the wave.

3 All medicines act by thy decree,
Receive commission all from thee;
And not a plant which spreads the plains
But teems with health, when heaven ordains.

4 Clay and Siloam's pool, we find
At heaven's command restored the blind;
And Jordan's waters hence were seen
To wash a Syrian leper clean.

5 But grant me nobler favors still,
Grant me to know and do thy will,
Purge my foul soul from every stain,
And save me from eternal pain.

6 Can such a wretch for pardon sue?
My crimes, my crimes arise in view;
Arrest my trembling tongue in prayer,
And pour the horrors of despair.

7 But thou, regard my contrite sighs,
My tortured breast, my streaming eyes;
To me thy boundless love extend,
My God, my Father, and my Friend.

8 These lovely names I ne'er could plead,
Had not thy Son vouchsafed to bleed;
His blood procures our fallen race
Admittance to the throne of grace.

9 When sin has shot its poisoned dart,
And conscious guilt corrodes the heart,
His blood is all-sufficient found
To draw the shaft and heal the wound.

10 What arrows pierce so deep as sin?
What venom gives such pain within?
Thou great Physician of the soul
Rebuke my pangs, and make me whole.

11 O, if I trust thy sovereign skill,
And bow submissive to thy will,
Sickness and death shall both agree
To bring me, Lord, at last to thee.

---

To Father, Son, and Holy Ghost,
The God whom earth and heaven adore,
Be glory, as it was of old,
Is now, and shall be evermore.

## HYMN 122. C. M.

LIVERPOOL. WAINWRIGHT.

## HYMN 123. L. M.

ANGEL'S HYMN. KNAPP.

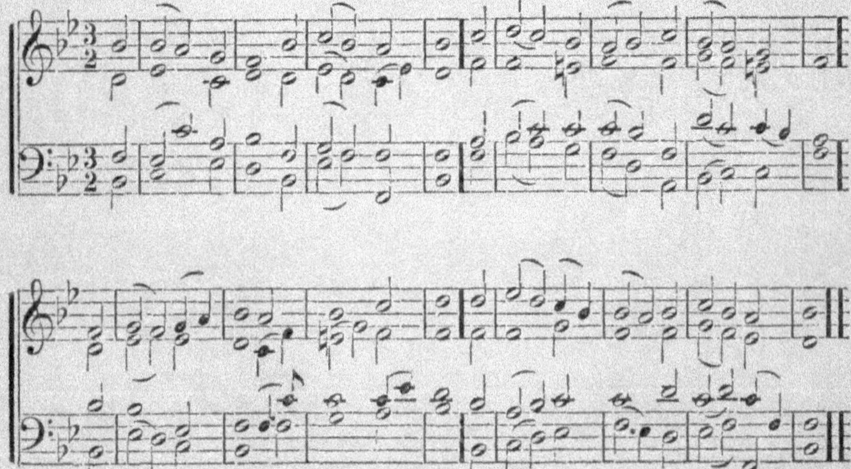

**HYMN 122. C. M.**

*On Recovery from Sickness.* WATTS.

1 WHEN we are raised from deep distress,
Our God deserves our song;
We take the pattern of our praise
From Hezekiah's tongue.

2 The gates of the devouring grave
Are opened wide in vain,
If he that holds the keys of death,
Command them fast again.

3 When he but speaks the healing word,
Then no disease withstands;
Fevers and plagues obey the Lord,
And fly, as he commands.

4 If half the strings of life should break,
He can our frame restore,
And cast our sins behind his back,
And they are found no more.

5 To him I cried, "Thy servant save,
Thou ever good and just;
Thy power can rescue from the grave,
Thy power is all my trust."

6 He heard, and saved my soul from death,
And dried my falling tears;
Now to his praise I'll spend my breath,
Through my remaining years.

---

To Father, Son, and Holy Ghost,
The God whom we adore,
Be glory, as it was, is now,
And shall be evermore.

**HYMN 123. L M.**

*On the Same.*

1 MY God, since thou hast raised me up,
Thee I'll extoll with thankful voice;
Restored by thine Almighty power,
With fear before thee I'll rejoice.

2 With troubles worn, with pain opprest,
To thee I cried, and thou didst save;
Thou didst support my sinking hopes,
My life didst rescue from the grave.

3 Wherefore, ye saints, rejoice with me,
With me sing praises to the Lord;
Call all his goodness to your mind,
And all his faithfulness record.

4 His anger is but short: his love,
Which is our life, hath certain stay;
Grief may continue for a night,
But joy returns with rising day.

5 Then, what I vowed in my distress,
In happier hours I now will give,
And strive that in my grateful verse,
His praises may for ever live.

6 To Father, Son, and Holy Ghost,
The blest and undivided Three;
The One sole giver of all life,
Glory and praise for ever be.

---

To Father, Son, and Holy Ghost,
The God whom earth and heaven adore,
Be glory, as it was of old,
Is now, and shall be evermore.

## HYMN 124. C. M.

CHINA. SWAN.

## HYMN 125. C. M.

DARLINGTON. GARNETT.

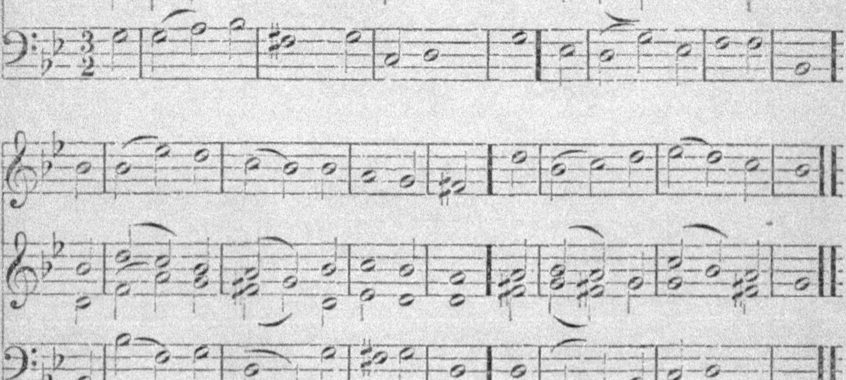

FUNERALS.

## HYMN 124. C. M.

WATTS.

1 HEAR what the voice from heaven declares,
To those in Christ who die:
Released from all their earthly cares,
They'll reign with him on high.

2 Then why lament departed friends,
Or shake at death's alarms?
Death's but the servant Jesus sends
To call us to his arms.

3 If sin be pardoned, we're secure,
Death hath no sting beside;
The law gave sin its strength and power;
But Christ, our ransom, died.

4 The graves of all his saints he blessed,
When in the grave he lay;
And, rising thence, their hopes he raised
To everlasting day.

5 Then, joyfully, while life we have,
To Christ, our life, we'll sing,
"Where is thy victory, O grave?
And where, O death, thy sting?"

---

To Father, Son, and Holy Ghost,
The God whom we adore,
Be glory, as it was, is now,
And shall be evermore.

## HYMN 125. C. M.

A. STEELE.

1 WHEN those we love are snatched away
By death's resistless hand,
Our hearts the mournful tribute pay
That friendship must demand.

2 While pity prompts the rising sigh,
With awful power impressed;
May this dread truth, "I too must die,"
Sink deep in every breast.

3 Let this vain world allure no more:
Behold the opening tomb;
It bids us use the present hour,
To-morrow death may come.

4 The voice of this instructive scene
May every heart obey!
Nor be the faithful warning vain
Which calls to watch and pray.

5 O let us to that Saviour fly,
Whose arm alone can save;
Then shall our hopes ascend on high
And triumph o'er the grave.

---

To Father, Son, and Holy Ghost,
The God whom we adore,
Be Glory, as it was, is now,
And shall be evermore.

## HYMN 126. C. M.

CURFEW. NOVELLO.

## HYMN 127. L. M.

NAIN. T. WOOD.

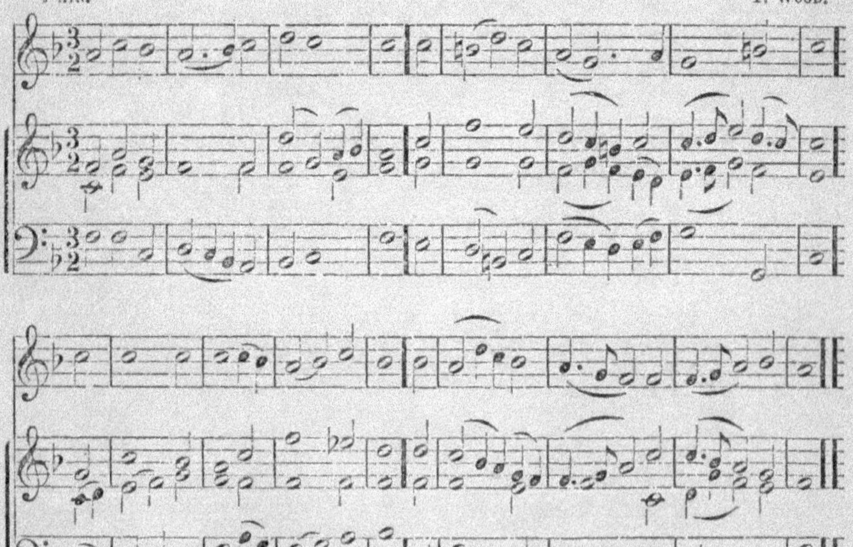

### HYMN 126. C. M.

*Death of a Young Person.* MUHLENBURG.

1 How short the race our friend has run,
Cut down in all *his* bloom!
The course but yesterday begun
Now finished in the tomb!

2 Thou joyous youth! hence learn how soon
Thy years may end their flight;
Long, long before life's brilliant noon
May come death's gloomy night.

3 To serve thy God no longer wait,
To-day his voice regard;
To-morrow mercy's open gate
May be for ever barred.

4 And thus the Lord reveals his grace
Thy youthful love to gain;
The soul that early seeks my face
Shall never seek in vain.

---

To Father, Son, and Holy Ghost,
The God whom we adore,
Be glory, as it was, is now,
And shall be evermore.

### HYMN 127. L. M.

*Death of an Infant.* CUNNINGHAM.

1 As the sweet flower that scents the morn,
But withers in the rising day;
Thus lovely was this infant's dawn,
Thus sweetly fled its life away.

2 It died ere its expanding soul
Had ever burnt with wrong desires,
Had ever spurned at heaven's control,
Or ever quenched its sacred fires.

3 It died to sin, it died to cares,
But for a moment felt the rod:
O mourner, such, the Lord declares,
Such are the children of our God!

---

To Father, Son, and Holy Ghost,
The God whom earth and heaven adore,
Be glory, as it was of old,
Is now, and shall be evermore.

## HYMNS 128 & 129. III 1.

ANGELUS. HANDEL.

## VIII. INVITATION AND WARNING.

### HYMN 128. III 1.

J. WESLEY.

1 SINNERS, turn, why will ye die?
God, your Maker, asks you why?
God, who did your being give,
Made you with himself to live;
He the fatal cause demands,
Asks the work of his own hands;
Why, ye thankless creatures, why
Will ye cross his love, and die?

2 Sinners, turn, why will ye die?
God, your Saviour, asks you why?
He, who did your souls retrieve,
Died himself that ye might live.
Will you let him die in vain?
Crucify your Lord again?
Why, ye ransomed sinners, why
Will ye slight his grace, and die?

3 Sinners, turn, why will ye die?
God, the Spirit, asks you why?
He, who all your lives hath strove,
Wooed you to embrace his love:
Will ye not his grace receive?
Will ye still refuse to live?
O, ye dying sinners, why,
Why will ye for ever die?

Holy Father, Holy Son,
Holy Spirit, Three in one!
Glory, as of old, to thee,
Now, and evermore shall be.

### HYMN 129. III 1.

T. SCOTT.

1 HASTEN, sinner, to be wise;
Stay not for the morrow's sun:
Wisdom, if you still despise,
Harder is it to be won.

2 Hasten, mercy to implore;
Stay not for the morrow's sun:
Lest thy season should be o'er,
Ere this evening's stage be run.

3 Hasten, sinner, to return;
Stay not for the morrow's sun:
Lest thy lamp should cease to burn
Ere salvation's work is done.

4 Hasten, sinner, to be blest;
Stay not for the morrow's sun;
Lest perdition thee arrest,
Ere the morrow is begun.

---

Holy Father, holy Son,
Holy Spirit, Three in One!
Glory, as of old, to thee,
Now, and evermore shall be!

## HYMN 130. II 3.

PEACE. MAZZINGHI.

## HYMN 131. S. M.

HANDEL. HANDEL.

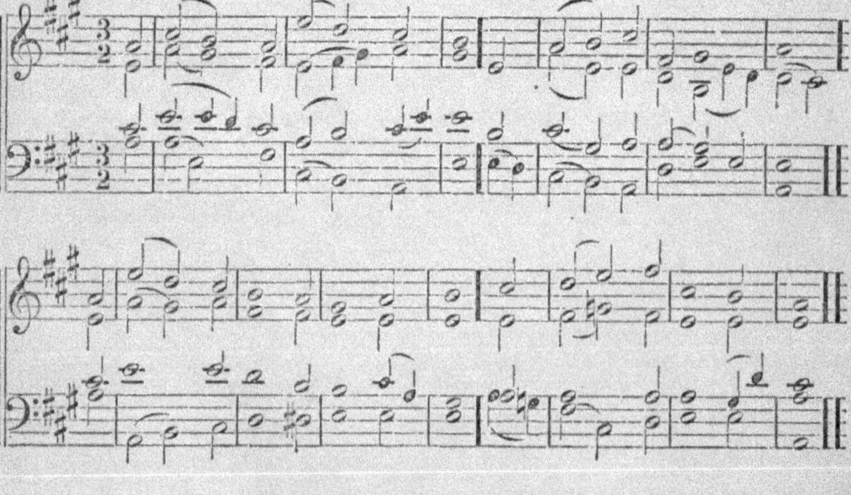

### HYMN 130. H 3.

1 Peace, troubled soul, whose plaintive moan
Hath taught each scene the note of woe;
Cease thy complaint, suppress thy groan,
And let thy tears forget to flow:
Behold the precious balm is found
To lull thy pain and heal thy wound.

2 Come, freely come, by sin oppressed,
On Jesus cast thy weighty load;
In him thy refuge find, thy rest,
Safe in the mercy of thy God:
Thy God's thy Saviour! glorious word!
O hear, believe and bless the Lord!

---

To God the Father, God the Son,
And God the Spirit, Three in One,
Be glory in the highest given,
By all in earth and all in heaven,
As was through ages heretofore,
Is now, and shall be evermore.

### HYMN 131. S. M.

Rev. xxii: 17, 20. H. U. Onderdonk.

1 The Spirit, in our hearts,
Is whispering, Sinner, come;
The Bride, the church of Christ proclaims
To all his children, come!

2 Let him that heareth say
To all about him, come!
Let him that thirsts for righteousness,
To Christ, the fountain, come.

3 Yes, whosoever will,
O let him freely come,
And freely drink the stream of life.
'T is Jesus bids him come.

4 Lo, Jesus, who invites,
Declares, I quickly come.
Lord! even so; I wait thy hour:
Jesus, my Saviour, come!

---

To God the Father, Son,
And Spirit, glory be,
As 't was, and is, and shall be so,
To all eternity.

## HYMN 132. C. M.

BETHEL. LEACH.

## HYMNS 133 & 134. C. M.

CHARMOUTH. WAINWRIGHT.

### HYMN 132. C. M.

A. STEELE.

1 YE humble souls, approach your God
With songs of sacred praise;
For he is good, supremely good,
And kind are all his ways.

2 All nature owns his guardian care,
In him we live and move;
But nobler benefits declare
The wonders of his love.

3 He gave his Son, his only Son,
To ransom rebel worms;
'T is here he makes his goodness known
In its diviner forms.

4 To this dear refuge, Lord, we come,
'T is here our hope relies;
A safe defense, a peaceful home,
When storms of trouble rise.

5 Thine eye beholds, with kind regard,
The souls who trust in thee;
Their humble hope thou wilt reward
With bliss divinely free.

6 Great God! to thy almighty love
What honors shall we raise;
Not all th' angelic songs above
Can render equal praise.

---

To Father, Son, and Holy Ghost,
The God whom we adore,
Be glory, as it was, is now,
And shall be evermore.

## IX.—CHRISTIAN DUTIES AND AFFECTIONS.

PRAYER.

### HYMN 133. C. M.

NEWTON.

1 APPROACH, my soul, the mercy-seat,
Where Jesus answers prayer;
There humbly fall before his feet,
For none can perish there.

2 Thy promise is my only plea,
With this I venture nigh;
Thou callest burdened souls to thee,
And such, O Lord, am I.

3 Bowed down beneath a load of sin,
By Satan sorely pressed;
By war without, and fear within,
I come to thee for rest.

4 Be thou my shield and hiding-place;
That, sheltered near thy side,
I may my fierce accuser face,
And tell him, "Thou hast died."

5 Oh! wondrous love, to bleed and die,
To bear the cross and shame,
That guilty sinners, such as I,
Might plead thy gracious name.

---

To Father, Son, and Holy Ghost,
The God whom we adore,
Be glory, as it was, is now,
And shall be evermore.

### HYMN 134. C. M.

MONTGOMERY.

1 PRAYER is the soul's sincere desire,
Uttered or unexpressed;
The motion of a hidden fire,
That trembles in the breast.

2 Prayer is the burden of a sigh,
The falling of a tear;
The upward glancing of an eye,
When none but God is near.

3 Prayer is the simplest form of speech
That infant lips can try;
Prayer, the sublimest strains that reach
The Majesty on high.

4 Prayer is the Christian's vital breath,
The Christian's native air,
The watchword at the gates of death:
He enters heaven with prayer.

5 Prayer is the contrite sinner's voice,
Returning from his ways;
While angels in their songs rejoice,
And cry, "Behold, he prays!"

6 In prayer, on earth, the saints are one;
They're one in word and mind,
When with the Father and the Son,
Sweet fellowship they find.

7 O thou, by whom we come to God,
The Life, the Truth, the Way,
The path of prayer thyself hast trod;
Lord, teach us how to pray.

---

To Father, Son, and Holy Ghost,
The God whom we adore,
Be glory, as it was, is now,
And shall be evermore.

## HYMN 135. L. M.

St. Luke's. Jer. Clarke.

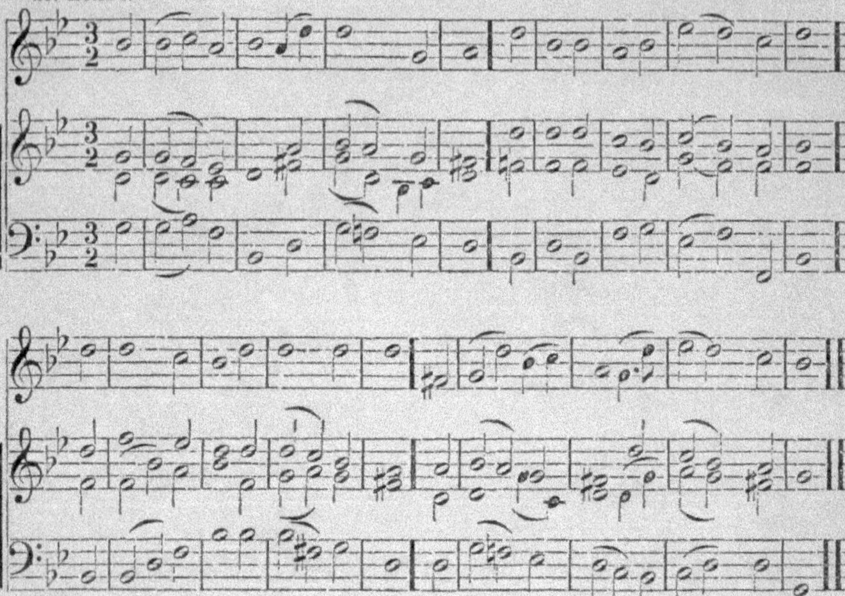

## HYMNS 136 & 137. L. M.

Rodgers. Rodgers.

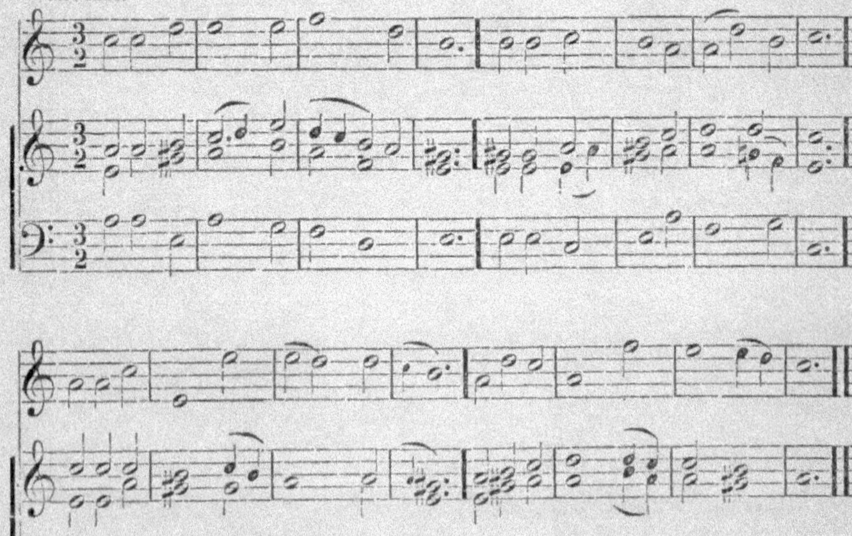

REPENTANCE.

### HYMN 135. L. M.

WATTS.

1 O THOU that hear'st when sinners cry,
Though all my crimes before thee lie,
Behold them not with angry look,
But blot their memory from thy book.

2 Create my nature pure within,
And form my soul averse to sin;
Let thy good Spirit ne'er depart,
Nor hide thy presence from my heart.

3 I can not live without thy light,
Cast out and banished from thy sight;
Thy holy joys, my God, restore,
And guard me that I fall no more.

4 Though I have grieved thy Spirit, Lord,
Thy help and comfort still afford;
And let a wretch come near thy throne,
To plead the merits of thy Son.

5 A broken heart, my God, my King,
Is all the sacrifice I bring;
The God of grace will ne'er despise
A broken heart for sacrifice.

6 My soul lies humbled in the dust,
And owns thy dreadful sentence just;
Look down, O Lord, with pitying eye,
And save the soul condemned to die.

7 Then will I teach the world thy ways;
Sinners shall learn thy sovereign grace;
I'll lead them to my Saviour's blood,
And they shall praise a pard'ning God.

8 O may thy love inspire my tongue,
Salvation shall be all my song;
And all my powers shall join to bless
The Lord, my strength and righteousness.

---

To Father, Son, and Holy Ghost,
The God whom earth and heaven adore,
Be glory, as it was of old,
Is now, and shall be evermore.

### HYMN 136. L. M.

C. WESLEY.

1 STAY, thou insulted Spirit, stay,
Though I have done thee such despite,
Nor cast the sinner quite away,
Nor take thine everlasting flight.

2 Though I have most unfaithful been,
And long in vain thy grace received;
Ten thousand times thy goodness seen,
Ten thousand times thy goodness grieved.

3 Yet, oh! the mourning sinner spare,
In honor of my great High Priest;
Nor in thy righteous anger swear
To exclude me from thy people's rest.

4 My weary soul, O God, release;
Uphold me with thy gracious hand;
Guide me into thy perfect peace,
And bring me to thy promised land.

---

To Father, Son, and Holy Ghost,
The God whom earth and heaven adore,
Be glory, as it was of old,
Is now, and shall be evermore.

### HYMN 137. L. M

C. WESLEY.

1 O THAT my load of sin were gone!
O that I could at last submit,
At Jesus' feet to lay it down!
To lay my soul at Jesus' feet!

2 Rest for my soul I long to find;
Saviour of all! if mine thou art,
Give me thy meek and lowly mind,
And stamp thine image on my heart.

3 Break off the yoke of inbred sin,
And fully set my spirit free;
I can not rest till pure within,
Till I am wholly lost in thee.

4 Fain would I learn of thee, my God;
Thy light and easy burden prove,
The cross, all stained with hallowed blood,
The labor of thy dying love.

5 I would, but thou must give the power,
My heart from every sin release;
Bring near, bring near the joyful hour,
And fill me with thy perfect peace.

---

To Father, Son, and Holy Ghost,
The God whom earth and heaven adore,
Be glory, as it was of old,
Is now, and shall be evermore.

## HYMN 138. C. M.

WAINWRIGHT. WAINWRIGHT.

## HYMN 139. III 2.

ST. AUSTIN'S. REV. R. CECIL.

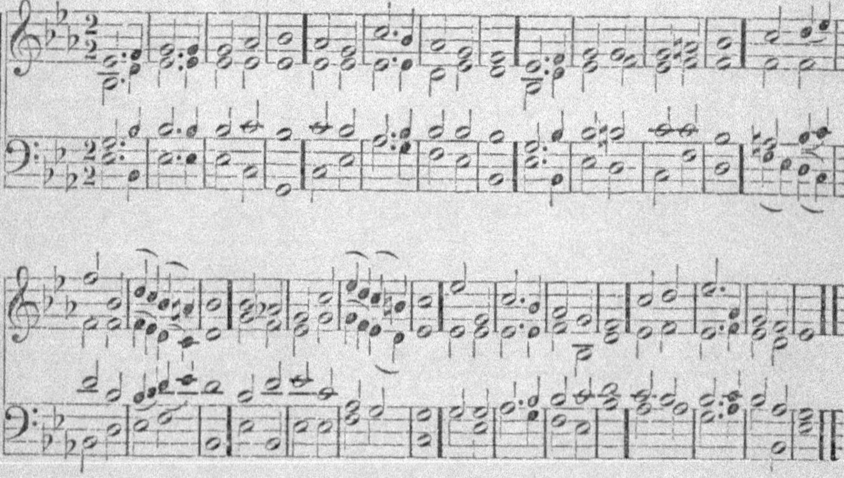

### HYMN 138. C. M.

*Penitential Gratitude.* WHITFIELD.

1 RISE, O my soul, the hours review,
When awed by guilt and fear,
To heaven for grace thou durst not sue,
And found no rescue here.

2 Thy tears are dried, thy griefs are fled,
Dispelled each bitter care;
For heaven itself has lent its aid
To save thee from despair.

3 Hear, then, O God! thy work fulfill,
And, from thy mercy's throne,
Vouchsafe me strength to do thy will,
And to resist mine own.

4 So shall my soul each power employ,
Thy mercy to adore;
While heaven itself proclaims with joy—
"One pardoned sinner more."

---

To Father, Son, and Holy Ghost,
The God whom we adore,
Be glory, as it was, is now,
And shall be evermore.

FAITH.

### HYMN 139. III 2.

1 ROCK of ages! cleft for me,
Let me hide myself in thee;
Let the water and the blood,
From thy side, a healing flood,
Be of sin the double cure,
Save from wrath, and make me pure.

2 Should my tears for ever flow,
Should my zeal no languor know,
This for sin could not atone,
Thou must save, and thou alone;
In my hand no price I bring,
Simply to thy cross I cling.

3 While I draw this fleeting breath,
When mine eyelids close in death,
When I rise to worlds unknown,
And behold thee on thy throne;
Rock of ages! cleft for me,
Let me hide myself in thee!

---

Praise the name of God most high,
Praise him, all below the sky,
Praise him, all ye heavenly host,
Father, Son, and Holy Ghost;
As through countless ages past,
Evermore his praise shall last.

## HYMN 140. L. M.

St. Wilfred. Widdop.

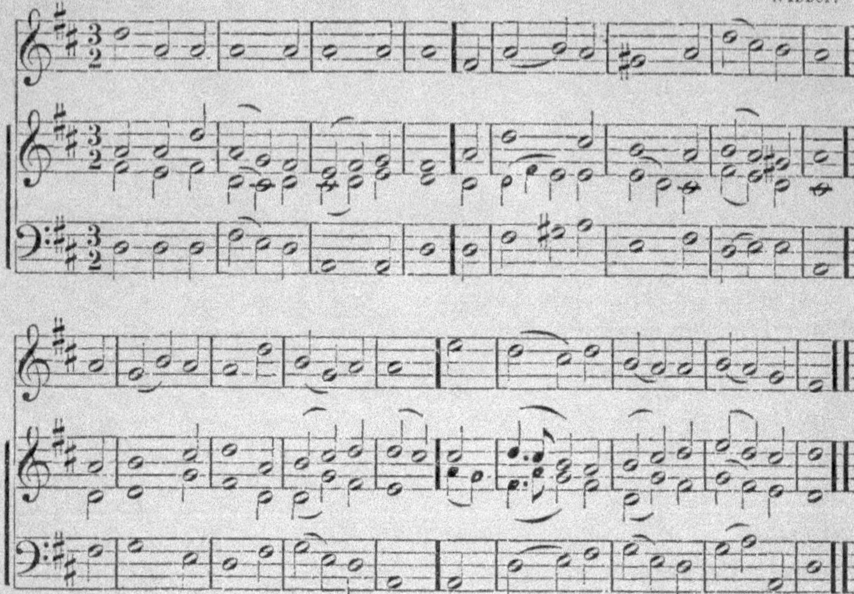

## HYMN 141. C. M.

Havens.

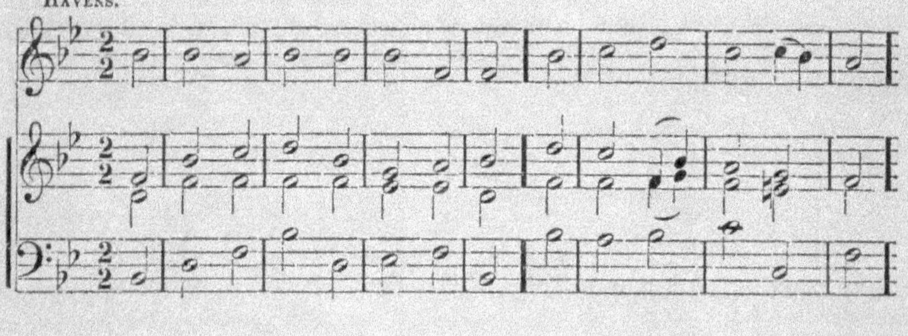

### HYMN 140. L. M.

WATTS.

1 FAITH is the Christian's evidence
Of things unseen by mortal eye;
It passes all the bounds of sense,
And penetrates the inmost sky.

2 Things absent it can set in view,
And bring far distant prospects home;
Events long past it can renew,
And long foresee the things to come.

3 With strong persuasion, from afar
The heavenly region it surveys,
Embraces all the blessings there,
And here enjoys the promises.

4 By faith a steady course we steer,
Through ruffling storms and swelling seas,
O'ercome the world, keep down our fear,
And still possess our souls in peace.

5 By faith we pass the vale of tears
Safe and serene, though oft distressed;
By faith, subdue the king of fears,
And go rejoicing to our rest.

---

To Father, Son, and Holy Ghost,
The God whom earth and heaven adore,
Be glory, as it was of old,
Is now, and shall be evermore.

### HYMN 141. C. M.

Rom. viii: 31-34. LOGAN.

1 O LET triumphant faith dispel
The fears of guilt and woe;
If God be for us, God the Lord,
Who, who shall be our foe?

2 He who his only Son gave up
To death, that we might live,
Shall he not all things freely grant,
That boundless love can give?

3 Who now his people shall accuse?
'T is God hath justified;
Who now his people shall condemn?
The Lamb of God hath died.

4 And He who died hath risen again,
Triumphant from the grave;
At God's right hand for us He pleads,
Omnipotent to save.

---

To Father, Son, and Holy Ghost,
The God whom we adore,
Be glory, as it was, is now,
And shall be evermore.

## HYMN 142. C. M.

LYSTRA. C. WESLEY.

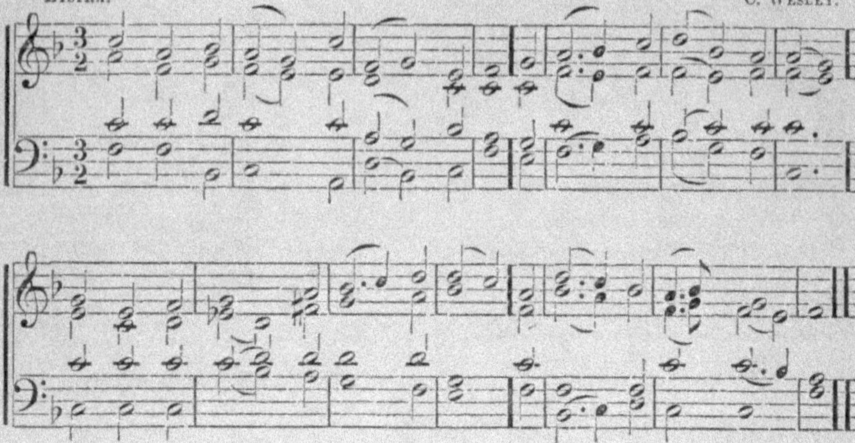

## HYMN 143. III 1.

HOTHAM. MADAN.

### HYMN 142. C. M.

*Dead Faith.* WATTS.

1 DELUDED souls, that dream of heaven,
And make their empty boast
Of inward joys, and sins forgiven,
While they are slaves to lust.

2 Vain are our fancies, vain our flights,
If faith be cold and dead;
None but a living power unites
To Christ, the living Head.

3 The faith which new-creates the heart,
And works by active love,
Will bid all sinful joys depart,
And lift the thoughts above.

4 God from the curse has set us free,
To make us pure within;
Nor did he send his Son to be
The minister of sin.

---

To Father, Son, and Holy Ghost,
The God whom we adore,
Be glory, as it was, is now,
And shall be evermore.

### HYMN 143. III 1.

*Christ our Refuge.* C. WESLEY.

1 JESUS, Saviour of my soul,
Let me to thy bosom fly,
While the waves of trouble roll,
While the tempest still is high;
Hide me, O my Saviour, hide,
Till the storm of life is past;
Safe into the haven guide;
O receive my soul at last.

2 Other refuge have I none,
Hangs my helpless soul on thee:
Leave, ah, leave me not alone,
Still support and comfort me:
All my trust on thee is stayed,
All my hope from thee I bring;
Cover my defenseless head
With the shadow of thy wing.

---

Holy Father, Holy Son,
Holy Spirit, Three in One!
Glory, as of old, to thee,
Now, and evermore shall be!

## HYMN 144. IV 4.

HINTON.

## HYMN 145.

AMSTERDAM. DR. NARES.

### HYMN 144. IV 4.

KENNEDAY.

1 How firm a foundation, ye saints of the Lord,
Is laid for your faith in his excellent word;
What more can he say than to you he hath said,
You who unto Jesus for refuge have fled:

2 Fear not, I am with thee, O be not dismayed,
I, I am thy God, and will still give thee aid;
I'll strengthen thee, help thee, and cause thee to stand,
Upheld, by my righteous, omnipotent hand.

3 When through the deep waters I call thee to go,
The rivers of woe shall not thee overflow;
For I will be with thee, thy troubles to bless,
And sanctify to thee thy deepest distress.

4 When through fiery trials thy pathway shall lie,
My grace, all-sufficient, shall be thy supply;
The flame shall not hurt thee, I only design
Thy dross to consume, and thy gold to refine.

5 The soul that to Jesus hath fled for repose,
I will not, I will not desert to his foes;
That soul, though all hell shall endeavor to shake,
I'll never—no, never—no never forsake.

O Father Almighty, to thee be addressed,
With Christ and the Spirit, one God ever blessed,
All glory and worship from earth and from heaven,
As was, and is now, and shall ever be given.

HOPE.

### HYMN 145.

WHITFIELD.

1. RISE, my soul, and stretch thy wings,
Thy better portion trace;
Rise, from transitory things,
Toward heaven, thy destined place.
Sun, and moon, and stars decay,
Time shall soon this earth remove;
Rise, my soul, and haste away
To seats prepared above.

2 Cease, my soul, O cease to mourn,
Press onward to the prize;
Soon thy Saviour will return,
To take thee to the skies:
There, is everlasting peace,
Rest, enduring rest in heaven;
There, will sorrow ever cease,
And crowns of joy be given.

---

To the Father, to the Son,
And Spirit ever blessed,
Everlasting Three in One,
All worship be addressed:
Praise from all above, below,
As throughout the ages past,
Now is given, and shall be so
While endless ages last.

## HYMN 146. III 1.

TUSCANY.

## HYMN 147. C. M.

MISSIONARY. T. WALKER.

### HYMN 146. III 1.

CENNICK.

1 CHILDREN of the heavenly King,
As we journey, let us sing:
Sing the Saviour's worthy praise,
Glorious in his works and ways.

2 We are traveling home to God
In the way the fathers trod;
They are happy now, and we
Soon their happiness shall see.

3 Banished once, by sin betrayed,
Christ our advocate was made;
Pardoned now, no more we roam,
Christ conducts us to our home.

4 Lord, obediently we'll go,
Gladly leaving all below;
Only thou our leader be,
And we still will follow thee.

---

Holy Father, Holy Son,
Holy Spirit, Three in One!
Glory, as of old, to thee,
Now, and evermore shall be.

### HYMN 147. C. M.

WATTS.

1 WHEN I can read my title clear
To mansions in the skies,
I'll bid farewell to every fear,
And wipe my weeping eyes.

2 Should earth against my soul engage,
And fiery darts be hurled,
Then I can smile at Satan's rage,
And face a frowning world.

3 Let cares like a wide deluge come,
Let storms of sorrow fall;
So I but safely reach my home,
My God, my heaven, my all.

4 There, anchored safe, my weary soul
Shall find eternal rest;
Nor storms shall beat, nor billows roll
Across my peaceful breast.

---

To Father, Son, and Holy Ghost,
The God whom we adore,
Be glory, as it was, is now,
And shall be evermore.

## HYMN 148. C. M.

BRADFORD. HANDEL.

## HYMN 149. S. M.

VIGIL. LEACH.

JOY.

### HYMN 148. C. M.

NEWTON.

1 Joy is a fruit that will not grow
In nature's barren soil;
All we can boast, till Christ we know,
Is vanity and toil.

2 A bleeding Saviour, seen by faith,
A sense of pard'ning love,
A hope that triumphs over death,
Give joys like those above.

3 These are the joys which satisfy
And purify the mind;
Which make the spirit mount on high,
And leave the world behind.

4 No more, believer, mourn thy lot,
O thou who art the Lord's,
Resign to those that know him not,
Such joy as earth affords.

---

To Father, Son, and Holy Ghost,
The God whom we adore,
Be glory, as it was, is now,
And shall be evermore.

### HYMN 149. S. M.

WATTS.

1 Come ye that love the Lord,
And let your joys be known;
Join in a song with sweet accord,
And thus surround the throne.

2 Let those refuse to sing
Who never knew our God;
But children of the heavenly King
May speak their joys abroad.

3 The God of heaven is ours,
Our Father and our love;
His care shall guard life's fleeting hours,
Then waft our souls above.

4 There shall we see his face,
And never, never, sin;
There, from the rivers of his grace,
Drink endless pleasures in.

5 Yes, and before we rise
To that immortal state,
The thoughts of such amazing bliss
Should constant joys create.

6 Children of grace have found
Glory begun below;
Celestial fruits on earthly ground,
From faith and hope may grow.

7 The hill of Zion yields
A thousand sacred sweets,
Before we reach the heavenly fields,
Or walk the golden streets.

8 Then let our songs abound,
And every tear be dry;
We're traveling through Immanuel's
ground,
To fairer worlds on high.

---

To God the Father, Son,
And Spirit, glory be,
As 't was, and is, and shall be so,
To all eternity.

## HYMN 150. III 3.

HAMBURG. MENDELSSOHN.

## HYMN 151. III 1.

LAWRENCE. NEUKOMM.

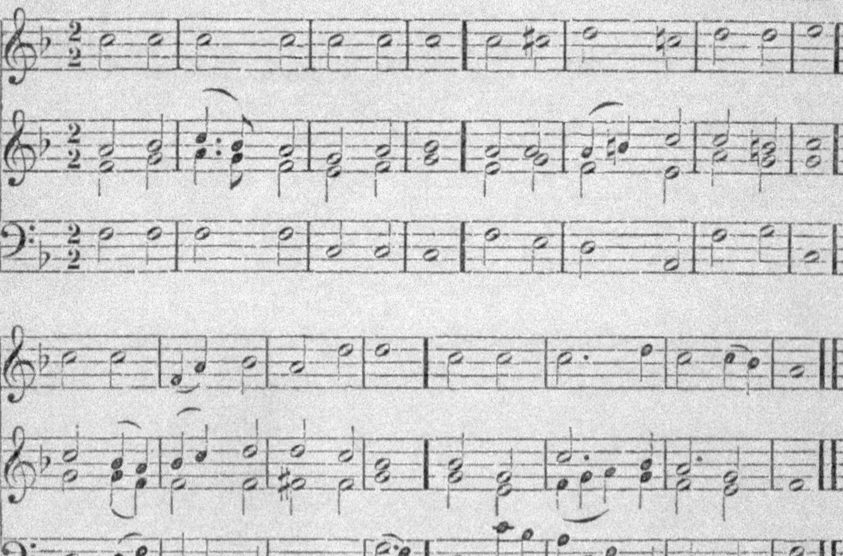

LOVE.

### HYMN 150. III 3.

F. S. Key.

1 Lord, with glowing heart I'd praise thee,
For the bliss thy love bestows;
For the pard'ning grace that saves me,
And the peace that from it flows:
Help, O God, my weak endeavor;
This dull soul to rapture raise;
Thou must light the flame, or never
Can my love be warmed to praise.

2 Praise, my soul, the God that sought thee,
Wretched wanderer, far astray;
Found thee lost, and kindly brought thee
From the paths of death away;
Praise with love's devoutest feeling,
Him who saw thy guilt-born fear;
And, the light of hope revealing,
Bade the blood-stained cross appear.

3 Lord, this bosom's ardent feeling
Vainly would my lips express;
Low before thy footstool kneeling,
Deign thy suppliant's prayer to bless;
Let thy grace, my soul's chief treasure,
Love's pure flame within me raise;
And since words can never measure,
Let my life show forth thy praise.

---

Praise the Father, earth and heaven,
Praise the Son, the Spirit praise,
As it was, and is, be given
Glory through eternal days.

### HYMN 151. III 1.

Newton.

1 Lord, my God, I long to know,
Oft it causes anxious thought;
Do I love thee, Lord, or no?
Am I thine, or am I not?

2 Could my heart so hard remain,
Prayer a task and burden prove,
Any duty give me pain,
If I knew a Saviour's love?

3 When I turn mine eyes within,
O how dark, and vain, and wild!
Prone to unbelief and sin,
Can I deem myself thy child?

4 Yet I mourn my stubborn will,
Find my sin a grief and thrall;
Should I grieve for what I feel,
If I did not love at all?

5 Could I love thy saints to meet,
Choose the ways I once abhorred,
Find at times the promise sweet,
If I did not love thee, Lord?

6 Saviour, let me love thee more,
If I love at all, I pray;
If I have not loved before,
Help me to begin to-day.

---

Holy Father, Holy Son,
Holy Spirit, Three in One!
Glory, as of old, to thee,
Now, and evermore shall be.

## HYMN 152.

HEBRON.

## HYMN 153. IV 3.

JUBELATE. DR. HOWARD.

PRAISE.

## HYMN 152.

OLIVER.

1 THE God of Abraham praise,
Who reigns enthroned above;
Ancient of everlasting days,
And God of love:
Jehovah, Great I AM,
By earth and heaven confessed;
I bow and bless the sacred Name,
For ever blessed.

2 The God of Abraham praise,
At whose supreme command
From earth I rise, and seek the joys
At his right hand:
I all on earth forsake,
Its wisdom, fame, and power;
And Him my only portion make,
My shield and tower.

3 He by himself hath sworn,
I on his oath depend,
I shall, on angel-wings upborne,
To heaven ascend:
I shall behold his face,
I shall his power adore,
And sing the wonders of his grace
For evermore.

4 There dwells the Lord, our King,
The Lord, our righteousness,
Triumphant o'er the world and sin,
The Prince of Peace;
On Zion's sacred hight
His kingdom he maintains,
And, glorious with his saints in light,
For ever reigns.

5 The God who reigns on high
The great archangels sing;
And "Holy, holy, holy," cry,
"Almighty King,
Who was, and is the same,
And evermore shall be;
Jehovah, Father, Great I AM,
We worship thee."

6 The whole triumphant host
Give thanks to God on high;
"Hail, Father, Son, and Holy Ghost,"
They ever cry:
Hail, Abraham's God and mine,
I join the heavenly lays;
All might and majesty are thine
And endless praise.

## HYMN 153. IV 3.

Psalm C. MONTGOMERY.

1 BE joyful in God, all ye lands of the earth,
O serve him with gladness and fear;
Exult in his presence with music and mirth,
With love and devotion draw near.

2 For Jehovah is God, and Jehovah alone,
Creator and ruler o'er all;
And we are his people, his scepter we own;
His sheep, and we follow his call.

3 O enter his gates with thanksgiving and song,
Your vows in his temple proclaim;
His praise with melodious accordance prolong,
And bless his adorable Name.

4 For good is the Lord, inexpressibly good,
And we are the work of his hand;
His mercy and truth from eternity stood,
And shall to eternity stand.

---

All praise to the Father, all praise to the Son,
All praise to the Spirit, thrice blessed;
The holy, eternal, supreme Three in One,
Was, is, and shall still be addressed.

## HYMN 154. L. M.

WINCHESTER. CROFT.

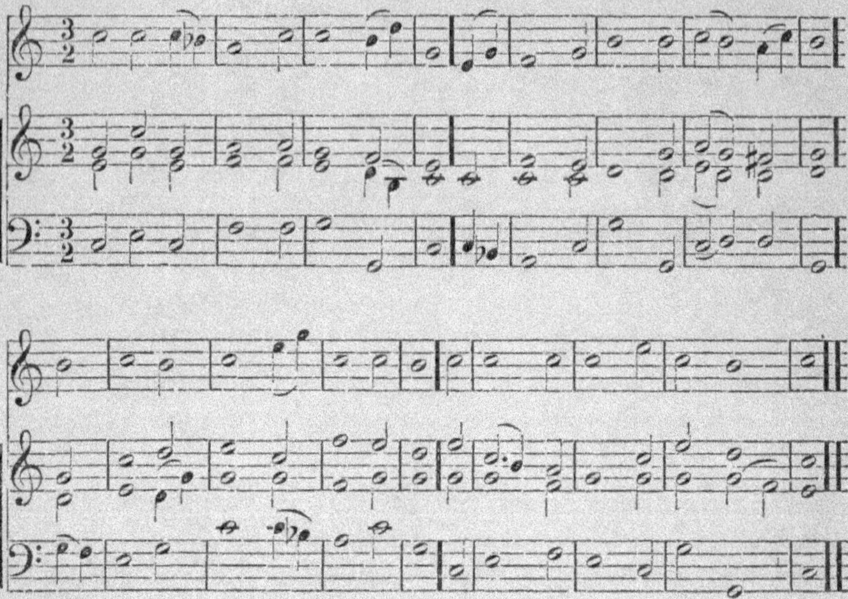

## HYMN 155. III 1.

CLARK. CLARK.

### HYMN 154. L. M.

Psalm c. WATTS.

1 BEFORE Jehovah's awful throne,
Ye nations, bow with sacred joy;
Know that the Lord is God alone;
He can create, and he destroy.

2 His sovereign power, without our aid,
Made us of clay, and formed us men;
And when, like wand'ring sheep, we strayed,
He brought us to his fold again.

3 We are his people, we his care,
Our souls, and all our mortal frame;
What lasting honors shall we rear,
Almighty Maker, to thy name?

4 We'll crowd thy gates with thankful songs,
High as the heaven our voices raise;
And earth, with her ten thousand tongues,
Shall fill thy courts with sounding praise.

5 Wide as the world is thy command,
Vast as eternity thy love;
Firm as a rock thy truth must stand,
When rolling years shall cease to move.

---

To Father, Son, and Holy Ghost,
The God whom earth and heaven adore,
Be glory, as it was of old,
Is now, and shall be evermore.

### HYMN 155. III 1.

*Songs of Praise.* MONTGOMERY.

1 *Songs of praise* the angels sang;
Heaven with hallelujahs rang,
When Jehovah's work begun,
When he spake, and it was done.

2 *Songs of praise* awoke the morn,
When the Prince of Peace was born;
*Songs of praise* arose when he
Captive led captivity.

3 Heaven and earth must pass away;
*Songs of praise* shall crown that day;
God will make new heavens and earth;
*Songs of praise* shall hail their birth.

4 And shall man alone be dumb
Till that glorious kingdom come?
No;—the church delights to raise
Psalms and hymns, and *songs of praise.*

5 Saints below, with heart and voice,
Still in *songs of praise* rejoice;
Learning here by faith and love,
*Songs of praise* to sing above.

6 Borne upon their latest breath,
*Songs of praise* shall conquer death;
Then, amid eternal joy,
*Songs of praise* their powers employ.

---

Holy Father, Holy Son,
Holy Spirit, Three in One!
Glory, as of old, to thee,
Now, and evermore shall be!

## HYMN 156. C. M.

LYSTRA. C. WESLEY.

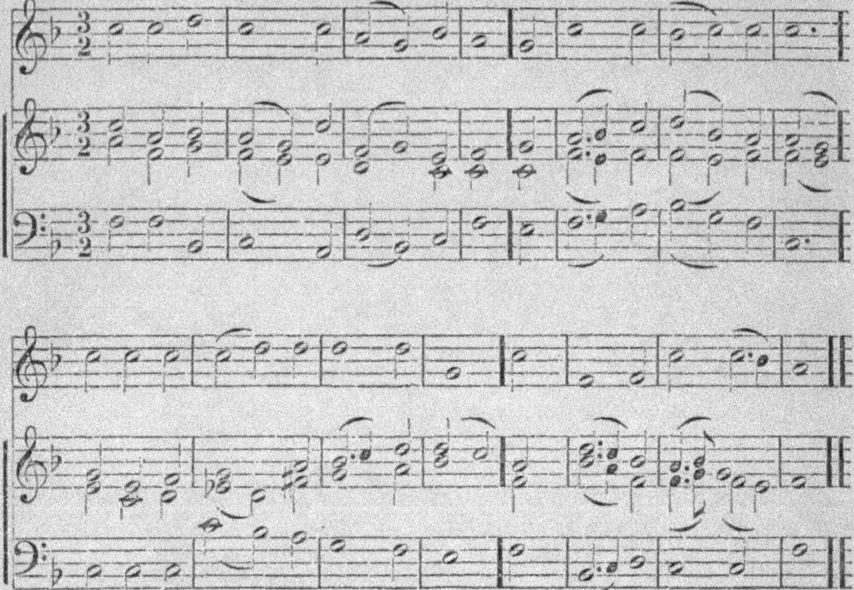

## HYMN 157. L. M.

ST. WILFRED. WIDDOP.

CONTENTMENT.

## HYMN 156. C. M.

STEELE.

1 Father, whate'er of earthly bliss,
Thy sovereign will denies,
Accepted at thy throne, let this,
My humble prayer arise—

2 Give me a calm and thankful heart,
From every murmur free;
The blessings of thy grace impart,
And make me live to thee.

3 Let the sweet hope that thou art mine,
My life and death attend,
Thy presence through my journey shine,
And crown my journey's end.

---

To Father, Son, and Holy Ghost,
The God whom we adore,
Be glory, as it was, is now,
And shall be evermore.

## HYMN 157. L. M.

NEWTON.

1 Be still my heart! these anxious cares,
To thee are burdens, thorns, and snares;
They cast dishonor on thy Lord,
And contradict his gracious word.

2 Brought safely by his hand thus far,
Why wilt thou now give place to fear?
How canst thou want if he provide,
Or lose thy way with such a guide?

3 When first before his mercy-seat,
Thou didst to him thy all commit;
He gave thee warrant from that hour,
To trust his wisdom, love, and power.

4 Did ever trouble yet befall,
And he refuse to hear thy call?
And has he not his promise past,
That thou shalt overcome at last?

5 Though rough and thorny be the road,
It leads thee home apace to God;
Then count thy present trials small,
For heaven will make amends for all.

---

To Father, Son, and Holy Ghost,
The God whom earth and heaven adore,
Be glory, as it was of old,
Is now, and shall be evermore.

## HYMN 158. C.M.

CURFEW. NOVELLO.

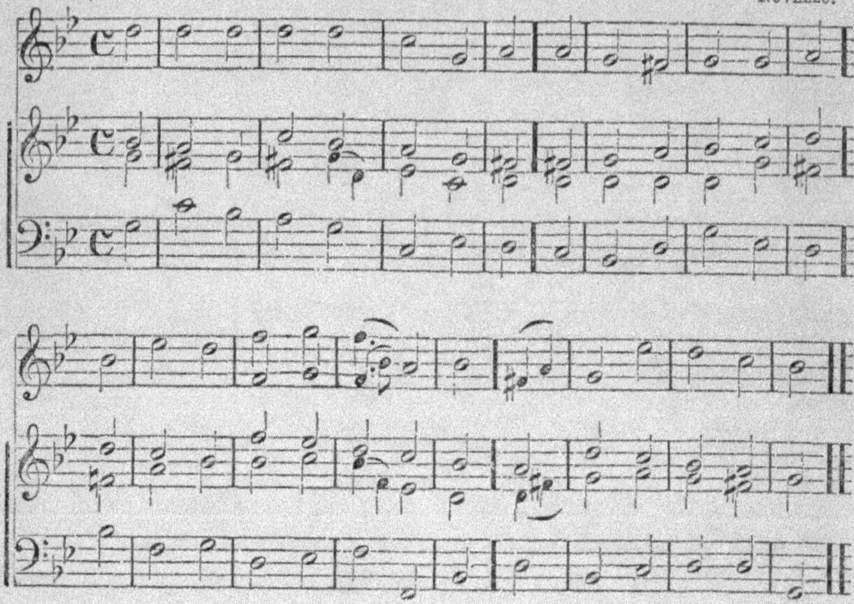

## HYMN 159. II 3.

BRIGHTON.

IN AFFLICTION.

### HYMN 158. C. M.

A. STEELE.

1 HEAR, gracious God! my humble moan,
To thee I breathe my sighs;
When will the mournful night be gone?
When shall my joys arise?

2 Yet, though my soul in darkness mourns,
Thy promise is my stay;
Here would I rest till light returns:
Thy presence makes my day.

3 Come, Lord, and with celestial peace
Relieve my aching heart;
O smile, and bid my sorrows cease,
And all their gloom depart.

4 Then shall my drooping spirit rise,
And bless thy healing rays,
And change these deep, complaining sighs
For songs of sacred praise.

---

To Father, Son, and Holy Ghost,
The God whom we adore,
Be glory, as it was, is now,
And shall be evermore.

### HYMN 159. II 3.

Psalm xlii: 1-5. BOWDLER.

1 As, panting in the sultry beam,
The hart desires the cooling stream,
So to thy presence, Lord, I flee,
So longs my soul, O God, for thee;
Athirst to taste thy living grace,
And see thy glory face to face.

2 But rising griefs distress my soul,
And tears on tears successive roll;
For many an evil voice is near,
To chide my woe and mock my fear,
And silent memory weeps alone
O'er hours of peace and gladness flown.

3 For I have walked the happy round
That 'circles Zion's holy ground,
And gladly swelled the choral lays
That hymned my great Redeemer's praise,
What time the hallowed arches rung
Responsive to the solemn song.

4 Ah, why, by passing clouds oppressed,
Should vexing thoughts distract thy breast?
Turn, turn, to Him, in every pain,
Whom suppliants never sought in vain;
Thy strength, in joy's ecstatic day,
Thy hope, when joy has passed away.

---

To God the Father, God the Son,
And God the Spirit, Three in One,
Be glory in the highest given,
By all in earth, and all in heaven,
As was through ages heretofore,
Is now, and shall be evermore.

## HYMN 160. II 3.

WHITE. HAYDN.

## HYMN 161. L. M.

GERMANY. BEETHOVEN.

## HYMN 160. II 3.

*A compassionate High-Priest.*

Hebrews iv: 15. GLENELG.

1 WHEN gathering clouds around I view,
And days are dark, and friends are few,
On Him I lean, who, not in vain,
Experienced every human pain;
He feels my griefs, he sees my fears,
And counts and treasures up my tears.

2 If aught should tempt my soul to stray
From heavenly wisdom's narrow way,
To fly the good I would pursue,
Or do the ill I would not do;
Still He, who felt temptation's power,
Shall guard me in that dangerous hour.

3 When vexing thoughts within me rise,
And, sore dismayed, my spirit dies;
Then He, who once vouchsafed to bear
The sickening anguish of despair,
Shall sweetly soothe, shall gently dry,
The throbbing heart, the streaming eye.

4 When sorrowing o'er some stone I bend,
Which covers all that was a friend,
And from his voice, his hand, his smile,
Divides me for a little while;
Thou, Saviour, seest the tears I shed,
For thou didst weep o'er Lazarus dead.

5 And, oh, when I have safely passed
Through every conflict but the last,
Still, still unchanging, watch beside
My bed of death, for Thou hast died:
Then point to realms of endless day,
And wipe the latest tear away.

To God the Father, God the Son,
And God the Spirit, Three in One,
Be glory in the highest given,
By all in earth, and all in heaven,
As was through ages heretofore,
Is now, and shall be evermore.

## HYMN 161. L. M.

*Sanctified Affliction.* COWPER.

1 Lord, unafflicted, undismayed,
In pleasure's path how long I strayed;
But thou hast made me feel thy rod,
And turned my soul to thee, my God.

2 What though it pierced my fainting heart,
I bless thy hand that caused the smart;
It taught my tears awhile to flow,
But saved me from eternal woe.

3 O, hadst thou left me unchastised,
Thy precepts I had still despised,
And still the snare in secret laid
Had my unwary feet betrayed.

4 I love thy chastenings, O my God,
They fix my hopes on thy abode;
Where, in thy presence fully blest,
Thy stricken saints for ever rest.

---

To Father, Son, and Holy Ghost,
The God whom earth and heaven adore,
Be glory, as it was of old,
Is now, and shall be evermore.

## HYMN 162. II 3.

BROWNELL. HAYDN.

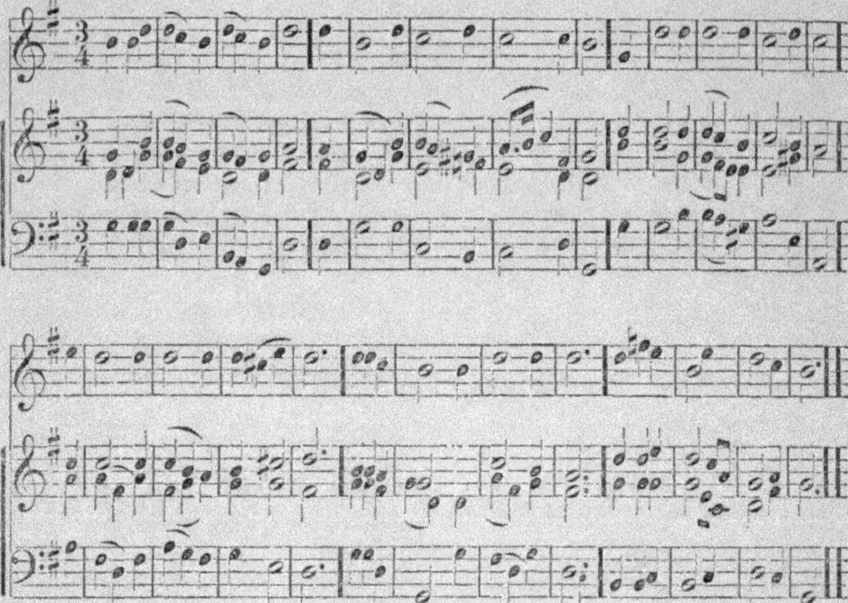

## HYMN 163. L. M.

GERMANY. BEETHOVEN.

DAILY DEVOTION.

## HYMN 162. II 3.

*Daily Dependence.* SIR. R. GRANT.

1 WHEN, streaming from the eastern skies,
The morning light salutes mine eyes,
O Sun of Righteousness divine,
On me with beams of mercy shine;
Chase the dark clouds of sin away,
And turn my darkness into day.

2 When to Heaven's great and glorious King
My morning sacrifice I bring;
And, mourning o'er my guilt and shame,
Ask mercy, Saviour, in thy Name;
My conscience sprinkle with thy blood,
And be my advocate with God.

3 As every day thy mercy spares
Will bring its trials and its cares,
O Saviour, till my life shall end,
Be thou my counselor and friend:
Teach me thy precepts, all divine,
And be thy pure example mine.

4 When pain transfixes every part,
Or languor settles at the heart;
When on my bed, diseased, oppressed,
I turn, and sigh, and long for rest;
O great Physician, see my grief,
And grant thy servant sweet relief.

5 Should poverty's destructive blow
Lay all my worldly comforts low;
And neither help nor hope appear,
My steps to guide, my heart to cheer;
Lord, pity and supply my need,
For thou, on earth, wast poor indeed.

6 Should Providence profusely pour
Its varied blessings on my store;
O keep me from the ills that wait
On such a seeming prosperous state:
From hurtful passions set me free,
And humbly may I walk with thee.

7 When each day's scenes and labors close,
And wearied nature seeks repose,
With pardoning mercy richly blest,
Guard me, my Saviour, while I rest:
And as each morning sun shall rise,
O lead me onward to the skies.



8 And, at my life's last setting sun,
My conflicts o'er, my labors done,
Jesus, thy heavenly radiance shed,
To cheer and bless my dying bed;
And from death's gloom my spirit raise,
To see thy face and sing thy praise.

---

To God the Father, God the Son,
And God the Spirit, Three in One,
Be glory in the highest given,
By all in earth, and all in heaven,
As was through ages heretofore,
Is now, and shall be evermore.

## HYMN 163. L. M.

*"I have set God always before me."*

Psalm xvi: 9. GISBORNE.

1 SAVIOUR, when night involves the skies,
My soul, adoring, turns to thee:
Thee, self-abased, in mortal guise,
And wrapt in shades of death for me.

2 On thee my waking raptures dwell,
When crimson gleams the east adorn,
Thee, victor of the grave, and hell,
Thee, source of life's eternal morn.

3 When noon her throne in light arrays,
To thee my soul triumphant springs;
Thee, throned in glory's endless blaze,
Thee, Lord of lords, and King of kings.

4 O'er earth, when shades of evening steal,
To death and thee my thoughts I give,—
To death, whose power I soon must feel,
To thee, with whom I trust to live.

---

To Father, Son, and Holy Ghost,
The God whom earth and heaven adore,
Be glory, as it was of old,
Is now, and shall be evermore.

## HYMN 164. L. M.

MORNING HYMN. CROFT.

## HYMN 165. L. M.

LUTON. BURDER.

### HYMN 164. L. M.

*Morning Hymn.* KENN.

1 AWAKE, my soul, and with the sun
Thy daily course of duty run:
Shake off dull sloth, and early rise
To pay thy morning sacrifice.

2 Redeem thy misspent time that's past;
Live this day as if 'twere thy last;
To improve thy talents take due care;
'Gainst the great day thyself prepare.

3 Let all thy converse be sincere,
Thy conscience as the noonday clear;
Think how the all-seeing God, thy ways
And all thy secret thoughts surveys.

4 Wake, and lift up thyself, my heart,
And with the angels bear thy part;
Who all night long unwearied sing,
Glory to thee, eternal King!

5 I wake, I wake, ye heavenly choir;
May your devotion me inspire;
That I like you my age may spend,
Like you may on my God attend.

6 May I like you in God delight,
Have all day long my God in sight;
Perform like you my Maker's will;
O! may I never more do ill.

7 Glory to thee, who safe hast kept,
And hast refreshed me while I slept;
Grant, Lord, when I from death shall wake,
I may of endless life partake.

8 Lord, I my vows to thee renew;
Scatter my sins as morning dew;
Guard my first spring of thought and will,
And with thyself my spirit fill.

9 Direct, control, suggest, this day,
All I design, or do, or say,
That all my powers with all their might,
In thy sole glory may unite.

10 Praise God, from whom all blessings flow,
Praise him, all creatures here below;
Praise him above, ye angelic host;
Praise Father, Son, and Holy Ghost.

---

To Father, Son, and Holy Ghost,
The God whom earth and heaven adore,
Be glory, as it was of old,
Is now, and shall be evermore.

### HYMN 165. L. M.

*Morning.* S. J. SMITH.

1 ARISE, my soul, with rapture rise!
And filled with love and fear, adore
The awful Sovereign of the skies,
Whose mercy lends me one day more.

2 And may this day, indulgent Power!
Not idly pass, nor fruitless be;
But may each swiftly flying hour
Still nearer bring my soul to Thee.

3 But can it be? that Power divine
Is throned in light's unbounded blaze;
And countless worlds and angels join
To swell the glorious song of praise;

4 And will he deign to lend an ear,
When I, poor abject mortal pray?
Yes, boundless goodness; he will hear,
Nor cast the meanest wretch away.

5 Then let me serve thee all my days,
And may my zeal with years increase;
For pleasant, Lord, are all thy ways,
And all thy paths are paths of peace.

---

To Father, Son, and Holy Ghost,
The God whom earth and heaven adore,
Be glory, as it was of old,
Is now, and shall be evermore.

## HYMN 166. C. M

MATINS.

## HYMN 167. III 1.

LAWRENCE. NEUKOMM.

### HYMN 166. C. M.

*Morning.* DRENNAN.

1 To thee let my first offerings rise,
Whose sun creates the day,
Swift as his gladdening influence flies,
And spotless as his ray.

2 This day thy favoring hand be nigh,
So oft vouchsafed before;
Still may it lead, protect, supply,
And I that hand adore.

3 If bliss thy providence impart,
For which, resigned, I pray,
Give me to feel a cheerful heart,
And grateful homage pay.

4 Affliction should thy love intend,
As vice or folly's cure,
Patient to gain that gracious end,
May I the means endure.

5 Be this and every future day
Still wiser than the past,
And when I all my life survey,
May grace sustain at last.

To Father, Son, and Holy Ghost,
The God whom we adore,
Be glory, as it was, is now,
And shall be evermore.

### HYMN 167. III 1.

1 Now the shades of night are gone,
Now the morning light is come,
Lord, may we be thine to-day;
Drive the shades of sin away.

2 Fill our souls with heavenly light,
Banish doubt and clear our sight;
In thy service, Lord, to-day,
May we labor, watch, and pray.

3 Keep our haughty passions bound;
Save us from our foes around;
Going out and coming in,
Keep us safe from every sin.

4 When our work of life is past,
O receive us then at last;
Night and sin will be no more,
When we reach the heavenly shore.

---

Holy Father, holy Son,
Holy Spirit, Three in One!
Glory, as of old, to thee,
Now, and evermore shall be.

## HYMN 168. L. M.

EVENING HYMN. TALLIS.

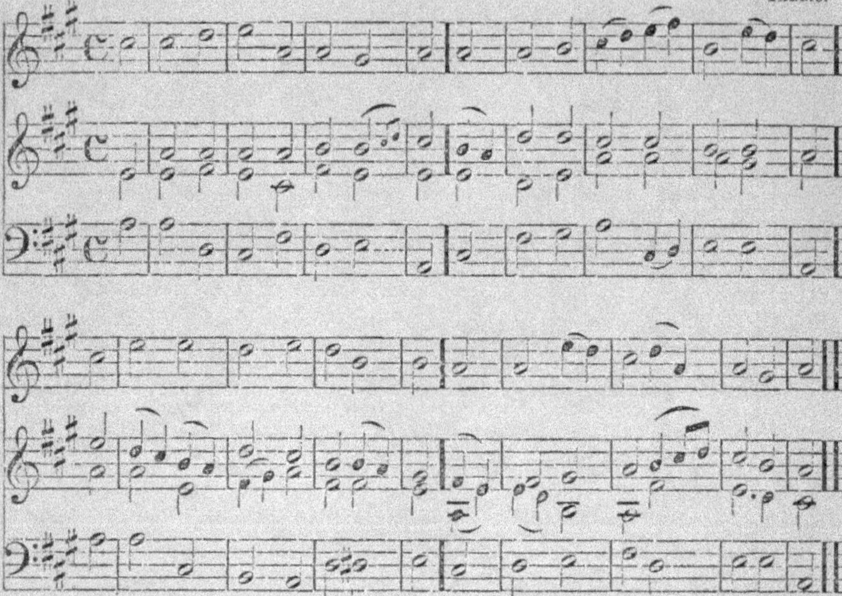

## HYMN 169. L. M.

VESPER. GARNETT.

### HYMN 168. L. M.

*Evening Hymn.* KENN.

1 GLORY to thee, my God, this night,
For all the blessings of the light;
Keep me, O keep me, King of kings,
Under thine own almighty wings.

2 Forgive me, Lord, for thy dear Son,
The ills that I this day have done;
That with the world, myself, and Thee,
I, ere I sleep, at peace may be.

3 Teach me to live, that I may dread
The grave as little as my bed;
Teach me to die, that so I may
Triumphing rise at the last day.

4 O may my soul on thee repose,
And with sweet sleep mine eyelids close;
Sleep, that may me more vigorous make
To serve my God, when I awake.

5 When in the night I sleepless lie,
My soul with heavenly thoughts supply;
Let no ill dreams disturb my rest,
No powers of darkness me molest.

6 O when shall I, in endless day,
For ever chase dark sleep away,
And hymns divine, with angels sing,
Glory to thee, eternal King?

7 Praise God, from whom all blessings
flow,
Praise him, all creatures here below;
Praise him above, ye angelic host,
Praise Father, Son, and Holy Ghost.

To Father, Son, and Holy Ghost,
The God whom earth and heaven adore,
Be glory, as it was of old,
Is now, and shall be evermore.

### HYMN 169. L. M.

*Evening.* MRS. STEELE.

1 GREAT God! to thee my evening song
With humble gratitude I raise;
O let thy mercy tune my tongue,
And fill my heart with lively praise.

2 My days, unclouded as they pass,
And every onward rolling hour,
Are monuments of wondrous grace,
And witness to thy love and power.

3 And yet this thoughtless, wretched
heart,
Too oft regardless of thy love,
Ungrateful, can from thee depart,
And from the path of duty rove.

4 Seal my forgiveness in the blood
Of Christ, my Lord; his Name alone
I plead for pardon, gracious God,
And kind acceptance at thy throne.

5 With hope in him, mine eyelids close,
With sleep refresh my feeble frame;
Safe in thy care may I repose,
And wake with praises to thy name.

---

To Father, Son, and Holy Ghost,
The God whom earth and heaven adore,
Be glory, as it was of old,
Is now, and shall be evermore.

## HYMN 170. C. M.

BRADFORD. HANDEL.

## HYMN 171. S. M.

SUTTON.

### HYMN 170. C. M.

*Evening.* MASON.

1 Now from the altar of our hearts,
Let flames of love arise;
Assist us, Lord to offer up
Our evening sacrifice.

2 Minutes and mercies multiplied
Have made up all this day;
Minutes came quick, but mercies were
More swift, more free, than they.

3 New time, new favors and new joys,
Do a new song require:
Till we shall praise thee as we would,
Accept our hearts' desire.

---

To Father, Son, and Holy Ghost,
The God whom we adore,
Be Glory, as it was, is now,
And shall be evermore.

### HYMN 171. S. M.

C. WESLEY.

1 THE day is past and gone;
The evening shades appear:
O may we all remember well
The night of death draws near.

2 We lay our garments by,
Upon our beds to rest,
So death shall soon disrobe us all
Of what is here possessed.

3 Lord, keep us safe this night,
Secure from all our fears;
May angels guard us while we sleep
Till morning light appears.

---

To God the Father, Son,
And Spirit, glory be,
As 't was, and is, and shall be so,
To all eternity.

## HYMN 172. III 1.

ADOPTION. PLEYEL

## HYMN 173. IV 2.

HERTFORD.

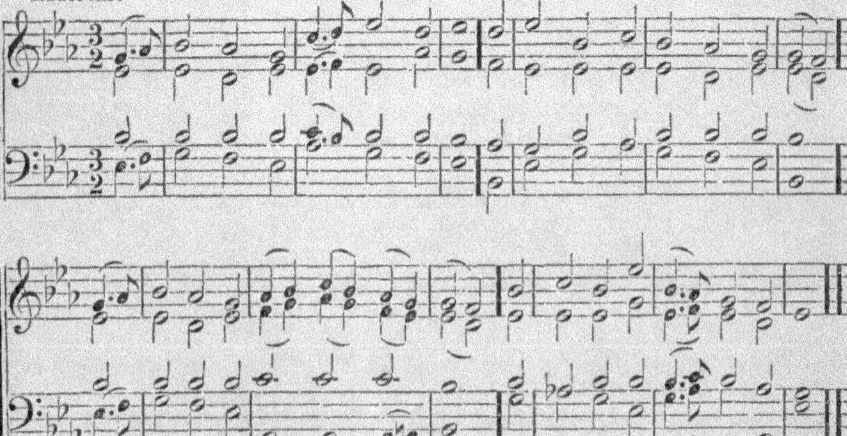

## HYMN 172. III 1.

Psalm cxli : 2. DOANE.

1 SOFTLY now the light of day
Fades upon my sight away;
Free from care, from labor free,
Lord, I would commune with thee.

2 Thou, whose all-pervading eye
Nought escapes without, within;
Pardon each infirmity,
Open fault, and secret sin.

3 Soon, for me, the light of day
Shall for ever pass away;
Then, from sin and sorrow free,
Take me, Lord, to dwell with thee.

4 Thou who, sinless, yet hast known
All of man's infirmity;
Then, from thine eternal throne,
Jesus, look with pitying eye.

---

Holy Father, Holy Son,
Holy Spirit, Three in One!
Glory, as of old, to thee,
Now, and evermore shall be!

## HYMN 173. IV 2.

*Evening.* TOPLADY.

1 INSPIRER and hearer of prayer,
Thou shepherd and guardian of thine,
My all to thy covenant care
I, sleeping or waking, resign.

2 If thou art my shield and my sun,
The night is no darkness to me;
And, fast as my minutes roll on,
They bring me but nearer to thee.

3 A sovereign protector I have,
Unseen, yet for ever at hand;
Unchangeably faithful to save,
Almighty to rule and command.

4 His smiles and his comforts abound,
His grace, as the dew, shall descend;
And walls of salvation surround
The soul he delights to defend.

---

All praise to the Father, the Son,
And Spirit, thrice holy and blessed,
The eternal, supreme Three in One,
Was, is, and shall still be addressed.

## HYMN 174. C. M.

DUNDEE. RAVENSCROFT, 1621.

## HYMN 175. L. M.

STILLORGAN.

## X.—THE CHRISTIAN LIFE.

### HYMN 174. C. M.

*Renouncing the World.* NEWTON.

1 LET worldly minds the world pursue,
It has no charms for me;
Once I admired its follies too,
But grace has set me free.

2 Those follies now no longer please,
No more delight afford;
Far from my heart be joys like these
Now I have known the Lord.

3 As by the light of opening day
The stars are all concealed,
So earthly pleasures fade away
When Jesus is revealed.

4 Creatures no more divide my choice,
I bid them all depart;
His name, and love, and gracious voice
Shall fix my roving heart.

5 Now, Lord, I would be thine alone,
And wholly live to thee;
Yet worthless still, myself I own,
Thy worth is all my plea.

To Father, Son, and Holy Ghost,
The God whom we adore,
Be glory, as it was, is now,
And shall be evermore.

### HYMN 175. L. M.

*Not ashamed of Christ.* GRIGG.

1 JESUS! and shall it ever be,
A mortal man ashamed of thee!
Ashamed of thee, whom angels praise,
Whose glories shine through endless days!

2 Ashamed of Jesus! sooner far
Let night disown each radiant star;
'T is midnight with my soul till he,
Bright Morning Star, bids darkness flee.

3 Ashamed of Jesus! O, as soon
Let morning blush to own the sun;
He sheds the beams of light divine
O'er this benighted soul of mine.

4 Ashamed of Jesus! that dear Friend
On whom my hopes of heaven depend:
No; when I blush, be this my shame,
That I no more revere his Name.

5 Ashamed of Jesus! empty pride;
I'll boast a Saviour crucified;
And, O, may this my portion be,
My Saviour not ashamed of me.

To Father, Son, and Holy Ghost,
The God whom earth and heaven adore,
Be glory, as it was of old,
Is now, and shall be evermore.

## HYMN 176. S. M.

PELHAM. GIARDINI.

## HYMN 177. III 3.

CALVARY. STANLEY.

### HYMN 176. S. M.

*Prayer for Christian Graces.* Wesley.

1 Jesus, my strength, my hope,
On thee I cast my care;
With humble confidence look up,
And know thou hear'st my prayer:
Give me on thee to wait,
Till I can all things do;
On thee, Almighty to create,
Almighty to renew.

2 I want a sober mind,
A self-renouncing will,
That tramples down, and casts behind
The baits of pleasing ill:
A soul inured to pain,
To hardship, grief, and loss;
Ready to take up and sustain
The consecrated cross.

3 I want a godly fear,
A quick, discerning eye,
That looks to thee when sin is near,
And sees the tempter fly;
A spirit still prepared,
And armed with jealous care,
For ever standing on its guard,
And watching unto prayer.

4 I want a heart to pray,
To pray and never cease,
Never to murmur at thy stay,
Or wish my sufferings less;
This blessing, above all,
Always to pray I want,
Out of the deep on thee to call,
And never, never faint.

5 I want a true regard,
A single, steady aim,
Unmoved by threatening or reward,
To thee and thy great name;
A jealous, just concern
For thine immortal praise;
A pure desire that all may learn
And glorify thy grace.

6 I rest upon thy word,
The promise is for me;
My succor and salvation, Lord,
Shall surely come from thee;
But let me still abide,
Nor from my hope remove,
Till thou my patient spirit guide
Into thy perfect love.

---

To God the Father, Son,
And Spirit, glory be;
As 'twas, and is, and shall be so,
To all eternity.

### HYMN 177. III 3.

*Prayer for Guidance.* Robinson.

1 Guide me, O thou great Jehovah,
Pilgrim through this barren land;
I am weak, but thou art mighty;
Hold me with thy powerful hand.

2 Open now the crystal fountains
Whence the living waters flow;
Let the fiery, cloudy pillar,
Lead me all my journey through.

3 Feed me with the heavenly manna
In this barren wilderness;
Be my sword, and shield, and banner,
Be the Lord my righteousness.

4 When I tread the verge of Jordan,
Bid my anxious fears subside;
Death of death, and hell's destruction,
Land me safe on Canaan's side.

---

Praise the Father, earth and heaven,
Praise the Son, the Spirit praise,
As it was, and is, be given,
Glory through eternal days.

## HYMN 178. L. M.

LUTON. BURDER.

## HYMN 179. S. M.

VIGIL. LEACH.

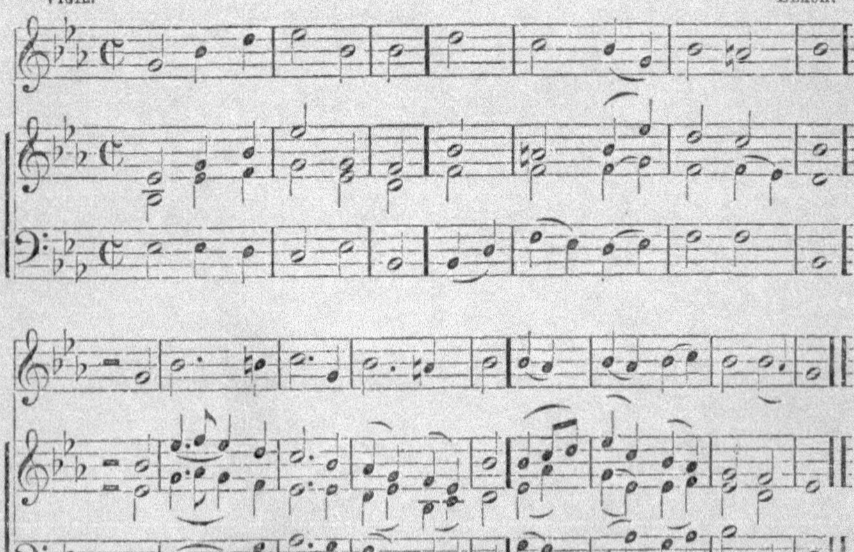

### HYMN 178. L. M.

*Following the Example of Christ.* MRS. STEELE.

1 WHENE'ER the angry passions rise,
And tempt our thoughts or tongues to strife,
To Jesus let us lift our eyes,
Bright pattern of the Christian life.

2 O how benevolent and kind!
How mild, how ready to forgive!
Be this the temper of our mind,
And these the rules by which we live.

3 To do his heavenly Father's will
Was his employment and delight,
Humility and holy zeal
Shone through his life, divinely bright.

4 Dispensing good where'er he came,
The labors of his life were love:
Then, if we bear the Saviour's name,
By his example let us move.

5 But ah! how blind, how weak we are,
How frail, how apt to turn aside!
Lord, we depend upon thy care;
We ask thy Spirit for our guide.

6 Thy fair example may we trace,
To teach us what we ought to be;
Make us by thy transforming grace,
O Saviour, daily more like thee.

To Father, Son, and Holy Ghost,
The God whom earth and heaven adore,
Be glory, as it was of old,
Is now, and shall be evermore.

### HYMN 179. S. M.

*Duties.* C. WESLEY.

1 A CHARGE to keep I have,
A God to glorify;
A never-dying soul to save,
And fit it for the sky.

2 From youth to hoary age,
My calling to fulfill:
O may it all my powers engage
To do my Master's will.

3 Arm me with jealous care,
As in thy sight to live,
And O, thy servant, Lord, prepare
A strict account to give:

4 Help me to watch and pray,
And on thyself rely;
Assured, if I my trust betray,
I shall for ever die.

---

To God the Father, Son,
And Spirit, glory be,
As 't was, and is, and shall be so,
To all eternity.

## HYMN 180. C. M.

CHRISTMAS. HANDEL.

## HYMN 181. C. M.

DUNDEE. RAVENSCROFT, 1621.

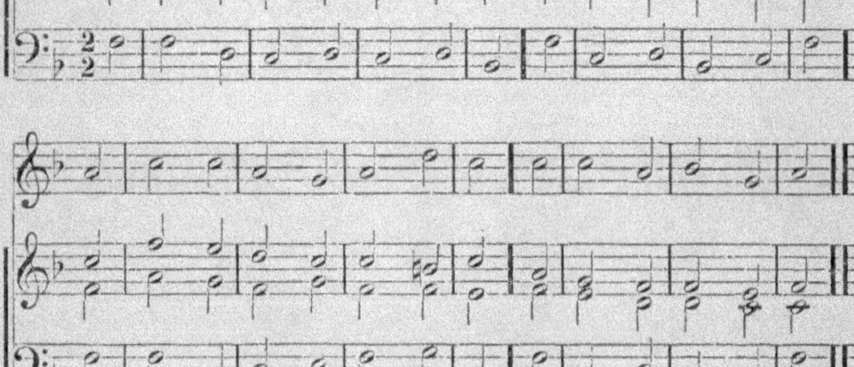

### HYMN 180. C. M.

*"Forgetting those things which are behind," etc.*

Phil. iii: 13, 14. DODDRIDGE.

1 AWAKE, my soul, stretch every nerve,
And press with vigor on;
A heavenly race demands thy zeal,
And an immortal crown.

2 A cloud of witnesses around,
Hold thee in full survey;
Forget the steps already trod,
And onward urge thy way.

3 'T is God's all-animating voice
That calls thee from on high;
'T is his own hand presents the prize
To thine uplifted eye.

4 Then wake, my soul, stretch every nerve,
And press with vigor on;
A heavenly race demands thy zeal,
And an immortal crown.

---

To Father, Son, and Holy Ghost,
The God whom we adore,
Be glory, as it was, is now,
And shall be evermore.

### HYMN 181. C. M.

*Doubting.* COWPER.

1 THE Lord will happiness divine
On contrite hearts bestow;
Then tell me, gracious God, is mine
A contrite heart, or no?

2 I hear, but seem to hear in vain,
Insensible as steel;
If aught is felt, 'tis only pain
To find I can not feel.

3 My best desires are faint and few,
I fain would strive for more;
But when I cry, "My strength renew,"
Seem weaker than before.

4 I see thy saints with comfort filled,
When in thy house of prayer;
But still in bondage I am held,
And find no comfort there.

5 O make this heart rejoice or ache;
Decide this doubt for me;
And if it be not broken, break;
And heal it, if it be.

---

To Father, Son, and Holy Ghost,
The God whom we adore,
Be glory, as it was, is now,
And shall be evermore.

## HYMN 182. C. M

DORCHESTER. STANLEY.

## HYMN 183. III 1.

PLEYEL'S HYMN. PLEYEL.

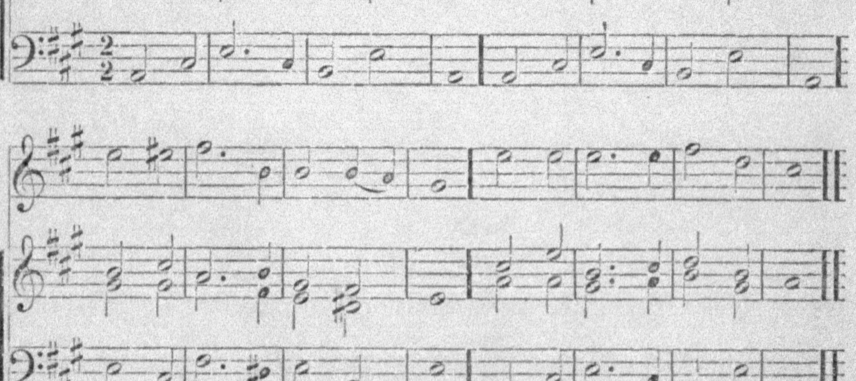

### HYMN 182. C. M.

*Desires after renewed Holiness.* COWPER.

1 O FOR a closer walk with God,
A calm and heavenly frame!
A light to shine upon the road
That leads me to the Lamb!

2 Where is the blessedness I knew
When first I saw the Lord?
Where is the soul-refreshing view
Of Jesus and his word?

3 What peaceful hours I then enjoyed;
How sweet their memory still;
But now I feel an aching void
The world can never fill.

4 Return, O holy Dove, return,
Sweet messenger of rest;
I hate the sins that made thee mourn,
And drove thee from my breast.

5 The dearest idol I have known,
Whate'er that idol be,
Help me to tear it from thy throne,
And worship only thee.

6 So shall my walk be close with God;
Calm and serene my frame;
So purer light shall mark the road
That leads me to the Lamb.

To Father, Son, and Holy Ghost,
The God whom we adore,
Be glory, as it was, is now,
And shall be evermore.

### HYMN 183. III 1.

*Trials.* COWPER

1 'T IS my happiness below,
Not to live without the cross;
But the Saviour's power to know,
Sanctifying every loss.

2 Trials must and will befall;
But with humble faith to see
Love inscribed upon them all—
This is happiness to me.

3 Did I meet no trials here,
No chastisement by the way,
Might I not with reason fear
I should be a cast-away?

4 Trials make the promise sweet;
Trials give new life to prayer;
Bring me to my Saviour's feet,
Lay me low, and keep me there.

---

Holy Father, Holy Son,
Holy Spirit, Three in One!
Glory, as of old, to thee,
Now, and evermore shall be.

## HYMN 184. C. M.

BRATTLESTREET. PLEYEL.

### HYMN 184. C. M.

*Habitual Devotion.* MISS H. M. WILLIAMS.

1 WHILE thee I seek, protecting Power,
Be my vain wishes stilled;
And may this consecrated hour
With better hopes be filled.

2 Thy love the power of thought bestowed,
To thee my thoughts would soar:
Thy mercy o'er my life has flowed,
That mercy I adore.

3 In each event of life, how clear
Thy ruling hand I see!
Each blessing to my soul more dear,
Because conferred by thee.

4 In every joy that crowns my days,
In every pain I bear,
My heart shall find delight in praise,
Or seek relief in prayer.

5 When gladness wings my favored hour,
Thy love my thoughts shall fill;
Resigned, when storms of sorrow lower,
My soul shall meet thy will.

6 My lifted eye, without a tear,
The gathering storm shall see;
My steadfast heart shall know no fear,
That heart will rest on thee.

---

To Father, Son, and Holy Ghost,
The God whom we adore,
Be glory, as it was, is now,
And shall be evermore.

## HYMN 185.

WEBSTER. WEBSTER.

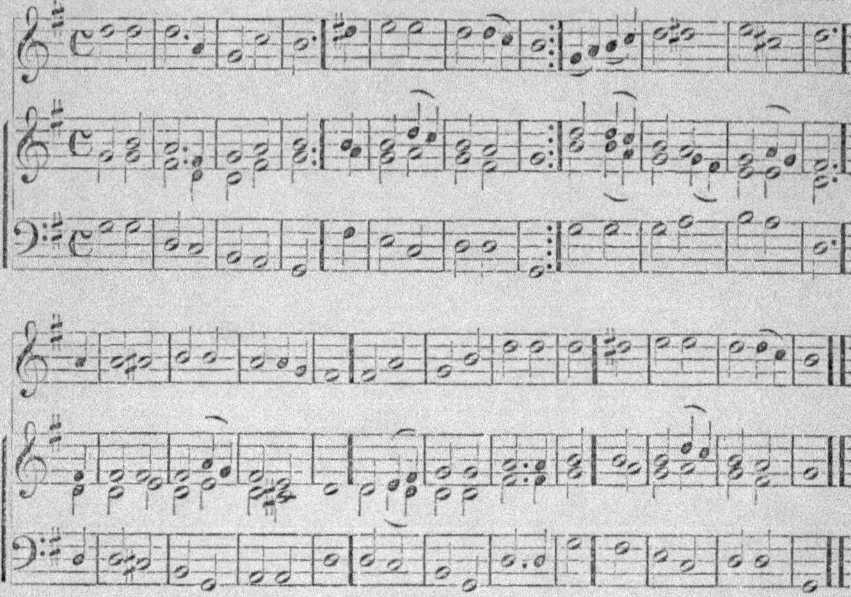

## HYMN 186. L. M.

ZORAH. HANDEL.

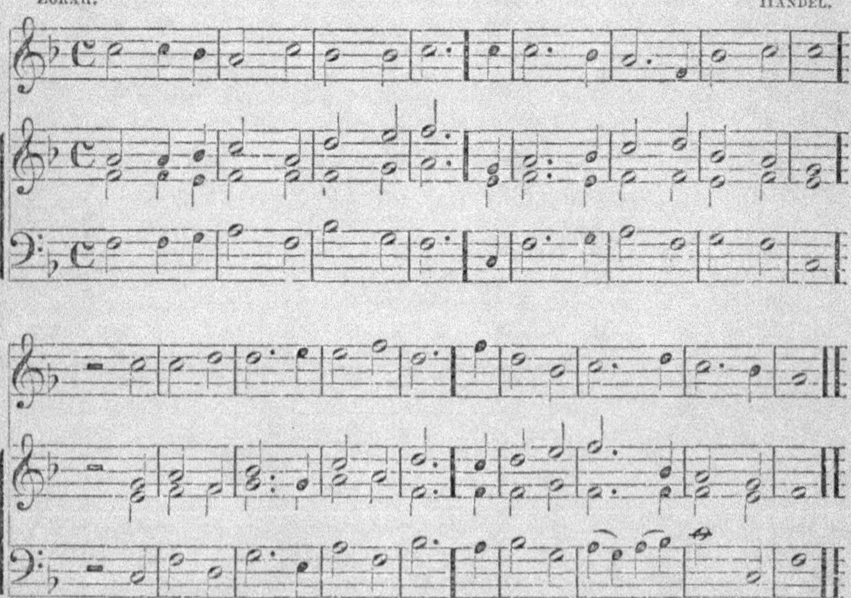

### HYMN 185.

*Walking with God.*

1 Since I've known a Saviour's name
And sin's strong fetters broke,
Careful without care I am,
Nor feel my easy yoke;
Joyful now my faith to show,
I find his service my reward,
All the work I do below
Is light for such a Lord.

2 To the desert or the cell
Let others blindly fly,
In this evil world I dwell,
Nor fear its enmity;
Here I find a house of prayer,
To which I inwardly retire;
Walking unconcerned in care,
And unconsumed in fire.

3 Oh that all the world might know
Of living, Lord, to thee,
Find their heaven begun below,
And here thy goodness see;
Walk in all the works prepared
By thee to exercise their grace,
Till they gain their full reward,
And see thee, face to face.

---

To the Father, to the Son,
And Spirit ever blessed,
Everlasting Three in One,
All worship be addressed:
Praise from all above, below,
As was throughout the ages past,
Now is given, and shall be so
While endless ages last.

### HYMN 186. L. M.

*Heaven seen by Faith.* Newton.

1 As when the weary traveler gains
The hight of some commanding hill,
His heart revives, if o'er the plains
He sees his home, though distant still.

2 So when the Christian pilgrim views
By faith his mansion in the skies,
The sight his fainting strength renews,
And wings his speed to reach the prize.

3 The hope of heaven his spirit cheers;
No more he grieves for sorrows past,
Nor any future conflict fears,
So he may safe arrive at last.

4 O Lord, on thee our hopes we stay,
To lead us on to thine abode;
Assured thy love will far o'erpay
The hardest labors of the road.

---

To Father, Son, and Holy Ghost,
The God whom earth and heaven adore,
Be glory, as it was of old,
Is now, and shall be evermore.

## HYMN 187. IV 4.

SEHNSUCHT.

## HYMN 188. C. M.

BURFORD. PURCELL, 1680.

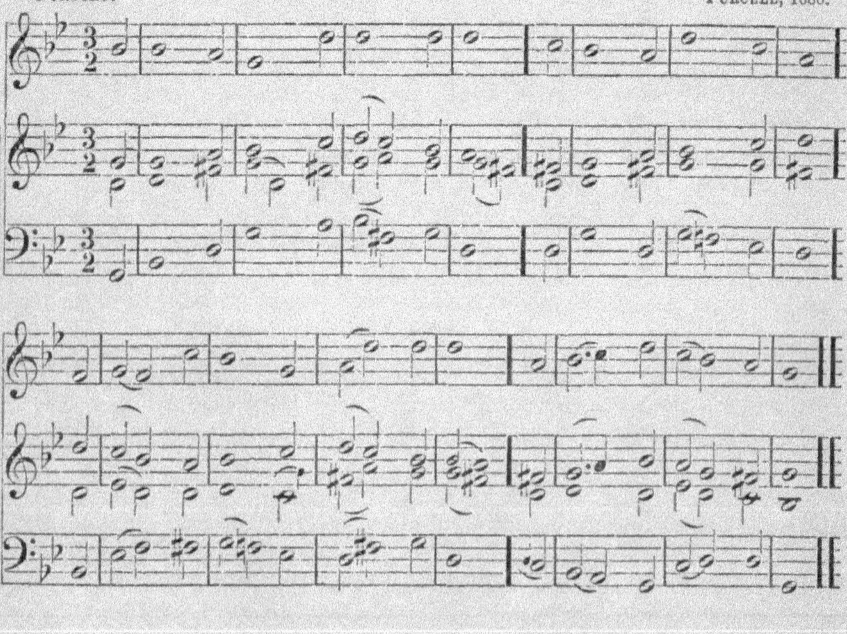

### HYMN 187. IV 4.

MUHLENBURG.

"*I would not live alway.*"—Job vii: 16.

1 I WOULD not live alway; I ask not to stay
Where storm after storm rises dark o'er the way;
The few lurid mornings that dawn on us here
Are enough for life's woes, full enough for its cheer.

2 I would not live alway, thus fettered by sin,
Temptation without, and corruption within;
E'en the rapture of pardon is mingled with fears,
And the cup of thanksgiving with penitent tears.

3 I would not live alway; no, welcome the tomb,
Since Jesus hath laid there, I dread not its gloom;
There, sweet be my rest, till he bid me arise
To hail him in triumph descending the skies.

4 Who, who would live alway, away from his God;
Away from yon heaven, that blissful abode,
Where the rivers of pleasure flow o'er the bright plains,
And the noontide of glory eternally reigns:

5 Where the saints of all ages in harmony meet
Their Saviour and brethren, transported to greet;
While the anthems of rapture unceasingly roll,
And the smile of the Lord is the feast of the soul.

---

O Father Almighty to thee be addressed,
With Christ and the Spirit, one God ever blessed;
All glory and worship from earth and from heaven,
As was, and is now, and shall ever be given.

## XI.—DEATH.

### HYMN 188. C. M.

Job xiv: 1-6. LOGAN.

1 FEW are thy days, and full of woe,
O man of woman born;
Thy doom is written, "Dust thou art,
To dust thou shalt return."

2 Behold the emblem of thy state
In flowers that bloom and die;
Or in the shadow's fleeting form,
That mocks the gazer's eye.

3 Determined are the days that fly
Successive o'er thy head;
The numbered hour is on the wing,
That lays thee with the dead.

4 Great God! afflict not in thy wrath,
The short allotted span
That bounds the few and weary days
Of pilgrimage to man.

---

To Father, Son, and Holy Ghost,
The God whom we adore,
Be glory, as it was, is now,
And shall be evermore.

## HYMN 189. C.M.

CHINA. SWAN.

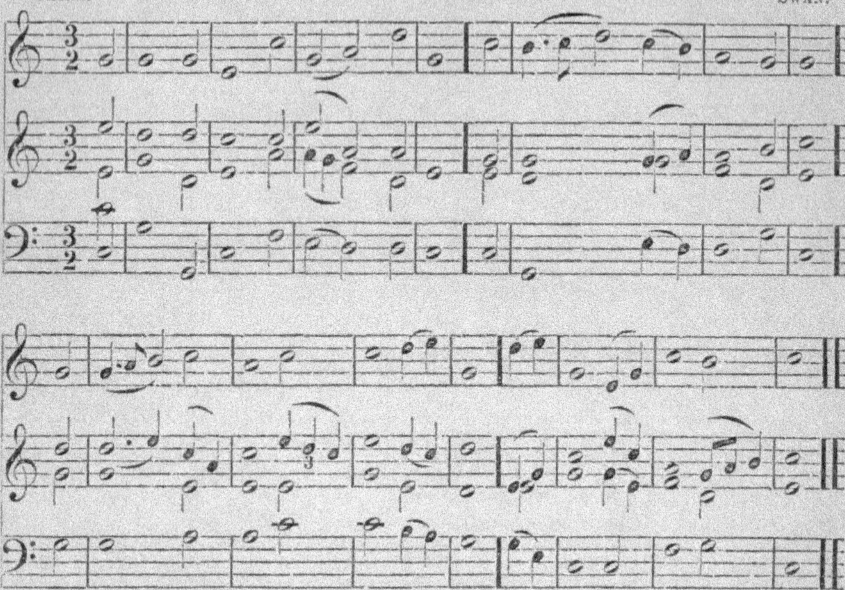

## HYMN 190. S.M.

LITTLE MARLBORO.

### HYMN 189. C. M.

WATTS.

1 HARK! from the tombs a mournful sound;
Mine ears attend the cry;
Ye living men come view the ground
Where you must shortly lie.

2 Princes, this clay must be your bed,
In spite of all your towers;
The tall, the wise, the reverend head
Must lie as low as ours.

3 Great God, is this our certain doom?
And are we still secure?
Still walking downward to the tomb
And yet prepare no more?

4 Grant us the power of quickening grace
To raise our souls to thee,
That we may view thy glorious face
To all eternity.

---

To Father, Son, and Holy Ghost,
The God whom we adore,
Be glory, as it was, is now,
And shall be evermore.

### HYMN 190. S. M.

Job xiv: 11-14. LOGAN.

1 THE mighty flood that rolls
Its torrents to the main,
Can ne'er recall its waters lost
From that abyss again:

2 So days, and years, and time,
Descending down to night,
Can thenceforth never more return
Back to the sphere of light:

3 And man, when in the grave,
Can never quit its gloom,
Until th' eternal morn shall wake
The slumber of the tomb.

4 O may I find in death
A hiding-place with God,
Secure from woe and sin; till called
To share his blest abode.

5 Cheered by this hope, I wait,
Through toil, and care, and grief,
Till my appointed course is run,
And death shall bring relief.

---

To God the Father, Son,
And Spirit, glory be,
As 't was, and is, and shall be so,
To all eternity.

## HYMN 191.

TURIN. GIARDINI.

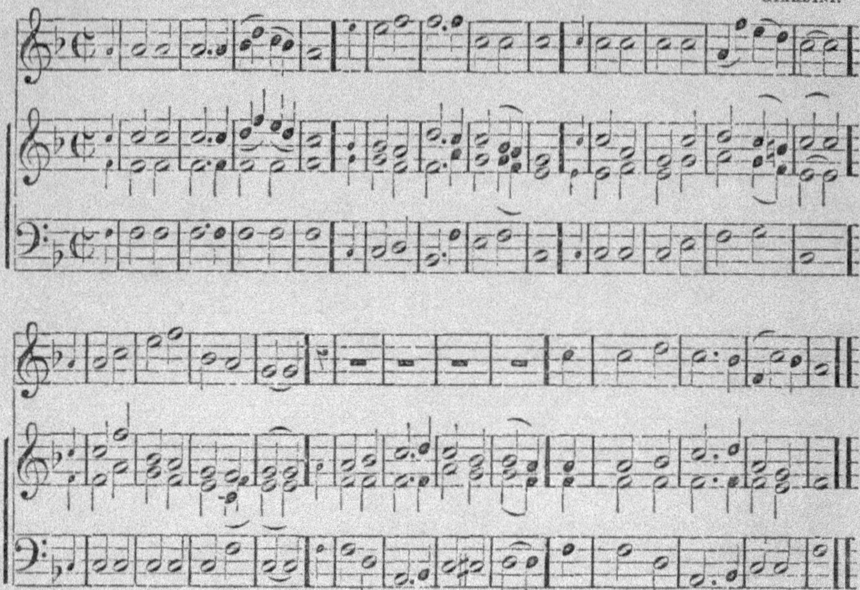

Use small notes for last stanza.

## HYMN 192. C. M.

DUNDEE. RAVENSCROFT, 1621.

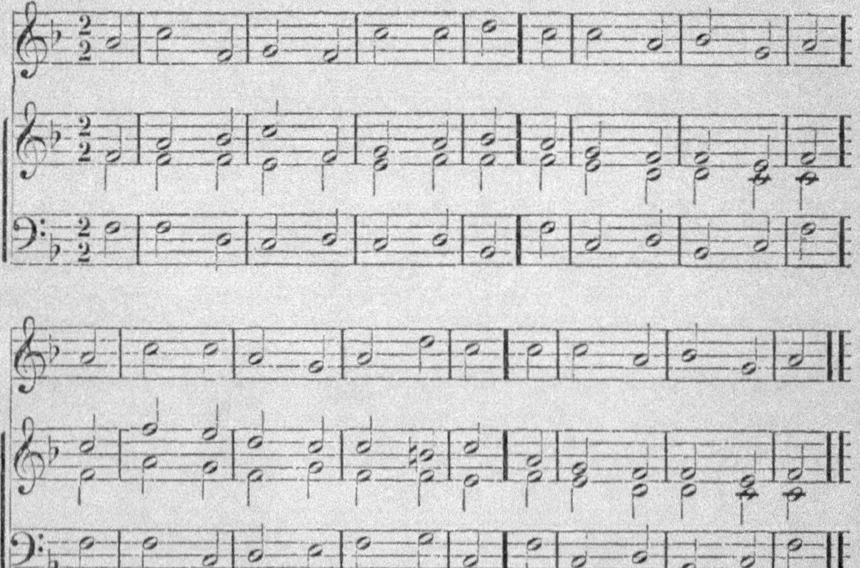

### HYMN 191.

POPE.

1 VITAL spark of heavenly flame,
Quit, O quit this mortal frame;
Trembling, hoping, lingering, flying,
O the pain, the bliss of dying!
Cease, fond nature, cease thy strife,
And let me languish into life.

2 Hark, they whisper, angels say,
Sister spirit, come away!
What is this absorbs me quite,
Steals my senses, shuts my sight,
Drowns my spirit, draws my breath?
Tell me, my soul, can this be death?

3 The world recedes, it disappears;
Heaven opens on my eyes; my ears
With sounds, with sounds seraphic ring:
Lend, lend your wings; I mount, I fly;
O grave! where is thy victory?
O death! O death, where is thy sting?

## XII.—JUDGMENT.

### HYMN 192. C. M.

SIR R. STEELE.

1 WHEN, rising from the bed of death,
O'erwhelmed with guilt and fear,
I see my Maker face to face;
O, how shall I appear?

2 If yet, while pardon may be found,
And mercy may be sought,
My heart with inward horror shrinks,
And trembles at the thought;

3 When thou, O Lord, shalt stand disclosed
In majesty severe,
And sit in judgment on my soul,
O how shall I appear?

4 But thou hast told the troubled mind,
Who does her sins lament,
That faith in Christ's atoning blood
Shall endless woe prevent.

5 Then never shall my soul despair
Her pardon to procure,
Who knows thine only Son has died
To make that pardon sure.

---

To Father, Son, and Holy Ghost,
The God whom we adore,
Be glory, as it was, is now,
And shall be evermore.

## HYMN 193. S. M.

ST. BRIDE'S. DR. HOWARD.

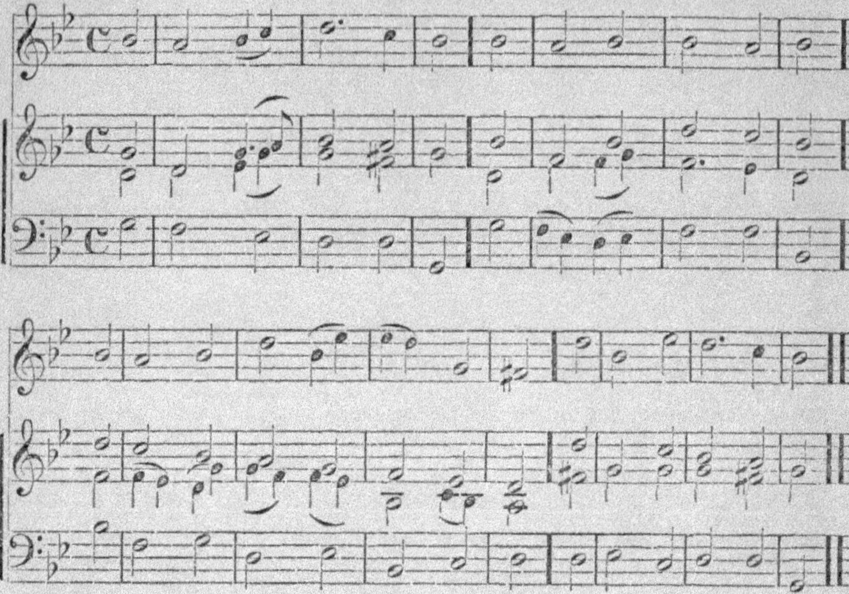

## HYMN 194. II 7.

LUTHER'S HYMN. LUTHER.

## HYMN 193. S. M.

DODDRIDGE.

1 AND will the Judge descend?
And must the dead arise?
And not a single soul escape
His all-discerning eyes?

2 And from his righteous lips
Shall this dread sentence sound;
And through the numerous guilty throng,
Spread black despair around.

3 "Depart from me accursed,
To everlasting flame,
For rebel angels first prepared,
Where mercy never came."

4 How will my heart endure
The terrors of that day;
When earth and heaven before his face
Astonished shrink away?

5 But, ere the trumpet shakes
The mansions of the dead,
Hark, from the gospel's cheering sound
What joyful tidings spread!

6 Ye sinners, seek his grace,
Whose wrath ye can not bear;
Fly to the shelter of his cross,
And find salvation there.

7 So shall that curse remove,
By which the Saviour bled;
And the last awful day shall pour
His blessings on your head.

---

To God the Father, Son,
And Spirit, glory be,
As 't was, and is, and shall be so,
To all eternity.

## HYMN 194. II 7.

LUTHER.

1 GREAT God! what do I see and hear?
The end of things created;
The Judge of man I see appear,
On clouds of glory seated:
The trumpet sounds; the graves restore
The dead which they contained before:
Prepare, my soul, to meet him.

2 The dead in Christ shall first arise
At the last trumpet's sounding,
Caught up to meet him in the skies,
With joy their Lord surrounding;
No gloomy fears their souls dismay,
His presence sheds eternal day
On those prepared to meet him.

3 But sinners, filled with guilty fears,
Behold his wrath prevailing;
For they shall rise, and find their tears
And sighs are unavailing:
The day of grace is past and gone;
Trembling they stand before the throne
All unprepared to meet him.

4 Great God! what do I see and hear?
The end of things created!
The Judge of man I see appear,
On clouds of glory seated:
Beneath his cross I view the day
When heaven and earth shall pass away,
And thus prepare to meet him.

---

To Father, Son, and Spirit blessed,
Supreme o'er earth and heaven,
Eternal Three in One confessed,
Be highest glory given,
As was through ages heretofore,
Is now, and shall be evermore,
By all in earth and heaven.

## HYMN 195. III 1.

PLEYEL'S HYMN. PLEYEL.

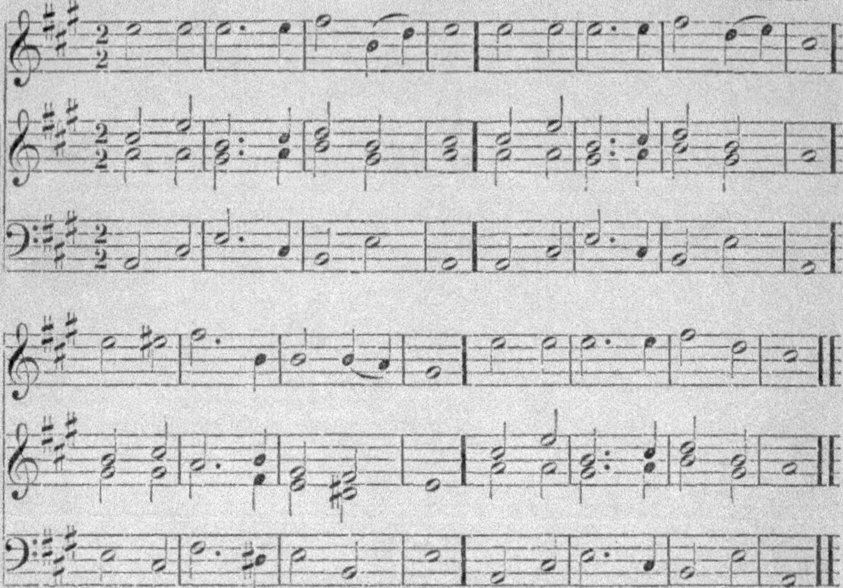

## HYMN 196. S. M.

LITTLE MARLBORO.

### HYMN 195. III 1.

St. Luke xiii: 21-27. ONDERDONK.

1 SEEK, my soul, the narrow gate,
Enter ere it be too late;
Many ask to enter there,
When too late to offer prayer.

2 God from mercy's seat shall rise,
And for ever bar the skies:
Then, though sinners cry without,
He will say, "I know you not."

3 Mournfully will they exclaim—
Lord! we have professed thy Name,
We have ate with thee, and heard
Heavenly teaching in thy word.

4 Vain, alas! will be their plea,
Workers of iniquity;
Sad their everlasting lot;
Christ will say, "I know you not."

---

Holy Father, Holy Son,
Holy Spirit, Three in One!
Glory, as of old, to thee,
Now, and evermore shall be.

## XIII. ETERNITY.

### HYMN 196. S. M.

MONTGOMERY.

1 O WHERE shall rest be found?
Rest for the weary soul?
'T were vain the ocean's depths to sound,
Or pierce to either pole.

2 The world can never give
The bliss for which we sigh:
'T is not the whole of life to live,
Nor all of death to die.

3 Beyond this vale of tears
There is a life above,
Unmeasured by the flight of years,
And all that life is love.

4 There is a death, whose pang
Outlasts the fleeting breath:
O what eternal horrors hang
Around the second death!

5 Lord God of truth and grace,
Teach us that death to shun,
Lest we be driven from thy face,
For evermore undone.

---

To God the Father, Son,
And Spirit, glory be,
As 't was, and is, and shall be so,
To all eternity.

## HYMN 197. C. M.

BRADFORD. HANDEL.

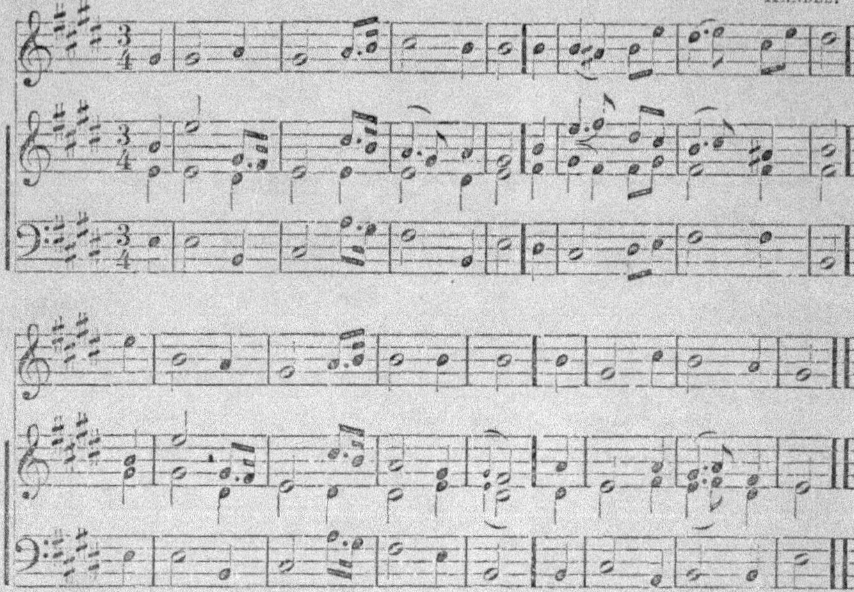

## HYMN 198. C. M.

ARLINGTON. DR. ARNE.

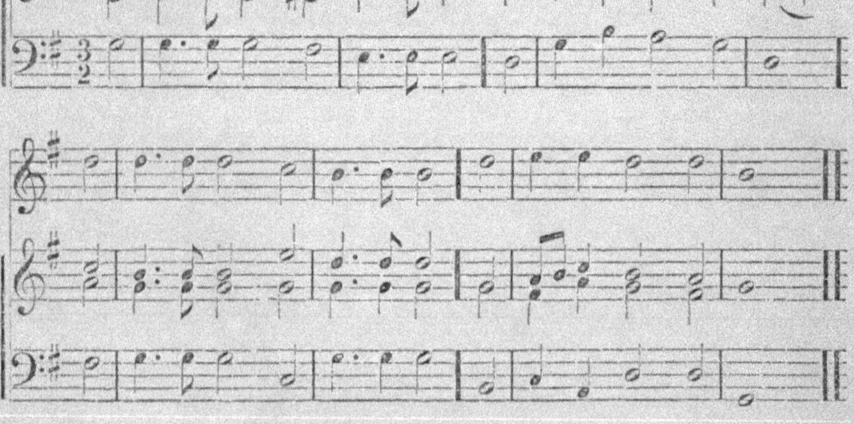

## HYMN 197. C. M.

2 Cor. iv: 18. A. STEELE.

1 How long shall earth's alluring toys
Detain our hearts and eyes,
Regardless of immortal joys,
And strangers to the skies?

2 These transient scenes will soon decay,
They fade upon the sight;
And quickly will their brightest day
Be lost in endless night.

3 Their brightest day, alas! how vain,
With conscious sighs we own;
While clouds of sorrow, care, and pain,
O'ershade the smiling noon.

4 O, could our thoughts and wishes fly
Above these gloomy shades,
To those bright worlds beyond the sky,
Which sorrow ne'er invades!

5 There, joys unseen by mortal eyes,
Or reason's feeble ray,
In ever-blooming prospects rise,
Unconscious of decay.

6 Lord, send a beam of light divine,
To guide our upward aim:
With one reviving touch of thine
Our languid hearts inflame.

7 Then shall, on faith's sublimest wing,
Our ardent wishes rise,
To those bright scenes where pleasures spring
Immortal in the skies.

---

To Father, Son, and Holy Ghost,
The God whom we adore,
Be glory, as it was, is now,
And shall be evermore.

## HYMN 198. C. M.

A. STEELE.

1 COME, Lord, and warm each languid heart,
Inspire each lifeless tongue;
And let the joys of heaven impart
Their influence to our song.

2 Sorrow, and pain, and every care,
And discord there shall cease;
And perfect joy, and love sincere,
Adorn the realms of peace.

3 The soul from sin for ever free,
Shall mourn its power no more;
But, clothed in spotless purity,
Redeeming love adore.

4 There, on the throne (how dazzling bright!)
The exalted Saviour shines;
And beams ineffable delight
On all the heavenly minds.

5 There, shall the followers of the Lamb
Join in immortal songs;
And endless honors to his Name
Employ their tuneful tongues.

6 Lord, tune our hearts to praise and love,
Our feeble notes inspire;
Till, in thy blissful courts above,
We join the angelic choir.

---

To Father, Son, and Holy Ghost,
The God whom we adore,
Be glory, as it was, is now,
And shall be evermore.

## HYMN 199. C. M.

BETHEL. LEACH.

## HYMN 200. C. M.

LYSTRA. C. WESLEY.

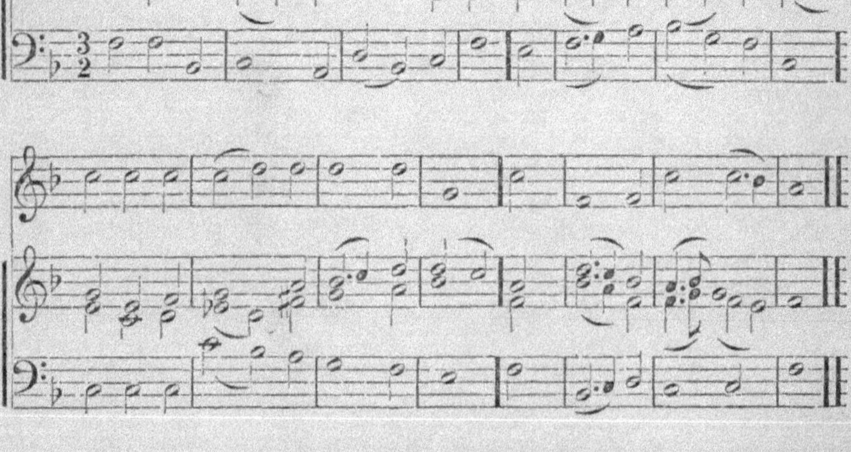

## HYMN 199. C. M.

WATTS.

1 There is a land of pure delight,
Where saints immortal reign;
Eternal day excludes the night,
And pleasures banish pain.

2 There, everlasting spring abides,
And never-fading flowers;
Death, like a narrow sea, divides
This heavenly land from ours.

3 Bright fields, beyond the swelling flood,
Stand dressed in living green;
So to the Jews fair Canaan stood,
While Jordan rolled between.

4 But timorous mortals start, and shrink
To cross the narrow sea;
And linger, trembling on the brink,
And fear to launch away.

5 O could we make our doubts remove,
Those gloomy doubts that rise,
And see the Canaan that we love,
With faith's illumined eyes!

6 Could we but climb where Moses stood,
And view the landscape o'er,
Not Jordan's streams, nor death's cold flood,
Should fright us from the shore.

---

To Father, Son, and Holy Ghost,
The God whom we adore,
Be glory, as it was, is now,
And shall be evermore.

## HYMN 200. C. M.

A. STEELE.

1 Should nature's charms, to please the eye,
In sweet assemblage join,
All nature's charms would droop and die,
Jesus, compared with thine.

2 Vain were her fairest beams displayed,
And vain her blooming store;
Her brightness languishes to shade,
Her beauty is no more.

3 But, ah! how far from mortal sight
The Lord of glory dwells;
A vail of interposing night
His radiant face conceals.

4 O, could my longing spirit rise
On strong immortal wing,
And reach thy palace in the skies,
My Saviour and my King!

5 There, thousands worship at thy feet,
And there, divine employ,
The triumphs of thy love repeat
In songs of endless joy.

6 Thy presence beams eternal day
O'er all the blissful place;
Who would not drop this load of clay,
And die to see thy face?

---

To Father, Son, and Holy Ghost,
The God whom we adore,
Be glory, as it was, is now,
And shall be evermore.

## HYMN 201. III 1.

ADOPTION. PLEYEL.

## HYMN 202. C. M.

LIVERPOOL. WAINWRIGHT.

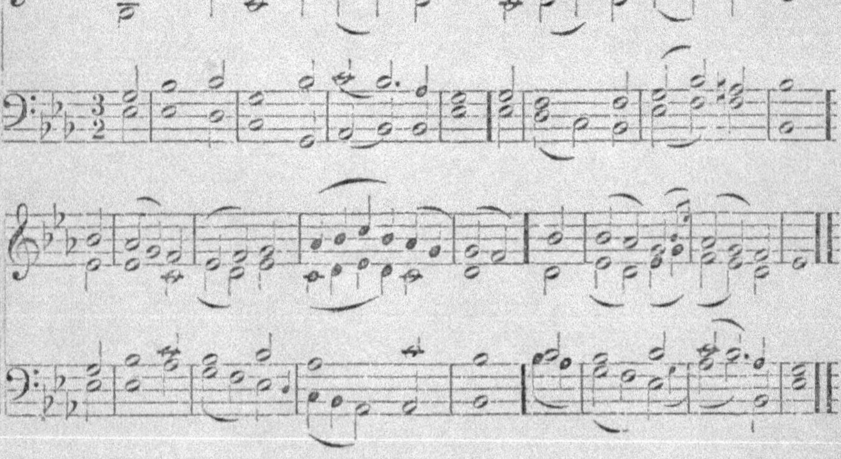

### HYMN 201. III 1.

Revelation vii: 9, etc. MONTGOMERY.

1 WHO are these in bright array?
This innumerable throng,
Round the altar night and day
Tuning their triumphant song?
"Worthy is the Lamb once slain,
Blessing, honor, glory, power,
Wisdom, riches, to obtain
New dominion every hour."

2 These through fiery trials trod,
These from great affliction came;
Now before the throne of God,
Sealed with his eternal name:
Clad in raiment pure and white,
Victor palms in every hand,
Through their great Redeemer's might
More than conquerors they stand.

3 Hunger, thirst, disease unknown,
On immortal fruits they feed;
Them the Lamb amid the throne
Shall to living fountains lead:
Joy and gladness banish sighs;
Perfect love dispels their fears;
And for ever from their eyes
God shall wipe away their tears.

---

Holy Father, Holy Son,
Holy Spirit, Three in One!
Glory, as of old, to thee,
Now, and evermore shall be.

## XIV.—MISCELLANEOUS.

### HYMN 202. C. M.

Gen. xxviii: 20, 21. LOGAN.

1 GOD of our fathers! by whose hand
Thy people still are blest,
Be with us through our pilgrimage,
Conduct us to our rest.

2 Through each perplexing path of life
Our wandering footsteps guide;
Give us each day our daily bread,
And raiment fit provide.

3 O spread thy sheltering wings around,
Till all our wandering cease,
And, at our Father's loved abode
Our souls arrive in peace.

4 Such blessings from thy gracious hand
Our humble prayers implore;
And thou, the Lord, shalt be our God,
And portion evermore.

---

To Father, Son, and Holy Ghost,
The God whom we adore,
Be glory, as it was, is now,
And shall be evermore.

## HYMN 203. III 3

HAMBURG. MENDELSSOHN.

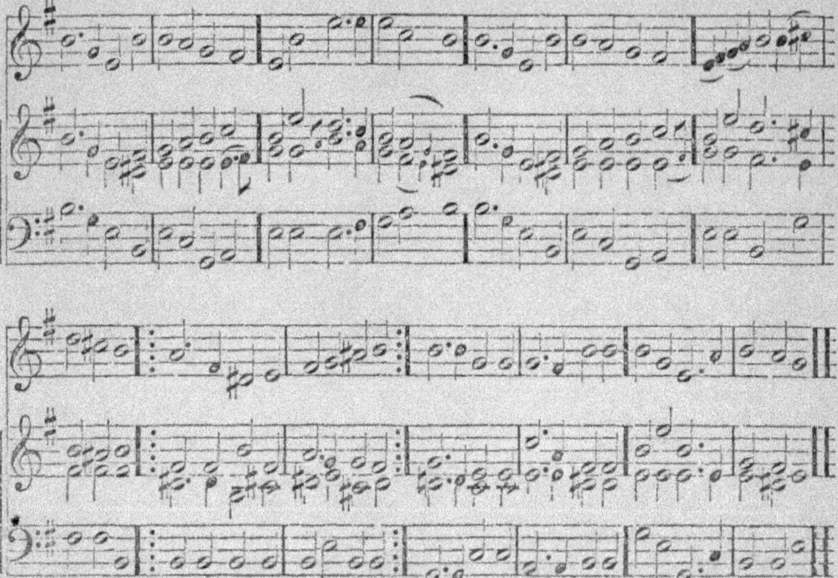

## HYMN 204. C. M.

ST. MARTIN'S. TANSUR, 1742.

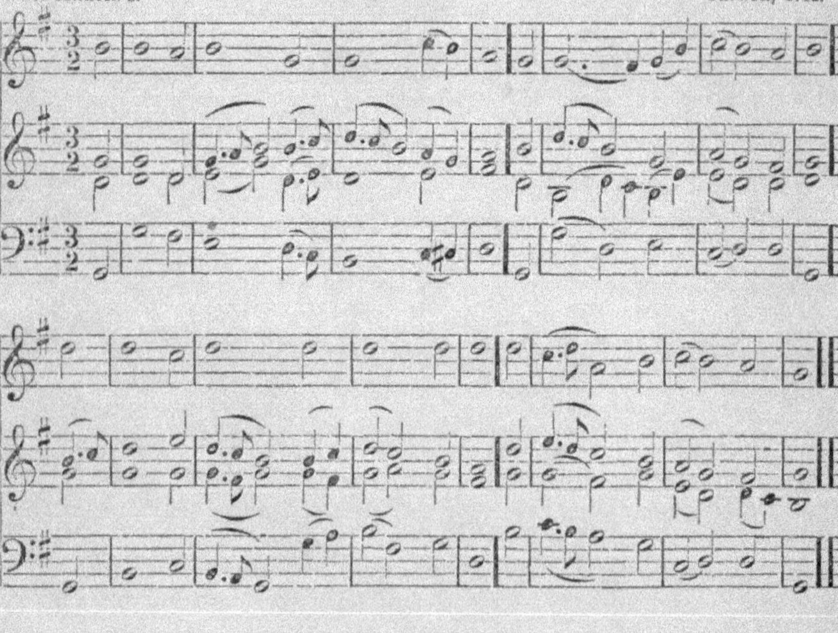

### HYMN 203. III 3.

Chron. xxix: 10-13. ONDERDONK.

1 BLESSED be thou, the God of Israel,
Thou, our Father, and our Lord!
Blessed thy majesty for ever!
Ever be thy name adored!

2 Thine, O Lord, are power and greatness,
Glory, victory are thine own;
All is thine in earth and heaven,
Over all thy boundless throne.

3 Riches come of thee, and honor,
Power and might to thee belong,
Thine it is to make us prosper,
Only thine to make us strong.

4 Lord our God! for these, thy bounties,
Hymns of gratitude we raise;
To thy Name, for ever glorious,
Ever we address our praise!

---

Praise the Father, earth and heaven,
Praise the Son, the Spirit praise,
As it was, and is, be given
Glory through eternal days.

### HYMN 204. C. M.

Prov. iii: 13-17. LOGAN.

1 O HAPPY is the man who hears
Religion's warning voice,
And who celestial wisdom makes
His early, only choice.

2 For she has treasures greater far
Than east or west unfold;
More precious are her bright rewards
Than gems or stores of gold.

3 Her right hand offers to the just
Immortal, happy days;
Her left, imperishable wealth
And heavenly crowns displays.

4 And, as her holy labors rise,
So her rewards increase;
Her ways are ways of pleasantness,
And all her paths are peace.

---

To Father, Son, and Holy Ghost,
The God whom we adore,
Be glory, as it was, is now,
And shall be evermore.

## HYMN 205. L. M.

SEASONS. PLEYEL.

## HYMN 206. C. M.

NEWTON. JACKSON.

### HYMN 205. L. M.

Isaiah xl: 6-8. S. WESLEY.

1 THE morning flowers display their sweets,
And gay their silken leaves unfold;
As careless of the noonday heats,
And fearless of the evening cold.

2 Nipped by the wind's unkindly blast,
Parched by the sun's more fervent ray,
The momentary glories waste,
The short-lived beauties die away.

3 So blooms the human face divine,
When youth its pride of beauty shows,
Fairer than spring the colors shine,
And sweeter than the opening rose.

4 But, worn by slowly rolling years,
Or broke by sickness in a day,
The fading glory disappears,
The short-lived beauties die away.

5 Yet these, new rising from the tomb,
With luster brighter far shall shine;
Revive with ever-during bloom,
Safe from diseases and decline.

6 Let sickness blast, and death devour,
If heaven shall recompense our pains;
Perish the grass, and fade the flower,
If firm the word of God remains.

---

To Father, Son, and Holy Ghost,
The God whom earth and heaven adore,
Be glory, as it was of old,
Is now, and shall be evermore.

### HYMN 206. C. M.

Isaiah xl: 27-31. LOGAN.

1 WHY mournest thou, my anxious soul,
Despairing of relief,
As if the Lord o'erlooked thy cares,
Or pitied not thy grief?

2 Hast thou not known, hast thou not heard,
That firm remains on high,
The everlasting throne of him
Who made the earth and sky?

3 Art thou afraid his power will fail
In sorrow's evil day?
Can the Creator's mighty arm
Grow weary or decay?

4 Supreme in wisdom as in power
The Rock of Ages stands;
Thou canst not search his mind, nor trace
The working of his hands.

5 He gives the conquest to the weak,
Supports the fainting heart;
And courage in the evil hour
His heavenly aids impart.

6 Mere human energy shall faint,
And youthful vigor cease;
But those who wait upon the Lord,
In strength shall still increase.

7 They, with unwearied step, shall tread
The path of life divine;
With growing ardor onward move,
With growing brightness shine.

8 On eagles' wings they mount, they soar
On wings of faith and love;
Till, past the sphere of earth and sin,
They rise to heaven above.

---

To Father, Son, and Holy Ghost,
The God whom we adore,
Be glory, as it was, is now,
And shall be evermore.

## HYMN 207. C. M.

HAVANA. HARRINGTON.

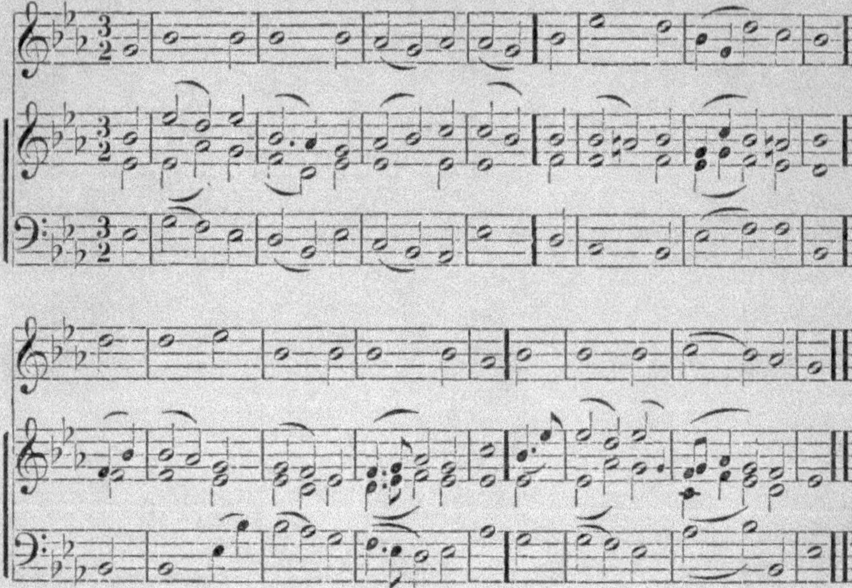

## HYMN 208. II 1.

CLINTON. ISAAC.

### HYMN 207. C. M.

Isaiah lvii: 15. LOGAN.

1 THUS speaks the High and Lofty One:
My throne is fixed on high;
There, through eternity, I hear
The praises of the sky.

2 Yet, looking down, I visit oft
The humble, hallowed cell;
And, with the penitent who mourn,
'T is my delight to dwell.

3 My presence heals the wounded heart,
The sad in spirit cheers;
My presence, from the bed of dust,
The contrite sinner rears.

4 I dwell with all my humble saints
While they on earth remain;
And they, exalted, dwell with me,
With me for ever reign.

---

To Father, Son, and Holy Ghost,
The God whom we adore,
Be glory, as it was, is now,
And shall be evermore.

### HYMN 208. H 1.

Habakkuk iii: 17-19. H. U. ONDERDONK.

1 ALTHOUGH the vine its fruit deny,
The budding fig-tree droop and die,
No oil the olive yield;
Yet will I trust me in my God,
Yea, bend rejoicing to his rod,
And by his grace be healed.

2 Though fields, in verdure once arrayed,
By whirlwinds desolate be laid,
Or parched by scorching beam;
Still in the Lord shall be my trust,
My joy; for, though his frown is just,
His mercy is supreme.

3 Though from the fold the flock decay,
Though herds lie famished o'er the lea,
And round the empty stall;
My soul above the wreck shall rise,
Its better joys are in the skies;
There God is all in all.

4 In God my strength, howe'er distrest,
I yet will hope, and calmly rest,
Nay, triumph in his love:
My lingering soul, my tardy feet,
Free as the hind he makes, and fleet,
To speed my course above.

---

To Father, Son, and Holy Ghost,
The God whom heaven's triumphant host
And saints on earth adore;
Be glory, as in ages past,
As now it is, and so shall last,
When time shall be no more.

## HYMN 209. C. M.

WESTHAM. DR. HOWARD.

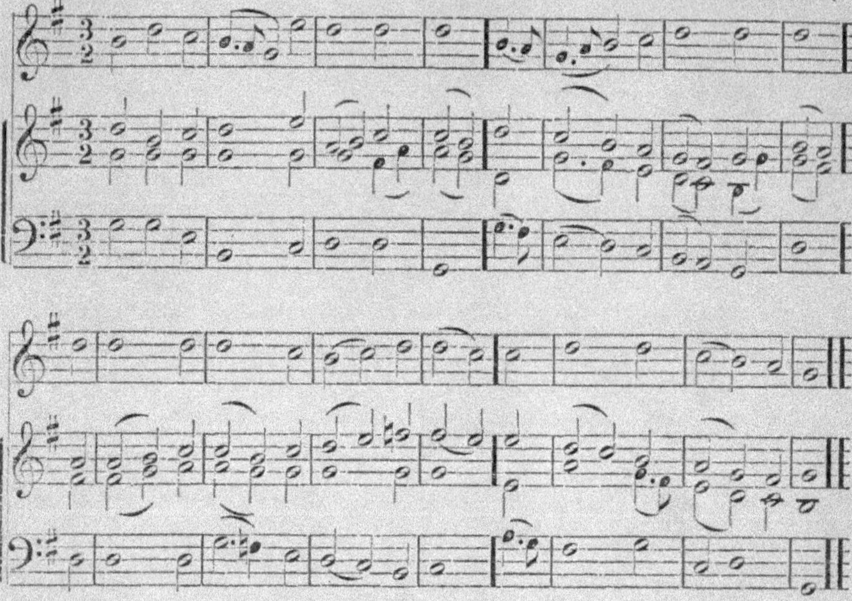

## HYMN 210. S. M.

SUTTON.

### HYMN 209. C. M.

St. John xiv: 6. DOANE.

1 THOU art the Way, to thee alone
From sin and death we flee;
And he who would the Father seek,
Must seek him, Lord, by thee.

2 Thou art the truth, thy word alone
True wisdom can impart;
Thou only canst inform the mind,
And purify the heart.

3 Thou art the life, the rending tomb
Proclaims thy conquering arm;
And those who put their trust in thee
Nor death nor hell shall harm.

4 Thou art the Way, the Truth, the Life;
Grant us that way to know,
That truth to keep, that life to win,
Whose joys eternal flow.

---

To Father, Son, and Holy Ghost,
The God whom we adore,
Be glory, as it was, is now,
And shall be evermore.

### HYMN 210. S. M.

Philippians ii: 12, 13. BEDDOME.

1 HEIRS of unending life,
While yet we sojourn here,
O let us our salvation work
With trembling and with fear.

2 God will support our hearts
With might before unknown;
The work to be performed is ours,
The strength is all his own.

3 'T is he that works to will,
'T is he that works to do;
His is the power by which we act,
His be the glory too!

---

To God the Father, Son,
And Spirit, glory be,
As 't was, and is, and shall be so,
To all eternity.

## HYMN 211. III 1.

WELDON. WELDON.

## HYMN 212. C. M.

WESTHAM. DR. HOWARD.

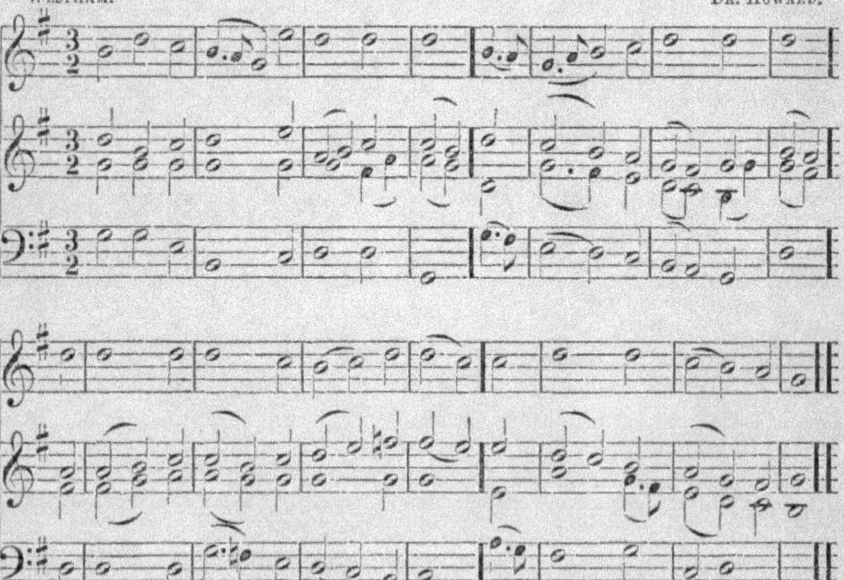

### HYMN 211. III 1.

Ephesians v: 14–17. ONDERDONK.

1 SINNER, rouse thee from thy sleep,
Wake, and o'er thy folly weep;
Raise thy spirit dark and dead,
Jesus waits his light to shed.

2 Wake from sleep, arise from death,
See the bright and living path:
Watchful tread that path; be wise,
Leave thy folly, seek the skies.

3 Leave thy folly, cease from crime,
From this hour redeem thy time;
Life secure without delay,
Evil is the mortal day.

4 Be not blind and foolish still;
Called of Jesus, learn his will;
Jesus calls from death and night,
Jesus waits to shed his light.

---

Holy Father, Holy Son,
Holy Spirit, Three in One!
Glory, as of old, to thee,
Now, and evermore shall be.

### HYMN 212. C. M.

Heb. xii: 1, 2. LOGAN.

1 Lo! what a cloud of witnesses
Encompass us around;
Men once like us with suffering tried,
But now with glory crowned:

2 Let us with zeal like theirs inspired,
Strive in the Christian race;
And, freed from every weight of sin,
Their holy footsteps trace.

3 Behold a witness nobler still,
Who trod affliction's path,
Jesus, the author, finisher,
Rewarder of our faith:

4 He, for the joy before him set,
And moved by pitying love,
Endured the cross, despised the shame,
And now he reigns above.

5 Thither, forgetting things behind,
Press we to God's right hand;
There with the Saviour and his saints,
Triumphantly to stand.

---

To Father, Son, and Holy Ghost,
The God whom we adore,
Be glory, as it was, is now,
And shall be evermore.

# TABLE OF FIRST LINES OF HYMNS.

# TABLE OF FIRST LINES OF PSALMS.

# INDEX OF TUNES.

CPSIA information can be obtained
at www.ICGtesting.com
Printed in the USA
LVHW111239230223
740172LV00005B/384

9 783382 307189